Praise for Brenda Minton and her novels

"Minton's characters are well crafted."
—*RT Book Reviews*

"[A] satisfyingly emotional story."
—*RT Book Reviews* on *The Cowboy's Courtship*

"This return to Dawson, Okla…tells the story of two people…learning to accept…the will of God in their lives."
—*RT Book Reviews* on *The Cowboy's Sweetheart*

"This easy, sensitive story…is quite touching. Don't miss [it]."
—*RT Book Reviews* on *His Little Cowgirl*

"A lovely story of faith, trust and taking one day at a time."
—*RT Book Reviews* on *A Cowboy's Heart*

BRENDA MINTON

The Cowboy's Courtship
and
The Cowboy's Sweetheart

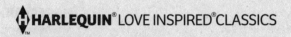
HARLEQUIN® LOVE INSPIRED®CLASSICS

Recycling programs
for this product may
not exist in your area.

ISBN-13: 978-0-373-60206-3

The Cowboy's Courtship and The Cowboy's Sweetheart

Copyright © 2016 by Harlequin Books S.A.

The publisher acknowledges the copyright holder
of the individual works as follows:

The Cowboy's Courtship
Copyright © 2010 by Brenda Minton

The Cowboy's Sweetheart
Copyright © 2010 by Brenda Minton

Printed in U.S.A.

CONTENTS

Brenda Minton lives in the Ozarks with her husband, children, cats, dogs and strays. She is a pastor's wife, Sunday school teacher, coffee addict and sleep-deprived. Not in that order. Her dream to be an author for Harlequin started somewhere in the pages of a romance novel about a young American woman stranded in a Spanish castle. Her dreams came true, and twenty-plus books later, she is an author hoping to inspire young girls to dream.

Books by Brenda Minton

Love Inspired

Martin's Crossing

A Rancher for Christmas
The Rancher Takes a Bride
The Rancher's Second Chance
The Rancher's First Love

Lone Star Cowboy League

A Reunion for the Rancher

Cooper Creek

Christmas Gifts
"Her Christmas Cowboy"
The Cowboy's Holiday Blessing
The Bull Rider's Baby
The Rancher's Secret Wife
The Cowboy's Healing Ways
The Cowboy Lawman
The Cowboy's Christmas Courtship
The Cowboy's Reunited Family

Visit the Author Profile page
at Harlequin.com for more titles.

THE COWBOY'S COURTSHIP

God be merciful to us, and bless us, and cause
his face to shine upon us, That your way may be
known on earth, your salvation among all nations.
—*Psalms* 67:1–2

This book is dedicated to Doug, my real-life hero, because he's always there for me.

Chapter 1

Until one month ago, Alyson Anderson hadn't even known that Etta Forester existed. Now she was sitting on a street just outside the small town of Dawson, Oklahoma, squinting through the windshield of her car at a yellow Victorian house with white gingerbread trim, shrubs that were pruned and flower gardens overflowing with pastel blooms.

She pulled her car into the driveway next to the house and parked. For a moment she sat there, not sure what her next move should be. Her hands shook on the steering wheel and her insides were quaking.

A mower reverberated in the quiet afternoon, and rolling down the window, Alyson could smell fresh-cut grass. She had lived in a lot of places, but never in a place like this.

Never in a place so quiet. She stepped out of her

car, pulling off her sunglasses and clutching her purse under her arm. This was it, the moment she had been planning in her mind for nearly a week.

No, she'd been planning something like this for years. She had always planned to walk away someday. She'd been saving for this and waiting until the time was right, until no one else was depending on her.

Because she'd tried once before, but it had been a day on the road and she'd felt guilty because other performers, younger kids, had depended on her for guidance. No one else understood what they were going through, not like she did.

The mower she'd heard got louder.

A man walked around the corner of the house pushing it, not paying attention to her. She watched as he stopped and moved the garden hose, still not seeing her. She liked that, that he didn't notice her.

She liked watching him, a man in jeans, work boots and a stained T-shirt. A gardener perhaps. A gardener who looked a lot like England's Prince Harry, whom she'd met only twice. This man was older, but with the same light reddish-blond hair, the same tawny complexion.

He looked up, ending her quiet reflection. He killed the engine on the mower and paused, staring at her as if she was some type of unknown species.

He took off leather work gloves and half stuffed them in the front pocket of his jeans. He walked toward her, with a slight limp, smiling, looking like Harry, but more mature, with more defined features. His smile was just as charming, with a little spark of mischief.

She'd had enough of charming to last her a lifetime. Charming wasn't loyal. Charming ran off with another woman. Instead of tears, she unearthed a healthy dose of anger that made the betrayal easier to deal with.

"Can I help you?" He stopped just feet away.

"I'm here to see Etta Forester."

"Etta isn't here." His eyes narrowed, drawing in his nearly blond brows.

"She isn't?" That hadn't been one of the scenarios she'd played through her mind during the two-day drive to Oklahoma. She glanced around, at the green lawn, the big house, the fields behind the house. "She has to be here."

Rejection had been a scenario she'd worked through, and she'd even felt angry when the image of the woman she had never met told Alyson she wasn't welcome here. She had worked through indifference, in case that was the reaction. She had even played through a scene in her mind in which she was welcomed with open arms.

But Etta not being here—that wasn't something she had planned on.

"She's in Florida. She's always in Florida until the end of June." He looked at his watch. "She'll be home in about four weeks."

He knew more than Alyson did. And she still didn't know his name. But then again, he didn't know hers. And he didn't know that her heart had an empty space, and her hands wouldn't cooperate on the piano keys. He didn't know that her father had been raised in this house.

But maybe he did know that. He didn't know that she might have been raised here, had things been different. Whatever *different* meant.

She thought he probably knew that her father was dead. A man she'd never met, the loss tightened in her throat, aching in her heart, hurting worse than losing Dan.

"Are you okay?" He took a step closer, watching her with brown eyes that were deep and earthy. He continued to stare. She was so tired of being the center of attention, the elephant in the room.

She was that dust collector that got put on a shelf, the odd thing that everyone talked about, wondered where it had come from and why it was there. Sometimes they wondered how it worked. If it quit working, they wondered about that, too.

She was obviously broken. Or maybe cracked. Who would ever know if she was cracked, since they'd never thought she was normal to begin with?

He had asked if she was okay. What did she tell a stranger? How much did she tell? She'd always kept conversations to a minimum—it saved a lot of explanation. She smiled, "I'm fine, just unsure."

"Unsure?"

The unsure part had fallen into the "too much" category. She was a social moron, inept, unable to carry on a conversation without spacing out, going in odd directions that caused her mother to give her "the look."

If she'd thought that being in Oklahoma would suddenly make her normal, she'd been way off. Being here, in middle America, didn't make her the person who suddenly fit in.

"Well?" He continued to watch her, so she smiled, as if everything were okay. And it wasn't. Her legs were trembling and she didn't know what to do with the rest of her life.

She was twenty-eight and a has-been.

"Where do I go from here? I mean, I really didn't

think about her not being here. I planned on staying with her."

"And you didn't call?"

No, she hadn't called. She hadn't wanted a rejection on the telephone. She had wanted to escape. If it couldn't be here, it would be somewhere else.

No matter what, she was going to find a place where she could discover who she was. Not knowing about this part of her past, she had thought this would be the best place to start fitting the puzzle of her life together.

"No, I didn't call. It was going to be a surprise."

He liked surprises. Jason Bradshaw started to tell her that, and that he also knew how to listen if she wanted to talk. She looked like a woman who needed someone to talk to. She also looked a lot like Andie Forester. But Andie was wild, a little out of control and somewhere in Colorado running that crazy horse of hers around barrels.

This woman was dressed in a shell-pink cashmere sweater, dove-gray pants and shoes so pointed he wondered how she got her toes shoved into them. She looked hot, not fashionably *hot*, but *sweltering in the Oklahoma heat* kind of hot. And she looked pretty unhappy.

Beautiful but unhappy, with pale ivory skin, clear-blue eyes and feathery blond hair that hung to her shoulders. Back in the day, he had flirted with women like her and they would either smile and give him a look that invited more flirting, or they gave him the look she'd just given him. It was the "rolled up newspaper on the nose" look, meant to send him back to a corner or under the table.

Not much had sent him running back then. He'd

dated, never thinking about the future, settling down or maybe even having a family. He'd thought about riding the next bull, dating the next woman, getting to the next event.

Until God reined him in.

"I'm sure Etta would have liked the surprise." Jason finally came up with something to say. The woman standing in front of him looked about to wilt. Had she told him her name? "Do you want a glass of ice water? I have the key."

He pulled the key to the house out of his pocket and held it up. She glanced at it, and then at the front door, and something lit up in her eyes, something like hopefulness. He wasn't sure what to do with her.

"Who'd you say you're here to see?"

She shot him a look and he knew that had been the wrong question.

Something that sounded like Beethoven rang from inside her purse. He looked at the pink leather bag that probably cost more than most people spent on groceries in a week and waited for her to answer. She stared at him, like she didn't hear it. But she did. He saw the quick flick of those blue eyes, down to the purse and then back to his face.

Her brows shot up in a look that asked "What?"

"You going to answer that?"

She shook her head. He had to think hard to put their conversation back together. People should start calling him Humpty Dumpty. He was the bull rider who'd fallen on his head, and all of the surgeons had tried to put him back together again.

"Fine. So you planned on staying with Etta?" He walked up the stairs of the front porch, right leg first because his left ached from pushing the mower. She came up behind him, smelling as soft and sweet as the sweater she was wearing.

And he had thought he'd left his girl-chasing days behind. This was his new life, detoured from bull riding, and looking for the adult Jason. When he stopped having headaches from the concussion, he'd get on with that adult thing. As soon as he could remember any thought for more than five minutes.

"I had planned on staying here. If she…" She sighed, her chest heaving and she looked away, her gaze wandering down the country road.

"I see." He pushed the door open and motioned her inside the shadowy interior of the house. It was cool inside, even without the air conditioner turned on, and it smelled as if Etta had been home that morning, slicing cantaloupe and baking muffins.

As they walked, he noticed that she slowed to look into each room. What if she was some kind of classy cat burglar? What if she was casing the joint? Maybe he should call Andie and tell her to come home, or have her contact someone to stay in the house for a few days.

"What's your name?" she asked as they walked down the long hallway to the kitchen at the back of the house. She paused to look at pictures on the wall.

She was taking too much interest in the pictures to be a mere cat burglar. He waited for her to finish. "I'm Jason Bradshaw. I live about a mile down the road. And that's a picture of Etta's son and daughter."

"Son and daughter?"

"Alana is in Florida. James passed away a few years ago."

"I see." Her word was quiet, barely a whisper. She blinked a few times and shook her head. "The water?"

"Are you okay?" He started to reach for her arm, but didn't. She nodded.

"I'm fine." Soft voice, and blue eyes that shimmered. He didn't push for more. He remembered what it was like, to fight that hard to show people he was fine.

He knew what it was, to smile when smiling was the last thing he wanted to do, or felt like doing. He knew how it was to put on an act for so many years that the act became his life.

"In here." He flipped on the light and walked to the fridge. "So, what's your name?"

"Alyson." She looked away, pale and surreal in this country kitchen with the crocheted dishrags, needle-point verses hanging framed on the walls and the oak, butcher-block table.

"Well, Alyson, here's your water." He handed her a glass of ice water and she took it, sipping and look-ing away from him. Her hands shook and she looked even paler than she had in the yard. "Why don't you sit down?"

"Thank you." She didn't immediately go to the table. Instead, she stopped at a needlepoint verse, touching it, reading the Bible verse. "Do you know if she did this?"

"Etta?"

She nodded.

He pointed to the initials in the corner. "I think her granddaughter Andie did that for her."

"Andie?" She turned, setting the water down on the table, droplets splashing over the side.

"She's James's daughter. Etta raised her because James worked away from home."

Alyson, with no last name, sat down. She moved the glass and held it between hands that trembled. Jason sat down across from her, trying to think of something that would make her laugh, or smile. He couldn't handle tears.

But he didn't know her, didn't know how to make her laugh.

"You look like Andie." More than looked like her. He thought maybe that was a piece of the puzzle that he was starting to put together.

"How old is she?"

He had to think about that. "A few years younger than me. Maybe twenty-seven or twenty-eight. She's on the rodeo circuit. She's a barrel racer."

"So no one is here." She lifted the glass again.

"I'm here." He winked.

"I'm afraid you don't count. Sorry." She said it with a smile that lifted shadows from her eyes. Aha, a sense of humor. She might be related to Andie after all.

"What were you wanting with Etta?"

She didn't answer right away. She looked out the window, out gingham curtains that had been closed long enough to let dust coat them. The housekeeper only came in once a month. Alyson, with a well-manicured hand, nails painted the same light shade as her sweater, pulled the curtains back to peer outside.

"I wanted to meet her." She bit into her bottom lip and he wondered if she would cry. She didn't. "I'm…"

He waited.

She turned to face him, smiling a little. "I'm her granddaughter, too."

And that's how she knocked the floor out from under him.

* * *

"Stop staring." Alyson slapped the palm of her hand on the table to get the attention of the handsome cowboy sitting across from her. She was still a little shocked, she didn't need his overreaction to her announcement.

She had a sister.

She hadn't found that information in the box inside her mother's desk when she'd been digging for her bank book.

A sister. That was the missing piece of her life, that part of her she had never been able to connect with. Andie. A memory, fuzzy, faded, but always in the back of her mind. She had thought it was her imagination, not a real memory.

She was still trying to figure out why she'd told the man sitting across from her that she was Etta Forester's granddaughter. Was she that needy? Or was it just easier to share with this man she didn't know?

She had other secrets, but those were hers, locked away where no one could use them against her.

"Okay, no longer staring." He looked out the window, avoiding eye contact. She smiled, because he was trying to make this easy. It was anything but.

She wanted to find a life, a family, and instead she'd found more secrets than she knew how to process. She had enough to deal with. This was supposed to be easy, a place to hide, to get control of her life.

"What am I going to do?"

He looked up. "Can I make a suggestion?"

"Please."

"We can call Etta. She always has solutions to problems. I do think that if you're her granddaughter, she'd want you to stay."

"Okay. We can call her." It wasn't the homecoming she'd planned, but it seemed like the only option. She'd brought money with her, but not enough to rent a house, stay in a hotel, whatever might happen if Etta Forester couldn't be reached. Or worse, didn't want her.

He stood and walked to an old rotary-dial phone on the wall. He lifted a piece of paper, found a number, squinted and dialed. Each time the round rotary dial swished back into place, she cringed. This was it, time to learn the truth, the depth of her mother's lies.

"I'm going to wait in the other room." She pushed herself up from the chair. "I don't think I want to listen to you talk about me."

He nodded, but didn't respond. Alyson walked out of the room, walking into what must have been the parlor. A love seat sat in front of a fireplace and a baby grand piano was in the corner of the room, dust covered, ancient, but beautiful.

Alyson touched the keys and her fingers trembled. She sat down and waited for the fear that always came. But it didn't, not this time, not here. She played softly, for herself, for no one else, the way she had played as a child.

She closed her eyes and tried to bring back a memory, one from childhood, of a piano, a woman with a big smile. Had it been this piano, this house? Had that woman been her grandmother?

It was easy to play this piano, without pressure. Here, in this parlor, she wasn't the golden one. She was no one.

"Beautiful. I've never heard it played like that. Andie tried, but she had absolutely no talent for anything other than riding horses and getting into trouble."

She moved her hands from the keys and turned to

face the man who stood in the doorway. He moved his hand, bracing it against the doorframe.

"It's a beautiful piano."

"Your grandmother is on a cruise. Alana is going to try and get hold of her. She's sure her mother will be here as soon as she hears. Alana says she'll try to come as well."

"Okay, that's that. Is there a hotel somewhere?"

"Not in Dawson. But I'm sure your grandmother would want you to stay here. Alana said the same thing—that you should stay."

"I don't know her." She ran her fingers over the keys one last time and walked out from behind the piano. "They don't know me, or if I'm even who I say or think I am."

"I'm pretty sure we all know who you are."

At least they knew. She wondered how that was possible, since she didn't even know who she was. She had always been Alyson Anderson, the pianist. That was the box she fit in. It was her sole identity. Now she wanted more.

Now she had a birth certificate that gave her real name: Alyson Forester. And she had paperwork from the adoption that took place when her mother married Gary. She had her father's signature, signing away his parental rights. As if she were a possession, something to be passed off to another person.

Why had he done that?

"Alana asked me to take you to town to get groceries."

Groceries. Well, that posed a problem. "Isn't there a restaurant?"

"The Mad Cow."

The Mad Cow. She'd learn to cook if that was her only option. But looking at the man in front of her, perspiration-stained and rugged, she thought driving herself would be the best idea.

"I think I'll be fine." She said it with a smile and walked him to the door. He drove away after promising to be back tomorrow to check on her.

Then she was alone in a house where she thought she might have memories. A house where she might learn clues about herself. And her sister, Andie. Her twin? She wasn't sure, but couldn't wait to find out....

Chapter 2

"Jas, where are you going?"

Jason didn't turn the key in the ignition of his truck. Instead, he waited for his sister to hurry across the drive, coming from the direction of the barn where she'd been doctoring a sick mare.

He only knew that because he'd just talked to his dad. At least he remembered one conversation that took place five minutes ago. That showed an improvement. He'd take anything at this point.

"I'm running into town." He tried to think of something funny, something that would wipe the concern from her eyes. He was used to making her laugh. Beth with her short, no-nonsense brown hair, serious brown eyes and a smile that wiped all that seriousness away.

When she smiled. Which wasn't that often.

"Could you get antibiotics for the mare? I called the

feed store. They have some in stock." She pulled a tablet out of her pocket and scribbled a note. "Stick that to your nose so you don't forget."

He took the note and nodded. "Will do, Fancy."

"Don't call me that." She socked his arm.

"We've always called…"

She shook her head. "Not since I was ten. Okay?"

"Okay, *Beth*."

"Thanks." She jumped up on the running board of the truck and kissed his cheek. "Where were you going, anyway?"

He glanced down at the paper on the seat next to him. "Grocery store and I'm going to check on Etta's house, feed her horses. I think I need to mow." He sighed. "I think there's something else, but I don't know."

"Me, neither. But it'll come to you." She squinted. "Weren't you mowing at Etta's two days ago? Are you graining her horses? With all the grass they've got?"

"I mowed already?" Of course he had. "I wish I could tell you what I need to do there, Sis, but I can't. I just know that I have to run by her place."

He was suddenly five. Man, he hated this. He'd never had a temper, never wanted to be the guy hitting walls when a ride didn't go well, when the bull won and he lost.

He'd always been the one keeping the family together, making them smile when they wanted to cry. He was the guy who had found faith and shrugged off his old ways.

At least God's memory wasn't lacking the short-term program. Even if it did occasionally feel as if He'd forgotten Jason.

"It'll get better." Beth's hand was on his arm. She

was six years younger than him, and she should have been loved by someone who would cherish her.

"Yeah, it'll get better. I have my name and number pinned to my shirt in case I get lost. I'll see you later."

She laughed a little, but he knew she wasn't sure if she should. He grinned and winked, "Laugh, Beth, that was funny."

"Okay, yeah, funny."

"Don't forget to pray for me."

"Right, now I know you've lost it." She walked away and he finally started the truck and headed down the drive.

Toward Etta's. He rubbed the back of his head, still feeling the place where one month ago staples had held his scalp together. He had his long-term memory. Etta wasn't a blur or a memory he had to dig up. He laughed a little, because who could ever forget Etta? But the reason for driving to her house, that one was lost somewhere in his scrambled brain.

Scrambled. He didn't remember the ride that had put him in the hospital. He barely remembered his stay there and then rehab where he'd learned the coping techniques he was still using.

One month and he still couldn't get from point A to point B without a note to tell him why he was going. He could leave the living room and walk into the kitchen, and in the one minute that took, he would forget what he needed. He'd had to move back in with his dad and sister because he couldn't remember to turn off the stove, or that he'd put something in the oven.

He was thirty-one years old and he didn't know how to get his life back. He gripped the steering wheel a little tighter because it felt good to have that control back—at least that.

At least he could drive. He could still ride a horse. He could work cattle. It might hurt a little, but he could cowboy through the pain.

He still had his life. His career, not so much. But maybe it was time to make some decisions about the future. He had a ranch that he hadn't spent nearly enough time on. Maybe it was about time to raise cattle and settle down.

The drive through Dawson didn't take five minutes. There was the one stop sign at the intersection of Main Street and the highway that led to Tulsa. A half-dozen cars were parked in front of the Mad Cow Café and the feed store was busy the way it usually was when the men around town took a break to get out of the afternoon heat. They'd spend the afternoon sitting at the feed store, drinking Coke out of a bottle and telling stories about each other.

He turned and drove down the side road to Etta's. What he'd known before the accident wasn't lost. He knew that Etta was out of town. So why was a car parked in the drive? Why was the front door open?

He parked next to the house and sat there for a minute, staring at the back end of an Audi convertible with Massachusetts plates. Time to think back, to try to retrieve the memory. He pulled his notebook out to see if he'd written himself a note, something to tell him why he would feel the need to check on Etta's house. Nothing.

An alarm sounded, and it had nothing to do with memories, or lost moments. He threw the door open and jumped out of the truck. As he ran up the front walk, windows went up in the living room. The alarm continued to squawk.

He opened the door and the woman in the hallway turned. She glared at him and ran on, into the parlor. She pushed at the bottom of the window.

"Those won't open." He leaned against the doorway, watching her, knowing her, but not. The stench of something burnt clung to the humid air.

She turned, her hair in her face, her cheeks pink. Blue eyes flashed shards of anger, like shattered glass.

"Why won't they open?"

She grabbed a magazine and fanned her face.

"Painted closed. The glass is old and thin. Opening them might break it, so Etta painted the windows closed. Do you have the kitchen windows open?"

"Yes, and the window in the screen door."

He flipped a switch on the wall and an instant rush of air swept through the house. The woman in the pink T-shirt and white Bermuda shorts shot him another look and then she tossed the magazine back on the table.

"What's that?" She walked into the hall and looked up, squinting at the louvered opening.

"Attic fan." He thought *he* was clueless. "It'll have this cleared out in a minute." He sniffed. "What is that lovely aroma?"

"My lunch."

"Smells, um, appetizing." He followed her down the hall. "What are you doing in Etta's house?"

She stopped, stood frozen for a minute and then turned.

"Excuse me?" She shook her head a little. "You're the one who let me in."

He had let her in? Well, at least he remembered that

he had unfinished business here, even if he didn't remember what it was. That was an improvement. "I let you in?"

"Yes, you let me in. You called Alana and then told me it was okay if I stayed here."

"That's good." He could honestly hide his own Easter eggs and not find them.

She made a little growl and walked into the kitchen. When she opened the door to the oven, black smoke rolled out. She sputtered, coughed and grabbed a towel to put over her face.

"I think you're not going to be eating that." He opened the drawer where Etta kept oven mitts and pulled the smoldering box out of the oven.

"No kidding." She pointed to the sink and he tossed it in with dirty dishes and a half-eaten bagel.

"You know you're supposed to take it out of the box, right?" He turned off the water she had turned on to put out the still smoldering pizza.

"But the frozen dinners that I bought go in the oven, box and all. She doesn't have a microwave."

Jason cleared his throat and focused on the window over the sink. He had a feeling that laughter might provoke some kind of really bad reaction from the woman standing in front of him.

"Yeah, so, pizza has to be taken out of the box." He explained. "It can go on the rack or on a baking sheet, but it definitely has to be taken out of the box. And the plastic wrap has to be removed."

"Great. Okay, you've had your laugh, you can go now."

"Look, don't be mad. You have to admit, it is kind of funny." He winked, hoping he still had a little charm left.

She smiled and then she laughed, not a lot, but enough for him to see that she looked a lot like Etta's granddaughter Andie.

"Yeah, okay, it's a little funny. But…"

"But now you're hungry." He opened the freezer and pulled out another frozen pizza. "We can try it again. I'll help, if you'll tell me who you are."

"You really don't know?"

"I really don't know." And he no longer felt like laughing. Even the class clown had his moments.

Alyson watched the cowboy standing in her grandmother's kitchen. Maybe he wasn't a cowboy, but he looked like one, in faded jeans, cowboy hat and boots. He unwrapped the frozen pizza, opened the oven door and slid the pizza onto the wire rack.

He turned around and she didn't know what to do now, because he didn't seem to know her and she couldn't forget him. Last night as she wandered through this big house, discovering her family for the first time, she'd thought of him.

She'd thought of him all day yesterday, when she'd been alone in this big house, not knowing anyone, and not really knowing herself. Two days ago she'd found out she had a sister. She was still reeling from the depths of her mother's deception.

"You were going to tell me your name." He leaned against the counter, arms crossed over his chest, the cowboy hat on his head cocked a little to the side.

"Alyson Anderson. I'm Etta's granddaughter."

"You're Etta's granddaughter?"

"I am." And she had a sister who looked so much like her, it ached in her heart to know that she'd missed out knowing her all these years, and she didn't know why they'd been separated.

Instead of the answers she thought she'd find here, she had more questions.

Last night she had looked at photo albums of a family she couldn't remember, a family she had been taken from. She had cried because the father who had held her in those pictures, pictures taken when she was a toddler, was gone. And she had been denied the opportunity to ever know him.

"Alyson, Etta's granddaughter." He nodded, still leaning against the counter. "And Andie must be your sister."

"I'm assuming that's the case."

"Assuming? You don't know?"

She shook her head and turned away from him, concentrating on the pitcher of tea she'd made that morning, pretending she stood in country kitchens every day, pouring iced tea into glasses shaped like kegs with wooden handles. The mugs were the most normal thing she'd found in the kitchen.

Her grandmother was a little different. Or so she'd decided in her exploration of the quaint Victorian. Her grandmother had shelves of books. She had Bibles and she had books on living off the land in the sixties. There were pictures of a commune in one photo album. She'd found a spinning wheel upstairs and wool. She was wearing a pair of socks she'd found in a basket next to the spinning wheel. Itchy wool socks, but they were somehow comforting.

And too hot for late May. But she didn't care.

"What are you doing here?" He opened the oven door and peeked in at the pizza. "Almost done."

"I'm here to see my grandmother."

"Right."

He said it in a way that implied he didn't believe her. And she guessed he was right. She wanted to meet her grandmother, but she had more reasons for showing up in Dawson, Oklahoma.

She was running away. Did twenty-eight-year-old women run away? Did they pack up without telling anyone where they were going and take off without saying goodbye? Did they ignore the phone when it rang, refusing to talk to family? Her younger sister had done something similar, but Laura had taken something important with her.

Laura had taken Dan.

That was hard to forget. She could work on the forgiving part. That was the consensus—she needed to forgive. People said it as if she should be able to sweep the vastness of her pain under a rug, along with the dust she'd shaken out of her mother's box of secrets.

That was something no one knew—that she'd found that box. They assumed that all of her pain had to do with Laura and Dan. But that box had pushed her to finally leave. She had packed up her clothes, left the key to her apartment with the doorman and walked away.

Jason rummaged through the cabinets, pulling out a baking sheet and a spatula. She watched as he opened the oven and slid out the rack. It seemed easy for him, sliding the baking sheet under the pizza and pulling it out. Of course she could have done it.

She would do it next time. And next time she wouldn't burn the house down.

"Do you want me to cut this?" He opened a drawer and pulled out a knife.

"Might as well. Why didn't you remember me?" Should she be afraid of him? But her grandmother seemed to trust him. He was mowing her lawn and he had a key to the house.

He had probably known her grandmother his entire life.

He pushed the knife into the pizza and glanced up at her, smiling. "I had an accident."

She nodded and watched as he worked the knife through the pizza, not as easily as he should have, or as easily as she would have imagined. She thought about offering to help, but she didn't because he seemed to be the type of man who always wanted to be strong.

"What kind of accident?" She took a step, putting herself next to him.

"A bull." He gave her a sideways look and went back to work on the pizza. "I'm a bull rider."

"I see. Wouldn't it be better to ride a horse?"

He laughed and turned, pushing up the cowboy hat that had kept her from getting a good look at him, at his brown eyes. He had eyes that were a mix of laughter and pain. He had stories.

She wanted his stories, not her own.

"You don't know what bull riding is?" He grabbed a paper plate off the holder on the counter and handed it to her. "Eat your pizza."

"I know what it is." She shrugged, hoping to look smart, like she really did know what the sport entailed. She'd seen pictures. She had seen it on TV.

She slid pizza onto the plate and handed it to him. "Are you going to eat?"

"No." But he took the plate. "Sure, why not."

She followed him to the table. "So, what happened when you were riding the bull?"

"I got stepped on." He sat down across from her. His hand went to the back of his head. "Let's pray."

He took off his hat and sat it on the chair next to him.

"Pray?" She looked at the hand he'd reached out for hers. She met the intent gaze, brown eyes with flecks of green.

"Bless our food." His hand grasped hers and he bowed his head. And she stared, not meaning to stare. She'd met so many people in her life. She'd never met the type of man that held her hand and bowed his head to pray over frozen pizza.

Until today.

His head was bowed. She followed, bowing hers. His strong, warm hands held her hands and soft words thanked God for their food. For frozen pizza. At his "Amen," she pulled her hands back.

"The bull stepped on you." Back to something easy to talk about. For her.

It probably wasn't easy for him.

"The bull. Yes. I was unconscious for..." He looked up and then shook his head. "Sorry, I can't find it."

"It?"

He looked at her. "I lose words. It's like having a bucket with a hole in it. I keep trying to fill it up, but it keeps leaking out. Twelve hours. I was out for twelve hours."

"I'm sorry."

He shrugged. "No need. I'm alive. It upset my plans a little, but, since I can't remember most of them, I'll survive."

His smile said it was a joke, as if it didn't matter. But it had to matter.

"Aren't you angry?"

Her plans had fallen apart in April. Her wedding would have been two weeks ago. She should have been in Europe on her honeymoon.

She had a note with the scrawled handwriting of her sister, begging forgiveness. Alyson looked at it every day, trying to figure out why she'd been tossed aside, and how her sister could have done this to her.

Dan had called to tell her that Laura knew how to enjoy life. As if Alyson didn't. It wasn't about not knowing how, it was about never getting the chance.

"No, I'm not angry." He reached for his hat, but he didn't put it back on. "That isn't true. Sometimes I am mad. Isn't that what happens when things don't go the way we expected?"

Alyson had never thought of herself as an angry person. Lately she'd been angry. Or maybe bitter. She stood, picking up the paper plate and empty mug.

"Will your memory improve?" She tossed the paper plates in the trash and opened the door of the dishwasher to stick the forks in the basket.

"It's getting better. They don't have answers about how far I'll progress, when or how. Physical therapy helped the physical problems, or is helping, but the other…" He shrugged.

"When did this happen?"

"Five weeks."

"April?"

He nodded.

April had been a bad month. April Fool. That was what she'd called herself when she got the note. She walked to the door and looked out, at the backyard, at the barn and the fields. She turned back to face him and he was watching her.

"There are horses in the field," she said, but of course he knew that.

"Yeah, the horses. I'm here to check them." He pulled a small notebook out of his pocket. "And your name is…"

She smiled this time because he glanced up at her, a little lost, unsure. "Alyson Anderson."

He wrote it down in his notebook and whispered it a few times. "I won't forget."

She was forgettable, so she thought he might.

Jason walked down the hall and flipped off the attic fan. The rush of air through the house stilled immediately. He glanced into the sitting room where Etta spent most of her time, usually knitting or quilting, and sometimes painting. Photo albums were scattered across the sofa.

The woman next to him turned a little pink. "I found them."

"I'm sure it's okay if you look at them." He rubbed his cheek, feeling the raspy growth of whiskers he'd forgotten to shave that morning.

"I don't know the people in those pictures." She didn't look at him.

"How did that happen?"

She shrugged. "I'm not really sure. I'm still trying to put it all together, why they're here, and I'm not."

"I can look at the album with you, if you like." Sit next to her on the sofa, with her soft, floral scent floating around him, reminding him of something, someone.

He nearly laughed, because he was sure that the memory was of her. It was her perfume that brought it back.

"The horses," she reminded him.

"You can help me feed. I'll help you with the pictures."

She nodded and he followed her to the sofa. She picked up the three albums and stacked them on the coffee table. When he sat down next to her, she picked up the first one and opened it to a page with Andie's baby pictures.

"Is this Andie?" She touched a picture of a toddler and her hands trembled, so did her voice.

"I think." He glanced at her. "Or it could be you."

She ignored the comment that pointed out the obvious.

"What's she like?"

It was a little ironic that he had no short-term memory, and the woman sitting next to him knew nothing about her life. Or at least about her family.

He flipped through the album and found several pages of Andie at different rodeo events.

"She's wild." He grinned, drawing up memories of a girl who had outrun the cops and hid her truck in his barn. "She's a little rebellious."

"What does she like to do?" Alyson pulled out a picture of Andie on her barrel horse. "Other than rodeos."

"That's about it. She fishes and hunts. I've seen her ride a bull. She's a little crazy."

She'd broken hearts all over the county. Not his.

He'd steered clear of Etta's granddaughter. If he were in his right mind, he'd steer clear of the one sitting next to him.

She put her hand on the page and stopped him from turning. Her finger dropped on the photo of James Forester, Andie's dad.

"Who is that?"

"I think that must be James. It's an older picture, probably before you were born. And the woman next to him is Alana, your aunt."

"Oh." She looked out the window and he didn't know what to do. She was a stranger. She had stiff shoulders and her chin was up, like she was holding it together as best as she could. He didn't know how to make her smile. He didn't know her well enough to make her laugh.

He definitely didn't know her well enough to put his arms around her and tell her that she could cry if she needed to cry. As he waited, her hand went up, flicking at her cheek, at tears he couldn't see.

"I'm not sure why I'm here," she whispered, still looking away from him, out the window. He wasn't sure if the words were for him. She turned and smiled. "I'm sorry, you didn't come here for this."

Jason stood, not sure, really not sure. He hadn't had a lot of experience with that feeling, not until last month. Lately it seemed as if his whole life was about being unsure.

In this case, he took a step back, knowing it was better to leave well enough alone. He'd always heard that saying. He could honestly say that this was the first time in his life that he really got what it meant.

He'd rather face a charging bull than this woman and her well of emotions.

"I'll go on out and feed the horses. If you need anything…"

"Thank you." She turned and there were tears sliding down her cheeks. What should he say? She'd found her family, and lost a dad, all in a span of a twenty-four hours.

"I'm sorry."

She nodded. And he left her there alone, sitting on Etta's satin sofa, the photo album in her lap.

Chapter 3

Alyson didn't want to need a cowboy. She didn't want to need anyone. Not now, when she was determined to find out who she was without her family planning her life, without a publicist or the media telling her who they thought she was. She was twenty-eight. She was going to figure out what she liked, what she wanted.

She would find out what it meant to be Alyson Forester, from Dawson, Oklahoma, and not Alyson Anderson, child prodigy.

She didn't want to need anyone, but she also didn't want to be alone, not with her heart aching and her throat still constricted tight and painful with grief over losing a father she'd never had the chance to know.

But if she closed her eyes and breathed deep in this house, was it his scent that she remembered? Did she remember a moment when her father had held her tight and told her he loved her and he was sorry? It was a vague memory, or maybe wishful thinking.

Being here made it all real, unlike at home when she'd searched for his name on the internet, tracing him here through articles about his rodeo life, and his death in a car accident.

He'd been a stranger she'd read about. Now, being here, he was real. Her memories, fuzzy and unfocused, were becoming clear.

And she had a sister, a sister who was probably more like their father. Andie had spirit. She looked like someone who knew how to fight for what she wanted. Alyson wondered if there was any of that within her, that fighting spirit that grabbed at life, at dreams.

Of course she had that in her. She was here. She had finally walked away from her life. She had contacted the lawyer friend who had helped her for the last ten years, secretly guiding her in how to keep her money safe, how to keep her schedule her own. He had encouraged her, and told her it was time to go.

And she'd walked away, taking her clothes and her only other rebellion, the iPod downloaded with Martina McBride and Miranda Lambert songs. Now that she thought about it, it was funny how she'd always loved country music. Maybe that had been a clue about her life, and who she really was.

She walked to the back door of her grandmother's house. On the wall was another needlepoint verse. This one said: Trust in the Lord with all your heart and lean not unto your own understanding.

Trust in a God she had never really understood. He was a cathedral, aging artwork in museums and a name people muttered when they were angry.

Her grandmother trusted. Obviously trusted.

Alyson didn't know how to trust a God she didn't know. Not when she barely knew herself.

Four days ago she had left Boston. She wasn't going to call it running away, like the message her mother had left on her phone, that she had run away and she had responsibilities. Children ran away—not grown women.

Alyson wouldn't let them call this running away, or a breakdown. This was finding herself. She was doing what she wanted to do, maybe for the first time in her life.

She had a feeling that twenty-five years ago she had wanted to stay here.

Outside was a world she knew so little about. It was hard to know real life when her childhood, her teen years, had been spent with a piano, or on a stage. She'd always lived in a bubble.

She hadn't even wanted to marry Dan. He had just seemed like the right choice. He had been the next step. He was a composer. He loved music. He loved to travel.

He loved her sister.

It wasn't a broken heart that ached inside her when she thought of that. It was something deeper. It was betrayal.

It might be bitterness.

If she stayed in Dawson, she could buy a little house on a quiet corner, get some cats and be the crazy cat lady people in town talked about fifty years from now. She could bake cookies for neighbor children who were afraid to come in her yard, and talk to herself at the store.

She'd give everyone something to talk about.

Crazy people probably didn't plan going crazy. So maybe she was still sane.

Through the window on the back door she watched the barn and saw the cowboy, Jason, as he walked out of a shed and across the lawn to a corral. She had walked out there that morning, taking her cup of coffee to watch as wispy fog covered the valley and horses grazed, tails switching at flies. The sun had touched it all with a golden hue. It had been something, to sit on a bench in the yard and watch the sun rise and the fog dissipate.

She pushed the door open now and walked out, knowing it was a mistake, to go out there, to follow that man around the barn, wanting to be around him, around someone.

As she walked across the lawn a dog joined her. He was tall, leggy and had wiry black hair. She stepped back, unsure. The animal wagged its tail and she took a few careful steps. It followed.

Her chest did a familiar squeeze, a painful clench that didn't belong here, not in Oklahoma in this peaceful setting. She closed her eyes and took a deep breath. When she opened them, the dog was still there. Her breath still felt caught in her lungs.

"Okay, dog, I'm not sure if you're friendly or not, so back off. Go on."

A whistle called the dog away from her. She turned toward the barn and he was there, standing in the opening. He was a little bowlegged, in the cowboy way, and it was appealing, cute. He held a hand out to the dog, sliding fingers through the hair at the back of the animal's neck.

He was Robert Redford rugged, standing in the doorway of a barn, petting a dog, but smiling at her. And she had never experienced life like this.

"That's a look." The cowboy with the Oklahoma drawl spoke when she got closer. "The dog isn't mean."

"Is he yours?" Could he be Etta's dog?

"He doesn't belong to anyone, but everyone feeds him. They toss him scraps at the Mad Cow. The convenience store gives him leftovers. Everyone in town looks out for Mutt."

"Why?"

His head tilted to one side. "Because he doesn't have anyone. He got dumped a year or so ago. People started feeding him and the vet gives him medical care, keeps him updated on his shots. He's just a good dog and he's refused to stay at any one house."

"Oh. So I can feed him?"

"You can. I'm sure Etta does."

She reached to pet the dog and its tail wagged hard enough to shake its back end. "Can I help with the horses? I can feed them so you don't have to drive over here."

"Come on, I'll show you what to do." He glanced back. "It's probably a good idea. You never know when I'll forget."

She followed him back into the barn. She had been in stables, but this barn was different. It was old. It was tall, with a hayloft in the top. Dust swirled in the light that shined through the front door. It smelled of animals, hay and the past.

The dog ran around the barn, sniffing in empty stalls and then barking a shrill bark when he found something. Alyson glanced at Jason and he shrugged.

"Probably a mouse or a cat." He walked into the

corner stall where the dog had something cornered. "Kitten."

Alyson peeked inside as Jason picked up the yellow tabby by the scruff of the neck. The kitten yowled and hissed, spitting and angry. Alyson reached for it and it slashed little claws at her hand.

"Did it get you?" Jason kept hold of the spitting little feline.

"No. What do we do with it?"

"Grab a towel out of the feed room and we'll wrap him up and see if we can calm him down."

He nodded toward an open door. She stepped into the feed room and glanced around, finally finding a pile of old towels, folded and shoved in a cabinet. She grabbed a couple and walked back outside. He was still holding the kitten out from him, but it wasn't hissing now, just looking around.

"Won't that hurt it, holding it that way?"

He shook his head. "This is how the momma cat carried him. He probably got a little big for his britches and ran off. He's old enough to be on his own."

He took the towel and wrapped it tight around the kitten.

"Now what?" She touched the kitten's head. Her first step toward being the neighborhood cat lady.

"Take him. Just keep the towel around him so he can't scratch you."

Alyson took the kitten. She'd always loved cats. They were funky and independent. This one struggled a little against her, but the towel around his legs kept him from clawing.

"Should I feed him?"

"Probably a good idea. You'll have to run to town

and get cat food. Or if you have bread and eggs. Sometimes my sister tears up bread and beats an egg into it."

"I can do that. I'll get food tomorrow. The lady at the Mad Cow said I should go to Grove for groceries, not to the convenience store."

"She's right. The convenience store doesn't carry much." He slipped a knife out of his pocket and cut the string on a bale of hay he must have tossed down from the hayloft.

"My grandmother just leaves her horses here when she goes to Florida? How long is she gone?"

"A few months. I watch them, or Beth, my sister, does. We ride them when the weather is warm. And they get a lot of attention from neighbor kids."

"What about Andie? Doesn't she live here?"

"She's gone a lot. She barrel races, and she has friends around the country. She's…"

"She's what?"

"She's always been a free spirit."

"I see." She held the kitten close and heard a soft purr. "I think he's calming down."

"Yeah, probably. But if you let him go, he'll be gone." He picked up a few flakes of hay and walked out the back door of the barn. Alyson followed.

The horses were there, waiting. There were three of them, one brown, one a light gold and one with spots on his rump. She liked that one. He had gentle eyes and had nuzzled her hand this morning.

"What kind of horses are they?"

He glanced back at her and then he pointed to the brown horse. "That one with the black mane and tail is a bay, that's her color. She's an Arabian, though. Etta bought her somewhere outside of Tulsa. She saw this horse, half-starved in a round pen and she pulled into the drive of the house and told the people to name their price. Goldie here is a Palomino. She's Andie's old barrel horse. This Appaloosa, with the white rump is the mare that Etta rides."

"They're beautiful. Maybe while I'm here I can ride."

"How long are you staying?" He glanced back at her as he dumped the hay in piles a good distance apart. "Or have you already told me?"

"I don't know how long I'll stay." She hadn't thought about it. How long did it take a woman to find herself? How long would her grandmother want her here, in this house, this town?

What if she didn't want Alyson at all? Maybe there was a reason Alyson's mother had taken her away and left Andie behind.

Jason pulled out his list, marking off feeding Etta's horses. He shoved the notebook back into his pocket and watched as Alyson leaned over the fence, trying to pet the Appaloosa while still holding the yowling kitten. The horse moved a little closer and Alyson scratched its neck.

"I need to take a drive out to the youth camp. Do you want to go along?"

"Youth camp?" She turned from the horse and leaned against the fence.

"Camp Hope. A good friend of mine and her husband run it." He ran a thought through his mind. "You could volunteer if you're here for a while."

She held the kitten tight, like a five-year-old with a new pet. That's what it was about her—she acted as if everything was new. "What could I do there?"

"I don't know, maybe play the piano."

Her eyes widened and she shook her head. "No, I don't play the piano."

He closed his eyes, trying to drag the memory back, surprised that it had been there at all. He remembered. She'd been playing a hymn, probably from one of Etta's songbooks. That's why the memory had stuck with him. He knew the song. It was one his mother had sung, a long time ago.

"I remember you playing."

"You didn't even remember me being here." She walked past him and he caught up with her.

"I remember you playing the piano." He followed her through the barn and across the yard to the house, his walk a kind of skip as he tried to keep up. "I can hear the song you were playing. I think it might have been 'It is Well.'"

"It was." They reached the house and he opened the back door for her. She slid through, still holding the cat.

"So, you'll go with me. You might as well get out and see what's going on in the community. It'll get old, sitting in this house waiting for Etta to get back."

"I won't get bored. I love having nothing to do, nowhere to go. You have no idea."

No, he didn't. "So, tell me, why do you want to be here, with nothing to do?"

She glanced back, over her shoulder, her eyes a little narrowed. She looked like the kitten, about to hiss. He laughed a little, because that was Andie, always ready to strike out at someone or something.

"I lived in Boston." She held the kitten in one arm and opened the fridge door. "I've lived in San Francisco. I've lived in Seattle."

"And now you're here? That's a big change."

"I've never lived here, or not since I was little. I want to know what this place is like. This was my father's world."

He nodded and somehow he retrieved the memory. His head was starting to pound. "James. He was here when he wasn't on the road."

"Where else did he go?" She turned quick, spilling a little of the milk she had opened to pour in a bowl.

"Not too much milk, it'll make him sick." Jason opened the loaf of bread she must have bought at the convenience store. It was half-stale and had a price tag on it that was twice what she should have paid. He pulled the piece of bread into pieces and dropped them in with the milk. She had cracked an egg to add to the mixture.

"What about my dad, about James Forester?" She opened a drawer and pulled out a fork.

"Years ago he was a saddle bronc rider. Later he drove a truck. He also worked offshore oil rigs. He was gone a lot."

"Who took care of my sister?"

"Etta raised her when James was gone. But he came into town and he lived here when he wasn't working."

Alyson glanced away. He followed her gaze to the frame with a dozen or so family pictures. And not one of them was of her. That was a shame. There was a picture of Etta and Andie dressed up for the Fourth of July celebration a few years back. They'd won first place in that competition. They'd been a pair, always having fun, and fighting.

"Would I like her?" She turned her attention back

to him, serious blue eyes locking on him, expecting answers.

He hadn't expected this, to get dragged into what should have been personal. But she was waiting, holding that kitten against her and the bowl in the other hand.

"Etta is a free spirit. Andie is, too. You'll like them both."

Alyson put the bowl of milk and eggs on the floor and sat the kitten on the ground next to it. They stepped back and watched as the ragged little guy hissed and slurped in turn. And then he was gone, running out of the kitchen and down the hall, paws sliding on the polished hardwood floors.

"What now?" Alyson went after the cat.

"You'll never catch him and Etta is going to be ticked. She hates cats."

Alyson turned, her face a little pale. "Now you tell me?"

He grinned. "Head injury, remember?"

"What do I do?"

He shrugged. "You'll catch him and Etta will forgive you."

How could she not forgive her granddaughter?

He shook off the mental wandering that could only lead to trouble. He didn't have enough space in his brain for that kind of trouble. "I have to go."

"To the camp?"

"Yeah, of course." He pulled the notebook out of his pocket. "First to the feed store."

He held the notebook up and the words blurred and then doubled. The ache in the back of his head tripled. He slipped the notebook back into his pocket and blinked a few times to clear his vision.

"Are you okay?" A female voice from too far away. He looked up and she was watching him, her eyes focused and full of concern. He managed a smile.

"Of course I am."

"You look pale." She rummaged through the cabinet and while he tried to get it together, she ran water into the mug and held it out. "Drink this."

He pulled off the hat that suddenly seemed too tight and wiped a hand across his forehead. She pushed the water into his hand and he took it, because she was determined.

"Thanks." He set the cup on the counter.

A cool hand was on his arm, holding him closer than he should have been to her, to someone who smelled like lavender and roses on a summer day.

She led him down the hall to the parlor. He let her, because of lavender and roses, and because he couldn't undo her hand from his arm. And he didn't really want to.

Which meant he wasn't too far gone.

"Sit down."

She backed him up to the wing chair next to the piano. He sat, closing his eyes and leaning his head back to rest, just for a minute.

The screen door slammed and he didn't want to open his eyes. But there were footsteps and perfume that hung over the air like some kind of heavy-duty air freshener. He opened his eyes.

"What in the world is going on here?" Etta Forester stood in the doorway of the parlor, a vision in tie-dyed clothes, lavender hair and a floppy, wide-brimmed hat.

It was a bad time to be seeing double.

The woman standing next to his chair looked like she

was about to faint. He barely remembered her name, but he felt a lot like the ten-year-old Jason after he'd gotten caught playing house with Amy Baxter, his next-door neighbor at the time.

This was her grandmother? Alyson had thought she was coming to a normal, sane world. She thought she had left crazy behind. Maybe the town cat lady wasn't as far-fetched as she thought. A giggle sneaked up on Alyson, surprising her, and she laughed. And then her grandmother laughed.

"Girl, I've wanted to hug you for twenty-something years. Come here." Etta Forester took the few steps that brought them together and then her arms were around Alyson, holding tight.

Etta stepped back. "Well, it don't look like they ruined you too awful bad. A little too much like a spit-polished boot, but you'll do. I'd say you've had your first scuff marks in the last few weeks. Is that what..."

Etta jerked around, and then leaned to look under the sofa. "What in the world. Is that a nasty old cat in my house?"

Another laugh, this one deep, male. Alyson glared at the man sitting in her grandmother's velvet wingback.

"Yes, it is a cat. He told me to bring it in and feed it."

"I didn't tell you to let it go." He struggled to sit up. Alyson held out a hand and he pulled himself to his feet.

And he didn't let go of her hand, not for a long moment, and it wasn't easy, to untangle herself from the emotion that happened in that moment. The connection between them started in her fingers and slid down her arms, straight to her heart. She couldn't breathe, couldn't move away from his touch.

"Jason Bradshaw, what is the matter with you? Bull get you down?"

"Just a little. Some head—"

Etta waved her hand. "I read about it on the internet. Concussion and some torn ligaments in your knee. How's your noggin?"

"My noggin hurts and you're pretty lucky that I remember you."

Etta patted his cheek. "Honey, you couldn't forget an old bird like me."

"You *are* unforgettable." Jason rubbed the back of his head and Alyson wondered if he was as okay as he pretended.

"There's that cat again." Etta pointed to the love seat. "Get that thing outta here. My goodness, you're here for what, two days and you're already dragging in strays. You always were animal crazy."

Alyson turned, she held her grandmother's gaze and she couldn't look away. "I was animal crazy?"

"Of course you were. Drove your mother insane. Well, everything drove that high-maintenance female insane."

"I'm sorry about the kitten. It was hungry." She glanced at Jason. "And it wasn't his fault."

Being around her grandmother seemed to push both of them back in time about twenty years, Alyson realized. They were suddenly children, apologizing and trying to make excuses for their bad behavior.

"The kitten doesn't have to go, but you'll need a litter box and some food for the mangy-looking thing."

"Since Etta is here, I think I can go now." Jason walked to the door. He paused at the opening and leaned against it a little and Alyson remembered he'd done that yesterday. She realized now that it wasn't about being relaxed. He was holding himself up.

"Jason, do you need a ride home?" Etta was more observant. It didn't take her two days to notice when a man wasn't as strong as he pretended to be.

"No, I think I'm fine. I just need a minute to get my legs back under me. Take care of each other. Etta, I'm glad you're home."

"Well, thanks to you I came back early and cut short a perfectly lovely cruise with friends."

"I did that?" Jason shook his head. "I guess I probably did."

"We'll blame it on Alana. She called the ship. I got off at the next port and flew to Tulsa."

"You didn't have to do that." Alyson found it hard to believe that anyone would do that. And as she was taking it all in, Jason was saying goodbye. Her one familiar link in this town, a man who couldn't remember her name.

He left, walking down the sidewalk to his truck, slow, even steps, and still that cowboy swagger. Alyson watched through the gauzy curtains as he got into his truck, pulling himself into the seat and sitting for a minute.

"We should probably drive him," she whispered.

A hand touched her shoulder. Her grandmother stood behind her, staring out the window with her. "He wouldn't thank you for that. A cowboy likes to take care of himself. He's stronger than most. He's been through a lot and came out just fine."

"What's he been through?"

"Now, honey, if I told you that, then you wouldn't

have the fun of getting to know him. Getting to know a man, that's part of the adventure."

Alyson watched him drive away. "I'm not here to get to know a man. I'm here to find out who I am."

Her grandmother put an arm around her shoulders. "I'm glad you're home, Alyson girl, glad you're home."

Chapter 4

Alyson stood in the center of her grandmother's parlor and thought about Etta's words. *Glad she was home.* Was this home? Or just a place to hide for a little while, until she figured out her next move, where she went from here?

"Are you going to tell me what happened?" Etta flipped on a light and pulled the drapes open, sending a light cloud of dust across the room.

Alyson sneezed a few times as sunlight poured into the room, the beams catching the particles of dust that had flown from the drapes. Etta didn't seem to be bothered by the sunlight or the dust. She swiped her finger across the windowsill and shook her head before turning back to face Alyson.

"Well?" Alyson's grandmother was a tall, thin woman with hair that wasn't gray, but a shade of lavender. Silver hoops dangled from her ears and her clothes were breezy and tie-dyed, like the ones Alyson had found upstairs in the room with the spinning wheel.

"I needed to find you."

Etta's brows went up and she shook her head. She pointed to the photo albums on the sofa and glanced back at Alyson. And then it hit her, that maybe she shouldn't be here. Maybe she should have run to anyplace but Oklahoma. She knew people in California. She had friends in Chicago. She could have gone anywhere.

And she'd picked Dawson, Oklahoma. She'd picked Etta. She wanted answers to questions that had lingered in the back of her mind for years. There had always been flashes of memory, missing pieces and unanswered questions.

She had tried to do research a few years earlier, when she'd first moved into her own apartment, but she'd hit dead ends. Maybe because she hadn't really known what she was searching for. It was hard to search for something that felt like childhood dreams—nothing real, nothing tangible.

"You're here because something happened." Etta sat down on the piano bench and ran her fingers over the keys. "You played it when you were a little bitty thing. I knew then, when you were barely talking, that you had a gift."

A gift, or was it a curse? Etta couldn't know the pressure. She couldn't know what it felt like, to never really have a childhood, to always be playing, to always be *on* for the people around her. Her weekends had been spent with her mother, poring over articles written about her performances. Nothing was more fun for an eight-year-old than to read about every wrong note she'd played.

And what happened to the prodigy when she became an adult, with hands that trembled and fear that squeezed the air from her lungs? What did she do when the pills stopped working?

"I didn't know about you, about my family here." Alyson walked to the window, she looked out at the quiet country lane. A truck pulling a trailer loaded with hay lumbered down the road, a Border Collie standing on the bales of hay.

Alyson turned to face her grandmother. "I had memories that I couldn't figure out. I stopped questioning my mother years ago. She wouldn't answer."

"I'm sorry." Etta stood, closing the cover over the keys of the piano and walking up behind Alyson. An arm, comforting and strong, wrapped around Alyson's shoulders and pulled her close. "You and Andie were the victims. I couldn't stop what they did, the way they decided to end things. I just prayed that someday you'd come back."

"I guess your prayers have been answered." The words were empty, because Alyson had never prayed, not real prayers that counted. She'd prayed to go to Europe, to have a pony and to survive. That had been a prayer that counted. She just hadn't realized it at the time.

"Yes, my prayers have been answered. But it isn't all about having you here. It's about having you happy."

Alyson walked away from the window, away from her grandmother's embrace. She stopped in front of the photo albums she'd left on the coffee table. She'd found pictures of herself in those albums, a toddler who smiled.

How did she tell her grandmother about the pills she took for anxiety, and about falling apart? How did she talk about how it felt to look in the mirror and see a fraud, someone so far from the perfect person everyone thought she was, that she didn't even recognize the person looking back at her?

She picked up the album and opened to pictures of her father and her sister. Andie. She whispered the name and closed her eyes. There were so many missing pieces of her life she wondered how she had ever felt whole.

Had she ever felt whole?

She wasn't sure that she was even there yet, not even with this knowledge, with this family she had missed out on, and with Etta standing next to her.

"He loved you."

Alyson closed her eyes and tried to remember that love, those arms, and how it had felt to be a part of their lives, a part of Etta's home and her family. Vaguely, she vaguely remembered him tossing her into the air and catching her.

There were other memories, memories that made her want to cry. She shook her head to clear the images of driving away. Images that had been explained away as childhood nightmares.

"I wish he would have come after me, after us." Alyson didn't mean to make it an accusation against a man who could no longer defend himself, but it happened.

"Aly, he couldn't. They made a deal. Your mother and father were two different people. James was a country boy. Caroline was city. He grew up in church. Your mother didn't. They couldn't find a middle ground."

"So he let her leave? With me?"

"That was the deal. He took Andie, she got you."

"*Parent Trap* was cute and funny, and it had a happy ending. My parents really did this to their children." As if they were property, as if their feelings hadn't mattered.

"I know." Her grandmother's voice was soft, unlike her image in those tie-dyed clothes.

And now the most difficult question. "How did they decide who kept whom? Why did he keep Andie?"

Etta sighed. "Andie wouldn't have survived your mother."

Alyson shook her head. Did that make her a survivor? Did they honestly see her as the strong one? When she looked at those pictures of Andie, smiling, laughing on the back of a horse, and then she thought of her own childhood, she didn't get that.

Andie looked stronger than Alyson had ever felt.

"How is Andie?"

"Andie's good. She's a free spirit, going all over the country, from rodeo to rodeo. She's going to love you, though."

The empty space in her heart grew and there didn't seem to be a way to fill it. This could have been her world, her life, and instead she had been her mother's prized possession, but never a daughter—that position had gone to her younger siblings.

Alyson's childhood had been spent performing. She had been paraded on programs, on stages, where they would test her with a song and then she'd play it. She remembered them trying to trick her, to break her with a song she might not know.

She had worn the responsibility of not letting her parents down, not letting her family down.

"We'll work through this, Alyson. I want you here, and you can stay as long as you'd like." Etta smiled big. "Honey, you can stay forever if that's what you want. It's whatever you decide."

Alyson could decide. Of course she could, but she also knew that there were obligations looming that she couldn't avoid. Sooner or later she would have to return to her life.

But for now, Alyson Anderson was Alyson Forester and that required a change.

"Do you think we could go shopping?"

Etta smiled. "Honey, now you're speaking my language."

As they turned to walk out of the room, the kitten shot past them, a ragged little feline with cobwebs on his whiskers.

"I can't believe you brought that animal into my house."

"He's cute, though."

Etta laughed. "Mangy is never cute. Now don't let me forget that we need comfortable shoes if we're going to work at Camp Hope."

The shift in conversation took Alyson by surprise. "When do we do that?"

"Next week." Etta grabbed her purse and keys that she'd dropped on the table just inside the front door. "We'll stop by later and talk to Jenna and Adam."

As they walked out the door, Alyson was thinking of Camp Hope, then her thoughts turned to Jason Bradshaw. She wanted him to remember her, because memories shouldn't be one-sided.

* * *

Jason landed wrong when he jumped out of his truck at Camp Hope. Too bad the pills he'd taken for his head weren't going to undo this. He leaned against his truck and flexed his leg, grimacing at the pull in his knee. He had more problems with his body than someone thirty years older than him. Or that's what the doctor had said the last time Jason had kept an appointment.

And with that verdict the doctor had also told him it was about time for him to think about retiring from bull riding. Jason shrugged off the advice, and didn't want to think about it, even now.

He limped away from his truck and started toward the dorm where Clint and Adam were working. Clint was on the ladder. Distracted, Jason didn't see the two boys running toward him until they hit him head on, wrapping six-year-old arms around his waist and nearly knocking him off his feet.

"Whoa, guys, what's up?" He hugged them close and they did what they'd always done, each claimed a leg to hug and he would walk with them holding tight.

"We've missed you." Both boys shouted. This must be what a sugar high looked like.

"I missed you guys, too. But did you maybe have too much candy today?" He stopped, grimacing because they were heavier than when they'd started this game a few years back. "Do you think you could give an old guy a break and walk with me today?"

They let go of his legs and sat back on the ground, staring up as if he'd lost his mind. "Do we gotta?" David asked.

"Yeah, sorry guys, today we gotta." He held out his

hands and the two grabbed, one on each hand. "Where is everybody?"

As in their parents, Jenna and Adam, and their uncle Clint.

"They have to get this place ready for kids." Timmy, always the mimic.

"They're fixing the roof of the dorm." David, more serious and quiet. "Cleaning, guttering."

"Let's head that way. Maybe they need my help."

"You won't remember, will you?" Timmy asked. "Because you've damaged stuff inside your head."

"Yeah, I guess I have."

A truck pulled down the drive of Camp Hope. Beth. What in the world would she be doing there? The camp was too much like church for his sister's comfort.

"Is that Beth?" David stood next to him, leaning in slightly, his bare feet scrunching in the dirt.

"Yeah, it's Beth."

"Are you serious?" Timmy shouted. "She wouldn't come near here with a ten-foot pole."

Jason laughed, because that was pretty close to right. "Let's see what she wants."

"Do we hafta?" Timmy pulled loose from his hand. "We kind of wanted to play with tanks and stuff, or maybe play with you. But we don't want to talk to a girl."

"Fine, I'll catch up with you." Jason headed back in the direction of his sister. She was getting out of her truck and looked about as happy as Timmy had. "What's up, Sis?"

"Antibiotics?"

"Antibiotics?"

"For my horse. You were going to pick them up and

bring them home. You drove past the house, so I thought I'd better run over here and see if you remembered."

If he remembered. He rubbed a hand over his face and tried to think back, to the remembering part. Nothing. He closed his eyes and worked backward, retracing where he'd been. And he could only remember one thing, lavender and roses.

"Jason, this isn't good. You really need to go back to the neurologist." Beth walked him over to his truck. "I'll go with you."

"I know you would." He opened the door of the truck as his phone rang. Beth climbed in, he took the call. As she hunted through his truck, he walked away.

Beth chased after him, catching him as he ended the call.

"Who was that?" She held the antibiotics up for him to see. "You remembered."

"That's good to know." He slipped the phone into his pocket. "That was Roy Cummings. He wanted to know how I'm feeling and if I plan on getting back on tour."

"You can't." Beth shook her head. "Jason, you can't be thinking about it, can you?"

"I don't know. What else can I do, Beth? I'm a bull rider."

"You're a bull rider who suffered a serious head injury. You could get hurt worse. You could…"

Jason hugged her. "I know what could happen. I've talked to the sports medicine team. I've talked to the neurologist. My short-term memory is damaged, Beth. I know all that. But I also know that I can't throw it all away without trying to fight back."

"Why do you need this so much?" Beth glanced over

her shoulder at a car coming up the drive. "Seriously, Jason, you have your ranch. You have this community."

Jason couldn't give her the answer she wanted.

All his friends were settling down, having families and building lives. And he couldn't remember going to the store for his sister.

A car pulled up the drive and parked. Etta's car. He couldn't remember the name of the woman getting out of the passenger's side. But he knew her.

"Is that the reason you had to go to Etta's this morning?"

He had no trouble remembering his sister, standing there staring at him, a smirk of a smile on her face. He pulled the paper out of his pocket and glanced over it, at the note telling him to go to the feed store and at the bottom of the page, the name Alyson.

"Yeah, I think so. That's Alyson. She's Etta's granddaughter."

"Some things haven't changed. You can still remember a woman's name." She watched Etta and her granddaughter. "But since she's with Etta, I think you should be careful. Break her heart and Etta will break your neck."

"You think?"

"I'm pretty sure of it. Did you know that someone bought the old church on Back Street?"

"I guess I didn't know that."

The church they had attended with their mother. It had been closed down for years. People had left the small country church behind, looking for more. If he closed his eyes, he could remember in detail the inside of that old building. He could remember how it felt to sit next to his mom and sing "In the Garden."

The fact that church interested his sister was more of a surprise than the fact that someone had bought the building. Their father had jerked her out of church about ten years ago and she hadn't been back. Now he thought she stayed away because of the recent past, not the distant.

"The sign in front of it says Sold." She looked up at him, and then glanced back at Etta. "She looks like Andie."

"She's Andie's sister. I think they might be twins." He glanced down and smiled. "How's that for short-term?"

"Good. When did Etta get home?"

"I didn't say the memory was perfect." He pointed to his head. "Remember, head injury."

"You need a keeper."

"I'm starting to realize that." He definitely needed someone to keep him on track until his memory returned to normal. If it ever did. He paused at that thought. Not long enough to let it get to him. He was an expert at not letting things get to him. "Are you here to work?"

"You know I'm not. Jas, do you want me to drive you home?"

"Why would I need that?"

"You look pale and you're limping."

"I'm good."

"Yeah, you're always good." She hugged him. "I'm heading home. Call if you need me."

She took the paper from his hand and wrote on it. "In case you forget."

"I won't forget."

As she walked away, he turned back to Etta and Alyson. Something had changed. He studied the woman in worn jeans, a T-shirt and flip-flops. He didn't remember her being like that. He remembered cashmere. And pink.

Of course Alyson's grandmother led her directly to Jason Bradshaw. In the few hours the two had spent together, Alyson had learned that her grandmother did her own thing.

On the way to Grove, they had talked about how a younger Etta had backpacked across Europe, lived in a commune during the early seventies and then found Jesus in a real way and settled in Dawson with Henry Forester.

He died when her children were young and she started a business making tie-dyed clothing.

And now she was making a beeline for Jason Bradshaw, holding tight to Alyson's wrist, as if she thought her granddaughter might try to escape. And Alyson couldn't lie and say the thought hadn't crossed her mind.

"What is it we need to do here, at the camp?" Alyson thought her question might pull her grandmother back and get her on track.

"Well, we're going to check on Jason and then we're going to ask Jenna and Adam what we can do to help them get started next week when the first campers arrive."

"I see." Alyson had never been to camp, and now she was going to volunteer at one.

"Jas, honey, are you here to work?"

"I think I probably am." He winked at Alyson. She looked away, scanning the camp, the buildings, the fields.

"There's Jenna and the guys." Etta pointed to a woman with a round belly. There were two men with her. One had a protective arm around her waist. The other was stepping onto a ladder.

"She sure looks pretty pregnant." Etta smiled at Jason, not at Alyson. "Adam's a lucky guy."

"I'm happy for them, Etta."

"I know you are, but a few of us thought…"

He limped ahead of them, ignoring her grandmother's unspoken question about what people thought. But Alyson wanted to know. What had people thought? Had there been something between Jason and Jenna?

"They were only friends," Etta answered. "I just don't know what's wrong with that boy. He's never had a serious relationship. Always been that way."

"Maybe he doesn't want to get serious with anyone." It made sense to Alyson. So did changing the subject, but something else she'd learned about her grandmother was that Etta was relentless.

"Well, that doesn't even make sense. Of course he wants to get serious with someone." Etta made a face, drawing in her brows and scrunching her mouth and nose. "Why aren't you married?"

"I…"

"Well?"

"I was engaged."

"I see." Etta stopped walking. "Is that why you're here?"

"No, not really. I mean, it's part of it. I wanted to find you."

"And you wanted to find a place to hide. We're more than a shelter in the storm, Alyson, we're your family.

We're going to be here, even when the storm passes. Make sure you remember that."

Alyson nodded. "I know. And I'm not here to hide. I'm here because I found you."

As they approached the group gathered at the corner of the dorm, Jason spoke to the woman, and then glanced toward Alyson and Etta. She couldn't hear what they were saying, but he looked away, and he looked uncomfortable.

"Etta, you're back." The woman, round and pregnant, hugged Alyson's grandmother.

"Well, of course I am. I had a surprise waiting for me." Etta slipped an arm through Alyson's. "Honey, this is Jenna, her handsome husband, Adam Mackenzie. And that guy on the ladder is her brother, Clint."

"Nice to meet you all."

"Are you here for long?" Jenna spoke, her hand going to her belly.

"I'm not sure."

Etta shot her a look that questioned her answer, but Alyson couldn't explain. How could she give answers when she had no idea what her future held? She couldn't explain to her grandmother about her fears.

For a little while she wanted to be a girl from Dawson. She might want to be that person forever. But wanting didn't undo the realities of her life and a schedule that couldn't be undone.

Jason smiled at her, making her answer okay. He winked and his hand went to the ladder, shaking it a little, distracting the people looking at her, waiting for answers. Clint Cameron grabbed the edge of the roof that he was working on.

"Give a guy a break when he's standing on a ladder."

Jason looked up, pushing his hat back. "Sorry, Clint, just making sure it's steady."

"Right." Clint took another step up the ladder. "Try to hold it steady."

"Jenna, we're here to volunteer." Etta stepped closer to the group, pulling Alyson with her. "I know you've got camp starting on Monday. If you need unskilled labor, Alyson and I will be here."

"We can always use help." Jenna's smile was sweet, and she held on to her husband as if he was the best thing in the world. "I know that I'm not going to be a lot of use, so we could really use kitchen help."

"Kitchen would be great." Etta wrapped an arm around Alyson's shoulders and squeezed. "It'll be fun, won't it?"

Alyson made a weak attempt at smiling and Jason laughed. He shot her a look and shook his head. "I don't know if you want her in your kitchen."

"Why is that?"

"I don't remember a lot, but I do remember putting out a fire in Etta's kitchen."

"Kittens, fires—what in the world kind of trouble are you going to drag out of your hat tomorrow?" Etta asked, still holding Alyson close.

"I'm sure she can think of something." Jason held the ladder as Clint climbed down.

"Are *you* going to work in the kitchen?" Alyson directed the question at Jason, who was standing by the ladder, pretending it wasn't holding him up. She knew that it was. She had him figured out. He deflected to keep the focus off him.

She had realized a long time ago that she learned more watching than she did talking.

"I'm not sure what I'll be doing." Jason stepped away from the ladder.

"Are you going back on tour when the doctor gives you the okay?" Clint asked as he pulled off work gloves. "We could really use your help here, with the junior rodeo at the end of camp."

Jason shrugged. "I've been thinking about it. If I can go on tour, I probably will. I need to get on some practice bulls and see how it feels. Or I might try some smaller, local events."

"You can't," Jenna spoke up and Alyson wanted to agree, even if it wasn't her business. "Jason, come on, is it really worth it?"

"Jenna, I don't have a family. I'm a bull rider."

"I hope you'll think about this," Jenna spoke softly, and then seemed to let it go.

Alyson listened but she wasn't going to comment on someone else's career, not when her own was going down the drain fast. And she didn't want them to know that she'd fed her curiosity about Jason Bradshaw.

She'd used her computer to search his name and information about his accident. He'd been unconscious when they took him from the arena. He hadn't regained consciousness for twelve hours. He had suffered a traumatic brain injury with symptoms that included short-term memory loss, headaches and dizziness.

He was the kind of person who faced his fears. She had never been that type of person.

But she was here, she reminded herself. She was in Oklahoma. She had left Boston, driven for two days, and made it here. She hadn't asked anyone's opinion, hadn't cleared it with anyone. She had just left.

Because her life wasn't about fear, or playing the

piano. This was her life, too. She was Alyson Forester. And she knew that, deep down inside, she was strong.

She was strong enough to meet the gaze of a cowboy with a slightly wicked smile and brown eyes that flashed with humor when he winked at her.

Chapter 5

He had to stop flirting with Alyson Anderson. Jason watched her walk away with Etta and Jenna. The three of them were going to the kitchen to talk about what they should expect next week. He didn't look away, not even when Clint cleared his throat to get his attention.

"If you mess with that, Etta will be on your doorstep with a shotgun," Adam warned.

"I know." Jason turned back to the two other men and ignored the strong desire to seek Alyson out, to get to know her better. "What's up with the camp?"

"We're going to have a great summer, Jason. We'd really like for you to be part of this." Adam nodded in the direction of the barns and stable. "Come on out and I'll show you what we're working on. Clint?"

"I'm going to get these gutters finished and head home."

"Okay, thanks. I'll see you tomorrow." Adam started walking and Jason followed.

They stopped at the gate next to the barn. Jason leaned against the top rail and looked out at the field, and then in the direction of the indoor arena.

"You've come a long way with this place."

Jason watched the two dozen horses grazing in the field, cows with calves a short distance away. A little over a year ago, there had been nothing here but a few of the buildings. Adam had arrived to find the place half-finished and the money to finish the rest had been spent by his cousin.

What a difference a year could make.

And a year ago, Jason was working hard, fast on the track for a world title. This should have been his year. It probably would have been, if it hadn't been for the wreck of the season that ended with him in the hospital for a couple of weeks.

Adam Mackenzie wanted him here, working at Camp Hope. It meant more than people realized. It meant staying, being involved. A guy couldn't do something like this halfway, without total commitment.

Of course, a guy had to be pretty committed to staying full time on the back of a bull, too.

Maybe he was better at commitment than he realized.

Or maybe it was because bulls weren't people and didn't expect much from him.

He figured he was an expert at being detached. He'd learned it from the best, his father. Detachment was not getting too close to a mother that fought cancer for a dozen years. Because Jason had known, even before anyone had said it, that he wouldn't always have her.

He remembered the little ways he had pushed her out

of his life. And now he recognized that he'd been a kid trying to protect himself from being hurt.

She had always pushed right back, insisting on hugging him when he was scared, insisting on being at school programs. Later, close to the end, she had talked to him about not being afraid to love someone.

He shook past that thought because it hadn't gotten any easier over the years. He'd become an expert at being unattached. There were exceptions, he realized. Beth, of course, his sister had always counted on him. They'd relied on each other.

And Jenna. She had needed a friend and he'd been there for her. And she'd figured out a few of his secrets along the way.

"Adam, this camp is a big deal and you know I want to support you." Jason let his gaze wander—to the dorms, to the steeple of the open-air chapel.

"Yeah, I know. But we're looking for more than a check, Jason."

"Right." A rangy-looking colt walked up to the fence, inching his nose out. Jason scratched the horse's face and rubbed its neck. "That's about the ugliest horse I think I've ever seen."

Adam laughed. "Yeah, he's Jenna's favorite. Some spooky mare of hers had this thing last fall."

"She would like it." Jason patted the horse's neck one last time and turned away from the fence. "I'll do what I can for the camp. I have a doctor's appointment next week. I've got people pressuring me about riding next month. And then I've got people telling me I'd be crazy to ride."

"And the sponsors always have to be happy." Adam

walked next to him, slowing his mammoth stride. "I get that."

"Yeah, I know you do."

"I won't pressure you, I just want you to know that there's a spot for you if you decide this is where you're supposed to be." Adam turned and they started the walk back to the main campus area.

Jenna was waiting for them at the dining hall. The boys were playing on the swing that hung from the oak tree nearby. She watched, but her hand kept going to her belly.

Jason shoved aside the moment of envy. Not because Adam had Jenna, but for what the two of them shared. How could he envy something he had never wanted?

It was the epidemic of love and marriage that was getting to him. Everyone had caught the illness, and he was the last one with any immunity. Cody, Adam, Clint—they were all married now with kids, or kids on the way. Clint and Willow were working on adopting child number two.

There were so many happy-ever-afters, a single guy had to keep his guard up. It kind of gave him the willies when he thought about it.

"How's your memory?" Adam asked as they sat down on the bench next to Jenna.

"Another reason you wouldn't want me working with kids. What if I put one on a horse and forgot he couldn't ride. Or forgot that the horse wasn't broke." He tried to smile, as if it were a joke.

Jenna patted his shoulder. "We'll get you a helper."

"Thanks." Jason stretched, straightening his leg out and taking a deep breath when the pain hit. Adam had asked him a question. "My memory is improving, though."

He had remembered Alyson. More specifically, he remembered her perfume, and a cashmere sweater.

"I should head home." Jason stood up. "I'll pray about helping."

He lifted his hand in farewell and walked across the big lawn toward his truck. He worked up a memory of Alyson in blue jeans, flip-flops and a T-shirt. She hadn't been dressed like that the day he first saw her.

A memory had never felt so good. But some strange twist to his gut told him the memory was dangerous.

After talking to Jenna, Alyson and Etta stopped at the Mad Cow. Alyson walked through the door of the café with her grandmother. It felt better than it had the previous evenings, when she'd come here alone. This time people smiled. They still stared, but it wasn't like before when everyone was trying to figure who she was and why she was in their town.

Today she was one of them. Kind of.

And she'd never been that before. At least not like this. She'd been in a group of children who all had spectacular musical gifts, so much so that people would pay to see them, to listen to their music.

"You okay?" Etta gave her a gentle push toward a booth in the corner, pausing for a moment to say hello to a friend and introduce her. And wasn't it wonderful to have her in town?

Alyson smiled, but her lips trembled and it was hard to breathe.

"Hold it together, kiddo," Etta whispered as they sat down on opposite sides of the booth.

Alyson blinked to clear her vision. It was the restaurant that caused a little bit of a light-headed feeling. The walls were painted with black-and-white splotches, like the hide of a cow. The booths were black. The tabletops were black Formica. And the tiles on the floor, black and white.

Vera, owner of the Mad Cow, came out of the kitchen carrying an order pad and two menus. She wore black pants, a white top and black-and-white spotted boots.

"Etta, great to have you back in town. And wasn't this a wonderful surprise? Alyson is back with us. Remember how she loved chocolate ice cream when she was a little thing? Goodness, always neat and tidy, too. And Andie couldn't ever eat a bowl of ice cream without getting half of it on her face or clothes."

Alyson blinked a few times, because last night Vera had been pleasant, but hadn't shared personal stories with her. Even her grandmother had been vague on personal stories. But this story—maybe it explained why Andie wouldn't have survived their mother.

"She's still pretty neat and tidy, Vera." Etta smiled at Alyson. "But from the looks of my kitchen, cooking isn't one of her skills."

"That's okay. She has other gifts." Vera patted her shoulder. "What can I get you ladies for supper?"

Alyson started to order a salad, but her grandmother shot her a look. "Good heavens, child, do you really want to eat a salad when you could have Vera's chicken fried steak, smothered in gravy?"

It sounded like an artery-clogging special to Alyson. But her mouth watered and her body chanted something that sounded like, Must. Have. Carbs.

And she agreed. She nodded. "I'll take it."

Vera smiled big and scribbled on the order pad. "Now that's more like it, sweetheart. A person can't live on salad alone. You having the same, Etta?"

"No, honey, I'm having her salad."

Vera laughed. "So, does Andie know her sister is home?"

"I called her this morning." Etta smiled and Alyson got the impression there was more to the call.

When Vera walked away, Etta stopped smiling. "There's something you learn in a town like Dawson. You don't ever give all the facts unless you want everyone to know your business."

"So what is our business?"

Etta poured sugar in her coffee and stirred it. "I called, but Andie didn't answer. She doesn't always."

"Oh."

"But she'll be home. She'll see my number on the caller ID and she'll call." Etta smiled big, as if everything was perfect, but it wasn't.

Alyson smiled back, but apprehension tugged at her stomach and she couldn't believe she was about to eat chicken fried steak smothered in gravy.

There were too many thoughts racing through her mind. She was thinking about Andie, about seeing a sister she hadn't seen since they were not quite three years old. And she couldn't help but think about Jason Bradshaw.

He was the last thing she should have been thinking about. She'd been dumped a month ago. She'd fallen apart, walking off the stage halfway through a concert, leaving a stunned symphony orchestra trying to pick up the pieces of a shattered performance.

The next day she'd read the article about what how

she'd had a nervous breakdown. But she hadn't. It had been just the opposite. She had finally walked away from something that she should have walked away from years ago.

Jason woke up the next morning with a pretty clear head and notes next to his bed telling him what he needed to do that day. After a cup of coffee, he walked out to the barn. His dad was coming out with an old saddle.

"What do you need me to do today?" Jason glanced at his watch. The notebook had outlined chores at his own place, a trip to town and stopping by Camp Hope.

"I can't think of a thing." Buck Bradshaw tossed the saddle into the Dumpster next to the barn. "Been meaning to throw that thing away for ages."

A thirty-year-old saddle that had belonged to Jason's mother. The two men didn't discuss it, just went on. That's how they dealt with things in their family. Jason's dad probably hadn't planned on anyone seeing him throw the saddle in the trash.

But why now? Jason didn't ask questions. He wouldn't have gotten answers anyway.

"How you feeling?" Buck paused at the door to the barn.

"Feeling good, Dad." Jason glanced one last time at the Dumpster. "I need to run into town, get a few things done. If you need me, just call."

"I'll do that."

Jason was heading down the drive when he saw Andie driving toward town, her truck pulling the horse trailer with the living quarters that she spent most of her time in.

He eased onto the road and followed her. Not the best move—he knew that. He should have driven on out to Camp Hope. He had it on his notepad. He had talked to Adam yesterday and promised to pray about working at the camp.

And Alyson's name was written on the bottom of that page. Etta's other granddaughter. He hadn't forgotten her.

He almost wished he could. If he could forget her, he could drive on past Etta's. He could take a side road that would lead him to Camp Hope and away from a situation that wasn't going to be pretty.

This had to be from the brain injury, this sudden need to be involved in everything, and his own crazy inability to walk away. It had nothing to do with a woman who reminded him of a summer day, kind of breezy, warm and easy to be around.

She even smelled like a summer day.

She was Andie's sister. And Andie was about to get the surprise of her life. There was no telling what she'd do when she walked through the doors and saw Alyson in her home, with their grandmother. People assumed life didn't bother Andie. Jason knew better.

The truck and trailer ahead of him turned into the driveway at Etta's and pulled down to the barn. He stopped next to the house and got out of his truck. As he walked, Andie jumped down out of her truck. It took him by surprise, how much she looked like her twin. He hadn't seen it before. They weren't identical, but they were close.

Andie was tough. She was country, the real deal, with her jeans tucked into leather boots, her T-shirt said something about being raised country. Her soft edges were hidden by a sharp personality, a sharp attitude.

"What are you doing here so early?" She walked back to the end of the horse trailer, sprang the latch and then flipped up the bar that kept the doors safely latched.

"Saw you driving by." Thought she might need a friend. He doubted that now.

"Cool." She walked into the empty side of the trailer, down to the end, where her horse was tied. She pulled the lead rope and freed him. "Back up."

The horse obeyed. When he backed out of the trailer, Andie had the lead rope. Her gaze shifted, to the back door of the house. Her eyes widened. Jason waited.

"What's she doing here?" Those were Alyson's sister's first words to her in over twenty-five years. So much for happy family reunions.

"She's found us," Etta said, reserved, smiling. "She found out who she is and she came looking for us."

Andie stared and Alyson waited, not knowing what to do. At least having a twin wasn't a surprise for Andie. Alyson's gaze shot to Jason Bradshaw and she wondered why he was there. For her sister, no doubt. They'd always known each other. They were friends.

And now, Alyson knew that she was the one who wasn't supposed to be here. Andie sighed and held her horse close. Andie, who had had this life, these people, their father, the horses and a childhood.

"Andie, I'm glad you're home. I've been hoping…" Etta started.

Andie shook her head. "Right. I need to put my horse up. He's had a long trip."

Alyson made a move to follow her sister but a hand on her arm stopped her. Jason's hand. "Give her a few minutes alone. You've had a few days to adjust. She needs a little time, too."

"Okay." Alyson watched Andie walk through the doors of the barn and disappear into the darkness.

And she knew what her sister was feeling. She knew the emptiness. She knew betrayal, and the feeling that everyone knew something she didn't. It was a deep down hurt. Alyson felt it, too.

"How about a cup of coffee, Jason?" Etta, quick to get it together again. Her outfit today was jeans and a tie-dyed T-shirt. Her lavender/gray hair was held back with a scarf. "Did you already eat?"

"I had coffee, but I need to head out to Camp Hope." He pulled a notebook out of his pocket and Alyson smiled as he read it off to them. "Camp Hope, a bridle that Dad ordered and dog food. If I don't see you all today, I'm sure I'll see you at church tomorrow."

Church. Alyson watched him walk away and she had another moment of not knowing what to do. Church? She glanced from her grandmother to the barn. Her sister did needlepoint verses. She probably understood faith.

Jason pulled out of the drive, waving as he took off down the road. Andie was still taking care of her horse. Or maybe waiting it out until they were gone.

Etta looked at the barn, and then back to Alyson. "We might as well go inside and wait. I guess I should have left a message on her phone, but I didn't want to tell her like that."

Alyson nodded because she didn't know what to say. She followed Etta to the house. Her grandmother had stirred up bread dough earlier and now she dumped it out on a cutting board. Alyson was pouring herself a second cup of coffee when Andie walked through the back door, the screen banging softly as it closed behind her.

Etta turned to smile. She was kneading the dough, the white glump sticking to her hands and the cutting board. Alyson sat down on a stool to watch, and to wait for her sister to say something.

Andie poured herself a cup of coffee, spooned in several spoons of sugar and looked from her grandmother to Alyson. She shook her head and then took a sip of the coffee.

"So, you're back." Andie set the cup down and backed up to the counter. With hands braced on the edge of the countertop, she hopped once and sat. Etta shot her a look that didn't seem to stop her.

"I guess I'm back. It happened suddenly, finding out about my family here. And then learning that I had a sister, too." She had learned that from Jason.

"What does that mean?" Andie reached for her coffee, and Etta supplied the answer, dough sticking to her hands.

"Alyson didn't know about us. She found out by accident."

"She didn't tell you about us?" Andie stared, and then she shook her head. "She didn't tell you that she took the perfect kid and left behind the defective one?"

"That's enough." Etta shot Andie a look. She was pulling dough off her hands. Finally, she walked over to the sink and used her arm to turn on the water. "We're family and we're going to treat each other with love and respect."

"Fine." Andie sighed. "Fine."

"I'm not sure what to say to you." Alyson wasn't sure how to take a deep breath, how to move forward. "I don't know why you're angry with me."

"Because she chooses to be." Etta picked up a towel and flipped it at Andie's arm. "Choosing to act like this is all about her. And I'm telling you right now, Andie, you're twenty-eight, not eighteen."

"Fine, it isn't all about me." Andie smiled a tight smile.

Alyson couldn't smile. This was the rejection part she had feared. "I didn't do this to us."

Andie jumped down from the counter, landing on the floor. When she smiled this time, it was a little softer. "No, you didn't. You had no idea. How'd you finally find out?"

"I was looking for my bankbook. I'd left it on the desk in my, *our* mother's office."

"And you found us in the desk?"

"I found a box that contained my real birth certificate, adoption papers and a couple of other papers."

"Wow, our mother is a piece of work."

"She…" How did Alyson defend their mother after all that she'd done to them? How did she tell Andie that the person who had given birth to them had gentle moments, sometimes.

"Don't defend her." Andie's smile faded. "Don't do that, not after everything she's done."

"I'm not defending her, Andie." Alyson stood up. "I'm not her. I'm your sister. I came here because I wanted to know my family."

"Fine, you know us. This is it. It isn't fancy. We're just country people and we go to church on Sundays."

Etta cleared her throat.

Andie laughed, real laughter, and it shifted her features. Her blue eyes danced. "Etta goes to church on Sundays. I'm the rebel. If you stay, you can't have that position in the family. You'll have to find your own niche." Andie looked her over, top to bottom. "I think you're probably still the good one. And I have chores to do. So if you don't mind, I'm going to get busy and when you're tired of pretending you're one of us and ready to *be* one of us, you let me know and I'll find something for you to do."

Andie walked out and Alyson stood there with her cup of coffee, watching out the window as Andie walked across the lawn to the barn. She was long legged, taking long strides. She was a part of this place in a way Alyson only wished to be.

She rinsed her cup and set it in the sink, ignoring Etta's knowing smile. "I'm going outside to help my sister with the chores."

When she reached the barn, Andie was waiting. She was leaning against the support post in the barn, messing with her fingernails. She looked up and smiled at Alyson.

"I thought that would get under your skin."

"Does this have to be our relationship?"

"Alyson, I got left here because you were the good one. You were the easy child. You didn't make messes. You probably even learned to read and I bet you can do long division without a calculator."

"Of course I…"

Andie looked away and Alyson got it. "She rejected me because I wasn't the perfect child. I don't think she could have known about my dyslexia, because my teachers didn't figure it out for years. They thought I was rebellious in school. But she knew that you were going to be special. You'd already proven that. And I've spent my life hearing it from everyone who met you—the sweetest toddler in the world. I can't live up to their perfect memories of my perfect twin."

Alyson reached for her sister, but Andie shook her head. "Don't. I'm not ready to hug you."

"Can I just say…"

Andie shook her head. "No, you can't. And even though I baited you to come down here, I don't want your help. I'm just cleaning out the trailer and I can do that alone. I need to be alone and I think Etta is probably ready to drive out to Camp Hope. Go with her."

Andie walked away and Alyson stood in the yard, watching her go. "I was just going to tell you that you had Etta. You had our father. And I've never been perfect."

But Andie didn't hear and Alyson didn't know if she'd ever listen. She turned back to the house, and Andie had been right. Etta was waiting.

Chapter 6

Jason walked through the stable, amazed by what Adam and Jenna had built in one year. They had built a place where dreams came true for kids who wouldn't ordinarily get to attend a summer camp, not one like Camp Hope.

And they wanted him to be a part of it.

In a couple of days a group of kids would arrive. He could stay here and teach those kids to ride, barrel race, rope calves and ride bulls.

He obviously wasn't going to be riding a bull for a while. So maybe it was worth thinking or praying about. Adam came out of the office, distracted.

"What's up?" Jason walked through the double doors and into the arena.

"I don't know. I've been trying to get hold of our accountant about some bills and a few checks from donors that haven't cleared." Adam shoved a few letters into his shirt pocket. "It's okay. Let's talk about camp."

"I'm thinking about it."

"It's a big commitment." Adam at least acknowledged that.

"Yeah, it is. And I haven't really thought about ending my bull-riding career this way."

"I get what you mean." Adam pointed to the mechanical bull at the end of the arena. "Were you wanting to try that thing out?"

Jason remembered Adam mentioning it. That was a huge improvement. "Yeah, I do. Give me a minute to stretch."

"Take your time."

Jason walked over to the mechanical bull. He would have touched his toes, but he couldn't manage it just yet. He raised his arms and swayed to the left and right. He bent his right knee, but the left pulled. He squinted against the sharp pain.

"Is he going to ride that?" It was Alyson's voice.

He turned and lifted his hat in greeting. "Yes. Do you want to give it a try?"

"Sorry, I'm pretty sure I'm not a bull rider."

He laughed at the look on her face. And then he remembered Andie.

"Andie came home, right?" He held his arms out and twisted right, and then left.

"Yes."

"You okay?" He stopped stretching and she nodded. "Sure you are."

Alyson approached, staring at the mechanical bull, and then turned her attention to him. Blue eyes caught and held his, and he forgot about pain.

"You're okay to do this?" Her gaze slid back to the bull.

"I'm good." Or at least he was about to find out if he was.

He climbed onto the mechanical bull and wrapped the leather around his hand, tight. He lifted his left arm and nodded once. Adam turned the machine on and controlled its moves. It bucked up and down, and then around.

Jason moved with the movement of the barrel. He kept his left arm up and his chin down. It wasn't easy, not as easy as it should have been. A mechanical bull didn't move like a real bull. It could do the unexpected, but it didn't take steps forward. It didn't come off the ground, all four legs in the air. It didn't land with a jarring thud that rattled a guy's brain.

But it did work him out. It did spin. It did buck. It didn't manage to unseat him. When it slowed to a stop, he climbed off. He stood there for a long second, waiting for the world to stop spinning. The vertigo shouldn't have lasted as long as it did.

Alyson headed his way. "Are you okay?"

He took off his hat and took a step toward her. "Of course. Do you want to give it a go?"

"Ride it?"

"That's what I mean." He liked the way she bit down on her bottom lip and studied the mechanical bull, her eyes narrowing as she considered his offer.

She nodded. "I think I can do that. You make it look easy."

He laughed. "It isn't easy."

He pulled off his glove and handed it to her.

"Do I put this on?"

"That's the idea of it. And when you get on that thing, you hold with your legs. You keep your head down and you don't let your right arm get straight on you. The momentum can fling you off the back end if you let yourself get pulled back."

"If I ride this, I can be a bull rider?" She said it with a smile that made his head stop spinning for a second.

"Yeah, you can be a bull rider. Come on, let me help you get your hand tied in." Jason took her hand and led her across the padding that surrounded the mechanical bull.

She stopped before they reached it. He glanced sideways and she was breathing in, eyes closed. He held on to her hand and her fingers squeezed a little. "I can do this," she whispered.

"Of course you can. It's a mechanical bull. We're controlling it and we're not going to let it go crazy on you."

"I know."

"You don't have to."

"I do have to." She opened her eyes and managed a smile. "I'm ready."

She climbed on and he helped her get settled. She met his gaze and her eyes were bright, sparkling like blue topaz. He really wanted to kiss her. He wanted to pull her close and undo the clips that kept her blond hair in a tidy little knot at the nape of her neck. Instead, he pulled a few tendrils loose to frame her face and he stepped back.

He didn't know if he could get far enough away from her to feel safe.

"Remember what I said," he warned as he moved away.

"I can do this."

He nodded and walked away, because he understood. It was something she had to do. He glanced toward the box with the controls, ready to give Adam the signal. Adam was gone.

The two of them alone shouldn't have been a problem for Jason, but suddenly it was. Walking away from her, he battled a strong urge to hold her close and kiss her. He let out a sigh as he stepped behind the controls of the bull.

"Ready?" He smiled as he looked up at the woman on the back of the mechanical bull, her smile teetering on the edge of tears. But her chin was set at a stubborn angle. "Tuck your chin and put your left hand up. Use it for balance. And don't worry, I'm not going to let that bull get you down."

"It isn't a real bull," she called out and she did what he'd told her to do. Head down, hand up. "Go."

She was ready for this. Alyson's heart picked up speed as the bull started to move, and she had to focus, to concentrate on the way the thing moved. That was hard to do when her brain seemed to suddenly warp out, sending her mind on a field trip of some sort.

She couldn't stop thinking about a cowboy who had smiled at her, winking when she felt the most fear. She had never felt stronger.

She could do this.

Her brain whirled back to center, back to the task at hand. She could ride a bull. It jerked and spun. She kept her head down, but her arm above her head flung back, threatening to take her with it. She leaned a little, pulling it back.

"Don't touch the bull or you're disqualified." The

words of warning came in wafts as she spun and she couldn't nod to let him know that she'd heard.

The mechanical bull, a barrel with a head and horns, twisted and bucked.

And then it stopped, and her heart was racing and her legs shook. It took her a few minutes to adjust to the end of the ride, to where she was. She was sitting on a mechanical bull. The big, open arena enclosed them, but outside was the vastness of the Oklahoma countryside.

"You okay?"

She turned and gave a short nod of her head. "I did it."

She slid off the back of the bull and her legs buckled a little. He was there to reach for her, his hands steady on her arms.

She knew how to anchor herself. She knew how to stay grounded and steady. But at that moment, reasoning fled. Grounded and steady were the last two things she wanted to be. She didn't want to be the person who planned every moment of her life—not today.

She wanted to experience life. And she wanted to experience what it was like to be held by a cowboy.

She looked into deep-brown eyes and he winked. She'd seen movies and read books. She played country music when no one was around to listen. Cowboys were good at holding a woman. She ignored other thoughts, that they were also good at breaking hearts, good at leaving, and not good at staying.

The cowboy standing toe to toe with her believed she was strong. He had allowed her that moment, to prove it to herself.

As she tried to get her thoughts together, his hands moved to the clip at the back of her neck and her hair came loose. He clipped it to the hem of her shirt and then his hands moved to the back of her neck, winding through her hair.

She could have stopped him, but she didn't. Instead, she leaned a little toward him, breathing in deep of a cowboy who smelled like soap and leather. His hands were gentle but calloused, brushing her neck.

"I like it better this way," he whispered as he leaned in.

And she felt everything, all at once. She wanted to tell him to wait, to let this moment be one she'd never forget, because she'd never really been kissed, not like she knew he would kiss her.

And before she could tell him, his lips touched hers and she was lost. He held her close, and everything changed, because she could only think about him, not anything else but being in his arms. She sighed and stopped thinking.

He whispered something she couldn't understand, and then he kissed her again.

Bull riding was nothing compared to that moment in the arms of a cowboy.

"I…" Jason didn't know what to say. He hadn't planned that.

He hadn't realized that it wouldn't be enough, that he wouldn't want to let her go. Ever.

That was a new experience for him, not wanting to let go.

He slid his hands around her back and drew her to him, holding her in a loose hug, and resting his cheek against the blond hair that he'd released from its clip.

He thought back to the kiss. He'd felt undone in a

way he hadn't expected, in a way he'd never experienced.

He stepped back. She looked up at him, blinked a few times and then shook her head.

"I don't think we should have done that," she whispered.

"I know." But he really didn't know. He knew less at that moment than he'd ever known. He had just kissed a woman, the kiss had been the sweetest, the most innocent and the most memorable. And by tonight, he probably wouldn't remember.

He let out a sigh and repeated to her that he knew.

He let the memory of the kiss replay in his mind. He replayed it more than once, wanting to keep it in his memory, and angry deep down, because he hated being weak, he hated not knowing.

"I should go." She slipped away and he didn't stop her.

He went back to the mechanical bull and climbed on, pretending for a few seconds that this was two months ago, he was still at the top of the world standings, and he still knew the name of the woman who had just changed his life with a kiss.

"Want to try it again?" It was Adam's voice, and at first Jason didn't know what he meant. Try what again? Try to kiss her again? Try to remember her name?

Ride the bull. He secured his hand, because the deep down anger needed to find a release. He pounded the leather over his hand, like this ride was for real, like the eight seconds would count. As if his career wasn't over.

"Go."

The mechanical bull didn't leap from the gate, shuffle and start to spin, like the real thing would have done. Instead, it twisted and turned, but always stayed in one place. It wasn't the real thing, but it boosted his confidence. When he got off, his head didn't pound and his vision was clear, even if his left arm did feel like spaghetti.

"Feel okay?" Adam called out, past the fog of memories Jason was trying to recall, trying to keep tethered in his brain so he wouldn't forget.

A kiss. A man should never forget a kiss that shifted his life in directions he hadn't expected.

"Jason?"

"Yeah, great."

"Want to talk about it?" Adam flipped off the power switch to the bull and waited for him. Jason walked over and dropped the glove on the shelf.

"Not much to talk about." Weakness wasn't cool, wasn't easy to admit to.

"Look, Jason, this can't be easy for you. I've had to let go of a career. I get it. I get it when things are out of your control and you can't do a thing about it."

Jason shrugged it off.

"I'm trying to make sense of it, to see what God has planned. I'm not letting go of my career until I absolutely know that I have to. But if I do... That's life."

He was used to letting go. He'd walked out of his mother's room, refusing to watch as they turned off the life support that had kept her breathing for days after hope was lost.

It had been easier to walk out of the room than to watch her leaving them.

He knew how it felt to open the door one morning and find his little sister standing on the porch, her jaw bruised and swollen, a parting gift from the man that seven years earlier she'd thought was a handsome prince with a Harley.

He had wanted to kill that man. Beth had just wanted a place to heal. She was still healing. He was still letting go of being angry.

He could at least say that he'd found faith, found a way to forgive himself and to overcome the rocky moments that had gotten him to this place in his life.

But no one liked to feel like they'd lost control, that they couldn't make choices for themselves the way they had always made choices.

He wanted to be the guy that slammed a fist into the wall, the guy that threw something. For a moment, just long enough to let go of the frustration that sometimes built up inside him, he wanted to be that guy.

Instead, he did what their pastor had taught them, more than once, because it wasn't an easy lesson. Jason let God…

Whatever God was doing, Jason knew enough to let God do it.

Through the open doors of the arena, he could see the retreating back of Alyson, nearly to the picnic table where her grandmother was sitting with a group of women who had worked in the kitchen that morning. Let God. He thought she probably didn't know how.

If he could remember, he would help her in that journey. And then he'd do what he did best, walk out of the room before it got too tough, before letting go wasn't easy.

"I'll see you tomorrow." He walked out of the arena, not sure where he was heading, or why. As he crossed the large expanse of lawn that led to the dining hall and dorms, he saw Etta and Alyson getting in Etta's car, leaving.

"If you don't want to work in the kitchen, Jenna said they could use you in the stable. She thought you might like to work down there, with the horses," Etta said as she parked the car under her carport at the side of the house.

Alyson nodded but didn't know what to say. She could have said that she knew that Jason had decided to work at the camp, in the stable. She could even tell her grandmother that she didn't need the help of matchmakers.

Instead, she followed Etta up the sidewalk that was cracked in places, with grass and dandelions growing up in the broken areas. The kitten, banished from the house after it was caught sharpening its claws on an antique stool, ran from the shed, mewing for food.

More to comfort herself than the cat, Alyson scooped up the kitten and held it close. It purred loudly, working tiny claws in her shoulder as it snuggled close.

The back door opened and Andie walked out, her short hair catching in the light breeze. "There's cat puke in my room."

"Hi to you, too." Etta shot a look back at Alyson and the kitten. "You get to clean that up."

"I will."

Andie smiled a little. "I made chocolate chip cookies."

Etta shook her head. "I'm going to sit in my room with a book and the ceiling fan on. You two enjoy the cookies."

Alyson followed her sister into the house. The cookies were on a tray and there was a pitcher of iced tea. "I thought the two of you would be ready for a break."

Andie was considerate. It was crazy to learn this stuff about her sister now, when Alyson should have always known. They should have had a lifetime of knowing these things about one another.

They walked down the hall to the front door and onto the wide front porch with its lavender-painted wicker furniture. The sweet scent of roses and other flowers drifted on the breeze. But there wasn't much of a breeze. Andie sat down on the wicker chaise lounge and drew her knees up. Her feet were bare and she had a flower tattoo on her ankle.

Alyson looked around, at the wicker chairs and the porch swing. She picked the porch swing, facing her sister. She reached for a cookie and set her glass of tea on the table.

Jason drove by, his truck pulling an empty horse trailer that rattled on the paved road. "Wonder where he's going," Andie mused as she lifted the glass to take a sip. And then she glanced at Alyson. "Why does the sight of Jason Bradshaw make you turn that lovely shade of pink?"

"It doesn't." Alyson didn't want to talk about Jason. She wanted to talk about two sisters who had lost so much of their lives together.

"You can stop looking at me with the big, sad eyes." Andie held her tea glass and stared out at the road.

"I'm not looking at you." Alyson sighed. "Okay, I am. You know, I don't remember you. I didn't have pictures. No one mentioned you to me."

"So you're saying that I had it better because I was

aware that my sister was taken by our mother and I was left here."

"Was here such a bad place?"

"No, here was a great place. The idea that I wasn't good enough for our mother, that I wasn't smart enough or talented enough, that can kind of wound a kid and make her feel a little inferior."

"I know, and I'm sorry. But you have to understand, that wasn't my fault."

"No, Alyson, being a brilliant child prodigy wasn't your fault."

Alyson stood up, her insides trembling. She'd never been so mad in her life. She stood there staring at her sister, and Andie staring back.

"*Child* prodigy, Andie. I was a *child* with a gift. And now I'm just another piano player. I have no skills. I have no life. I played the piano. I graduated early. I've never been to a prom or a homecoming. Now I have to figure out where I belong."

"Figure it out. You're an adult. No one is going to tell you who you need to be."

But for twenty-eight years people had told her who to be, so finding herself now didn't seem like such an easy thing to do.

"You make it sound easy. But you've always known who you were."

"Yeah, I guess I did." Andie picked up another chocolate chip cookie. "But I think you know who you are. You must be a Forester, because you got mad and left."

Alyson smiled at that and she sat back down. "Yes, but I planned it for over a week."

"Yeah, I would have just jumped in the truck and left."

"I'm glad you're my sister." Alyson didn't say it too softly, because Andie obviously didn't do soft.

"Yeah, about that. I'm okay with having you back, and I've missed having a sister. But what set you off? What suddenly sent you running?"

"We have a half sister named Laura, and a month ago she eloped with the man I thought I was going to marry."

"Ouch."

"Yeah, ouch. Too bad I don't miss him."

They both laughed, and it felt good to have that moment between the two of them, a moment that signified something, maybe healing.

"There are photo albums." Alyson loved those photo albums. She'd looked at them several times already, but not from Andie's perspective. "Would you look at them with me?"

"And take a trip down memory lane?" Pain hid within the sarcasm in Andie's tone.

"At least tell me something about our dad." Alyson swallowed. "Isn't there something you want to know about my life, about our mother or your half sisters?"

"Soon, but not yet. It isn't easy, knowing the reason she left me. I've always known and I've always had that resentment."

Alyson smiled. "She didn't get an easy out, Andie. She didn't trade you for a perfect child, or perfect children. I'm dyslexic, too. It drove her crazy, trying to force me to learn the way my sisters learned. And they drove her crazy with bids for attention that you won't believe."

Andie smiled. "Okay, let's share."

"What was he like?" Alyson had to start there, with her father.

"Always lonely." Andie offered but she looked away and Alyson saw the moisture gather in her eyes. "He always missed her and you."

"But he loved you?" Alyson wanted it to be a fairy tale. She wanted to believe what she'd told herself on the drive here, that there was this perfect parent who had missed her. He would have been her hero.

"He loved me. He loved us both." Andie said it the way a person dismissed trivial facts. "But he started drinking when I was five. And if the car accident hadn't killed him, I think drinking would have."

Alyson sighed, because she had wanted to believe that things here were different. There were no fairy tales. "I'm sorry."

"Don't be. I wasn't unhappy. He loved me. Granny loved me. I grew up riding horses and pulling crazy stunts." Andie turned to sit on the side of the chair. "What did you do?"

"I…" Alyson thought back to what she had done, something that sounded more exciting than hours at the piano, panic attacks before walking out onstage, or her mother telling her she was a disappointment. "I played in London for the queen."

Andie laughed. "I said, what did you do for *fun*?"

They both laughed. "I don't know if fun was allowed. While I played and performed, Dad—" She shook her head. "Gary would take Laura and Cindy places. I did see a lot of museums."

"If you're trying to make it sound bad so I won't be jealous, it's working."

"You have nothing to be jealous of." Alyson looked

up as a truck approached. Jason Bradshaw driving by with a horse in the back of his trailer. "What's Jason like?"

"If you're a pianist with big, blue eyes, he's a big, macho prince charming. If not, he's the guy down the road that you've always liked, because he's always been funny, always been easy to get along with. His mom died years ago. His dad is difficult. His sister ran away. Kind of a typical family with normal problems."

"As opposed to a mom who took one kid and left the other?"

"He's broken a lot of hearts, Alyson. And then he got religious and broke a few more. Don't let him break yours. He's looking for a good Christian wife these days. I don't think either of us fit that description."

Alyson shrugged it off. "I don't plan on getting my heart broken, and I don't plan on falling in love."

She didn't know what to say about being a Christian. She had agreed to attend church with Etta tomorrow. When she thought about it, her stomach did a small flip. It did another flip when she thought about seeing Jason there.

Chapter 7

Jason found a parking space near the doors of the church and got out, alone, as usual. Beth had quit going when she was a teenager and realized it made their father angry. Jason's dad had never been one to attend church, not even before. And in their world, *before* always meant before Elena Bradshaw died. They didn't talk about her death. They didn't really talk about her, or life without her.

Instead, Buck Bradshaw had created a new life for his family after his wife's death. She was gone, and he acted as if she had never been there. But she had, and the big hole in all their lives was evidence of the fact.

Jason was still thinking about the saddle that had gone in the Dumpster. It should have been thrown away years ago. Letting it go had to mean something.

He took the step from the parking lot to the sidewalk

and bit back some inappropriate words. Roping yesterday and riding a green broke horse hadn't been a good idea. He'd given it a try and jammed his knee worse than before. The fact that his jeans barely fit over his swollen leg was a pretty good indication that he wasn't going to be able to put off surgery much longer.

But it would have to wait because he wasn't going to miss out helping with camp. Not now that he'd decided he should do this. He'd keep weight off it a couple of days and then deal with it.

"What's wrong with you?" A familiar voice. He turned and smiled at Etta. And Alyson. That felt good, remembering her name, and remembering that her being there probably meant something.

"What do you mean, what's wrong with me?"

"Aren't there crutches in your truck for a reason?" Etta walked over to the door of his truck and gave it a yank. She pulled out the wooden crutches and handed them to him. "Stop being so stubborn and take care of yourself."

"I'm taking care of myself." He winked at Alyson. "I knew the two of you would be along to give me a hand."

"And if we hadn't, you would have fallen on your stubborn face." Etta nodded toward the church. "Head that way or we're going to be late."

"And that'll be my fault, too?" he mumbled, for Alyson's benefit. She laughed a little and he shot her a sideways glance, winking again, because he liked it when she turned that pretty shade of pink.

She was about the frilliest thing he'd ever seen, even in her new "country clothes." Her denim skirt swished around her ankles and her blouse was ruffled.

She smelled so good, he wanted to slide up close to her and see…

Or maybe just yank his thoughts back into check and remember that he was at church and she was searching for herself, not a relationship.

The stairs going up to the church were narrow and had been there since before Dawson was a town. The ramp, a new addition, required by the state, ran alongside the building. Alyson walked behind him, up that long ramp. He wondered if she always did what she thought was the right thing. This time the right thing was not letting him fall on his face.

"I really can make it on my own." He glanced back over his shoulder. Her gaze was down, studying the wood of the ramp.

"I know you can, but I thought—" she smiled up at him "—that I'd catch you if you fell."

He swallowed any fool reply that tried to slip out. He could tell her a hundred ways a man could fall, and it wasn't about hitting the ground. It was all about lace ruffles and perfume that wrapped around a guy's senses and drove him to sing the Lord's Prayer in his mind to keep his thoughts on holy things as he walked into church.

"You can catch me if I fall." He stood back, motioning with his hand for her to walk through the doors of the church ahead of him, and she didn't. Instead, she looked a little green, and he remembered panic attacks.

"Give me a minute." She glanced around, and people were watching.

He stepped closer, close enough that it became just the two of them, and he knew that people would talk.

But in a town like Dawson, that's just what people did. He didn't mind giving them something to talk about.

"Deep breath, darlin'."

"Okay." She closed her eyes, inhaling. He wanted to put his arms around her, but then she'd be the only thing holding him up and they'd both fall.

He hummed the Lord's Prayer and took a careful step back, trying not to tangle his legs, the crutches and the people walking past them.

"Why do you keep humming?" She looked up, distracted, and he hadn't realized he'd hummed out loud.

"I'll explain it someday." The church bell rang. "Ready?"

"As I'll ever be."

Etta appeared in the vestibule. "I saved us a seat, but thought the two of you might have changed your minds about coming inside."

"We're here." Jason wondered if Etta knew that her granddaughter had panic attacks. "No Andie, I see."

Etta shook her head. "Of course not. She guilted Alyson into coming, but she backtracked as soon as we got close to being ready. She said she's going to pick up another horse today."

"Sounds like Andie." He sat down on the end of the pew and stretched his leg out into the aisle.

"What happened?" Alyson asked as she reached for a hymnal.

"Bull bucked me off."

"That was a month ago. And my name is Alyson."

He laughed a little, because of her quirky smile and the way her brows arched when she was being funny, and then the hint of shyness, as if she had found out something new about herself.

"I know. I promise, I'm not going to forget you, not again. And I really do remember what happened. I did some calf roping with a friend and when I jumped off a horse I was trying out, I twisted my knee. I already have some torn ligaments, so…"

"You'll need surgery."

"Probably so." He put a finger to his lips and she nodded, but she kept looking at him, not at the front of the church.

Alyson glanced away from the cowboy sitting next to her. She swallowed emotions that surfaced, unfamiliar and consuming. She reminded herself of how it felt to be the person Dan left because she didn't know how to enjoy life. That note had changed her life more than his leaving her had. That note had hurt, because it had been the truth. And it hadn't been her fault that she'd become this person who lived by a schedule.

The pianist missed a note. Alyson looked up, catching the problem, shuddering a little, and not meaning to. The woman was doing a great job. There was something about the song, the way it lifted to the rafters of that little church. It wasn't polished, it wasn't perfect, but it was moving.

She listened as they moved from a song about the earth not being home, to a song she knew well. As the worship leader sang the words, "It is well, with my soul," Alyson wondered, as she had never really wondered before, what that meant. Before it had been a beautiful song, a song the piano brought to life. And now, listening, she realized it was about life and having something stronger than oneself to rely on.

And she didn't know if she could ever live through

disasters and sing that all was well with her soul. How did a person do that? How did a person find peace within their soul?

How could she ever find it when fear bounced around inside her, stealing any peace she managed to find, and bitterness welled up within her when she thought of the life she'd missed because of her mother's selfishness?

The message created more questions in her mind, more questions than she had answers for.

"Where are we going for lunch?" Etta asked as they walked out of church an hour later.

Alyson was still lost in the words of a song, still trying to make sense of peace, and her grandmother was moving on, as if this was all normal, as if everyone should understand and get this faith, this God that seemed to be such a part of these people's lives.

They assumed that everyone got it, that it was easy, but it wasn't. Maybe that was her, overthinking again.

A hand touched hers, fingers lightly brushing. She looked up, and his eyes held understanding. He winked.

"You with us?" He leaned into the crutches and his mouth tightened.

"Should you go to the emergency room?"

"For what?" He really looked confused.

"You fell off a horse, remember?"

He laughed, "I haven't forgotten. I just don't know why I'd go to the E.R. for that."

"Because that's what people do when they're hurt."

"Not this cowboy. I'll take some aspirin, put some ice on it and tomorrow be good as gold."

"While the two of you are talking, I'm going into a diabetic coma here." Etta sighed.

"You aren't diabetic." Jason took an easy step forward. "And if you'll join me at the Mad Cow, I'll buy lunch."

"I'm not a diabetic, but I'm definitely tired of waiting." Etta pulled keys out of her purse. "Alyson, can you drive him?"

"I got myself here, I think I can drive myself to the Mad Cow."

"And you'll wreck your truck and hurt someone."

Jason held his keys in a tight fist. "Etta, have you ridden in a five speed with your granddaughter? I bet she can't drive a stick shift."

"She needs to learn and who better to teach her?"

"Might as well drive my truck." Jason handed over the keys and Alyson didn't want to take them. "She won't give up."

"I can't."

"You've got to." He winked and walked away. As Alyson stood on the sidewalk, trying to figure out what to do, he was tossing crutches into the back and opening the door.

Okay, she was driving a truck. She opened the driver's side door and stared at the cowboy sitting in the passenger seat, a cute grin on his too handsome face. Smug. He definitely looked smug.

She climbed in and sat behind the wheel. Her feet were miles from the gas and brake, and the added pedal, the clutch. She felt queasy as she stuck the key into the ignition.

She started to turn the key and he stopped her.

"Foot on the clutch." He clicked his seat belt.

"Foot on clutch. Anything else?"

"Once it's started keep your foot on the clutch and shift into Reverse. And then give it a little gas and back up. Then you'll put your foot on the clutch again and shift into First."

"Got it."

Alyson started the truck, remembering to keep her foot on the clutch and then forgetting as she put the truck into Reverse. It jumped, choked and died.

"This is so hard on my truck."

"We could sit here and Etta would get the hint."

"She's already gone." Jason smiled. "We could go to my place and have a picnic."

A picnic. Alyson tried to remember the last time she'd done anything like that. She was tempted, and she knew he was teasing. It was just suggested as a way to get back at Etta, not because he thought it might be a good idea.

"Do you want to go on a picnic?" Jason turned, resting against the passenger-side door, his arm over the back of the seat.

"It would be fun, someday."

He pulled out his phone. "We'll invite Etta."

He was serious. She tried to stop him but he held up a finger to silence her and dialed. She started the truck again, not sure what to do next, so she sat there. A car drove around them, the people inside it stared, shaking their heads.

And of course Etta didn't want to go on a picnic, but encouraged the two of them to go ahead. She'd meet with friends. Alyson sat there, listening to the conversation on speaker. A picnic with Jason.

He put the phone away. "Now let's switch places."

They were still sitting in front of the church and everyone else was gone. "I can drive."

"Not on your life." He unbuckled his seat belt. "I'll slide over there, you come over here."

"I'll come around."

"Just climb over here." He shook his head and grinned. "Never mind, get out and go around."

When she got in on the passenger side, Jason was starting the truck. He did it with ease, shifting without so much as a chug or cough from the engine. Alyson watched out the window as farms rolled past, including the one where he lived with his dad and sister.

"Where are we going?"

"My place."

"When do you think you'll move back?"

"Soon. My memory is better. I still have headaches, some dizziness, but not as bad. It's little stuff now. Did I put the milk in the fridge, or mail the check for the electric bill? But every day is a little better. Maybe because I'm learning to cope better."

"You remember me."

"You're not short-term." He grinned. "I had to keep reminding myself of you. Even of that kiss."

She felt heat work its way up from her neck to her cheeks.

"That shouldn't have happened."

"I don't know why it shouldn't have happened, and I've reminded myself of it on a daily basis, so I won't forget that it was about the sweetest thing that ever happened to me."

"Do you really think you should ride a horse?" Alyson changed the subject with ease, and she didn't admit that she'd thought about him, and about that kiss, so often she was starting to question her sanity.

She was twenty-eight and she really thought this

might be her first crush. And if that was the case, it would end. That's what happened to a crush. At least she wasn't sixteen, so it wouldn't break her heart when it was over.

She knew about being dumped. She'd just never been dumped by a cowboy.

"Why wouldn't I ride a horse?" Jason stopped the truck in front of the house he'd built a year earlier. The farmhouse design was clean, with white siding, a green metal roof and porches that held empty flower baskets. He should have hired someone to take care of the place. Maybe he had planned to and had forgotten.

At least he could smile about it now.

"Your knee." Alyson broke into his thoughts with what sounded like a random phrase.

"My knee?"

"You asked me why I thought you shouldn't ride a horse."

"And the answer is, my knee?" And she was probably right. "Come on in, we'll get our lunch together and, I guess we'll drive the truck back to the creek."

"You think?"

She was pretty in her ruffled Western shirt and denim skirt. She wasn't country, but she was trying it on for size. Maybe someday she'd grow into it. Maybe she'd find out who she was in Dawson.

Or maybe she'd find that she really loved the city and her life was there.

"I think maybe you're coming out of your shell, Cashmere." He opened the door and before he could hop to the bed of the truck, she was there with the crutches. "Thanks."

"You're welcome. And thank you for suggesting a picnic."

"Been a while?"

"So long I don't remember the last time."

He pulled the key out of his pocket and unlocked the front door. After pushing it open, he motioned her inside. The house smelled clean, but deserted. He had Beth to thank for that. The hardwood floors were swept and mopped, the furniture was dusted. His sister, always looking out for him.

"I like your house." Alyson stood in the center of the living room. The furniture was plaid, and big rugs covered the hardwood. She zeroed in on the piano in the corner of the room. His mother's.

She crossed the room, forgetting him, but he didn't mind. He watched as she stood in front of it, her hands hovered over the keys and then dropped to her sides. He joined her, leaning the crutches against the wall and taking a seat on the bench. While she stood frozen in that space next to him, he played something he remembered, that he didn't have to open a book to play.

She sat down next to him, a frightened foal, not quite ready for contact. He knew that look in her eyes, that longing for something, and fear of reaching for it.

"I didn't know you played." Her shoulder brushed his.

"My mom taught me."

"Your mom?"

He gave her a sideways glance and then back to the keys of the piano, smooth from use. When he played, he remembered his mom, how it had felt to sit next to her before she got sick.

He played a hymn from church and she touched the

keys, playing with him. But then she stopped and he stopped, too.

"Why don't you play?" He closed the piano up, but they didn't move from the bench.

"I can't." She didn't look at him, and she didn't cry. "For twenty-five years the piano has been my life and for most of those twenty-five years, I've hated it. The pressure, the practice, the people staring at me. I wanted to be like all of the other girls. I wanted to be like my sister Laura. I wanted to go on dates, hang out at the mall and dance at the prom."

"I understand."

She looked up, her blue eyes penetrating, asking questions, and shadowed with the pain of a life lived for other people. He understood. He'd been an adult his entire life. He'd helped his mother with her medication because his dad had hidden in the barn. He'd held his sister when she cried, because their parents couldn't. He'd told stories, made people laugh. He'd learned to cook, to teach his sister the things she needed to know about life.

But he'd told jokes to keep people smiling, to keep them from noticing how much they hurt, and how much he hurt.

And now this woman, a woman with her own stories, wanted him to share his.

"We should get ready to go. Before long it won't be lunch, it'll be supper." He grabbed the crutches and she stood, as if she was still waiting for answers.

He wasn't going there.

He'd take her on a picnic and help her find the kid who should have grown up in Dawson. He'd teach her to ride. He'd even break the buckskin and give him to her. He could do those things.

She followed him through the big dining room with the French doors that led onto the back porch with its stone fire pit and outdoor kitchen. She stopped to look outside and he went on to the kitchen. He was pulling food out of the fridge when she walked into the room.

"What can I do?" She leaned against the counter and watched.

"You can get the chips down." He nodded in the direction of the cabinets. "They're up there. And if you could get the basket out of the lower cabinet."

"You keep food here, even though you don't live here."

"I have to eat when I'm over here working."

"I see." She had the basket out and she set it on the cabinet. "Do you work over here a lot?"

"Every day. The animals have to be fed. I have horses that need to be taken care of. This really is all new to you, isn't it?"

"I've always lived in cities." She glanced out the window. He followed her gaze, seeing what she saw, but not the same way. This had always been his life. The cattle, the open land, the rodeos.

She had always been city.

He didn't want to connect too much, not when it felt as if he wouldn't want her gone, not tomorrow, or even next week. She reminded him of a bird that just passes through, on its way to wherever it's supposed to be.

He'd seen one of those birds last week. Beth had pointed it out, asked him if he'd ever seen anything like it. He hadn't. And the bird hadn't stayed. It was going north, back where it belonged.

He was a broken cowboy without a career. What did a guy like him offer a woman like her? Why was he even thinking like that?

He had a brain injury, of course. He was thinking crazy thoughts. A man did that when he looked death in the face. It made him think about the future, like he needed to fill it up with something.

She wasn't the thing he was going to fill his life with. No matter how good she looked in his kitchen. He nearly laughed at the idea of her in an apron, tossing frozen pizzas in the oven.

"You okay?" She was standing close, and he really didn't need close.

"Good to go." He grabbed the basket and she took it from him.

"I can get it." She held it in front of her.

"I'll leave these here." He leaned the crutches against the wall and took a painful step without them.

"Have you ever been called stubborn?" she asked as he tried to take the picnic basket.

"More than once." He had the basket and he took another step. She walked next to him. Okay, so he'd done something pretty bad this time. He could feel his knee give with each step.

"Oh, come on, this is crazy. Cowboy or not, you have to use common sense." Alyson grabbed the crutches and came back with them.

"Cowboys have plenty of common sense." He exhaled and gave up on strong and whatever else he'd been trying to be.

Idiot came to mind.

"Okay, let's go, Cowboy."

She sashayed out the front door, carrying the picnic

basket and maybe his heart. But no, he didn't give that away. He'd never given that away.

Alyson sat next to Jason as the truck bounced through the field in the direction of a copse of trees at the far edge of the field. She'd kept her gaze averted for a minute or two, but now she was watching him again.

She enjoyed watching him, had enjoyed it from the first day when he'd come around the corner of Etta's house, a cowboy in faded jeans and a sweat-stained T-shirt. He still looked like that cowboy, rugged with that grin that hit a girl in the midsection.

She'd never met anyone like him. Maybe that was the attraction. It was just the experience, the newness of it all. Maybe it wasn't about the cowboy at all.

Sitting next to him, she felt like the kind of woman who could be strong. She felt like she could haul hay, break a horse, and hog-tie something. She felt like the kind of woman who cooked big meals on a Sunday afternoon.

She wasn't that woman, but he made her believe that about herself.

"You're quiet." He reached to turn down the radio, silencing a Kenny Chesney song about tractors and hay-lofts.

"I'm just thinking."

"About?"

Anything but him. Unfortunately, it wasn't working, this effort at distraction.

"You ask a lot of questions, but you don't talk about yourself."

His eyebrows shot up and he grinned. "That's because I'm a private kind of guy."

"Is that it?"

"Yeah, that's it. I don't like to share my stories."

"But I want to know them." She'd get to know him, bit by bit, Etta had said. That's how you found out a man's stories.

"I'm sure you do." He slowed as they got closer to the trees. She could see the creek and hear the crickets, or maybe grasshoppers. He stopped the truck.

They picked their way across ground that was rough, with heavy clumps of grass and a few big rocks. The trees at the edge of the creek were small and some were topped, as if someone had chopped the tops out.

"What happened to the trees?"

"Storms. Tornadoes." He nodded to a spot near the edge of the creek. "You can put the blanket there."

He'd pulled a blanket out from behind the seat of his truck and given it to her to carry. Alyson spread the blanket and took the picnic basket that he'd lugged along in his right hand, hobbling with one crutch under his right arm.

"Are there fish in the creek?" She held his arm and he lowered himself down, stretching out on the blanket. And then what? Was she supposed to sit next to him? Or maybe lean against a tree?

"Sit down." He shook his head and laughed a little. "I don't know about you, but I'm about to starve and you want to play twenty questions. No, there aren't any fish in the creek. My mom was probably one of the kindest women I've ever known, and she fought a twelve-year battle with cancer. I'm the oldest of two kids, and my dad is emotionally detached."

Alyson bit down on her bottom lip and fought the sting of tears, because she understood now why stories

should come in small pieces. And she got that sometimes a story didn't tell anything about a person. It was
just facts.

"I'm sorry."

"Alyson, sit down and relax. This picnic is for you.
Enjoy it."

She sat down next to him, pulling her knees up and
hugging them close as she watched the creek. A hand
touched her shoulder and she turned to look at him.

"I'm sorry, I'm not good at the whole 'kiss and tell'
part of relationships."

"I didn't expect kiss and tell. I wondered about you
playing the piano."

"How'd you know that I play?" He grinned, probably because her face lost all of its color. "Kidding."

"Cute."

"Thank you, Ma'am. I like to think I am." He leaned
back on his elbows, a piece of grass between his teeth.

"I was talking about your sense of humor, not you."
She pulled food out of the picnic basket. "You're definitely not cute."

He sat back up. "Really?"

"Really." She handed him the sandwich with mayo
and took the one without for herself. "We should eat."

"I left the room when my mom was taken off life
support."

His words stole her appetite. She put the sandwich
back in the baggie. "I'm sorry."

"It was my choice. I couldn't watch her leave. I knew
her faith. I knew that she believed she'd go to heaven.
But man, I didn't want her to go. I was so angry with
God for thinking He needed her more than us. She was

the person who kept our family together. Even when she was sick."

"Jason, I…"

He shook his head. "Let's not, okay. You wanted to know. I told you. End of story."

"I didn't mean to force this out of you."

He took in a deep breath and his expression shifted. With a tenderness deep down in his brown eyes, he touched her cheek and his smile returned. "It isn't something I like to talk about, but you didn't force me. I wanted to tell you. I want you to know me."

She tried to make sense of those words. He wanted her to know him. As she was making sense, he was moving closer.

He slid a hand behind her neck and pulled her to him, touching his lips to hers, holding her there for a moment that felt like forever. It was one of those moments, the kind that felt as if you'd caught a butterfly in your hand, or seen a meteor fall to earth. It felt suspended in time, and yet, not long enough.

The kiss was as soft as a whisper on a summer night. Alyson didn't plan on it ending, but felt the cold air between them when it did.

"I want you to know me," he whispered again near her ear and then grazed her lips with another sweet kiss. She'd never been kissed like that before, not in a way that touched her heart, that changed what she believed about herself, and about the person holding her close.

Her heart was melting.

Cowboys knew the right words. Cowboys were good at making a girl believe they loved her more than anything. And hadn't Andie warned her about him? Jason Bradshaw didn't do long-term relationships.

Her phone rang and, dazed, she reached for it, answering it without looking at the caller ID.

"Well, it's about time you answered." Her mother's voice.

Cold water in her face couldn't have been more effective in bringing Alyson back to reality.

"Mom."

Jason didn't move away. He sat next to her, filling their paper plates with food and twisting the top off a bottle of water before setting it next to her. Her mother's voice, tense and cool, edged out the warmth of the afternoon.

"So, I take it you're in Dawson?"

"I am."

"You need to come home. You have concert dates. You have family obligations."

"Mom, no one wants to hear me play. I'm twenty-eight. I'm not a child prodigy anymore. You don't need me."

Her shelf life had expired. Her father had other prodigies on his client roster. And yet, the guilt was still there because it had always been about doing the right thing for her family. Playing, even when playing was the hardest thing in the world to do.

"Alyson, Oklahoma isn't your life. You're not one of them. You're my daughter, not his."

"He's gone, Mom. And I'm trying to decide if this is my life."

Because she was suspended between who she had always been, and this new person she wanted to be, the person who made her own decisions, and kissed a cowboy until she couldn't breathe.

Chapter 8

On Wednesday afternoon, the third day of camp, Jason stood next to a little gray mare as a boy with boots a size too big and a cowboy hat falling over his eyes swung himself into the saddle, nearly falling over the other side.

"Careful there, Hoss." Jason grabbed the boy by the arm and smiled at the gap-toothed kid. "You can't be like Jell-O. You've got to keep your back straight without being stiff and keep your arms tucked to your side. No spaghetti arms, okay?"

The boy nodded and Jason smiled again. The kid was shaking like a sapling in a storm.

"What's your name?" Jason adjusted the stirrups and then fixed the reins in the kid's hands. He had probably asked the kid his name three times, but eventually it would stick.

"Bobby."

"Well, Bobby, this is Cheerio. She's a pretty good little horse and she's never thrown anyone. The two of you are going to be good friends."

"Okay."

"But you have to breathe a little, okay? 'Cause if you pass out, you're gonna fall off."

"Okay."

Jason led the boy to the arena where four other kids were already walking their horses around the perimeter of the enclosure. He gave the horse a little pat on the rump, the boy jumped and the horse took off at a sedate walk.

He'd already given them all pointers on commands and how to keep their seat. A few had some experience. Some claimed experience they didn't have. He leaned on the gate and watched, but his gaze traveled to the dining hall.

Alyson had worked in the kitchen for the last few days. He'd seen her at lunchtime, serving chicken nuggets and salad to the campers and staff. She had smiled at each one of those kids, and he knew how that smile made them feel. It probably made them all feel like a five-year-old with the greatest kindergarten teacher in the world.

But she hadn't talked to him. Their gazes had connected, but she'd looked away and he'd pushed his tray off the end of the counter. Salad and nuggets had gone everywhere and the kids had gotten a great laugh over the mishap.

He shook his head and gathered his wits, because he had kids on horses and he didn't have room in his mind for them and Alyson. It was better, thinking about the campers, the sun beating down on his back, and a youth rodeo. Anything but a woman.

"How's it going?" Adam Mackenzie walked up, his hat off and his hair plastered to his head.

"Hot, isn't it?"

Adam nodded. "I've been chasing two boys around the yard, trying to get some kind of little snake away from them."

"But you love it."

"Yeah, I do." Adam rubbed his brow with his sleeve and settled his hat back in place. "How's it going?"

"Pretty good. I mean, you're not going to have a lot of problems with horses like these."

"What about your knee?"

"Good to go." Jason didn't look at the other man. He kept his focus on the kids, on the horses, watching for problems.

"Right. What do you think about this group? Can we pull off a showdeo at the end of the two weeks?"

A showdeo. A combination between a rodeo and a horse show. They would have steer riding, pole bending, egg relay and a Western pleasure class. If he had the kids with the ability, they might try roping.

Jason shrugged. "I think so. I'm going to work with a few of the more skilled riders this afternoon. I have a couple who think they can learn to rope."

"You're going to build Rome in a day?"

"I'm going to turn these kids into rodeo stars in two weeks."

"I don't doubt you will. Jenna suggested you let Alyson help you out. She looks a little lost in the kitchen."

"And you think she'll be better off working with the horses?" Jason knew this game, and he wasn't playing.

He'd found out a long time ago that controlling situations solved a lot of problems before they happened. Walk away from an argument, no fight. Walk away from the girl, no problems when she got sick of you or you got tired of her. Walk out the door of the hospital room…

And pretend it never happened, that his mother hadn't lost her life with the turn of a switch.

He'd been accused of not letting himself feel.

And Sunday afternoon he'd learned that maybe people were right. Because Sunday, he'd felt everything. He wasn't about to admit that what he'd felt the most was scared to death.

For a guy who rode bulls for a living, that was a little unnerving.

"I think Alyson would like working out here." Adam cleared his throat a little. "I didn't really think you'd mind."

Jason laughed. "Thanks, but no thanks. I have enough problems keeping focused without having to keep her out of trouble."

"I'll pass that on. You know your objections are only going to make the women push harder, right?"

"Yeah, I get that." Jason shifted his weight to his good leg. "But maybe you could tell them to give me a break. No sense in having a woman feel forgotten. That wouldn't be good for her self-esteem."

"That's a good point." Adam stepped away from the gate. "I need to get a few things done in the office. Yell if you need help."

"Will do. It's time for this lesson to end. I'm going to let them trot a little, so they feel like they've done something."

"Thanks, Jason. This program will be better with you involved."

"I hope."

Jason strode into the arena and called the kids to the center. After a few minutes of instruction he turned them loose. Smiles split across serious faces when he gave the nod and they loosened the reins and gave their horses the nudge to move them at a faster gait. He laughed a little because several of them looked as if they'd bounce right off the back end of their horses if he didn't stop them soon.

But he remembered being a kid and escaping on the back of a horse. And these kids needed the escape, probably more than he ever had.

As he ended their lesson, his gaze swept across the open field, catching sight of movement. Alyson walked down the hill to the chapel and he wondered why.

Alyson walked through the open doors at the end of the chapel and stood for a moment in the dimly lit entrance. The building had a roof and screened walls to let the breeze flow through.

At the front, behind the pulpit was a giant cross. She stared at the cross, not really getting it, and yet...

It ached inside her heart, not understanding what everyone else believed and held on to. And she needed something. She needed something more than herself and something more than her career.

She reached into her pocket and pulled out her phone. She pushed the button that turned it off. She couldn't take another call from her mother, more pressure, more guilt.

Alyson walked down the aisle to the front of the

chapel. She sneaked a look around and hoped no one would be upset with her for being here. But when she'd left the kitchen, needing to be alone, to get away, the chapel had seemed like the place to go.

Last night she had sat in here with Etta, at the back, listening to Pastor Todd, the camp minister. He'd told funny stories, drawing the kids in with laughter. And then he'd brought them to a point where they understood faith, understood the point of a Father's love. An unconditional love.

She sat down on the piano bench and lifted the cover to expose keys that were faded and worn from use. She loved pianos like this one, the kind that had been played for so many years, by so many people.

She touched the keys, but she didn't play. Instead, she waited for the fear, the panic. With her eyes closed, she remembered what it felt like to be onstage and be consumed by that fear. But the fear hadn't been about the piano, it had been about the audience watching her. The fear had been about what they would think of her performance.

When the fear didn't grab hold she started to play. "Jesus Loves Me." The words were so simple, the melody was sweet. *Jesus loves me, this I know, for the Bible tells me so.*

Jesus loves me. Here, in this town, with her grandmother and these people, that love was natural. They all accepted it, as if it were a given. But how did she accept that He could love her that way?

Love her. She tried to remember feeling loved. And the only moment that came to mind was a picnic by a lake and a cowboy. That wasn't love, though. That was…

She didn't know what it was. It was more than her limited experience with life could really fathom. The one thing she knew for sure, it was a memory she would hold on to forever.

After walking the kids from his afternoon group back to the dining hall, where they met up with their counselor, Jason headed down the hill toward the chapel. He couldn't seem to convince himself to let it go.

He heard the piano before he got there. The tune was simple, "Jesus Loves Me," but it was sweet. Of course it was Alyson. He had watched her walking down there thirty minutes earlier.

He walked up the back steps and stood in the open doorway. She was sitting in front of the piano, playing with one finger, her eyes closed.

While she played, he stayed at the back of the chapel and watched. When she didn't notice him, he sat on the back pew and waited. Her hand came up and she wiped at her cheek.

He should go. Common sense told him that. There were a million things he could be doing. He had kids who wanted to learn to rope. He had cattle of his own that needed to be taken care of.

And instead of doing those things, he sat there, waiting, in case she needed him.

What made her cry? "Jesus Loves Me"? Or playing the piano. Maybe both?

She stopped playing but she stayed on the bench, her head bowed over the keys. He stood, not sure which door to exit from, or how to get away from her.

A sane man would have left, would have ignored her tears, would have called Jenna to talk to her. Calling Jenna was about the only thought he'd had that made sense.

He couldn't remember what he was doing half the time, and he had never been accused of making all the right choices. With her shoulders shaking gently, he moved forward, because he couldn't leave her there alone. And he didn't want anyone else at her side during this moment.

For a guy who knew when to exit a situation, he seemed to have lost all sense of timing.

When he sat down beside her, she did the unexpected; she turned into his arms. He sat there for a few seconds, unsure, and then he wrapped his arms around her and held her as she cried. He tried to tell her it would be okay. He whispered the words through emotion that settled in his throat, and he rocked, back and forth with her in his arms, waiting for her to tell him what she needed.

Strong arms wrapped around her and Alyson had never felt so safe. Jason held her against his solid chest, rocking her gently, his lips brushing against her temple as he whispered that everything would be okay.

After a few minutes, she pulled back and she knew that she had to be a mess, with tear-stained cheeks and swollen eyes. Her nose was probably red. She never looked good when she cried.

Jason smiled and then he wiped her eyes with his hand.

"Should I ask what's wrong, or just give you a shoulder to lean on?" His words melted her eyes into another round of tears. She brushed them away and leaned, resting her forehead on a shoulder that was strong.

"I guess that's your answer," he whispered.

She moved out of his embrace, even though staying would have been good. But that was the problem. If she stayed in his arms, she would want to stay in his life. And how did she do that?

A breeze picked up, and she closed her eyes. How did she explain a lack of faith to a man who had grown up here, surrounded by faith? How did she explain that her life had never been like his? For every moment that his father wasn't invested in his life, Alyson's mother was consumed with hers.

"You were playing the piano." He encouraged, nudging her with his shoulder as they sat side by side on the bench.

She touched the keys again. "Yeah, 'Jesus Loves Me.'"

"It's a good song."

"Is it a song, or does it mean more? 'Jesus loves me, this I know, for the Bible tells me so.' I don't know, Jason. I sat there this morning listening to the chapel service for the children, to a story so simple, and I've never heard it before. I've never heard these stories, about Jesus. Greater love hath no man than this, that he would lay down his life for a friend."

"For you."

She looked up, still conscious that her eyes would be swollen and her nose red. "Excuse me?"

"For you. He laid down his life for you. If you were the only person who ever accepted. If everyone else said a collective 'No, thank you,' He still would have done it. For you."

"It's like accepting that the world is round after years

of being told it is flat. How does a person change everything she's ever known or believed?"

"Baby steps. You start by opening the door to faith, and you let that faith grow. You take steps. You test it. It tests you. And you change. Your ideas about God change."

"You make it sound easy, maybe because you've always lived here, always heard the stories. But my world is so far from here. My world…was flat until today."

She couldn't explain it any other way. Her mother. The anger her mother had with the people here, with their beliefs, with their faith. How did Alyson reconcile those two worlds?

"I can't imagine myself in this world, with this faith. I don't know how to be this person." She played the song again. "Jesus Loves Me." "Why would He love me?"

"Because He created you."

She was trying to reconcile that morning's sermon, about a God who loves unconditionally with a mother whose love always seemed to have conditions.

Her lawyer had told her to walk away, to find a new manager and break that connection with her parents that gave them control of her career. And she hadn't known how, because she'd known what it meant to them, to her sisters, and to the other performers connected to them.

If it had been about her—her alone—it would have been easy.

She closed the lid down over the piano keys. Gift. It wasn't a gift; it was a curse. It was always having to be what other people thought she should be. It was performing because people expected it of her, even when she hated it. It was the stares, the lack of friends and relationships, because people didn't understand. They didn't get that she was just a person who played the piano.

"Have you always had faith?" She looked up, into his brown eyes that were deep with compassion, and she was moved in new directions that her heart didn't know how to react to, how to soak up.

"Not always. My mom had faith, enough for all of us, I guess. And then, when she was gone…"

He faltered and looked away, and she knew this was another part of him she was getting to know, the part that hadn't dealt with the death of his mother. This was a man who found it easy to comfort, to joke, but not easy to deal with his own loss and his own pain.

Or at least she thought that was who he was.

"I've had to work through a lot in order to get over being angry with God for taking her."

"Are you still angry?"

He looked away, to the back of the chapel, to a simple wooden cross hanging on the wall.

"No, I'm not." He took hold of her hands, cupping them in his as he lifted them to brush a kiss over her knuckles. "Are you?"

She didn't know how to answer. "I'm not as angry as I was. But it isn't easy, to let go of what my mother did. And then, in April, my sister eloped with my fiancé. Which I can now say I'm glad about, but…"

He blinked a few times. "Bad month, April."

"A little." She managed a smile. "But each day since has gotten better."

"Alyson, can I pray with you?" He still held her hands in his. His thumbs stroked her fingers. He had straddled the bench and was watching her, waiting. And she didn't know what to say, because this time it wasn't frozen pizza they were praying for. This time they were praying for her to find faith.

She nodded and emotion, so heavy it hurt to breathe, settled in her chest. "Please."

They bowed their heads. Ceiling fans hanging from the rafters swished the air downward, circulating but not really cooling. The chapel wasn't fancy. The piano was old and out of tune. The hymnals were held together with tape. But the moment was one that settled in Alyson's heart.

It all became real in that moment.

After he prayed, Jason touched her back and stood up. She remained on the bench, unsure of her next move. What did a person do after praying for faith? How did they meet the next moments of their life? It changed everything. It changed her heart. It changed how she looked at her future. Because she had faith.

"I want you to make sure that Etta knows that we prayed. This is the open door, Alyson. It's a starting point for change. Believe in yourself, in who God created you to be."

She nodded. "Jason, are you going to remember?"

He grinned and winked. "You bet. Even if I have to write it down. Today, Alyson found faith. I think that's something to remember."

Why was he leaving? She stood, wanting to ask that question, but afraid of the answer. She touched his hand and he met her gaze.

"Why are you walking away?"

He paused and she could see in his eyes that he didn't have an answer. "I don't know. Habit, I guess. Will you be okay?"

Walking away was a habit. She filed that away in her

memory, so she wouldn't forget, so she wouldn't let it hurt her. Andie had warned her.

She nodded, and then she stood there as he left. She couldn't follow him. She wouldn't be the woman that ran after a man who didn't want to be caught.

Jason made his way to the dining hall, and he'd never been so glad to get anywhere. He sat down at one of the picnic-style tables and put his foot up on the bench of the table across from him. He liked what they'd done with this room. It was decorated with photographs of the kids from the previous year.

Jenna left the kitchen and joined him.

"What's up with you?" She handed him a bottle of water.

"What do you mean, what's up?"

"You know, this memory thing is a problem, but I think that you remember what's going on and you know what I'm talking about. You look terrible."

"Thanks. I think my kneecap is no longer attached to my leg, the ligaments and tendons are slapping around loose, and you want to have a counseling session?"

"Yeah, that's rough."

He felt like an idiot. "I'm sorry, Jen."

"It's okay." She slapped her prosthetic leg. "I'm doing really well. And having a baby. Could life be better?"

"No, I don't think it could. You deserve this."

He remembered back, to Jenna when she was sixteen and afraid. The two of them used to sit together at night, talking about life, about how to make it. They'd never been in love. They'd been friends. She had been the person he talked to, and he was the person she'd turned to when she got into trouble.

"You deserve to be happy, too." She looked at him, not smiling. "I saw you in the chapel with Alyson."

"Great."

"She's pretty terrific. I mean, she has a lot to learn about living here, but she has potential."

"You like her?"

"What I think doesn't matter. You, on the other hand, are going to be working with her."

"Yeah, I've been told. Or warned. But really, she can't ride and she doesn't know a thing about rodeos. I'm sure she'd rather stay in here, in the air-conditioning."

"You think that about me?" Not Jenna's voice. Jason turned and Alyson was standing in the back doorway. Which was why he hadn't seen her come into the dining hall. "Are you the same guy who was in the chapel with me?"

Was Jenna humming, "Goin' to the Chapel"? He thought she might have hummed it as she walked away.

"Yes, I'm the same guy. I'm sorry, Alyson. But the kitchen is great. It's cool and clean. The stables are hot and dusty."

She sat down across from him. "I want to work in the stable."

"Okay, you want the stables. I can handle that." What he really wanted was to head out the door and escape the look in those blue eyes. Angry women, not his thing.

A woman he'd led to faith in God.

The reminder jerked him up by the scruff of the neck. It felt like a huge connection between them, and he didn't want her angry. He wanted her...

In his arms.

The door opened and Jason looked up as Adam

Mackenzie entered the building, looking like a big thunderstorm about to hit. The other man's face was a little red and his eyes showed his fury.

"That accountant stole our money!" Adam slammed a notebook down on one of the tables.

Jenna came back from the kitchen, her face pale. She leaned against the stainless-steel counter and waited. They all waited as Adam worked on getting a grip on his temper.

"What does that mean?" Jenna was the first to ask.

"The donations to the camp are gone, and so is Joseph Brooks. I think he left a few thousand dollars in the camp account. Nice of him, huh?"

"Have you called the police?" Jason turned to straddle the bench seat of the cafeteria table so he could face Adam.

"I just called. They're coming out. We're going to try and chase him down, but I have a feeling he and our money are long gone. I should have paid more attention." Adam brushed a hand through his hair and shook his head. He sat down at the table. Jenna walked up behind her husband and put her hands on his shoulders.

"We'll work something out." She leaned in and kissed his cheek.

"Work something out? We have kids here. We have more kids coming in two weeks. How do we work this out?" He shook his head. "I'll transfer money from our private account. We aren't going to let the camp go down."

"You could have a fund-raiser."

They all turned to look at Alyson, whose suggestion had come out of the blue. She was standing a short distance away, and she shrugged. "I'm sorry, I know it isn't any of my business, but that's what I know—charity events."

"I'm afraid all of our supporters are going to take their money elsewhere when they find out what I allowed to happen." Adam shook his head. "I can't believe I didn't catch it sooner. He handed me checks, showed me the books."

"How did you find out?" Jenna asked, as she sat down next to Adam.

"I wrote a check to pay the electric bill and the bank called. The weekly deposit wasn't made."

"Man, I'm really sorry." Jason could write a check. He could help them out. But he knew that his help wouldn't be enough, not when the camp was hosting six groups each summer and then weekend groups in the spring and fall.

"Nothing we can do about it. We'll just have to start over."

"A charity event would work. We could invite people from Tulsa and from this area." Jason smiled at Alyson. "We could headline a pianist from the East Coast and have the kids at camp serve dinner to those who attend. Nothing fancy, maybe spaghetti?"

"I can't…" Alyson shook her head, her eyes watery. "I mean, I don't think it would be a draw. People here don't know me."

"You're still a gifted pianist." Jason didn't get it. Hadn't she offered? He retraced the memory, and he wasn't sure.

"I can't."

"We could have the fund-raiser during the next camp, at the end of June," Jenna suggested, smiling at Alyson.

Jason let it go. And he let Alyson go. She smiled his way as she said her goodbyes. Etta was standing in the yard, waiting for her.

"The accountant emptied the accounts for Camp Hope." Alyson filled Etta and Andie in on the story as Andie cooked burgers on the grill.

"Do they know where the guy is?" Andie turned, her apron a cow with its tongue hanging out. She slipped the spatula into the tongue that was also a pocket.

"Not a clue." Alyson swirled her glass of iced tea. "I suggested they do a fund-raiser, some kind of charity event. They could incorporate the camp rodeo at the end of June, mixed in with the children performing songs or skits, maybe serve dinner."

"That's a great idea." Etta nodded her approval. "I could contribute a few things to sell or auction.

"In less than a month." Andie shook her head. "The two of you think you could pull that off in that short a time?"

"You could help, instead of telling us we can't manage to do it," Etta scolded. "And don't let the burgers burn."

"I can't believe we're having veggie burgers." Andie shook her head. "We live in Oklahoma. It should be a law that we only eat beef."

Alyson smiled, because this was family.

"What about you, Ms. La-Di-Dah?" Andie pointed the spatula her direction. "Are you going to perform?"

Then it wasn't amusing. "No, but I could help get it all organized. I have a lot of experience with events like this."

"Because you've performed in them?" Andie kept it going.

"I can't do it." Alyson stared at her sister. Andie glared back.

"Come clean, Sis. Tell us why you can't."

"Because I have panic attacks when I walk on stage." Alyson picked up her kitten to keep it from clawing its way up her pant leg. "Because until I came here I was on medication for anxiety. And I can't go back to being that person."

"So face your fears." Andie tossed it out, as if it would be that simple. "Figure out what you're afraid of. It can't be the piano."

"No, it isn't the piano." Alyson looked to her grandmother for support. On the ride home they had talked about faith, about trusting God. So how did she put that into action?

How did she become a person who trusted? Jason had said baby steps. A baby step was helping with a charity event. She could help the children with their talents.

She wasn't ready to get back on stage in front of people.

"Let's talk about this later." Etta pointed to the grill. "I think what you need to think about is how to keep those burgers from burning."

"And how to make them edible," Andie muttered as she flipped their dinner off the grill onto a plate.

Alyson smiled a "thank you" at her grandmother. But she knew the conversation wasn't over. This was a conversation she needed to have with herself, about facing her fears.

Eventually she would have to go back to her life as Alyson Anderson. She would have to go back to Boston, back on stage.

On Friday Alyson walked down to the stables of Camp Hope. Her first day working there. Jason wasn't around yet. She didn't mind. She loved the peacefulness and the quiet of the stable. It was a new discovery—her love for dusty barns, the sweaty smell of horses and the sweet scent of hay.

As she walked through the double doors, a horse whinnied a greeting. Alyson took that as an invitation. She stopped at the stall and the horse's head came over the top of the gate, rubbing against her arm. The gray with his dappled coat was one of her favorites.

"Have you ever been afraid?" She smiled as she rubbed the horse's ears. "Of course you haven't."

"Why are you afraid?" A voice asked from the open doorway of the stable. "Are you talking to the horse about the fund-raiser?"

Jason. She turned and then avoided him by letting the horse nip at her sleeve. She ran a hand down the soft, gray neck and breathed in the scent of horse.

"I am, and he's a good listener. It's hard to explain." She glanced over her shoulder at him. "It just happens."

"Alyson, it was your idea, the fund-raiser. Or did I miss something?"

"You didn't miss anything. A fund-raiser is always good. The kids can have the spaghetti dinner. I bet there are kids here who have talent. If they sing or play, we can showcase their talents. You can add the showdeo. It could be a great thing for the camp. We don't charge. We ask for donations to the camp."

"Right. It is a great idea. And yet, you ran the minute I mentioned your involvement."

"I can't play."

"Of course you can. I've heard you play."

She turned away from the horse and faced a man who was asking her about the things she kept hidden deep inside, out of the spotlight.

"I can't play." It was easier to say it, after having told Andie and Etta. "I walked off the stage a few weeks ago. I can't play."

Jason took his hat off and hung it on a hook nearby. He leaned against the wall, waiting. "Why did you walk off the stage?"

"I can't play on a stage without falling apart." She walked to the doors of the barn and he joined her. He was still limping and he leaned against the door, watching her. "I have panic attacks. When I left Boston I decided to end a ten-year relationship with medication for those attacks. I've only taken the pills because that's how I walk onstage. That's how I face a crowd." It was how she faced herself.

And now he knew the truth.

"It's okay to be afraid."

"It isn't okay when fear keeps you from doing what you have to do."

She looked out at the field, and then at the sky. There were clouds in the distance. Dark gray and eating up the blue sky as they moved north.

"Looks like a storm coming." Jason followed her gaze. "Think we ought to head back?"

She shook her head. She wasn't ready to head back. From where she stood, she could see the children with their group leaders. They had classes after breakfast and then craft time.

"Jason, I'll help plan the fund-raiser. I'll help the children in any way that I can. I'm not sure if I can play."

His arm slid around her waist and she wondered how his touch made her feel stronger, almost made her believe she could walk on stage and conquer her fear.

"No one is going to push you to do something you're not ready to do. I'm sorry if you felt like I was pushing. I didn't realize." His voice was low, husky and tinged with an Oklahoma accent that softened it all, making it easy to hear.

She turned to look up at him, at a cowboy with a Robert Redford smile and brown eyes so warm, so kind, she wanted to…to touch him. How had that happened, that twenty-eight years of holding back ended with this moment of wanting to let go and feel a little of what everyone else felt, even their pain? Even if it meant being afraid.

His pain. She sometimes saw flashes of it in the depths of his eyes. But he always wiped it away with a smile and a joke.

"George Strait," he whispered.

"What?"

"On the radio." He held her hand in his and his left hand went to her waist.

She paused, barely hearing the song that filtered from somewhere farther down in the stable. He held her close and they swayed to the music and then he twirled her in a circle under his arm and pulled her close again.

She reached up, touching his cheek, resting her palm there. His head bent and she waited, breathless in a way that was full of wonder and a fear that didn't create panic, but made her wait, expecting something beautiful.

The horse nuzzled her arm as she leaned back against the stall door, Jason in front of her, his eyes tender and warm, holding her captive.

His lips touched hers and she leaned into him. His hands cupped her cheeks as he made her breathless.

"Alyson, you are so beautiful," he said softly, holding her close as he kissed her again.

He made her feel beautiful, and strong.

When the kiss ended, she held him close as they returned to a world that was crashing with thunder, sweeping a breeze through the stable and kicking up dust in the field.

"Wow, did we do that?" He laughed a little shakily as he leaned on the door of the stall next to her, holding her with an arm wrapped around her waist.

"I think we must have." Her voice trembled and she wanted to sit down.

Outside lightning flashed across the sky, followed by a crash of thunder. She jumped a little.

"Come on, let's go down to the office and drag out a couple of chairs. We can't go anywhere until this is over, we might as well have a cup of coffee and enjoy watching it rain."

The two of them, alone, while her emotions were doing cartwheels and her brain was trying to drag her back to reality. Her brain and her emotions were clashing, creating a storm of their own that she knew she couldn't outrun.

In the beginning she had allowed herself to believe that it was the newness of being here, of knowing someone like Jason, that created the intensity of her emotions. But the more she knew him, the more she wanted to be near him.

She watched from the door of the office as Jason filled the coffeepot with water from the watercooler and then scooped coffee into the filter basket. He switched it on and then reached for a couple of folded canvas chairs.

He handed her the chairs and sidestepped out of the office, holding the doorframe as he eased down. He smiled at her, winking as he took the chairs back.

"I'm not getting any younger." He said it with a lightness that she had to wonder about. Did it really not bother him? Was he really capable of joking about an injury that could possibly rob him of his career?

Or was she right, and that's how he handled life? He made a joke of the things he didn't want to deal with, to smooth over his pain.

"It can't be that easy." She took one of the chairs and unfolded it in the doorway of the stable, back far enough to keep them out of the wind and rain, close enough to feel the cool breeze.

He sat down next to her. "I'm getting my memory back. My knee is probably going to need surgery, but it'll get better."

"I don't know if anyone is that strong." She didn't look at him. Instead, she watched the rolling clouds of the storm sweep across the vast openness that was Oklahoma. "I hope there aren't any tornadoes."

Gray skies and green grass met at the horizon line. The temperature cooled and Alyson shivered.

"Someone would come get us, or call my cell phone if there were." Jason reached for her hand. "Relax."

She sat for a moment, his hand strong and firm on

hers. She listened to the coffeepot as it gurgled and then was silent.

"I'll get our coffee."

"Thanks." Jason touched her arm before she could walk away. "And you're right. It isn't always easy."

Chapter 9

Jason drove up to the camp the morning after the storm had blown through, taking shingles off one of the dorms and knocking limbs from a few trees. And in a sense, doing things to his heart he hadn't expected. But that had been a storm of a different kind. That storm had happened inside the stable and it was still pounding at him, making him relive a moment when he'd held Alyson in his arms and he had realized something about himself.

He had realized that for the first time in years he was being honest with his emotions and the woman he had held shifted that for him, making him reach out instead of tucking it all inside. For a guy who rode bulls for a living, he had thrived on safe. Safe relationships.

Because as far back as he could remember, only a few people lasted. He had a few guys on the bull-riding circuit that were still friends. But being in that life, traveling from event to event, things were always changing. People came and went.

You got used to guys leaving due to injuries, or because they got bumped to the lower event levels. Some got married and gave it up.

And Jason had lived that life, traveling, dating the women he met on the road, and never really staying in anyone's life long enough to get attached.

He hadn't minded at all. It had suited him.

A storm had changed that for him. A storm had pushed him further into the arms of a woman than he'd ever been. Because there had been a moment when he'd held her that he couldn't imagine ever letting go.

He parked his truck in the grassy field that was the parking lot for Camp Hope. He sat for a minute, relieved that he could remember yesterday. And then wishing he could forget.

But he hadn't been able to forget her since she first arrived. Cashmere and lavender. How in the world had those two things led to his downfall? He'd never been the kind of guy to fall for cashmere. His women had worn jeans and knew how to rope a calf, brand a steer and drive a four-wheel drive truck through mud, with a stock trailer on the back.

Alyson had traded her cashmere for blue jeans and T-shirts.

He climbed out of his truck and headed up the driveway to the stable. It was early and the campers were starting to stir, but the place was still pretty quiet.

If he had time this morning, he wanted to do a little roping with one of the new horses that Adam had bought, just to make sure it was gentle enough for a novice rider.

He walked through the stable to the gated entry at the end. The horse in question, a big chestnut, burnished red and with a wide, white blaze running down his face was in the corral waiting. The animal trotted to the gate.

Jason snapped a lead rope onto the halter and led the horse through the gate, latching it closed behind them.

"Time for us to see what you can do."

"He's pretty gentle."

Jason turned and nodded at Adam. "Yeah, I think he'll be fine. There's a boy with a little riding experience. I'm going to teach him to rope and see what the two of them can do."

"Jenna talked to Alyson and she thinks we should plan the charity dinner and concert for the same day as the showdeo at the end of the next two week camp. That would be short notice, just three weeks, but it would bring in quite a few people."

Jason cross-tied the horse in the center aisle of the stable. He walked through the door into the tack room and flipped on the light. There were a dozen or more saddles, bridles and other tack, brushes, and buckets neatly stored inside the room. It smelled like leather and bug spray.

He walked back out with the bridle and saddle. "That would be good. I've already been making calls. But Adam, I don't know if Alyson can do this. She's willing to help with the planning, but she might not be up to the concert part."

"Why do you say that?"

"Just leave it up to her." Jason slid the saddle pad into place on the horse's back, then the saddle. The gelding twitched a little, stomped at a fly on his leg and then settled. Jason tightened the girth strap.

"Whatever you say." Adam gave him another look, and Jason ignored the grin on the other man's face.

"Yeah, whatever I say. Turn a calf loose in the arena."

The horse walked next to him, as if it had been his horse for years and knew exactly what was expected of him. The previous owners had said the horse had been used in small rodeos, but a guy never knew for sure.

The sun was burning the last of the dew off the grass and heating up the morning as Jason slid his foot into the stirrup and lifted himself into the saddle. His right leg went over the horse's back and he settled into the seat.

"Easy there, boy." Jason held the reins and waited for the gelding to settle. He could feel the shifting, feel the horse tense. "You aren't going to throw me, big guy."

The horse moved a few steps, stomping and then nodding his head a little as he fought the bit.

"Don't tell me I got ripped again." Adam stood outside the arena, leaning on the gate.

"No, he's just restless. And I think he's afraid of the calf." What kind of roping horse was afraid of a calf?

Like a pianist afraid to play the piano. It could happen.

Jason pulled back on the reins and the horse backed at his command. "Not bad."

He rested the reins on the animal's neck and put pressure on his left side. The horse turned to the right. Jason nodded and touched his heels into the horse's side. With that silent command the gelding broke into a slow trot. They circled the arena and the calf stayed ahead of them. When Jason was ready and thought the horse was ready he gave another light nudge and the animal broke into an easy lope, inside front leg leading, head down at a nice level. He adjusted, pulling back on the reins, and the horse walked.

Jason rode back to the gate. "He'll make a good pleasure class horse. Put a kid on him for that and he'll be fine. I'll try using him for roping, but if he's a Western pleasure horse, that's where I'd keep him."

The horse was meant to show, not rodeo. He had the gait, didn't have to be encouraged to lead off on the right leg. It was a no-brainer as far as Jason was concerned. He swung his leg over the saddle and dismounted.

He landed with a jolt that jarred his leg and he took in a quick breath. "Wow, that wasn't good."

"When are you going to have that surgery?" Adam opened the gate and Jason led the horse out.

"One of these days." He stopped while Adam latched the gate. Out of the corner of his eye he saw movement. Alyson and the boy who wanted to learn to rope. He had really thought the chestnut gelding would be a great fit. Back to the drawing board on that.

"Alyson, Trent, you guys are down here early."

Alyson shrugged a little and looked away, her cheeks flushed pink. "I work down here, remember?"

Oh yeah. She worked down here. And she was dressed for the occasion in clothes that looked right off the rack and boots that were still a little too shiny. She'd have blisters tonight and tomorrow she wouldn't be smiling. He'd seen a pair of boots in the tack room. If he could talk her into wearing those, she'd be a lot happier. Or at least more comfortable.

"You want to try this horse out, Trent?" Jason held

the reins of the saddled chestnut and waited for the boy to stop looking overwhelmed.

The kid, lanky and with hair the color of straw, finally shrugged. Man, Jason remembered that age. About thirteen, when everything felt awkward and there was a new experience every day, making a guy feel as if he might never understand life or girls.

Especially one like Alyson, who didn't give it all away with a smile and a look in her eyes. She kept a part of herself back and left something for a guy to discover.

He thought he might have to kiss her again later, just to get her to let go of that dangerous look she was wearing.

"I'd like to ride him." Trent finally found command of the English language, and then his face turned red and he looked down at the ground.

Jason got it then, the kid was in love with Alyson. Well, a guy couldn't blame him for that.

"Come on then, let's walk you into the arena and you can show me what you know. Now the thing about this horse is, I don't think he's a roping horse. He's more of a show horse. But we'll work on roping later."

"Thank you, sir." The boy followed Jason through the open gate. When Jason held the headstall of the bridle, the kid put his foot in the stirrup and then half climbed into the saddle.

The gelding twitched a little but he didn't out and out throw the kid. Trent thunked himself into the saddle and moved his legs a little too much in the stirrups. The horse still didn't move.

"First off, let's keep the movements to a minimum." Jason put the reins in Trent's hands.

"Yes, sir."

"Take it easy to start with. You know the basic commands from our lesson yesterday. So take him around the arena. One lap at a walk, once at a trot and then an easy lope. Don't let him take control."

The boy nodded and turned the horse away from the group of adults who were watching. As he rode away, they all seemed to let out a collective sigh of relief. Jason stayed inside the arena, just in case.

"Any news on the accountant?" He didn't turn to look at Adam, but kept his attention on the boy and the horse. They were still walking, plodding along. The boy held the reins correctly and rode with his back straight.

"They've got a few leads, but the money has been disappearing for months. I guess I never thought someone would embezzle from a camp for kids. And he was smart about it. The books looked clean. It seemed that everything was getting paid. But the biggest loss was through donations. Money that came in and never made it to our account."

"I'm really sorry." Jason nodded to the boy as he rode past. "Loosen up on the reins. That's the reason he's shaking his head."

The boy nodded and kept riding, but his hands moved a little and the horse settled into a trot, the head bobbing stopped.

"This too shall pass." Adam shrugged. "I was ready to go after the guy, but Jenna, man, she's all faith. She's positive God will take what this guy meant for bad and use it for good for us."

Alyson was shaking her head. "How can this be good? How can God let this happen to a camp that only does good things?"

Adam looked at Jason and Jason didn't know what to

say. He knew she needed an answer, because he knew her. He knew her life.

"Life happens, Alyson. People do things that we don't get. People hurt us. But we find faith." He shook his head. "That sounds like an easy answer, but it's the only one that I have. You pray. You find a way to forgive. You trust God to redeem the situation. And through it all, our faith grows. We get stronger."

"Forgive." She looked away, blue eyes the color of the blue sky and blond hair lifting in the light breeze. "That's the part that isn't easy."

"No, it isn't."

Jason reached to touch her shoulder, but he stopped himself.

Adam had walked away, into the barn, leaving them alone. Not too subtle, Jason thought. He turned his attention back to the horse and its young rider. The animal was in an easy canter, smooth and controlled. The rider looked a little less than confidant and kind of bouncy.

"Tighten up your legs and settle into the saddle," Jason called out. The boy nodded, just a little and Jason could see that he was trying.

The horse and rider came around the arena again and slowed to a stop in front of Adam. "Move with the horse. Find his rhythm and let that be your rhythm in the saddle. I know it sounds easy, but the more you focus on that, the easier this will be."

"Got it." Trent took in a deep breath, as if he could suck in confidence with oxygen. And maybe he could. Jason nodded in the direction of the arena.

"One more time. Walk once, canter once and bring him in."

"I told Jenna that I could make phone calls. I do

know people who could help with the concert." Alyson spoke as the boy rode away. "I want to help."

"I know you do." Jason opened the gate and walked out of the arena. "Listen, don't feel like you have to do this, Alyson. People will understand. Besides, the other help you can give will mean a lot."

"Right." She shot a glance past him, at the arena and Trent. "He's in trouble."

Jason turned back just as the horse started to side-step and then arch his back and buck. "Trent, hold tight with your knees. Don't let him throw you off. Keep his head up."

The horse bucked a few more times. The boy went forward in the saddle, but landed back in the seat. He kept his knees tight.

"Keep a firm hold and turn his head back this way. Distract him from wanting to buck." Sometimes that worked.

Trent followed every command and when they turned back, the horse broke into a stiff-legged walk, but obeyed his rider. Trent shook like a leaf on one of the maple trees during a good wind.

"Buddy, you stayed on him."

"I heard a bee." Trent looked a little pale and his voice trembled. "I think he got stung or something in the ear. His ears were really twitching."

Jason walked back through the gate. "Okay, come here, Red."

He took the bridle and nodded for the boy to dismount. When Trent was on the ground, Jason checked the horse over. Sure enough, he had a red mark in his ear where something had stung him.

"You did good, Trent. I'm proud of you. A horse like

Red needs a rider like you, one who isn't going to panic. Tomorrow we'll work on roping. I think he might be willing to do double duty for you."

Trent's face lit up. "You think?"

"I think." Jason handed the reins over to the teen. "Take him inside. Cross-tie him and take his saddle off. He'll need a good brushing and some grain before you put him out in the field."

"Yes, sir." Trent led the horse away, his back a little straighter.

That's why Jason was at Camp Hope. Moments like this made it all clear. It made sense, working with these kids, making their lives a little better, giving them a little more confidence. It hooked him, and how did a guy walk away from that?

How did he go back on the road, to airplanes, motels and a different city or town every weekend? How did Jason go back to his life?

And women. None of them knew him. They knew that he was a bull rider. They loved the excitement at an event. They wore little tops, tight jeans and polished boots, but they didn't care about him, about his life.

Some of that was his fault. He'd never really cared to share his life with any of them.

Alyson walked next to him, back to the barn. Sometimes she felt like a complication. Sometimes she felt like the best thing that had ever happened to him. He shook his head, because never in a million years would he have dreamed up this scenario.

But God had. Jason wouldn't have been home when she showed up if it hadn't been for the accident. He nearly stopped walking when that thought shifted through his mind.

"You're good with these kids." Alyson pulled him back to a hot summer day and her presence next to him.

"I enjoy working with them."

"More than bull riding?"

He glanced down, wondering how she could do that, how she could know what he was thinking. Of course she didn't. It was coincidence.

"I don't know. Bull riding has always been my career. It's been in my blood for a long time."

"Are you going to compete again?"

She was so formal about it. He wanted to laugh, but he didn't. Instead, he led her into the stable and they stood back and watched as Trent took care of his horse.

"I'm scheduled for an event in a month. I'm going to Clint's to get on practice bulls tomorrow morning."

"Is that dangerous?"

"No, not really. Come with me. I'll show you."

As soon as the invitation was out, he knew that it changed everything. He knew that it made her someone he wouldn't walk away from before it hurt.

Alyson walked past the chapel on her way to the dining hall. Jason was still in the stable, helping a few of the younger children learn to pole bend. She'd watched him set up the poles, spacing them a short distance apart in the arena, making a line that the horses would run through, weaving back and forth through the poles. She didn't quite get it, but he'd promised to let her try it tomorrow.

On a horse. She could ride one around the arena, or through the field. But around poles?

As she passed the chapel, she heard the piano. She glanced in and saw a few of the children gathered around it. They plunked at the keys and managed something that sounded like "Twinkle, Twinkle." Turning off the trail that led to the dining hall, she walked over to the chapel, through the open door at the end.

One of the girls looked up, eyes wide. "We were just playing."

"That's okay, keep playing." Alyson walked down the center aisle between the two rows of pews. There were four girls and two boys, Jenna's twins. She smiled at Timmy and David and they smiled back—big smiles that lit up their smudged faces.

"We were just playing the piano," said a smaller girl. She had curly brown hair and big brown eyes. "I've never played one and Timmy said we could touch this one."

"You can touch it." Alyson walked up behind the group. "Would you like for me to show you how to play?"

They all nodded. David's smile grew. "'Cause she's a professional piani..." He scrunched his nose. "Pianoist."

"Something like that. A pianist." She ran a hand over his blond head. His hair had been buzzed short and his feet were bare. "Where are your shoes?"

"Lost. The dog took 'em."

"Oh." She sat down and the children circled around her. Her heart pounded, but this time it wasn't fear, it was something like being filled up. She smiled and touched the keys, running her fingers over them and getting a thrill that had been missing for a long, long time.

What made it different?

She played a few children's songs, including "Twinkle, Twinkle."

"Don't you need a book?" The little girl with curly hair had settled on the bench next to Alyson.

"No, I don't. I play by ear." The songs had always been in her head. It was hard for anyone to understand. She could hear a song and know how to play it.

"Can you play the song 'In the Garden.'" The older girl that had originally explained their presence in the chapel moved forward. "I love that song."

"Can you hum it for me?"

The girl, in a sweet alto, sang the song. As she sang, Alyson started to play. The song was beautiful, the melody pure. The words, about walking in the garden with the Savior, reached deep into Alyson's heart, to her soul.

She had a savior. Tears clouded her vision as she played and the young girl sang about Jesus telling her she was His own.

The song ended and the girl leaned and hugged her close. "Are you okay, Miss Alyson?"

"I'm fine, sweetie. You know what I think? I think we should practice a song that you can do this Sunday."

The children nodded. One of the girls suggested a song that they all knew and Alyson listened to excited chatter. As they talked, the bell rang, signaling lunch.

The children scattered. David, one of Jenna's twins, was the last to leave. Before he turned to run after the other kids, he hugged her tight. And then he was gone.

Alyson wiped her tears and took a deep breath. Her fingers moved to the piano keys again. She played the song and this time she sang the words that she remembered.

Jason stood on the trail and listened to the music that drifted from the chapel. Sun beat down on his back and he moved into the shade of a tree and leaned against it for support. The song was "In the Garden." He closed his eyes and listened to a child singing the lyrics. And he knew that it was Alyson playing the piano.

His mother's song. They had even played it at her funeral.

The child's voice faded as the song ended. He stood there, listening to the children talk, and Alyson laughing to something they said. The lunch bell rang and the children ran from the chapel, up the hill to the dining hall. That had been his destination, too. He just hadn't made it.

Before he could step away from the tree, the piano picked up the tune again. This time it was Alyson who sang the words.

He walked down the trail to the chapel. This was different than the last time, when she had picked out the words to "Jesus Loves Me."

This time she was singing about something personal.

And he knew he should walk away. He had experience with walking out the door, not with staying to feel the pain. He liked his life uncomplicated.

It had been anything but since Alyson showed up at Etta's.

That should scare him, but it didn't.

She stopped playing and looked up, her gaze connecting with his. She closed the piano up and stood, no longer a woman from the city. She had transformed herself into what she wanted to be, a Forester.

Who was she really? He didn't think she had an answer to that question. As much as she wanted this transformation, he had to wonder if it was that easy to shed who she had always been.

"You're missing lunch." He stood at the back of the chapel and she walked down the aisle toward him. The sun peeked through the leaves of shade trees that had been left standing around the chapel. The golden beam found her, catching the blond of her hair in its light.

And Jason felt a tingle of fear, because of this woman, walking up the aisle of the chapel to join him. He swallowed hard and tried to think of something funny to say, and he couldn't get the words out, couldn't shove them past the lump in his throat.

"I was heading for the dining hall when I heard the children on the piano," she admitted as she got closer to him.

And then they were standing there, at the back of the chapel, and his eyes ached because of sunlight and because she had consumed the air around him.

Man, she obviously didn't get that he had a reputation for not getting trapped in relationships.

"I'll walk up with you," he offered. "You might have to pull me up the hill."

She glanced down, at his swollen knee and she shook her head. "You're a lost cause."

"Not too much." He hooked his arm through hers. "They're having a bonfire for supper tonight."

"I know, hot dogs."

"And s'mores." He leaned a little toward her, because her hair smelled like coconut and her lips sparkled with pink gloss.

"So, will you go with me?" he asked.

She shot him a look. "You're that cheap? You want me to accept an invitation to a bonfire that I'm already attending?"

He shrugged. "I did promise you a bonfire. This one is already being built and I don't have to do the work."

She looked up at him, smiling. That pink gloss was more temptation than any man could handle.

"That's pretty cheesy."

He pretty much agreed, but he didn't have anything better. He'd thought he could go for the broken cowboy routine. He'd had experience with that, and it had a way of working on women.

But Alyson was different, and he couldn't play those games with her.

"I'll pick you up at seven?" They were already at the dining hall and kids were filing in.

Alyson nodded a little, and he wasn't even sure if she was agreeing. But he planned on knocking on her door at six-thirty.

Chapter 10

Andie knocked on the frame of the open door of the bedroom and Alyson turned away from the mirror. Andie stepped into the room. She had a backpack flung over her shoulder and she'd been rushing through the house all afternoon, getting ready to leave.

"I'm outta here." Andie plopped down on the chair next to the window. "And you look like a woman getting ready for a date, not a bonfire at a Christian camp."

"Will you be back next week?" Alyson shifted the conversation, she hoped, to something neutral.

"Probably. Are you going to be here?" Andie propped booted feet on the window seat.

Would she be here? Alyson sat down on the edge of her bed and slipped her feet into flip-flops. "Of course I'll be here. I'm working at the camp. I'm not going to walk away from that."

She had talked to Jenna about working with the children, teaching them a few songs that they could sing. They were thinking of bringing these kids back for the fund-raiser, so they could participate. The kids were begging their own church to let them return.

"Alyson, can I give you a little advice, if it isn't too late?"

"Do I have a choice?"

Andie laughed. "Actually, no, you don't. I was just going to remind you to be careful with your heart, sister."

Jason. Of course that's what Andie meant with that advice.

"My heart is still intact. I've already been dumped and I'm not about to go through that again."

"Yeah, but I don't think you loved that guy."

"No, I probably didn't."

Andie dropped her feet to the ground and stood up. She leaned to kiss Alyson on the top of her head. "See you soon. And I don't want a message on my voice mail telling me you've eloped with a cowboy."

"That isn't going to happen."

As Andie walked out the door, she laughed. "We'll see."

Alyson mumbled that she didn't have to see, she knew. But because of Andie, she found herself thinking about Jason, and a night that felt like a first date.

She thought back, to dating Dan. It hadn't really been dating. He'd taken her to dinner twice a month. That had been their schedule. And each date had ended with a friendly kiss that hadn't shattered anything more than her dreams of what love should feel like.

Now she knew the truth. Dan had been comparing

her to her sister, to Laura's more dramatic beauty. Laura had dazzled him with her bright laughter and easy personality.

Alyson hated that she understood. She'd always been slightly dazzled by Laura, too. But she still loved her sister.

A truck rumbled down the road outside Etta's. Alyson listened as it turned into the driveway and pulled up to the house. He hadn't forgotten. She smiled, because she had hoped, just a little, that he might forget.

Instead, he was knocking on the front door and Etta was yelling up the stairs that her date was here. Her date. Alyson was twenty-eight and she felt as if she was going to the prom.

It wasn't the prom. It was hot dogs and a bonfire at Camp Hope. She stood up, shot a quick glance at the mirror, and walked out the door. He was waiting at the bottom of the stairs and for a second it felt like the prom. Except that she was in shorts and a T-shirt, he was in jeans, but tonight, no hat. He wore an unbuttoned short-sleeved shirt over a T-shirt.

He smiled up at her, and her heart tumbled down the stairs. She grabbed the rail to make sure she didn't follow and reminded herself that this was one night, and not forever.

"Ready to go?" He winked and she wondered if he had a clue how nervous she was.

"Of course." This was the new, stronger version of herself. Like a new computer program, updated and more sophisticated. Her less confident self reminded her that new programs were always full of bugs and tended to crash often. "Of course I'm ready."

She had reached the bottom of the stairs and he reached for her hand. "You're driving."

"I can't drive a truck." She glanced at Etta. "Tell him this is a bad idea."

"Of course you can. You need the practice." He handed her the keys.

"See you kids later." Etta was pushing them to the door, like they were sixteen. "Have fun and stop worrying."

And then the door was closing behind them. Jason took hold of her hand and held it tight as they walked to the truck. This had nothing to do with her needing experience driving a stick shift. She considered asking him the real reason, but he was as entitled to his secrets as she was to hers.

He stopped at the driver's side of his truck and opened the door for her. She climbed in, but she didn't let him close the door.

"We could take my car," she offered.

"Nope, not into the field." He closed the door and walked around to the passenger side. "Put your foot on the clutch and the gas, make sure it's in first gear and start your engines."

"No race car analogies, please."

Alyson started the truck, and that proved to be the easy part. Shift, clutch, brake, gas, shift, don't forget the clutch, grinding gears, man next to her mumbling under his breath and then trying to smile. On the highway outside of Dawson it got easier. She could put the truck in fourth gear and drive like a normal person.

"As we get close to the camp entrance, slow down, use the clutch and shift to Third. Then slow again, clutch, shift to Second."

"Okay." But it wasn't okay. Her hands, legs and insides were shaking.

He laughed. "You're doing great."

She shifted once, twice and on the third shift the truck bucked, jerked and died.

"Oops." She shifted into First and started it again.

He leaned back in the seat. "Up the driveway to the barn."

"And then you can take over?"

He shook his head. "You're doing a great job."

The gate was already open. She drove through, afraid she'd hit the truck against the posts on either side. And from the way he sucked in a breath, he had to be thinking the same thing.

In the distance she could see a stand of trees and a group of people. The fire was already burning, smoke swirling into the air and kids standing around it. The truck bounced as she drove across the field toward the group of people who had already gathered.

"Park at the end of the row." Jason pointed. There were several trucks and a tractor attached to a trailer. That was for the hayride they planned to have.

She parked the truck and started to turn the key, but Keith Urban was playing on the radio, and she liked his music. Jason opened his door and got out of the truck.

Alyson left the music on and stepped out. She started to reach in the back for their lawn chairs and the blanket Jason had brought along, but she didn't. Jason stood at the back of the truck, a hand on the tailgate and his head down.

She walked back to him. He opened his eyes and smiled, winking as if nothing had happened.

"You're not okay."

"Of course I am." He slipped an arm around her waist and walked her around the truck to where she'd left the chairs and blanket. Keith Urban was still singing and Jason swayed a little, catching himself on the side of the truck.

She started to comment, but he stopped her with a look.

"I think this song might be my favorite." He moved closer. "What about you?"

A love song, sung in pure Keith Urban style, twirling a woman's emotions. Alyson pretended the song didn't matter, and that this moment with the sun setting behind the dark green of the trees, turning the sky a brilliant orange and pink didn't matter. She was standing in a field with a man whose smile touched deep inside her and she really wanted it to not matter.

But it did.

Nothing had ever mattered more.

As he pulled her close, she no longer felt like a person coming unraveled, losing herself. For that moment, with Keith Urban singing and a cowboy holding her close, she felt the promise of a summer night.

He leaned, kissed her cheek and then whispered in her ear, "We'd better join the group before we forget why we're here."

"For s'mores," she whispered back.

"Exactly."

But she was breathless and his hand lingered on hers for a few seconds more.

Jason carried the chairs and walked next to Alyson, not reaching for her hand as they neared a group of people who wore openly curious expressions. He wasn't going to satisfy their curiosity. And he wasn't going to fall on his face from the bout of dizziness that had hit him about the time he left his house for Etta's to pick up Alyson.

He was waiting for the medication to kick in and praying it wouldn't take long.

He wasn't going to be able to keep making excuses, like telling Alyson she needed to practice driving. And then holding on to her instead of falling.

Alyson opened her chair and then she walked away, drawn to the rope swing the kids were using to swing out over the swimming hole. Some took longer to let go than others. Jason watched, laughing because the girl on the swing had been over the water twice and she was still hanging tight. Adam and Jenna were standing nearby, encouraging her to let go.

Let go. Jason shot a glance in Alyson's direction. She knew about letting go. When he'd held her in his arms, she had let go. He'd seen it in her eyes, that she was beginning to see who she was. She was Alyson Forester, from Dawson.

She was good at being that Alyson.

Not that he minded the Alyson who wore cashmere.

She probably wanted that cashmere right now, he thought. It wasn't cold, but she hugged herself as if she were chilled. He thought about offering the jacket he kept behind the seat of his truck, but knew she wouldn't take it. She wasn't cold, just trying to pull herself together.

He understood.

He could barely remember the first day he met her, but he knew that the shreds of memory he had retained meant something. He couldn't let go of seeing her standing at the edge of Etta's lawn, staring at him, at that big house, as if she'd just entered another dimension.

Or found something she'd lost.

And maybe she had lost something—herself. But he thought she was finding that person again. He also thought that when she found herself, she'd leave. Once her confidence was back and her life wasn't about fearing her gift, or fearing rejection, she'd return to the life she'd left behind.

He walked to the edge of the creek bank where she was standing. She glanced at him and then back up, at the rope swing.

"You should try it," he suggested, and she shook her head.

"I don't think I'm dressed for plunging into a creek." She watched as the next teenager took the rope, walked back and then glided forward, swinging over the water. This kid dropped on the first try. "Is it deep?"

"It's over their heads."

"I'd like to come back and try it. Someday." She sighed and didn't look at him. "Before I leave."

"Are you planning to leave?" Why did that question land somewhere in his gut?

"Eventually." She was still watching the kids on the rope. "I have a schedule that I can't walk away from."

"Yeah, I get that."

This time she looked at him, her blue eyes bright. "I knew this was temporary."

He nodded, because he'd known it, too. She should be easy to let go of. He'd go back on the road, back to riding bulls. She'd go back to her world.

Jenna called out for the kids, telling them it was time to eat. They walked out of the creek and hurried back to the fire, flinging towels around their shoulders. Alyson reached for his hand.

"Stop pretending." She spoke so softly he barely caught it.

"What?"

"You, acting like you're okay, like you just wanted to let me practice driving a stick shift."

He smiled and winked, because he didn't know what to say to someone who saw way too much.

"How do you like your hot dogs?" he asked as they got closer to the fire, to the group of people already shoving hot dogs on sticks. A few were standing close to the fire with sticks held close to the flames.

"Well, since I've never had one roasted on a fire, I'll let you help me with that. And I asked you a question."

He laughed. "I never thought you'd be this stubborn."

"You don't know me very well."

He looked at her, at a woman with a soft smile and blue eyes that held his attention. He knew her better than he had planned on knowing her.

"Then I guess I'll have to get to know you better." He moved a little closer and she stepped back, her eyes bright with laughter and her hair coming loose from the clip that held it in place.

She was definitely determined to get under his skin.

"Not so fast, Cowboy." She was still teasing, still smiling. "I have questions."

He shrugged. "Yes, I really am naturally this charming and cute."

"Oh, so you really are one of those love 'em and leave 'em types?"

He laughed. "Yeah, honey, that's me."

And it had been, for a long time.

"Funny, but I don't see you that way." Her smile dissolved and her eyes studied him, holding his gaze until he felt fifteen and unsure.

"How do you see me?" This wasn't working out the way he had planned, as a way to distract her.

He wasn't sure he wanted to know how she saw him. And really didn't want this conversation to take place with an audience. He smiled across the fire, at Willow and Clint, holding the little girl they'd adopted from China.

"I see you as a guy who is always laughing and smiling so he doesn't have to deal with how much he hurts on the inside."

"I think we should roast hot dogs."

"Exactly my point." And she took her roasting stick and walked away, leaving him as unsure as he'd ever been in his life.

From across the fire he saw Clint Cameron laugh and sign something to his wife. They were looking at him. Willow signed back and Clint nodded.

Married couples. They thought everyone should follow their example.

Alyson had joined Jenna on the lawn chairs a short distance from the fire. He thought about joining them, but instead he went the opposite direction, finding a place with a group of teenage boys who were intent on discussing the steer riding they would do the next day.

That was a lot safer than any other conversation Jason thought he could have at that moment. And definitely safer than spending too much time with Alyson.

Chapter 11

Alyson walked through the doors of the now familiar Mad Cow Café. The black-and-white painted walls were even starting to grow on her. So was Vera. It was only seven in the morning and the place was packed.

From a corner booth, Jenna waved to get her attention. That was the reason she was there, to meet with Jenna about the charity concert for the camp. They'd discussed it the previous evening at the bonfire, and decided it would be easier to talk at the Mad Cow, without camp responsibilities to distract them.

Alyson sat down across from Jenna, and Vera hurried across the room with the coffeepot. Alyson turned her cup and smiled up at the older woman, who no longer treated her like the stranger that had shown up in town.

Alyson was already a part of the community.

And last night her mother had left a message on her

cell phone that she was expected to play in Chicago in three weeks. The same weekend as the fund-raiser.

"That's a long face." Vera poured the coffee and dropped a couple of creamers on the table. Her smile was bright for so early in the morning.

Alyson couldn't imagine wearing that smile before noon.

"Sorry, I'm not great at mornings."

Vera laughed. "Honey, you'd better get used to them if you're going to stay around here. You are going to stay, right?"

"I don't know." Alyson stirred creamer into her coffee and ignored the way Jenna watched her, curious and concerned.

"You have to." Vera, not as subtle as Jenna. "Why, honey, we're all itching to get Jason Bradshaw married off. He isn't getting any younger, and he's a pretty decent catch."

Jenna laughed. "If he can remember your name."

"Oh, he's getting better." Vera pulled the order pad out of her apron pocket. "What can I get you girls for breakfast?"

"Poached eggs and toast." Alyson didn't have to open the menu.

"Omelet, hash browns and bacon." Jenna handed the menu back to Vera. "And milk."

"Eating for two." Vera winked and then she was gone, hurrying off to the kitchen, but refilling several cups of coffee along the way.

"Don't let it get to you." Jenna stirred sugar into her coffee. "This is hard to get used to, having just one cup of coffee in the morning."

"I can't imagine."

"About the matchmakers. Don't worry. They're harmless and they all know that it has to be God's will, not theirs. They love you or they wouldn't be trying to pair you up with Jason."

"I'm not anyone's match." Alyson tried to smile, to let the words sound light.

"Of course you are. You have to trust God, Alyson. I don't think you showed up here by accident."

Alyson looked up. "You really think that God, as busy as He is with this messed-up world, looked down and thought about me, and getting me here?"

"I do think that."

Alyson leaned back and it was okay to smile. "Maybe I'm here because God knew I could help with this fund-raiser."

"Maybe."

It felt right. God had brought her here to help these people. She liked that thought. And she also thought that she might not have found faith if she hadn't come here. It was new faith, but it was real enough for her to know that God would do this for Camp Hope, for Jenna and Adam.

If she put her time here in that box, then it made it easier to leave, easier to deal with what she thought she might feel for Jason. Because she didn't want to miss him when she left and she knew she would.

"I have an idea about the concert." Alyson steered the conversation back to the reason for meeting and Jenna shot her a knowing smile.

"Okay."

"I could work with the kids on a few songs."

"Sounds great to me."

"And they could display their artwork and photographs they've taken. We could do an art show for guests to look at, even bid on."

"Wow, great ideas." Jenna bit down on her bottom lip and then she leaned forward a little. "What about you, Alyson? Are you going to play?"

"I think the children would be the real attraction. People need to see what Camp Hope is all about."

"If you can't…"

She smiled at the young waitress who came around the corner with their food. She set their plates down in front of them and then promised to refill their coffee cups.

"Jenna, I really don't think I can."

Jenna switched the plates, giving Alyson her eggs. "It's okay. If you can help the kids and help me get the invitations out to the right people, I think that's going to be more than enough."

"Of course I'll do that." She buttered her toast and started to take a bite, but she put it down on the plate. "I want you to understand. It isn't that I don't want to. I just can't. And I'm not sure if I'll even be able to be here for the fund-raiser."

"I forgot that you mentioned that. It got lost in Vera trying to marry you off to Jason." Jenna put her fork down. "Why would you leave?"

"I have a career. As much as I don't want it, I can't walk away and leave everyone in a lurch."

Jenna nodded, thoughtful and sweet.

"I understand."

"I love it here, though." Alyson looked around the room, at tables full of people she had gotten to know. "I'm so glad I found this place, and found my family."

"Why can't you finish your obligations and come back home, to all of us?"

"I've thought about it."

"And you don't know if you will?"

Alyson shrugged. "I'm not sure. I came here looking for my family and I've found them. I know that I'll never lose them. But I have an apartment and I have my family in Boston."

There was so much she hadn't planned on. She hadn't planned on having a twin. She hadn't planned on Camp Hope. She definitely hadn't planned on Jason.

There were no easy answers for her future.

The arena was empty. Jason walked through the double doors, glad for a few minutes alone. He had seen the kids going from the dining hall to their dorms. He had a few minutes to get his act together and to get ready for the kids who were going to try their hands at steer riding.

He needed to be thinking about them, not about Alyson standing next to the bonfire last night, the glow of the flames flickering in her eyes. And when he'd dropped her off at home, she'd thanked him and walked inside. He remembered standing there in the cool evening air, with nothing.

He flipped on the lights and the arena changed from a dusky place, shadowy and quiet, to bright and ready for action. From a pen at the other end of the building low mooing erupted.

He walked along the outside edge of the arena to the pens where steers were being held. He flaked off hay and tossed it in. The steers, rangy and young, ran to the back of the pen. They eyed him, snorting and wide-eyed, and then came forward again, taking bites of hay.

They had water. Now they had food. And he had time on his hands.

He turned away from the steers as Adam and Clint led a group of about twenty kids into the arena. Adam pointed to the small riser of bleacher-type seats and the kids filed single file down the row and took seats.

"This is what we're going to do today." Adam leaned against the gate and addressed the kids. "Our rodeo is in a little over a week. You've learned to ride. You've learned to rope. And today we're going to put a few of you on steers. But before we do, Jason is going to do a demonstration on a bull."

Adam shot him a look. "You up to that?"

Jason shrugged. "Ready as I'll ever be."

Clint ran a bull into one of the chutes and held Jason's bull rope up for the teens to see it. "Here you go."

Jason walked to the chute, rethinking his involvement in this, in teaching kids, in the camp and bull riding. He had a nice piece of land, some livestock, a great house. Why in the world was he still riding bulls?

His dad had always said that someone needed to pound some sense into him. A couple of months ago, a bull had tried. So where was that sense? Shouldn't he be handing the rope to Clint, telling him to go for it, or find someone a little younger to climb on that big, red bull snorting in the chute.

The bull was one of Willow's older bulls. The animal snorted and pawed. It rammed against the metal gate and bellowed. Clint laughed a little as Jason stood on the platform overlooking the animal. Nearly a ton of bone-breaking ability caged inside a metal chute and about to be unleashed on him.

He hadn't been on a bull since the accident. He'd been on the mechanical bull at the camp. The kids had trained with him on it. He'd taught them the basics and knew their skill level would match the steers they were going up against today.

The steers were a third the size of and not nearly the man this bull was.

"If you're not ready?" Clint had his bull rope ready and Jason had to make the move.

"I'm ready." Jason climbed over the gate, trying not to think about the ride that had changed his life and how it had felt before he climbed on the back of that bull. He didn't remember the ride, just the way the animal snorted as he lowered onto its back.

He remembered the music. He lowered himself onto the back of the bull with Clint leaning over him, ready to pull the rope and help him get it tight.

Heavy metal music had been playing the night he got trampled into a hard-packed dirt arena in Arizona. There was no music today. The bull shifted beneath him, lowering its massive head and then leaning into the gate, pushing Jason's leg into the metal. Adam Mackenzie pushed from the outside of the gate, the arena side, moving the bull.

The rope was tight. Clint handed him the end and Jason wrapped it around his hand. The moment of truth. Could he get back into an arena without losing his nerve? When the gate opened, would he jump before the bull made its first jump?

Jason felt the bull settle. He nodded and Adam opened the gate. The bull turned out, bursting into the arena with two thousand pounds of fury and force. It bucked, hopped to the side and rolled its back a little to the left before settling into a spin that included a front jump with each revolution.

A few jumps felt as if the animal's back end was trying to meet up with its front end. Jason gritted his teeth and clenched his hand a little tighter. His spine felt as if it was being jammed into his brain.

Jason didn't wait for the eight-second buzzer. He loosened his hand from the rope and waited for the right moment to jump, knowing Clint and Adam would distract the bull as he fell to the ground.

When he landed, he landed on his feet, lost his balance and fell to his knees, but the bull was there, head just inches away, snorting, blowing hot air at Jason. He got to his feet, helped by Adam grabbing the back of his Kevlar vest. Clint pushed the head of the raging animal, giving Jason a few seconds to recover and climb the gate, out of the arena.

Alyson didn't realize how tightly her hands were clenched in her lap until Jenna patted her on the back and whispered for her to relax. As if she could. Her heart was pounding so hard she didn't know if it would ever return to its normal beat and she'd bitten into her bottom lip hard enough that it was probably bleeding.

That man who had sat on the back of that bull was a Jason Bradshaw she'd never met. He wasn't the same cowboy with the quick smile and easy laugh that she knew. This man was dead serious about his sport and willing to go head to head with a two-thousand-pound animal.

As he limped out of the arena, she moved toward

him, but Jenna grabbed her arm. "Not yet. Let him throw something or kick something."

"But what if he's hurt?" Alyson watched him walk out the gate, past the chutes and out a side door.

"He isn't hurt. He's mad because he didn't make the eight seconds. He's mad at his body for letting him down."

Alyson tried to get it, but it was a world far removed from the one she'd always lived in.

Clint was standing in the arena, talking to the kids who had showed up for their first day of riding real steers. The kids—all teenagers—were leaning forward, catching every word, bouncing with excitement.

"I'll be back." Alyson stood up and Jenna let her go. She walked down metal steps that vibrated with each movement.

With every step she questioned why she was doing this. He had friends. These people understood him. They knew when he needed to be left alone.

But maybe he'd convinced them that alone was where he belonged.

What did she know about the life of a bull rider? Or the life of a cowboy? She looked down at the boots that were starting to look a little worn. She was breaking in her country self, feeling more like Alyson Forester.

Jason was in the stable, pulling a saddle out of the tack room. He turned when she walked up. His smile spread easily across his face, but it didn't reach his eyes, didn't leave the crinkles at the corners that she was so used to.

"That was pretty amazing." She leaned against the wall, relieved that he couldn't see the way her insides shook.

"Yeah, amazing. At least I remember your name."
He winked and picked up the saddle. She followed him
to a stall that held a pretty black horse.

"That's good to know." She reached to pet the nose
of the horse. "Are you okay?"

He turned, still smiling. "Of course I am."

"Okay." But she knew he wasn't. Of course he
wasn't. He smiled. He made jokes. He deflected. "Are
you going for a ride, now? I mean, aren't you going to
stay and teach the kids to ride the steers?"

He put the saddle down. "I don't know."

"Oh."

"I can't even believe I'm here, teaching kids at a
camp."

"Did it ever occur to you that we're supposed to be
here?" She took a step closer, liking that he smelled
like soap and peppermint. "I'm here because my life
fell apart. You're here because your career got put on
hold. But we both needed to be here."

He shook his head and then smiled, reaching out, but
he didn't take her hand. And she had wanted him to.
Instead, he shoved his hand into his pocket.

"Thank you." He leaned, his hands still in his pocket,
and he dropped a kiss on her cheek. "You're right."

"But that doesn't make it any easier."

He laughed. "Not really, but it was sweet. Let's go
teach some boys to ride bulls."

He hooked his finger through her belt loop and his
first step tugged her back. She glanced to the side,
catching the grimace of pain.

"Do you think you need to go…?"

He shook his head. "Not yet. Let's get this camp over,
and then I'll get it taken care of."

"Right."

They walked back into the arena and Alyson walked up the steps to where Jenna was still sitting. Jason joined the guys. They had a steer in a chute and an older teen, not from the camp, standing on the platform, about to climb on the back of the animal. The steer, red-coated and thrashing his head back and forth, started bucking inside the chute, before the boy could get settled on his back.

Jason hauled the kid out by the back of his shirt.

"I'm not sure if I can watch." Alyson covered her face, but she peeked through her fingers.

Jenna's laughter was soft. "You get used to it. You have to understand that these guys know what they're doing. And the guys in the arena, they're tops at keeping a rider safe. They'll jump between the bull and the bull rider. That's the job of a bull fighter."

"They don't really fight the bull?"

"No, they distract him. They're in there to keep that cowboy safe. They'll pull him loose if his hand gets hung up in the rope. They'll jerk him off the ground and give him a shove if he needs it. I've seen them cover a fallen bull rider with their own bodies to keep the guy safe from those hooves."

"That's pretty amazing. And the kids from the camp are wearing helmets?"

Jenna nodded. "Helmets and Kevlar vests. Bull riders started wearing the bulletproof vest after Lane Frost got killed. A lot of cowboys have been saved by that vest."

Alyson let out a breath and told herself to relax. But her gaze kept going to Jason Bradshaw. She kept thinking of him on the back of that bull.

And she realized she would have jumped in there and saved him.

It felt as if he had already rescued her.

Jenna and Alyson left before Jason finished up with the kids. He had walked out of the arena and they were gone. From the distance he heard the piano in the chapel and he thought she might be there.

Rather than going there, to her, he left for the day. He hadn't been home before dark all week. And tonight he was moving back into his house. He could finish a sentence. He could remember where he was going, most of the time.

And he needed his house, his space.

He parked outside the garage and eased himself out of the truck. Hopping out was no longer the recommended exit strategy. He leaned against the truck for a minute and then turned and walked out to the barn. Someone was already there.

When Beth walked out, she smiled. He breathed out a sigh, because it was easy to see her now. The bruises were long gone. Her arm had healed. He didn't know about her heart. But she was smiling, and that counted for something.

"What are you doing here?" He stopped at the gate.

"I didn't know you'd be here so early. I was feeding for you. You have a new foal."

"The bay mare?"

Beth nodded in the direction of the twenty-acre field south of his barn. "Yeah, and she looks like her mother."

"That's what I hoped for. Let's walk out and take a look."

"I can't. I promised Dad we'd run into Tulsa tonight.

It's a little funny, but I think he feels bad for Marcie Ballentine."

"Dad and Marcie with the five kids?"

"That's the one." Beth pushed dark-brown hair back from her face, revealing the one scar that hadn't disappeared with time, right above her eye. "The kids are all grown. It isn't like he'd be raising them."

"Yeah, I guess. What does this have to do with Tulsa?"

"She's going with us. He says it's the neighborly thing to do, to take out a neighbor who is down."

"Wow." Jason latched the gate they had walked through. The grass was a little long. He'd had fewer horses on it than normal and it hadn't been eaten down the way it usually would have been by this time of the year.

The mare grazed and her foal, still damp and wobbly, stood at her side, trying to find dinner. Jason stopped, not wanting to interrupt.

"Pretty, isn't she?"

"She is." He smiled, because his thoughts took a sudden turn and he wasn't seeing the foal, it was Alyson's face that flashed through his mind, taking him by surprise.

Then again, it didn't surprise him.

Chapter 12

Alyson stuck a needle through the back of the cloth and pulled the thread through, adding another touch of color to what she hoped would be her first finished needlepoint. She'd been working on it all week, each night after she got home from camp.

Her grandmother had told her it was a relaxing pastime. That had sounded good after watching Jason ride the bull at camp.

Alyson poked the needle through again and this time it got hung up, the way it had been doing all evening, tangling thread at the back of what was supposed to be a picture of a cottage.

"You're supposed to relax when you're doing this." Etta laughed, but she didn't stop the movement of the spinning wheel. She'd bought wool and she was busy turning it into yarn. That was something else Alyson couldn't do. She couldn't spin. She'd tried and the ensuing tangle of wool had made her grandmother grumble just a little.

"I'm relaxed." She jabbed the needle through the cloth again. "Ouch."

She kissed her finger and put the needlepoint down on the table next to her. She loved this attic room with the tall eaves, the stained-glass window and the window seat. It was a fairy-tale room. She hoped she wouldn't prick her finger and sleep for one hundred years.

Because there weren't any handsome princes out searching for her—she was sure of that.

Not even a cowboy. Because the cowboy had gone off to a rodeo, just days before camp ended. A rodeo in Oklahoma City, where he hoped to garner points that would help him get back on track for the world championship.

"What's your mother up to? Didn't she call earlier?" Etta kept spinning, but cast a look back, over her shoulder.

"She called."

"She's been calling a lot."

"I know. She's reminding me that I have a career and I can't be gone forever." Alyson picked up the needlepoint again, but she didn't pick up the needle. "She reminded me that I have a concert in Chicago. In fifteen days."

The same weekend as the fund-raiser for Camp Hope. No amount of needlepoint was going to make her feel better about that, or about leaving.

She was torn between her two lives, and knowing which world she belonged in. She didn't know how to explain to Etta that Gary Anderson had raised her, and that he had been a fair man, buffering her from her mother's tangents.

She couldn't explain to her mother about the faith she had found in Dawson.

"No matter what, Alyson, you have family here. I know you have commitments you have to keep. That can't be undone, but she can't take Dawson out of you. You can take the girl out of the country, but you sure can't take the country out of the girl." Etta stopped spinning. "And you can't take her faith, either."

"I know." Alyson jabbed at the fabric again, fighting tears that clouded her vision. "It shouldn't be this difficult."

She closed her eyes, trying to breathe past the tightness in her throat and then she blinked away the tears.

Where would she put her new life, this new person she'd become, when she went back to Boston? Her heart ached, thinking about how it would feel to lose the person she'd become.

She wouldn't lose herself. She pulled the needle through the fabric again, adding another block to the chimney of the cottage. She was Alyson Forester. Alyson Anderson had ceased to be. That Alyson had been the creation of her mother.

The new Alyson knew what she wanted from her life. She knew who she was. That wouldn't change.

"Let's go downstairs and bake something." Etta's other antidote for stress. "Pizza."

Alyson laughed. "I think not."

A car rumbled up the drive. Etta got up to go look, "Maybe Andie is home early."

"That would be good."

"Nope, it's Jason Bradshaw. Imagine that."

Alyson didn't have to imagine. Not much. She'd been thinking about him all day. She glanced out the window and watched him get out of the truck that pulled a horse trailer.

"What's he doing?" Etta turned from the window. "I've never known that boy to be so hard to figure out. He's always been a pretty carefree guy."

Alyson couldn't agree with that comment. She thought that he'd always pretended to be carefree and that maybe no one had ever figured him out the way she had. Maybe they'd all been so glad to see him smiling, joking, being the great guy they all relied on, that no one had given him the chance to be the man she thought he might be.

Days ago he had whispered that he wanted her to know him. And she thought she did.

Jason led the Appaloosa gelding out of the trailer and tied him to the side. He went back in after his horse. When he turned from tying the big roan to the trailer, Alyson was standing behind him. He grinned and pushed his hat back.

"Thought you might like to go for a ride."

She looked up, at the dusky evening sky. "It's late."

"Only eight o'clock. It's the only time of day that's really cool enough for a longer ride."

He looked down at her flip-flops and back up, catching her smile. Her toenails were cotton candy pink and she wore a toe ring.

"I'd have to change."

"So change." He rested his arm on the rump of his red roan. The horse moved to the side a little and stomped at a fly. "I'll get these guys saddled and ready to go, you grab us a couple of bottles of water."

"And change."

He grinned. "Sure, but I really like the pink polish."

She turned about the same color as her nails and then she recovered. "You can borrow it."

He laughed and the horse moved abruptly to the right, knocking him off balance. "I think I'll leave the polish for you. We can share that way. You wear it, and I'll enjoy it."

"I'll be back."

He watched as she hurried up the sidewalk and then he turned back to the roan.

"Buddy, this isn't something a guy plans." The horse looked back and reached to nip at his arm. Jason pushed the horse away. "I don't think so."

He was saddling the Appaloosa when Alyson walked out the front door with Etta. He glanced back over his shoulder, catching a glimpse of Alyson and then returning his attention to the horse, tightening the girth strap, fiddling with the stirrups, whatever it took.

"I'm making brownies." Etta stopped next to the roan. "They'll be ready when you get back."

"Sounds great." His gaze traveled to Alyson. She had changed into a T-shirt and jeans. The toenails were no longer in sight. He was a little sorry about that. Maybe they should have put off riding and just sat on the porch with coffee and brownies.

"Ready?" Her tone was hesitant and she moved a little toward the Appaloosa, a dark almost black horse with a white blanket on its rump. The horse turned, nuzzling at her, a good fit for a beginning rider. He'd borrowed the gelding from Adam and Jenna.

"I'm ready. Do you have the…"

She held up two bottles of water. "Water?"

"Yep." He untied her horse and led it away from the trailer.

Alyson took the reins and grabbed the saddle horn. He cupped his hands for her foot and she ignored him. She slid her left foot into the stirrup and swung her right leg over the saddle.

"I can do it, but thanks." She grinned down at him.

He saluted and went to his horse. Etta was at the porch. She turned and watched, waving. And she looked worried. Jason felt that look in the pit of his stomach as he pulled himself onto his horse, settling in the saddle and glancing back at Alyson to make sure she was okay.

She looked as worried as Etta.

"Where to?" She eased her horse up next to his as they took off down the road.

"Church."

"Okay, that's strange."

He smiled a little. "They're having a trail ride from there."

"Oh, so it isn't just the two of us?" She looked away before he could see if the look on her face was disappointment or relief.

"No, not just the two of us. Maybe a dozen." All couples. He didn't tell her that part. That he'd made them a couple for this ride.

This was courting, Dawson-style.

The Appaloosa gelding was an easy horse to ride. He poked along, not too doggy, but Alyson didn't have to constantly control him, or worry about him. His head was up, ears pricked attentively.

"Nice horse." She eased into the ride, losing her nervousness, until she saw the crowd at the church. Not a crowd really, but a group, and all couples.

"It's a couples' ride." Jason shot her a grin that remained in his eyes, crinkling at the corners. And she didn't know what to say.

"Alyson, it isn't a big deal. It's just an easy way for people to get together, to do something on a muggy summer night when the Mad Cow—fine dining that it is—is closed. No one really wants to drive to Grove, or to Tulsa. We'll ride down the road, maybe stop at the creek to water the horses, and ride back."

"It does sound like fun."

Because Jason wasn't afraid of her. He didn't stumble, trying to find the right words. He wanted to spend time with her.

The others greeted them. One of the riders was Etta's neighbor. She couldn't remember his name, but he was rowdy and full of himself. She'd seen him talking to Andie and then he'd hopped in the truck with some pretty brunette and taken off.

Andie said he was her best friend. Alyson thought her sister might be fooling herself. And she was surprised to see him at church. She hadn't seen him there before.

"If everyone's ready, we can go." The guy on a big white horse rode to the front of the group.

Alyson turned her horse, looking for Jason. He rode up next to her, his smile easy, chasing away the nervousness that fluttered in her stomach.

"How was your rodeo?" she asked as they headed down the dirt road behind the church. She'd never seen a dirt road until she came here.

It was magical, riding down that tree-lined road, and dusk falling over the Oklahoma countryside. Horses plodded along, their hooves beating a rhythmic tune on the road, tails swishing.

"I didn't win." He shrugged as if it didn't matter. "I think I'm done. It hit me while I was out there. I've always been on the road. I didn't know what else to do with my life. And now I've found something else."

She glanced up, meeting brown eyes that were melted chocolate on a summer night.

"The camp." He smiled. "And a new friend. Leaving home isn't as much fun as it used to be."

When he was running. When it had been too much to be at home, with his dad hurting and his sister in California with an abusive husband. It had been hard to be at home then. She didn't say it, because it was his story and he knew.

But her grandmother had been wrong about one thing. Finding out his story wasn't fun. It was difficult, and it hurt to learn what his smile had hidden.

But she had also learned that Jason smiled because he had faith. He didn't let things keep him down, she realized. That's what his smile was all about. It was about dealing with whatever was going on in his life and finding the answers.

She wanted it to be that easy for her. But she felt torn, pulled in two directions. She loved her family, both sides of it. God had been working on her, healing her heart, helping her to remember good things about her parents, not just the deception and the pressure.

"It can't be easy to walk away from." She meant his bull riding, but it sounded as if she meant her own life as well. They had similar stories. "It's been a big part of your life."

He rode close and their knees brushed. His horse bit at hers and he pulled the gelding away. "I've had a couple of months to adjust. I've learned that it's okay to give it up."

"That's good."

They rode through an open gate and into a field. A deer jumped out of a stand of trees and raced across the field. Alyson pulled back on the reins and watched. A fawn followed the mother, jumping and darting across the field.

"I have to leave." There, she'd said it. The words were loud in the silence of that summer evening.

"Leave what?"

"I have concerts that I have to play or it'll leave everyone in a bind." Obligations that she'd run from, but she had to stop running.

She'd found herself. Now she had to literally go face the music.

"I see." He pulled his horse up and she stopped next to him. "What about the concert for Camp Hope?"

"I have a concert that weekend in Chicago. I'm going to try and make it back. I just don't know if I can."

The perfect summer evening crumbled in around her. Jason pushed his hat back and then he shrugged, as if it didn't matter. And he didn't say that he would miss her. He didn't ask her to stay.

It felt as if he had always planned on her leaving.

It shouldn't have bothered him so much. Jason was still telling himself that as they rode back to the church an hour later. A perfect summer evening, riding with a woman he'd come to know in a way he hadn't expected, and now this.

The great escape artist had had the tables turned on him.

She was the one leaving.

"Jason, I don't want to lose you."

He pulled his horse up next to the trailer and dismounted. She landed on the ground next to her horse, standing there in her Dawson persona, he thought. She had easily turned herself from Boston to Dawson in a matter of weeks.

And turned his life pretty much upside down in the process. His memory problems had been nothing compared to this. As a matter of fact, he almost wished for memory loss, so he could walk away and close the door on this relationship.

She tied her horse to the side of the trailer and stepped around his horse, putting herself next to him. "I came here looking for my family, and for myself. You were a big part of that journey."

"Right." He led his horse to the back of the trailer and turned to look at her. He felt about sixteen and she was the prom queen. But she'd never been to a prom. To a dance.

She'd been everywhere, but nowhere.

"Alyson, I…" He wasn't about to say it. The words settled in his stomach and crawled around like yesterday's lunch. He would bite his tongue before he told her he thought he might love her. He wasn't going to keep her here that way, with words. It had to be more than words.

He couldn't say it, not without really knowing. But

he thought he knew. And the idea of her leaving made it all the more clear.

But he wouldn't do that to her, either. He wouldn't make her feel guilty for doing what she had to do.

"You what?" She leaned against the trailer, watching him. Her booted foot was on the rail and her hair had come loose from the clip on top of her head.

"Nothing." He leaned in and kissed her cheek. It wasn't enough, that sweet kiss, but he wasn't going any further in this relationship. "We should get home."

Chapter 13

Alyson met with Jenna two mornings after that ride with Jason. They sat under the shade tree, watching kids play a game of baseball. Timmy and David were in the middle of it all, keeping the older kids laughing.

"So, you're leaving?"

Alyson nodded. She sighed, because the decision was a heavy weight on her heart. Jenna had become such a good friend, probably the best friend Alyson had ever had. But she was another friend that Alyson would have to walk away from. Because her family needed her.

Her entire life had been about what her family needed. Their lifestyle depended on her, had depended on her since they learned about her gift.

She didn't want to resent her talent. This gift that God had given her. She could see that now. So what did she do with it? How did she go forward, with a new faith, and a new attitude?

How did she go back to Boston with this faith?

She leaned forward, petting Jenna's dog named Dog. Or Puppy. Or Buddy. It depended on who you asked.

"Yes, I have to go." She scrunched her fingers through the silky soft fur at the dog's neck and wrinkled her nose because the animal had been into something and he smelled like a garbage dump. She pulled back and he nudged her with his nose.

"Go away, Dog." Jenna pushed him back. "I think he got into the kitchen trash again. You'll come back, though. Right?"

Back to their conversation. "I don't know when, but I want to come back. I plan on it."

"Getting married, having a few kids?"

Alyson laughed. "Buying an old house, being the crazy cat lady."

"Right, staying single, not falling in love." Jenna shook her head. "Keep telling yourself that."

She would have to keep telling herself that, because she didn't know her future. She didn't know when or how she would come back to Dawson. First she had to deal with the past and with the career that had been hers for as long as she could remember.

And now her father was trying to get her a record deal. She remembered a time when that had been her dream. Or at least it had been the dream her mother had put in her mind.

"It makes it easier to leave." Alyson stood up. "I have a few kids meeting me in the chapel for their last piano lesson."

"Thank you for doing that with them." Jenna stood

up, groaning in the process. "This kid can't come soon enough."

"I wouldn't have missed working here for anything. And, Jenna, if I can, I'll get back in time for the charity concert. And if you need anything, just call. I'll do what I can from the road."

"Thanks. I know this isn't easy for you. And believe me, I'll call."

"Good, because I'm going to miss you."

"We'll all miss you, Alyson. All of us."

Everyone would miss her.

Alyson walked away, down the path to the chapel. She saw the few kids with their camp counselor heading toward the chapel. They waved and she waved back.

Could this be the new plan, the new way of using her talent? The idea lightened her mood. She loved these children. She loved teaching them and watching them. What would it be like, to trade a career, a record deal, for this life?

What would they all say if she went home and told them she was through?

If it wasn't for obligations, she would have done just that. She wouldn't even have gone home; she would have called.

She would stay and be the crazy cat lady who taught local children to play piano. She smiled as she walked through the doors of the chapel. She loved that scenario. She could picture herself in a little house with a veranda, wicker furniture and Etta stopping by to visit. She could see herself in her grandmother's tie-dyed clothing, wearing big floppy hats and weeding her flower garden.

If only. It seemed as if her life had become a pattern of If Only.

The other thing she thought about was being onstage again. Sitting on the stage under bright lights, knowing the crowd sat in darkness, listening. Fear tightened in her chest and she breathed to release it.

She wasn't going to fear. She no longer had to fear. If she kept telling herself, she might believe it. She might believe that she wasn't afraid to leave here.

She couldn't be afraid to face the world. Not now. She had prayed about it, and as new as prayer was to her, she had to believe that God wasn't going to stay in this town, letting her face the world alone. He would be with her. No matter where she went.

The kids pulled her forward, out of her thoughts, and into their presence, where there was no room for fear. She let them lead her down the aisle to the piano. Their counselor, a woman from their home church, tried to calm them down.

"It's okay." Alyson hugged them close. "As soon as we start playing, they'll calm down."

They always did.

And so did she, now that she was playing for herself.

"Who's going first today?" Alyson asked.

Becky, a girl of about twelve, raised her hand. "Can I? I've been practicing."

"Go ahead." Alyson sat on the bench with the girl. They were working on simple songs. Of course they wouldn't learn a lot in two weeks of camp. But Alyson's hope was that they would go home and find a way to continue. She had talked to the youth pastor of the church about helping to find teachers in their area who might donate their time to needy children.

The girl played through the page of the book they'd been working on. As she played, Alyson looked up, catching sight of someone at the entrance to the chapel.

Jason. He tipped his hat and nodded. And then he walked away.

Jason walked out to the arena. In fifteen minutes Jenna would join him and they'd work with a group of girls who were going to barrel race in the rodeo, and the winner would come back in two weeks for the charity event.

He had fifteen minutes to get a lot of crazy out of his system. He really didn't like crazy. He'd had years of practicing keeping his cool, keeping his emotions under wraps.

To lose it now really didn't sit well with him.

Because of a woman. Man, how in the world had that happened?

As he walked through the stable, he found Adam. "Could you work the controls for me?"

"The bull?"

"What else."

"I thought you were giving that up." Adam closed the door to the tack room.

"I am. Or was. Who knows?"

"Hey, it's your choice." Adam led the way into the arena. The overhead lights were off. It was hot and a little dusty. Barrels had been set out in a triangle pattern for the girls who would be practicing.

Adam left his side and walked back to the control panel for the bull.

Jason grabbed a glove and walked over to the mechanical bull. He climbed on, cringing a little with the effort of actually swinging his knee. He settled onto the back of the bull and wrapped his hand in the rope.

It wasn't a real bull. It didn't stomp. It didn't rear up in the chute and try to cram his head into the gate. It wasn't going to try to lie down or roll over in a narrow enclosure with him on its back.

It was safe. When had he become about safe? He pounded his hand into the rope and pushed his hat down tight on his head.

All his frustration settled deep inside him. He would work it out on the back of a machine that couldn't really fight back. But he could fight through. This was familiar. He knew how to control this. He knew how to keep it together on the back of a bull.

And control felt good, even if it was this one thing, this moment.

He nodded his head and Adam gave the bull a crank and a twist. Jason felt the jolt, got strung out, his arm in the rope straightening and his left arm, his free arm going backward, jerking his body back, forcing him to lose his seat.

His head snapped forward and he fought to get control of his upper body. Chin tucked, he broke at the hips, bringing himself back to center on the next jump. The bull spun and he anticipated the move, holding steady, bringing himself forward when momentum tried to take him back again.

The bull slowed to a stop. He didn't have to jump, didn't have to escape pounding hooves or horns that would hit a guy upside the head. Instead, he climbed off. And for the first time since April, his vision refocused without dizziness, without spinning. His head didn't pound.

He limped off the platform and across the arena, remembering how it felt to be in an arena with a crowd, with a real bull blowing hot air down his neck and kicking dirt into his face as he rolled away from pounding hooves. He pushed his hat, loosening it, and looked up, meeting Adam's curious gaze.

"Well?" Adam asked.

"I'm only seeing one of you and I still remember where I am."

"I mean, did that solve your problems?"

"Nope." Because he could ride a bull but he couldn't shake a woman from his mind. He was no longer a love 'em and leave 'em kind of guy. It was a bad time to figure that out, when the woman in question was making plans to leave.

But maybe it wasn't her. Maybe it was just settling down that mattered.

He could date and find someone who wanted to settle down with him in Dawson, on a ranch, with a few horses, some cattle and a couple of kids.

Somehow that version of the future didn't make him feel better, either.

"The kids are on their way down." Jason could see them heading toward the stable, a handful of girls and Jenna.

He had considered bull riding again. But being here, at this camp. That was okay, too. Having his ranch, and really living there, also a pretty good feeling.

Nope, going on the road wasn't in his plans at all.

And before long, Alyson Forester would be a memory. He had kind of hoped he would forget her, but he'd never been able to forget Alyson.

* * *

Alyson left on Monday after the last day of camp and the rodeo. She had wanted to watch the final performance of kids whose lives she had been involved with. And it had been the best night of her life, watching those kids perform with confidence.

And now it was time to go. She stood on the porch with Etta, hugging her grandmother tight. A yellow house, lavender wicker furniture and a woman who loved her, no matter what. Unconditional love, something she'd learned in Dawson. Alyson held on to her grandmother, and the moment.

She tried not to think about Jason.

"You don't have to go." Etta walked down the stairs with her, across the lawn to the car.

Alyson's kitten ran across the lawn, brushing against her legs, tail twitching. She picked it up and held it close. She couldn't look at her grandmother. If Etta had tears in her eyes, Alyson knew she would cry, too.

She thought she'd probably cry anyway.

But she had to go. She had to face her fears. That's what it had come down to.

"I have to go." Alyson put the kitten down and opened the trunk of her car. She had packed up last night, but she had her overnight bag to store. There were more clothes than she'd come with. Her new wardrobe, clothes that made her a part of Dawson, less a part of Boston.

She closed the trunk and turned to face her grandmother, facing her tears. "I have to go. I have to face my fears. I have to face my parents and forgive them. I have to talk to my sister Laura. I want her to know that it's okay. She loves Dan. He loves her. They should be together."

"Will it be that easy?" Etta put an arm around Alyson's waist and pulled her close, hugging her again.

"It won't be that easy, but I've forgiven her. And I do love my mom. I know she loved us the best way she knew how."

She refused to acknowledge the smiling face that flashed through her mind. She refused to let herself think about him, about not talking to him for days, other than casual greetings as they passed one another at the camp. And she reminded herself of Andie's warnings, that he'd break her heart.

But it wasn't his fault. She'd made a decision to leave. But she would come back to Dawson. Maybe someday she'd come back and be the crazy cat lady who taught children to play the piano.

But first she had to be Alyson Anderson, pianist. Even if being that person scared her to death, shook her insides and made her want to run away, again.

"You're stronger than you realize, Aly." Etta kissed her cheek. "You're an amazing young woman and I'm proud of you. I'm proud that you're not running from your commitments. I'm proud of you for facing your fears. But don't forget that you have family in Dawson."

"I won't forget." She couldn't forget. Memories were strong and she knew that each time she smelled honeysuckle or petunias, she'd think of home. She'd think of Etta.

And each time she saw a man with an easy smile, she'd feel her heart break all over again.

"Goodbye, sweetie." Etta backed away from the car.

"I love you." Alyson got into the car and Etta closed the door.

* * *

Jason watched Alyson drive out of town, but he didn't go after her. Alyson had fears to conquer and she had a life that didn't include any of them. He had to let her go.

Even if it wasn't easy.

He walked into the Mad Cow and sat down at a table with a half-dozen local ranchers. They stopped talking when he sat down. But Clint Cameron finally spoke up.

"So, you're just going to let her leave?"

"She's a big girl." Jason turned his coffee cup over for the waitress to fill it. She pulled out her order pad and he shook his head. "Just coffee."

"Right." Johnny Foster laughed. "And you're an idiot if you let her leave."

"She's already gone." Wasn't that a country song? He shook it off and slid his attention back to the cup of coffee. He sipped the hot, black liquid.

"She doesn't have to be," Clint interjected.

"You know, I'd really like to talk about something other than Alyson." Jason pushed his coffee cup back. "I have to leave."

"Jason, come on. We're cool." Johnny Foster laughed. "It's just that we don't always have the chance to give you a hard time—not over a woman. We've never seen you like this."

"Right." Jason walked out the door, without a joke, without a comment to make things okay for his friends.

He didn't have a thing to say that would make anyone laugh. He was done trying to hide behind a smile. People expected him to always be okay, to roll with whatever hit him.

And he didn't think he could roll with this. The thought knocked him on his can.

Clint walked out the door, catching up with him. "You know, you could go after her."

"No, I can't."

"Send her roses. Make sure she knows that you're here when she decides it's time to come back."

"Is that what you did?" Jason pulled his keys out of his pocket, half wanting the answer, half wanting to sound like it didn't really matter, as if he didn't really mean it.

"No, I gave Willow room to be strong. I helped her realize she could make it. Oh, and that she couldn't stand to live without me."

"Right, well, Alyson is going back to Boston. She's going to return to the stage and be who she was meant to be. And that's her choice. That's me letting her be strong."

"And you think you're going to just stop loving her?"

A conversation between two cowboys shouldn't take this direction, that's what Jason thought. It sounded like an episode of *Oprah* or like some sappy chick flick that made women cry.

"You know, Clint, I realize you're married and Willow has helped you get in touch with your emotions, but I'm still kind of not so much into the whole touchy-feely stuff. So if you don't mind, I'm going to head to the ranch and ride a bull."

Because that felt like a man's way to deal with emotions when things got a little touchy-feely.

Clint laughed. And even though Jason laughed as he got into his truck, his mind kept running back to the word *love*.

Chapter 14

Alyson walked next to her mother through the concert hall in Chicago. It hadn't been an easy reunion. Alyson really thought that her mother would never understand the pain she'd caused. Her mother would never get that being a concert pianist had never been Alyson's dream.

But something good had come from all this. Alyson could now look at her family through eyes that saw more clearly. They didn't need her. Her father had a business managing musicians from all over the country.

For years Alyson's mother had told her that they depended on her. Maybe they had. They had needed her to build this business. They had needed her in the spotlight.

Now they didn't.

"What about your grandmother? Is she going to be here?" Caroline Anderson had held on to bitterness. It laced her tone, settled in her eyes.

"She has the flu. Andie is at home with her."

Andie, your other daughter, Alyson wanted to remind her mother. She let it go, because she knew their mother couldn't be pushed.

They'd had the conversation. Alyson had tried to get her mother to talk about Andie, about leaving her and taking Alyson. But the conversations had ended with Caroline saying she had done the best she could and hadn't Andie had a good life.

"I'm sorry she's sick. Alyson, about this recording contract. This is a chance that few people ever get. It's a once-in-a-lifetime opportunity."

"I don't want it. I didn't have a choice when I was younger, but now I do. This isn't my life."

"This is about Etta and Dawson. You're not thinking clearly." Her mother looked away. "I should have thrown that paperwork away. You wouldn't have known about them if I hadn't kept it. But I thought someday…"

"You knew that someday I'd want to know the truth."

"Yes." Her mom turned back around, her eyes swimming with unshed tears. "Whatever else you believe, you have to know I love you."

"I love you, too. But Mom, I love Dawson. I love a cowboy from Dawson. That's going to be my life."

"I understand, Alyson. I loved a cowboy from Dawson, too."

The words were whispered between them, it wasn't perfect, but it was a start.

"There's your sister." Caroline stepped away, straightening her jacket and it seemed as if she straightened her emotions, pulling herself together emotionally with that movement.

Laura walked down the hall to greet them, looking shy, young. And Alyson didn't resent her. Her sister was beautiful, with curly blond hair and a face that was beautiful and sweet. She'd never been a bad person, never mean. She'd always laughed and teased.

The wedding ring on her finger glinted in the lights of the hallway, mocking Alyson. But she wouldn't let it be about what had happened, not when they had saved her from a huge mistake.

"Alyson."

"Laura." Alyson took the first stop, hugging her sister. "I'm glad you're here."

Laura started to cry. "I'm so sorry. I should have talked to you. I should have told you how I felt. How Dan felt."

"You should have. It should have been more than a note, Laura. That hurt."

"I know that now. I hope you'll forgive me. Forgive us."

"I've already forgiven you." Because Alyson had experienced forgiveness. She knew how it felt, that moment when she learned that God had forgiven her. She knew how mercy felt.

She closed her eyes. And she knew how love felt. Her heart had been tripping all over that reality for a week. She had tried to tell herself that love didn't happen in weeks. In that short amount of time, she couldn't know a person so well that she thought he might be someone she wanted to spend her life with. But she did know Jason. And she knew without question that she loved him.

Did it really matter? He had let her go. He hadn't tried to stop her, or called to see if she would come back. She didn't know what that meant, but she knew what she felt. And when he had held her, it had felt like he might love her back.

If she went back to Dawson, what if he wasn't there? What if he had decided to go back on the road?

She could question herself all night and make herself doubt what she really wanted. She had made up her mind. No matter what, she was going back to Dawson. Even if she was just going back to work at Camp Hope, she was going back.

Tonight, though, she was going to face her fears. She was going to conquer this stage. She was going to be strong. This wasn't like before, when fear had controlled her because she had never felt as if she could be good enough. Now it wasn't about being good enough. It was about doing what she was meant to do.

She stood offstage and looked at the piano where she'd be performing. The stage was dark and the lights were still on in the auditorium as people took their seats. The symphony was performing tonight and she was their guest. Her mind raced back to the past, to standing in so many spots like this one, waiting.

Fearing.

Even now her heart raced. She remembered how much she'd disliked performing. The music had stopped mattering. It had stopped being an escape. It had become something she wanted to escape from.

And she'd taken pills for that escape.

The pills were gone. She'd flushed them before she left Boston. She had been tempted to take more than one. And that's when she'd realized she had a problem. Not an addiction, but it could have become one.

The pills had been her crutch. She hadn't dealt with her pain, or her fear, because she'd had that medication to rely on. It had become her way of coping with her unhappiness.

All of it became more clear standing there, facing the stage, facing those same fears.

Alyson turned to face her mother. "This is the end. My final performance as Alyson Anderson. I'm Alyson Forester and after tonight, I'm going home."

And she walked out onstage. When the lights came up and hit her in the face, she was nervous, but not afraid.

She peered out, almost believing Jason would be in the audience. That would be the perfect end to this evening, to see him. But he wasn't there.

And when the concert ended, there were no roses, no notes to tell her he'd see her soon. She told herself it didn't matter. She had made it through this last performance.

No matter what, she was strong.

Jason walked across his front porch and eased down the steps. He'd had surgery three days before. Not because he had wanted to, but because a horse had pushed him and his knee had finally given up. He hobbled with crutches, wishing he could have at least made it through this night before having the surgery.

Tonight was the fund-raiser for Camp Hope. He shifted the crutches under his arm and headed across the driveway to his truck.

He heard a vehicle slowing to turn into his driveway. He opened his truck door and grabbed the handle above the door to pull himself up into the seat.

Once he got in, he wasn't sure how he would drive. But it was Beth pulling up next to his truck. So maybe that was one problem solved. She stopped and rolled down the passenger-side window of her truck.

"Where are you going?"

"I'm going to Camp Hope. You wouldn't want to take me, would you?"

She laughed as she got out of her truck. "If I say no, are you really going to try to drive yourself?"

"Yes, I'm going to drive myself."

"I'm not sure what to think about this new Jason Bradshaw."

"What does that mean?" He scooted into the seat, managing to get his left leg in without bumping it on anything.

"It means, scoot over and I'll drive." Beth stood on the running board of the truck, leaning in the driver's side door. "It means that it's about time you lost control and wanted something so badly it's making you a little crazy."

"I don't know what you think I want that's making me crazy."

"You want Alyson Forester back. You want her back more than you ever wanted the world title. You're half crazy thinking she might be at the camp. I don't think she is, but if it'll calm you down a little, I'll take you up there."

"Whatever." But he did want her back. And he was tired of ignoring the fact that her silence was driving him crazy. "Okay, you're right."

"I know. So scoot and I'll drive you."

Jason moved and his sister climbed behind the wheel. She shifted into Reverse, turned the wheel and headed down the drive, hitting the road at a speed that made him cringe.

"Could you be a little careful?"

She shot him a look. "Fine, be picky."

"I just put new tires on this thing." He brushed a hand over his face. "I'm sorry."

"Don't mention it, I'm enjoying this. A lot." She laughed and shifted, picking up speed as the tires hummed on the paved road. "So, when you find her, what do you plan on doing? I mean, are you going to do the sweet thing and tell her how much you love her? Or the macho thing—the toss her over your shoulder and elope tactic?"

"I doubt I'll do either."

"Jason, stop trying so hard to hold it together. Stop. Stop. Stop."

"What do you want me to do?"

"Stop being the guy who thinks you always have to control your emotions. Let yourself fall in love and do something crazy."

He smiled at his sister's huge wave of emotion. She'd always been the one willing to jump into love. And his smile faded, because she still had the scars to prove it.

They pulled up the drive to Camp Hope. There were people everywhere, preparing for the charity concert and auction. They still had campers, too. Beth parked and he got out, reaching in the back of the truck for the crutches that he'd need for the next month or so.

They headed up the drive, toward the dining hall. Jenna saw him and she waved. He nodded and moved in her direction, but she turned and headed toward the stable.

"I guess she doesn't want to talk to you," Beth teased.

"I guess not."

And that's when he heard the piano. And it wasn't

the organist from church or one of the campers. He stopped and listened. Beth slipped away. He started to call her back, but she knew better than he did what his emotions were.

Alyson was here. She had come back. Maybe just for this weekend, for the concert, but she was back. And if he had anything to do with it, she would stay.

Even if he had to resort to Beth's macho man tactics.

Timmy and David rushed past him.

"Hey, guys, could you do me a favor?"

They put on the brakes and hurried back to his side. And he knew exactly what he needed, and what he was going to do. They accepted the mission he gave them and disappeared into the dining hall, returning a few minutes later with exactly what he'd hoped for.

Alyson played through the song again, preparing for the concert this evening. "It Is Well with My Soul." The song had been Etta's suggestion. She couldn't be here because she was still getting over a bad case of the flu, but she wanted Alyson to play the song for her.

Alyson smiled to herself, thinking back to the previous evening when she'd showed up on Etta's doorstep, surprising her with flowers and the news that she was home for good. Etta had cried. And even Andie had teared up a little.

None of them had mentioned Jason. Alyson hadn't wanted to hear from her sister that she'd been warned not to fall in love with him so she hadn't brought him up. If no one was mentioning him, there had to be a reason.

She played through the song again, embracing the lyrics.

Whatever my lot, thou has taught me to say, it is well, it is well, with my soul.

She closed her eyes and prayed those words would be true and the lyrics would have meaning in her life. She knew that she was where she was meant to be, and no matter what, it would all work out.

Even Jason. She couldn't stop loving him. She'd told herself to let it go. But she couldn't. She loved a cowboy with a Robert Redford smile. And there was a spark of hope in her soul, believing he might even love her.

She closed her eyes and played the song again.

"Could you play 'In the Garden'?"

She looked up, and there he was, leaning on metal crutches, watching her. That smile that wouldn't let her sleep at night was on his face. He managed the steps and headed across the stage to where she sat.

"I can play it." She inhaled a deep breath and couldn't let it out when he sat down next to her.

"I would like that." He leaned against her. She realized how much she had missed him. At that moment everything she'd thought she felt for him became very real.

Missing him had ached inside her. Loving him and not knowing what the future held had ached inside her.

She had been so afraid that it would turn out that it was just a summer romance. That fear of losing him had rivaled any stage fright she'd ever felt.

Because at twenty-eight, she finally knew who she was and what she wanted. The idea of him not wanting her back was more than she could think about.

She played his song, closing her eyes, but still aware of him sitting next to her. When she opened her eyes his hand moved from the spot next to the songbook. Something pink and plastic was sitting next to the hymnal.

"What's that?" She reached for it, and immediately knew what it was.

"It's the only ring I could get at the last minute. Shopping in Dawson is limited, you know, and I didn't want to face you empty-handed. I couldn't make it to Vera's or the convenience store to hit the quarter machine. It just so happened that Timmy and David were willing to get this out of the camp treasure box for me."

He took the ring from her hand and slipped it on her pinky finger.

Laughter and love and every other emotion she'd been holding in for days welled up inside her. Alyson wiped away her tears. She held up her hand and admired the plastic ring.

"It's beautiful. Does this mean we're going steady?"

He leaned a little and her breath caught and held. His lips caught hers, gentle, sweet, holding her captive for a long moment as his hands went to her back, keeping her close. It was a familiar place, being in his arms. It felt like forever when he held her like that.

"I couldn't get to Chicago, Alyson. I wanted to be there for you."

"I would have called, but I didn't want to make you feel as if you had to do something or say something."

"Something like, I love you?" He held her close. "Something like, I want to hold you forever and I'd like to replace that ring on your finger with a real one. Because I want more for us than going steady."

"What do you want?" She touched her forehead to his and waited, because she knew what she wanted.

"I would love to marry you. I'd love to make you Alyson Bradshaw."

"I was kind of planning on being the crazy cat lady living in town and teaching kids to play—"

"No, sorry, I don't think you'll be able to fulfill that role."

"I think you're right. I think I might want Alyson Bradshaw, wife of Jason Bradshaw, more than I want to be single with a dozen cats and a big hat."

"I'm glad to hear that." He kissed her again and again. "Because I think my sister wants me to throw you over my shoulder and elope."

"I think I want the same thing."

Because Alyson Forester loved a cowboy, and now she knew that he loved her back.

"I forgot something." Alyson pulled away from Jason and when he looked confused, she smiled.

"What did you forget, because I don't know if I can let you leave again."

She touched his cheek and then she leaned toward him, a little breathless as she kissed him, knowing he was hers forever.

"I forgot to tell you that I love you, too," she whispered.

* * * * *

Dear Reader,

Welcome back to Dawson, Oklahoma, to the lives of characters I've come to know. I hope you're enjoying them as much as I am. *The Cowboy's Courtship* is Jason Bradshaw's story, and some of you would say that it is about time he got to be a hero. I think he's always been a hero, but it took time for me to find the right woman for him.

Jason needed a woman in his life who would unlock the secrets of his past and help him to deal with his pain, the pain he's been hiding behind his smile and charm. He needed a woman who would settle him down and keep him in town. That woman happened to be Alyson Anderson, who arrived in Dawson looking for her past.

These two characters don't realize it when they meet, but they have a lot in common. Neither of them has ever really felt connected to another person. Once they meet, that ends for both of them, and the journey of finding themselves and finding love begins.

I hope you enjoy this new book in the cowboy series.

Brenda Minton

THE COWBOY'S
SWEETHEART

Let us therefore come boldly unto the throne of grace, that we may obtain mercy, and find grace to help in time of need.
—*Hebrews* 4:16

Dedicated to the readers, for the wonderful emails, letters and prayers. To the editors at Love Inspired, for the opportunity to write the books that I love and for encouragement along the way. You're the best. To my family, for all of the love and support you've given me. To God, for giving me the desires of my heart.

Chapter 1

You have to cowboy up, Andie. Get back on, even if it hurts.

Andie Forester swiped a finger under her eyes and took in a deep breath. She hit the control on the steering wheel to turn down the radio, because it was the fault of Brooks & Dunn and that song of theirs that she was crying. "Cowgirls Don't Cry."

Whatever.

The song made her think of her dad pulling her to her feet after a horse had thrown her. She remembered her world when he was no longer in it. And the song reminded her how it felt to have a sister so perfect the world couldn't love her enough.

Andie even loved Alyson. How could she not? Alyson had come to Dawson and back into her life, soft smiles and sunshine after a twenty-five-year separation.

Andie was home just in time to help her sister prepare for her wedding to Jason Bradshaw. A beautiful wedding, with the perfect flowers, the perfect dress.

At the moment Andie wanted to throw up because she was Andie Forester and she didn't think like that. She didn't think sunshine and lace. She thought leather boots and saddles. She thought hard and tough. She was a tomboy. She knew how to hang with the crowd, with cowboys and stock contractors, and guys from Dawson, Oklahoma.

But her dad had been wrong. Brooks & Dunn were wrong. Sometimes cowgirls did cry. Sometimes, on a dusty road in Oklahoma when there wasn't anyone around to see, cowgirls sobbed like little girls in pigtails.

Sometimes, when her best friend had hurt her in a way she had never thought he could, a cowgirl cried.

But she'd get it out of her system before she got to Dawson, and she'd be fine. Ryder Johnson wasn't going to get to her, not again.

That was another thing about Foresters. They learned from their mistakes. She shouldn't have made this mistake in the first place. That's what really got to her.

She downshifted as she drove through the tiny town of Dawson, all three businesses and twenty or so houses. The trailer hooked to her truck jerked a little and she glanced in the rearview mirror, smiling because even Dusty was glad to be home. The dusty gold of his nose was sticking out of the side window, his lips curled a little as he sniffed the familiar scents in the air.

Home was where people knew her. Yeah, they knew her secrets, they knew her most embarrassing moments, but people knowing her was good. The folks in Dawson had shaken their heads, sometimes laughed at her antics, but they'd always been there for her.

The end of September was a good time to return to Oklahoma. The weather would be cooling off and in a month or so, the leaves would change colors.

She would get back to normal. Home would do that for her.

Andie took in another deep breath, and this time she didn't feel the sting of tears. She was done crying. Her pep talk to herself had worked.

She slowed as she drove past the Mad Cow Café and pretended she wasn't looking for Ryder's truck. But she was. It was an old habit. She consoled herself with that thought. And with another one—his truck wasn't there. Hopefully he was still on the road. She didn't want to run into him, not yet.

They'd both been going in opposite directions as fast as they could, putting distance between them and their big mistake. He'd gone back to riding bulls or steer roping, whatever he was doing this year. She'd taken off for Wyoming and a rodeo event she hadn't wanted to miss. Even her trips home had been planned for the times she knew he'd be gone.

The last time Ryder had seen her, well, she'd done a lot of changing since then. She wasn't ready to talk to him about any of that.

At least Dawson hadn't changed. That was something Andie could count on. Her hometown would always be the safe place to land. Jenny Dawson, the town matriarch whose grandfather had started this little community, would always be in her front yard wearing a floral print housedress, digging in her flower gardens, a wide-brimmed hat shading her face from the Oklahoma sun. Omar Gregs would forever be in the corral outside his big barn, a shovel in hand, and that old dog of his sniffing at a rabbit trail.

And Granny Etta would always be at home, waiting.

She slowed as she drove past the Johnson ranch, past the drive that led to Ryder's house. Her best friend. Her heart clenched, the pain unfamiliar, sinking from her heart to her stomach. He'd never been the one to make her feel that way.

The truck jerked a little, evidence of a restless horse that had been in a trailer for too many hours. Andie downshifted as she approached the drive that led to the barn. It felt good to see the yellow Victorian she'd grown up in. It looked just the way it had the last time she was at home. Flowers bloomed profusely out of control. The lavender wicker furniture on the front porch was a sign that all was well in the world.

As she turned into the drive, Andie noticed a big sedan on the other side of the house, parked in the driveway that company used. Company, great.

Etta walked out the front door, waving big.

Andie's grandmother had hair that matched the furniture on the porch, kind of. It was the closest the stylist in Grove could get to lavender. And it clashed something horrible with Etta's tanned skin. A Native American woman with Irish ancestors didn't have the complexion to carry off lavender hair.

But tall and thin, she did have the ability to carry off some wild tie-dyed clothes. The clothing was her own design, her own line, and it sold nationwide.

Andie drove the truck down the drive and parked at the barn. Etta was fast-walking across the lawn, the wind swirling the yellow-and-pink tie-dyed skirt around her long legs.

Andie hopped out of the truck and ran to greet her grandmother. Andie was twenty-eight years old—almost twenty-nine—and a hug had never felt so good. When Etta wrapped strong arms around her and held her tight, it was everything.

It was a bandage on a heart that wasn't broken, more like bruised and confused. She hadn't expected it to take this long to heal.

"Sweetheart, it's been too long. And why that serious face and no smile? Didn't you call and tell me things were good?"

"Things *are* good, Gran."

"Well, now why am I not buying that?"

"I'm not sure." Andie smiled as big as she could and her granny gave her a critical stare before shaking her head.

"Okay, get Dusty Boy out of that trailer and let's go inside. I bet you're hungry."

"I am hungry." Starving. She'd been starving for the past few weeks. She was just sick of truck-stop and hotel-restaurant food. Even when she'd stopped in with friends, it hadn't been the same. Nobody cooked like Etta.

Andie moved the latch on the trailer and stepped inside, easing down the empty half of the trailer to unhook Dusty. He shook his head, glad to be free and then backed out, snorting, his hooves clanging loud on the floor of the trailer.

"Come on, boy, time for you to have a run in the pasture."

"Where'd you stay last week?" Etta was standing

outside, shading her face with her hand, blocking the glare of the setting sun.

Andie held tight to the lead rope, giving Dusty a minute to calm down. His head was up and his ears alert as he snorted and pawed the ground, eager to be back in the pasture with the other horses.

"I was at Joy and Bob's."

"You were in Kansas? Why didn't you just come on home?"

Because she didn't want to face Ryder and she'd heard he might be home. She'd planned her timing lately so that she was home when he wasn't. But how did she explain that to Etta?

She shrugged, "I was looking at a mare they have for sale."

Not a lie.

The roar of a truck coming down the road caught their attention. Dusty dipped his head to pull at a bite of clover, but he looked up, golden ears perked, twisting like radar as he tuned into the noises around him. He snorted and grabbed another mouthful of grass. Andie pulled on the lead rope and his head came up.

The truck slowed at their driveway. Etta beamed. "Well, there's that Ryder Johnson. He's been down here three times in the past week. He says he's checking on me, but I think he misses his running buddy."

"I'm sure. If he missed me that much…" He would have called. Two months, he could have called. He hadn't.

Etta shot her a look, eyes narrowing. "What's going on with you two kids?"

"Well, first of all, we're not kids. Second, he needs to grow up."

"Oh, so that's the way the wind blows."

"This might be Oklahoma, but the wind isn't blowing, Etta." Andie turned toward the barn, Dusty at her side. He rubbed his big head on her arm and she pushed him back. "Bad manners, Dusty."

"Where are you going?" Etta hurried to catch up.

"To put my horse up."

"Well, I guess I'll make tea."

Tea was Etta's cure for everything.

"Don't invite him for tea, Etta. I'll take care of this, but he doesn't need to hang out here."

"Nonsense." And Etta stormed off, like a wise grandmother who had dealt with her share of lovesick kids. Andie shook her head and unhooked the gate. She wasn't lovesick.

She was mad at herself. And mad at Ryder.

"Off you go, Dusty. Eat some green grass and I'll be back later."

She watched, smiling as her horse made a dash around the field, bucked a few times and then found a place to roll on his back. And then she couldn't put it off any longer. She turned, and there he was, walking toward her, his hat low over his eyes. She didn't need to see those eyes. Brown, long dark lashes. He had a dimple in his chin and a mouth that flashed white teeth when he smiled. He had rough hands that could hold a woman tight and a voice that sounded raspy and smooth, all at the same time.

Those were things she had just learned about him, eight weeks ago. Before that he'd had a voice that teased and hands that held hers tight when they climbed fences or arm wrestled. He had been the person she told her secrets to and shared her fears with.

More than anything she was mad that he couldn't be that person right now. Instead, he was the person she needed to talk about.

He was tall, a cowboy who wore faded jeans, ripped at the knees, and button-down shirts, plaid with pearl buttons. He was her best friend. They'd been friends for twenty-five years, since his family moved to Dawson from Tulsa. His dad had done something right with the stock market. His mom had inherited a chunk of cash. It hadn't been a perfect life though, and a little over five years ago his parents had died in a car accident.

She'd been there for him.

He'd buried his face into her shoulder and she remembered her fingers on soft, brown hair.

She remembered waking up weeks ago, knowing her life would never be the same. One night, one mistake, and her world had come unraveled.

And then God had hemmed it up again. She'd been running from God longer than she'd been running from Ryder. God had caught her first.

Ryder watched the changing expressions on Andie's face and he wondered what kind of storm he was about to face. Would it be the summer kind that passes over with little damage, or the other kind, the kind that happens when hot air meets cold?

He had a feeling that it was the hot-meets-cold kind. She had gone from something that looked like sad, to pretty close to furious, and now she was smiling. But the coldness in her eyes was still there. She had latched the gate and she was strong again.

She stood next to the barn, looking a lot like she had the last time he'd seen her. She was a country girl, born and raised in Dawson. Her idea of dressing up was changing into a new pair of jeans and boots that weren't scuffed. She was tall, slim, with short blond hair and brilliant blue eyes.

And she had every right to be angry.

He slowed a little, because maybe this wasn't a hornet's nest he wanted to walk into. It was going to get worse when she found out who was in the house waiting for her. She leaned back against the barn, the wind lifting her hair, blowing it around her face.

"Did you forget how to use a phone?" Yep, she was mad. Her voice was a little softer, a little huskier than normal.

"Nope. I just thought I'd give you a few weeks to get over being mad at me," he said.

"I wouldn't have been mad if you had left a note, called, maybe met up with me somewhere."

"I know." He cracked his knuckles and she glared. He took that to mean she wanted more than an easy answer. "I'm not good at relationships."

Understatement. And it was an explanation she didn't need from him. His parents had spent his childhood fighting, drinking and socializing. The ranch here in Dawson had saved him. At least he'd had horses to keep him busy and out from under their feet.

Away from his parents had usually been the best, safest bet for the kid.

He'd had Andie to run with and Etta's house as a safe haven. Right at that moment Andie looked anything but safe. Standing there with her arms wrapped around herself, hugging her middle tight, she looked angry, sad and about a dozen other female emotions he didn't want to put a name on.

"Relationship? This isn't a relationship, Ryder. This is us. We were friends."

"Oh, come on, we're still friends." He slipped an arm around her shoulder and she slid out of the embrace. "We'll go out tomorrow, maybe drive into Tulsa. It'll be like old times."

"Nope." She walked quickly toward the house. He kept up.

So, the rumors were true. "This is about church, isn't it?"

She stopped abruptly and turned. "No, it isn't about church. You think that going to church would make me mad at you? Don't be an idiot."

"Well, isn't that what people do when they feel guilty?" He winked. "They get right with God?"

"Shut up, Ryder."

She took off again, arms swinging, boots stomping on the dry grass.

"We've been friends forever."

"Right." She stopped and when she glanced up, before she could shake the look, he thought she looked hurt.

The way she'd looked hurt when he'd turned eleven and she'd been about ten, but not quite. He'd had a bunch of boys over and she hadn't been invited. He'd told her it was a guys-only party and she'd wanted to be one of the guys, because she was his best friend.

Now he realized that best friends shouldn't be easy to hold or feel soft in a guy's arms. Or at least he thought that was the case. He didn't want to lose someone who had always been there for him. He didn't want to turn her into his mom.

He sure didn't want to be his dad.

He wanted them to stay the way they were, having fun and hanging out. Not growing up, growing angry, growing apart. He didn't want to think about how self-ish that sounded, keeping her in his life that way.

"Andie, I didn't plan for this to mess up our friend-ship."

"Neither of us planned for that. And this isn't about…" She looked away. "This is about you not call-ing me back."

"Because I didn't know what to say."

"Ryder, you're almost thirty and I've heard you talk to women. You always know what to say." She looked down, shuffling her feet in the dusty driveway. "But you didn't know what to say to me?"

"I'm sorry." He hadn't known what to say and he still didn't. With other women, he just said what felt right at the moment. And man, he'd had a lot of nasty messages on his answering machine over the years, because he'd said what felt right, not what mattered.

"You don't have to apologize. We're both respon-sible."

"I know, but we made a promise. I made a promise." A promise to keep boundaries between them. "I don't know what else to say, except I'm sorry."

"You should have called." She had shoved her hands in her front pockets and she stared up at him, forcing his thoughts back to that. That night in Phoenix he'd found her standing behind her trailer, crying because she'd been rejected by her mother. He'd never seen her like that, hurt that way.

He shook his head, chasing off memories that were more than likely going to get him in trouble again.

"Come on, Andie, give me a break. You know me

better than anyone. You know that I'm not good at this. You know that we were both there. We both…"

"Stop. I don't want to talk about what we both did. I want to talk to you about us."

Heat crawled up his neck, into his face. "Andie, you sound like a woman."

"I am a woman."

"No." He took off his hat and swiped a hand through his hair. "No, you're not. You're my best friend. You're my roping buddy. You're not like other women. You've never been like other women, getting all caught up in the dating thing and romance."

"I'm still not caught up in those things."

"No, now you're caught up in religion."

"I'm not caught up in anything. This is about faith. And to be honest, I really needed some." She looked away.

"Whatever. I'm just saying, this isn't you."

"It's me. But for a lot of years, I've been trying to be who you wanted me to be. I've done a lot of things to make you feel better about being angry." Her voice was soft and sweet, reminding him of how easy it had been to kiss her. Maybe things had changed—more than he'd realized. Being on the road he'd been able to fool himself into believing that they could go right back to being who they'd always been.

"Go to supper with me at the Mad Cow. I'll buy you a piece of pecan pie." He nudged her shoulder and she nodded. He thought she might say yes.

But then she shook her head. "I'm tired. It was a long trip."

"Yeah, I guess it was. Maybe tomorrow?"

"Tomorrow's Sunday."

"And you're going to church?"

"Yeah, Ryder, I'm going to church."

"Fine, I've got to get home and get things cleaned up before Wyatt gets here."

"Wyatt's coming?"

Ryder pulled his keys out of his pocket. This was something she would have known, before. He would have called her to talk it over with her, to get her opinion. He guessed that was a pretty good clue that he'd been avoiding her, and telling himself a whole pack of lies.

Number one being that nothing had changed.

"Yeah, he's coming home."

And Ryder didn't know how it would work, with him, Wyatt and two little girls all in one big, messy house. The girls needed to be here, though. Ryder knew that. He knew his brother was falling apart without Wendy. Wyatt was caving under the guilt of his wife's death. A year, and he was still falling apart.

"If you need anything." Andie's voice was gentle, so was her hand on his arm.

"Yeah, I know you're here." He smiled down at her, winking, because he needed to find firm footing. "Gotta run. Let me know if you change your mind about, well, about anything."

About being this new person, this woman that he just didn't get.

"Right, I'll let you know."

The back door opened. He waved at Etta and tried to escape, but she left the back stoop and headed in their direction. And then he remembered why he'd driven down here. Because mad or not, Andie was about to need a friend.

"Don't you want to come in for tea?" Etta had been filling him with tea for years. Tea for colds, tea for his aches and pains, tea to help him sleep when his parents died. He'd turned to something a little stronger for a few years, until he realized that it was doing more than helping him sleep. It had been turning him into his dad.

He glanced at Andie, and she was still clueless. "I can come in for a minute. I have to get my house clean before Wyatt shows up."

Why'd he have to feel so old all of a sudden? Last week he'd still felt young, like he had it all, except responsibility. He had liked it that way.

"When's he going to be here?" Etta stepped a little closer.

"Tomorrow or Monday. I guess I'll have to call Ruby to get my house really clean."

"You'll be fine, Ryder." Etta's eyes were soft, a little damp.

"Yeah, I'm more worried about Wyatt." Ryder didn't want to think about the house and the girls, not all in the same thought.

And then the back door opened again.

Chapter 2

Andie had forgotten about that car in the drive. She shouldn't have forgotten. It was Ryder's fault and it would have felt good to tell him that. But she didn't have time because the woman standing on the back porch was now walking down the steps. She was nearing fifty and stunningly beautiful. And she was smiling. Andie hadn't expected the smile. She wanted this woman to be cold, to live up to Andie's expectations of her.

A woman that ditched a child couldn't be warm. She couldn't be loving. Andie replayed her list of words she used to describe her mother: *cold, unfeeling, hard, selfish.*

The list used to be more graphic, but Andie was working hard on forgiving. She'd started with the easy "need to forgive" list. She would forgive Margie Watkins for spreading a rumor about her. She could forgive

Blaine for gum in her notebook back in the fifth grade. She'd kept her mother on a list by herself, a final project. Saving the most difficult for last.

So now Andie knew that it was true—God had his own timing, reminding her that He was really the one in charge. She had really thought she'd wait a few months to contact Caroline.

"You okay?" Ryder stepped next to her. "I thought I ought to be here for you."

Cowgirls do too cry. They cry when the man they are the angriest with shows up and says something like that. They can cry when they see their mother for the first time in twenty-five years. She nodded in answer to his question and blinked away the tears, because she'd never cried this much in her life and she didn't like it.

She didn't like that her edge was gone.

Was this really the plan, really what God wanted? For her to forgive the person who had hurt her more than anyone else, even more than Ryder when he ignored her phone calls?

If so, it was going to take some time.

"Caroline wanted to see you." Etta's tone was noncommittal and Andie wondered if her mother had been invited or just showed up.

Oh, the wedding. Alyson's wedding.

"Did she?" Andie managed to stand tall. "Or is she here to see Alyson? To help plan the wedding."

It made sense that her mother would show up to help plan Alyson's wedding. She had never shown up for anything that had to do with Andie.

"I'm here to see you." Caroline was close enough to hear, to respond. And she had the nerve to smile like she meant it.

But really? Did she?

"That's good." Andie managed words that she didn't feel. Standing there in the yard, the sun sinking into the western horizon, red and glowing, the sky lavender. The sky matched Etta's hair. At least that lightened the mood.

"I know I should have come sooner." Caroline glanced away, like she, too, had noticed the setting sun. She stared toward the west. "I don't have excuses. I'm just here to say that I'm sorry."

"Really?" Apparently it was the day for apologies. Was it on the calendar—a national holiday?

"We should go in and have that tea." Etta gathered them the way a hen gathered chicks.

"Ryder, you should go." Andie squeezed his hand. "Thank you for being here."

"You're okay?"

"I'm fine. I'll see you at church tomorrow." She said it to watch the look on his face. She knew he wouldn't be there. He'd gone to church when he was a kid, until his dad's little indiscretion.

"That's one thing I can't do for you, Andie." He kissed the top of her head. "I'll see you around."

Why did it have to sound like goodbye, as if they were sixteen and breaking up?

She watched him get in his truck and drive away. And it wasn't what she wanted, not at all. She wanted her best friend there with her, the way he would have been there for her if Phoenix hadn't happened, if they hadn't spent weeks not knowing what to say to each other.

Watching his truck turn out of the driveway and head

down the road, she felt shaken, and her stupid heart felt like it was about to have a seizure of some kind.

And her mother was standing in front of her, waiting for her to pull it together. Caroline, her mother. But Etta had been that person to Andie. Etta had been the one who taught her to be a woman. Etta had taught her to put on makeup, and helped her dress for the prom. Etta had held her when she cried.

Caroline had been in some city far away, being a mother to Andie's twin, and to her half siblings. She'd left the less-than-perfect child with the less-than-perfect husband.

Issues. Andie had a lot of issues to deal with. But she wasn't the mess some people thought she should be. She'd had Etta. She'd had a dad who'd done his best. She'd been taught to be strong, to not be a victim. Now those seemed like easy words that didn't undo all of the pain.

"Come on." Etta took her by the hand and led her to the house.

"Of course, tea will make this all better," Andie whispered. As if tea could make getting steamrollered feel any better.

They walked through the back door into the kitchen decorated with needlepoint wall hangings that Andie and Etta had worked on together. They'd never had satellite, and only a few local stations until recently. Winters had been spent reading or doing needlepoint. It hadn't been a bad way to grow up.

"What's going on between you and Ryder?" Etta spooned sugar into the cup of tea she'd just poured. "If I didn't know better, I'd think that was a lovers' quarrel."

"We'd have to be in love for that to be the case."

Andie leaned in close to her grandmother, loving the way she smelled like rose talcum powder, and the house smelled like vegetables from the garden and pine cleaner.

It was her grandmother's house and it always felt like the safest place in the world.

Even with her mother standing across the counter from her, fidgeting with the cup that Etta had set in front of her it was still that safe place. Caroline looked up and Andie met her gaze.

"Well, it was just a matter of time," Etta whispered as she walked away.

"What did you say?"

"I said, I hope you don't mind sugar in this tea, and do you mind if it has thyme. It's good for you, you know."

"Right."

She sat down at the kitchen island and her granny slid the cup of tea across the counter to her. Etta sat down next to her, moving a plate of cookies between them. Peanut butter, nothing better.

Andie sipped her tea and set the cup down, not feeling at all better, not the way she usually did when she came home.

"I'm surprised to see you." Andie reached for a second cookie. "I'm the reject kid, right? The one you didn't want."

Caroline shuddered and Andie didn't feel better, not the way she'd thought she would feel the sense of satisfaction she'd expected. And now, not so much.

"You're not defective. You're beautiful, smart and talented," Etta spoke up, her voice having a loud edge.

Andie shot her grandmother a look, because they

both knew better. She and her father hadn't been good enough for Caroline. He'd been Caroline's one-night stand in college, and he'd married her. A cute country boy from Oklahoma. And reality hadn't been as much fun.

One-night stands didn't work. She sipped her tea and pushed the thought from her mind. Better to focus on Caroline and her father rather than on her own mistakes.

"I'm not the prodigy. I'm the kid who struggled to read." Andie no longer felt like the kid in school who didn't understand what everyone else got with ease. She had been fortunate to have great teachers, people who were willing to help and encourage her. She'd had Etta.

"You have a challenge, not a disability." Etta covered Andie's hand with a hand that was a little crooked with arthritis, but still strong, still soft, still manicured. "She took Alyson. I got to keep you. That wasn't so bad, was it? Being here with me and your dad?"

Caroline spoke up. "It wasn't bad, was it? I mean, I know Etta loves you. Your dad loved you."

"You can't comment. You weren't here." Andie closed her eyes and tried to let go of the sparks of anger that shot from her heart, hot and cold.

"I can comment." Caroline's hand shook as she set her cup on the counter. "I can comment, because I know what I did and why I did it. I couldn't take this life. I couldn't be a cowboy's wife and the mom to two girls. I couldn't be from Dawson."

Andie shook her head, feeling a little sick with guilt, with hurt feelings. "Really, would it have been that hard?"

"I don't know."

Andie finished off the last of her cookie and drained

her cup of tea, and she still didn't know what to say to Caroline Anderson—the woman who had never been her mother.

She'd thought about this two months ago when she'd slipped into a church service held at the rodeo arena after one of the events. She had sat there wondering how to put her life back together. The pieces were in her hands; Alyson, her mother and Ryder.

It was up to her to put it all back together. It was up to her to forgive.

Andie hopped off the stool. "I have to take care of my horse."

And she planned on spending the night in the camper of her horse trailer. It wasn't really running away. She was giving herself space and a little time to think.

Ryder woke up the next morning to the rumble of a truck in his driveway. He peeked out the window as Wyatt jumped out of a rented moving truck and then reached in for the two little girls who resembled their mom.

As he watched them cut across the lawn—Wyatt holding both girls, looking as sad as they looked—Ryder ran a hand through his hair and shook his head. Man, this was a lot of reality to wake up to.

He glanced at the clock on the coffeemaker as he walked through the kitchen. Nearly ten on a Sunday morning. And Etta's old Caddy was going down the road, because it was time for church. And for the first time in years, Andie was in the passenger seat.

Too much reality.

Too many changes. He was nearly thirty and suddenly everything was changing. Andie was going to church and she didn't want to talk to him. Not that he really blamed her.

But he wanted her back, the way it was before. He wanted it to be like it had been before their night in Phoenix, before her trip to the altar and God. Not that he had anything against God. He knew there was one. He'd been to church. He'd heard the sermons. He'd even prayed.

But his parents had gone, too. They'd picked a church in a neighboring town, not Dawson Community Church. And that had just about done him in on religion. His parents, their lifestyle and then the day in church when someone brought his dad forward. Man, he could still remember that day, the looks people had given him, the way it had felt to hear what his dad had done.

And he remembered the clapping of a few hands when his dad was ousted from the congregation, taking his family with him.

That had been a long time ago, almost twenty years. He shrugged it off, the way he'd been trying to shrug it off since the day it happened. He walked down the hall and met his brother at the back door, coming in through the utility room. It had rained during the night and Wyatt's boots were muddy. He leaned against the dryer to kick them off.

Ryder reached for three-year-old Molly but she held tight to Wyatt. It was Kat, a year younger, who held her arms out, smiling the way little girls should smile. With one less child, Wyatt could hold the door and kick off his boots.

They would never know their mom. They wouldn't even remember her. But then, even in her life, Wendy hadn't been there for the girls. She had changed after having them. She had lost something and before any of them had figured it out, it had been too late to get her back.

"Long trip?" Ryder settled Kat on his hip and walked into the kitchen. The two-year-old smiled because his cheek brushed hers and he imagined it was rough.

"The longest." A year. That's what Ryder figured. His brother had been on a journey that had taken the last year of his life, and brought him back to Dawson.

"You girls hungry?"

"We ate an hour ago, just outside of Tulsa," Wyatt said. "I think they're probably ready to get down and play for a while. Maybe take a nap."

Ryder glanced at the little girl holding tight to his neck as he filled the coffeepot with water. "You want down, Chick?"

She shook her head and giggled.

"Want cookies?" he asked. When she nodded, he glanced at Molly. "You want cookies?"

She shook her head. She had big eyes that looked like the faucet was about to get turned on. She'd be okay, though. Kids had a way of bouncing back. Or at least that's what he thought. He didn't have a lot of experience.

"They don't need cookies this early," Wyatt interjected.

Older, wiser, Wyatt. Ryder shook his head, because he'd never wanted to grow up like Wyatt. He'd never wanted to be that mature.

"Well, I don't have much else around here." Ryder looked in the fridge. "Spoiled milk and pudding. I think the lunch meat went bad two days ago. It didn't taste real good on that last sandwich."

"Did it make you sick?" Molly whispered, arms still around Wyatt's neck in what looked like a death grip. He hadn't been around a lot of kids, but she was the timid kind. That was fine, he was a little afraid of her, too.

He'd had enough experience to know that kids could be loud and destroy much if left to their own devices.

"Nah, I don't get sick." He bounced Kat a little and she laughed.

"I guess I'll have to go to the store." Wyatt sat down at the dining room table.

"No, I'll get ready and go." Anything to get out of the house, away from this. He flipped on the dining room light. "Make a list and I'll drive into Grove. When I get home, we can run down to the Mad Cow before the church crowd gets there."

"I need to have the girls back in church. They like going."

"Yeah, kids do." They liked the crafts, the stories. He got that. He had liked it, too. "I need to feed the horses and then I'll get cleaned up and run to the store."

He brushed a hand through his hair and for the first time, Wyatt smiled. "Yeah, you might want to get a haircut."

"Probably." He slid his feet into boots and finished buttoning his shirt. "I guess just help yourself to anything you can find. The coffee's ready."

A brother and two kids, living in his house. Now that just about beat all. It was really going to put a kink in his life.

But then, hadn't Andie already done that? No, not Andie, not really.

When he walked out the back door, his dog, Bear, was waiting for him.

"Bear, this is not our life." But it was. He could look around, at the ranch his dad had built. He could smell rain in the air and hear geese on a nearby pond.

It was his life. But something had shaken it all up, leaving it nearly unrecognizable. Like a snow globe, shaken by some unseen hand. He looked up, because it was Sunday and a good day for thinking about God, about faith. He didn't go to church, but that didn't mean he had forgotten faith.

So now he had questions. How did he do this? His brother was home—with two kids, no less. His best friend was now his one-night stand. He had more guilt rolling around in his stomach than a bottle of antacid could ever cure.

Did this have something to do with his crazy prayers before he got on the back of a bull a month or so earlier. Did the words *God help me* count as a prayer? Or maybe it was payback for the bad things he'd done in his life?

Whatever had happened, he had to fix it—because he didn't like having his life turned upside down. But first he had to go to town and get groceries, something to feed two little girls.

Church had ended ten minutes ago and Andie had seen Ryder's truck driving past on his way to the farm. But they'd been stalled by people wanting to talk with she and her grandmother. Caroline had managed to smile and hang at the periphery of the crowds.

"We need to check on Ryder and Wyatt." Etta started her old Caddy, smiling with a certain pride that Andie recognized. Her granny loved that car. She'd loved it

for more than twenty years, refusing to part with it for
something new.

What could be more dependable, Etta always said,
than a car that she'd taken care of since the day she
drove it off the lot?

Dependable wasn't a word Andie really wanted to
dwell on, not at that moment. Not when her grandmother was talking about Ryder.

"I think Ryder and Wyatt are able to take care of
themselves." After her mother climbed into the front
seat beside Etta, Andie slid into the back and buckled
her seat belt. Etta eased through the church parking lot.

It hadn't been such a bad first Sunday back in church.
The members of Dawson Community Church were
friends, neighbors and sometimes a distant relative.
They all knew her. Most of them knew that she'd gone
on strike from church when Ryder stopped going. Because they'd been best friends, and a girl had to do
something when her best friend cried angry tears over
what his father had done, and over a moment in church
that changed their lives. A girl had to take a stand when
her best friend threw rocks into the creek with a fury
she couldn't understand because life had never been
that cruel to her.

Her strike had been more imaginary than real. Most
of the time Etta managed to drag her along. But Andie
had let her feelings be known. At ten she'd been pretty
outspoken.

"How long have you known Ryder and Wyatt?" Caroline asked, and Andie wanted to tell her that she should
know that. A mother should know the answer to that
question.

"Forever." Andie leaned back in the seat and looked

out the window, remembering being a kid in this very car, this very backseat. Her dad had driven and Etta had sat in the passenger side. The car had been new then. She'd been more innocent.

She'd heard them whispering about what Ryder's dad had done. She'd been too young to really get it. When she got home from church that day she'd run down the road and Ryder had met her in the field.

"Forever?" Caroline asked, glancing back over her shoulder.

"We've known each other since Ryder was five, and I was three. That's when they moved to Dawson. I guess about the time you left."

Silence hung over the car, crackling with tension and recrimination. Okay, maybe she'd gone too far. Andie sighed. "I'm sorry."

Etta cleared her throat and turned the old radio on low. "We'll stop by the Mad Cow and get take-out chicken. Knowing Ryder, he doesn't have a thing in that house for Wyatt and the girls to eat."

"What happened to Wyatt's wife?" Caroline asked.

Stop asking questions. Andie closed her eyes and leaned back into the leather seat. She wouldn't answer. She wouldn't say something that would hurt. She was working on forgiving. God had to know that wasn't easy. Shouldn't God cut her a little slack?

Etta answered Caroline's question. "She committed suicide last year. Postpartum depression."

It still hurt. Andie hadn't really known Wendy, but it hurt, because it was about Ryder, Wyatt and two little girls.

"I'm so sorry." Caroline glanced out the window. "It isn't easy to deal with depression."

Clues to who her mother was. In a sense, Andie thought these might also be clues to who she was. She waited, wanting her mother to say more. She didn't. Etta didn't push. Instead she turned the Caddy into the parking lot of the Mad Cow. And Ryder was already there. He was getting out of his truck and a little girl with dark hair was clinging to his neck. He looked like a guy wearing new boots. Not too comfortable in the shoes he'd been forced to wear.

He saw them and he stopped. Etta parked next to his truck.

As they got out, Wyatt came around the side of the truck. The older of the two girls was in his arms. She didn't smile the way the other child smiled.

"We didn't beat the church crowd." Ryder tossed the observation to Wyatt but he smiled as he said it.

"No, you didn't, but you can eat lunch with us." Etta slipped an arm around Wyatt, even as she addressed the response at Ryder. "And you'll behave yourself, Ryder Johnson."

"I always do." He winked at the little girl in his arms and she giggled. And she wasn't even old enough to know what that wink could do to a girl, how it could make her feel like her toes were melting in her high heels.

Andie wished she didn't know what that wink could do to a girl. Or a woman. She didn't want to care that he looked cuter than ever with a two-year-old in his arms. He looked like someone who should have kids.

But he didn't want kids. He had never wanted children of his own. He said the only thing his childhood had prepared him for was being single with no one to mess up but himself.

"You look nice." He stepped closer, switching his niece to the opposite arm as he leaned close to Andie. "You smell good, too."

Andie smiled, because every answer seemed wrong. Sarcasm, anger, the words *"Is this the first time you've noticed how I look?"* and so on.

She didn't feel like fighting with him. She felt like going home to a cup of ginger tea and a good romance novel. She felt like hitching the trailer back to her truck and hitting the road with Dusty, because she could always count on her horse and the next rodeo to cheer her up. She could head down to Texas.

"You look a little pale." Caroline stood next to her, another problem that Andie didn't want to deal with. She felt like a tiny ant and people were shoveling stuff over the top of her, without caring that she was getting buried beneath it all.

"I'm fine."

"You really don't look so hot," Ryder added.

"You just said I look nice. Which is it, Ryder?"

"Nice, in a pale, illusive, gonna-kick-somebody-to-the-curb sort of way." He teased in the way that normally worked on her bad moods. Ryder knew how to drag her out of the pits.

But not today.

Today she wanted to be alone, to figure out the next phase of her life. And she didn't want to think about how Ryder would have to be a part of that future.

Or how he was going to feel about it.

Chapter 3

"Why aren't you eating?" Ryder had tried to ignore Andie, the same way she'd obviously been ignoring him. She had talked to Wyatt, to the girls, even to her mother.

She was ignoring him the same way she was ignoring the chicken-fried steak on her dinner plate. And her mother was right, She did look pale.

"I'm eating." She smiled and cut a bite of the gravy-covered steak. "See."

She ate the bite, swallowing in a way that looked painful.

"Are you sick?"

She looked up to the heavens and shook her head. "No, I'm not sick."

"You act sick." He grinned a little, because he just knew he had to say what was on his mind. He couldn't stop himself. "You look like something the cat yacked up."

His nieces laughed. Even Molly. At least they appreciated his humor. He sat back in his chair, his hands behind his head, smiling at Andie. Kat giggled as if she knew exactly what her Uncle Ryder had said. He hadn't expected to really like a two-year-old this much, but she already had him wrapped around her little finger.

He didn't think Andie was as thrilled with him. As a matter of fact she glared at him as if he was about her least favorite person on the planet. And with her mother, Caroline, sitting at the same table, he was pretty shocked that he'd be Andie's least favorite person.

"That's pleasant, Ryder. I'm sick of you asking me what's wrong. You haven't seen me in two months. Do you have something else you'd like to say to me?"

"Right here, right now?" That made his hands a little sweaty, especially when everyone at the table stared, including his nieces. Kat, who sat closest to him, looked a little worried. "No, I guess not. Well, other than wanting to know if you'd like to go the arena with me tonight. I could use a flank man."

"I'm not a man."

"Good point," Wyatt mumbled.

Ryder shot his brother a look. "Keep out of this."

Kat, two and innocent, clapped her hands and laughed.

A chair scooted on the linoleum floor. Ryder flicked his attention back to Andie. She was standing up, looking a little green and wobbly. Maybe it was the dress, or the three-inch heels. He stood, thinking he might have to catch her.

"What's wrong?" Etta started to stand up.

"I'm going outside. I need fresh air."

"I'll go with you." Ryder grabbed his hat off the back

of the chair and moved fast, because she was practically running for the door.

She didn't go far, just to the edge of the building. He stood behind her as she leaned, gasping deep breaths of air.

"What's going on with you?"

"Stop." She kept her face turned, resting her forehead against the old concrete block building. "I must have caught something from Joy's kids when I stopped in Kansas. One of them was sick."

"I could take you home," he offered quietly, because he had a feeling she didn't need more questions at the moment.

"I'm fine now. I would just hate to make the girls sick. They don't need that." She turned, smiling, but perspiration beaded along her forehead and under her eyes. She was still pale.

"No," he agreed, "the girls don't need to get sick. I don't think I could handle that."

"They're just little girls."

"Yeah, and I'm not anyone's dad. That's Wyatt's job. He's always been more cut out for the husband and father gig."

And saying the words made him feel hollow on the inside, because he remembered standing next to Wyatt at his wife's funeral. He remembered what it felt like to stand next to a man whose heart was breaking.

Ryder hadn't ever experienced heartbreak and he didn't plan on it. He enjoyed his single life, without strings, attachments or complications.

"You're good with the girls," Andie insisted, his friend again, for the moment. "Just don't slip into your old ways, not while they're living with you."

"Right." He slid his hand down her back. "I'll be good. So, are you okay?"

"I'm good. I'm going back inside." She took a step past him, but he caught her hand and held her next to him.

"Andie, I don't want to lose my best friend. I'm sorry for that night. I'm sorry that I didn't walk away…before. And I'm sorry I walked away afterward."

She didn't look at him. He looked down, at the ground she was staring at—at dandelions peeking up through the gravel and a few pieces of broken glass. He touched her cheek and ran his finger down to her chin, lifting her face so she had to look at him.

"I'm sorry, too," she whispered. "I just don't know how to go back. We've always kept the line between us, Ryder. This is why."

"We don't have to stop being friends," he insisted, hoping he didn't sound like a kid.

"No, we don't. But you have to accept that things have changed."

"Okay, things have changed." More than things. She had changed. He could see it in her eyes in the way she smiled as she turned and walked away, back into the Mad Cow.

A crazy thought, that he had changed, too. He brushed it off and followed her into the diner. He hadn't changed at all. He still wanted the same things he'd always wanted. Some things weren't meant to be domesticated, like raccoons, foxes…and him.

When they got home, Andie changed into jeans and a T-shirt and headed for the barn. She was brushing

Babe, her old mare, when Etta walked through the double doors at the end of the building.

"What's going on with you?" Etta, arm's crossed, stood with the sun to her back, her face in shadows.

The barn cat wandered in and Etta stepped away from the feline.

"There's nothing wrong." Andie brushed the horse's rump and the bay mare twitched her dark tail and stomped a fly away from her leg. "Okay, something is wrong. Caroline is here. I don't know what she wants from me. I don't know why she expects to walk into my life and have me happy to be graced with her presence."

"She doesn't expect that."

Andie stopped brushing and turned. "So now you're on her side."

"Don't sound like a five-year-old. I'm not on her side. I'm on your side. I want you to forgive her. I want you to have her in your life. I have to forgive her, too. She broke my son's heart. She broke your heart."

Andie shook off the anger. Her heart hadn't been broken, not by Caroline or anyone else.

"I'm fine." She brushed Babe's neck and the mare leaned toward her, her eyes closing slightly.

"You're not fine. And this isn't about Caroline, it's about you and Ryder. What happened?"

"Nothing. Or at least nothing a little time won't take care of."

Etta walked closer. "I guess it's too late for the talk that we should have had fifteen years ago," she said with a sigh.

Andie swallowed and nodded. And the words freed the tears that had been hovering. "Too late."

"It's okay." Etta stepped closer, her arm going around Andie's waist.

"No, it isn't. I messed up. I really messed up. This is something I can't take back."

"So you went to church?"

"Not just because of this. I went because I had to go. As much as I've always claimed I was strong, every time I was at the end of my rope, it was God that I turned to. I've always prayed. And that Sunday morning, I wanted to be in church."

"Andie, did you use…"

Andie's face flamed and she shook her head.

"Do you think you might be…"

They were playing fill-in-the-blank. Andie wanted option C, not A. She wanted the answer to be sick with a stomach virus. They didn't want to say the hard words, or face the difficult answers. She wasn't a fifteen-year-old kid. Funny, but until now she had controlled herself. She hadn't made these choices. She hadn't gotten herself into a situation like this.

She was trying to connect it all: her mistake, her relationship with God, and her friendship with Ryder. How could she put it all together and make it okay?

"Maybe it's a virus. Joy's kids had a stomach virus."

"It could be." Etta patted her back. "It really could be."

And then a truck turned into the drive. Ryder's truck. And he was pulling a trailer. Andie closed her eyes and Etta hugged her close.

"You're going to have to tell him."

"I don't know anything, not yet. I don't know if I can face this. I'm trying so hard to get my act together and I can't pull Ryder into this."

"Soon." Etta kissed her cheek.

"When I know for sure."

Ryder was out of his truck. And he was dressed for roping, in his faded jeans, a black T-shirt and nearly worn-out roper boots.

"You going with me?" He tossed the question before he reached the barn. His grin was big, and he was acting as if there was nothing wrong between them. Andie wished she could do the same.

"I don't know."

Etta's brows went up and she shrugged. "I'm going in the house. I have a roast on and it needs potatoes."

Andie watched her grandmother walk away and then she turned her attention back to Ryder. He scratched his chin and waited. And she didn't know what he wanted to hear.

"Come on, Andie, we've always roped on Sunday evenings."

It was what they'd done, as best friends. And they hadn't minded separating from time to time. She'd go out with James or one of the other guys. She'd watch, without jealousy, when he helped Vicki Summers into his truck. No jealousy at all.

Because they'd been best friends.

But today nausea rolled in her stomach and she couldn't think about leaving with him, or him leaving with Vicki afterward. And that wasn't the way it was supposed to happen.

"I can't go, not tonight."

"I don't want to lose you." He took off his white cowboy hat and held it at his side. "I wish we could go back and…"

"Think a little more clearly? Take time to breathe

deep and walk away?" She shook her head. "We can't. We made a choice and now we have the consequences of that choice."

"Consequences? What consequences? You're the one acting like we can't even talk. It's simple. Just get in the truck and go with me."

"I can't." She tossed the brush into a bucket and the clang of wood hitting metal made Babe jump to the side. Andie whispered to the mare and reached to untie the lead rope from the hook on the wall. "I can't go with you, Ryder. I'm sick. My mom is here. I'm going to go inside and spend time with Etta."

"Fine." He walked to the door. "I'm going to be pretty busy in the next few weeks. Wyatt and the girls are going to need me."

"I know." She watched him walk away, but it wasn't easy. She'd never wanted to run after a guy the way she wanted to run after him, to tell him they could forget. They could go back to being friends, to being comfortable around each other. But she couldn't go after him and they couldn't go back.

She stood at the gate and watched as he climbed into his truck and slammed the door.

Ryder jumped into his truck and shifted hard into first gear. He started to stomp on it, and then remembered his horse in the trailer. Man, it would have felt good to let gravel fly. If only he could be sixteen again, not dealing with losing his best friend to a one-night mistake.

Why couldn't she just get over it and go with him? This was what they did, they went roping together. They hunted together. They got over things together.

As he eased onto the road he let his mind drift back, to the night in Phoenix. Stupid. Stupid. Stupid. They'd both been hurting. He'd been upset by Wyatt's situation. She'd been hurting because her twin sister had arrived in town, bringing back the pain of being a kid rejected by her mother.

And then his thoughts made a big U-turn, shifting his memory back to the Mad Cow and Andie's pale face.

He was an idiot. An absolute idiot.

Consequences. He caught himself in time to keep from slamming on the brakes. He eased to the side of the road and stopped the truck. He sat there for a long minute thinking back, thinking ahead. Thinking this really couldn't be happening to him.

He leaned back in his seat and thought about it, and thought about his next move. A truck drove past and honked. He raised a hand in a half wave.

Glancing over his shoulder he checked the road in both directions and backed the trailer up, this time heading the way he'd come from, to Etta's and to Andie.

As he turned into the driveway, she was coming out of the barn. She stopped in the doorway, light against the dark interior of the barn, her blond hair blowing a little in the wind. She sighed, he could see her shoulders rise and fall and then she walked toward him. And he wondered what she would say.

He parked and got out of the truck, waiting because he didn't know what questions to ask or how to face the consequences of that night. It would have been easier to keep running. But this would have caught up with him eventually. It wasn't as if he could run from it.

When she reached him, they stared at each other. The wind was blowing a little harder and clouds, low and heavy with rain, covered the sun. Shadows drifted across the brown, autumn grass.

"You're back a little quicker than I expected." She smiled, and for a minute he thought it might have been his imagination, her pale skin, the nausea.

He rubbed his face and tried to think of how a man asked a woman, a friend, this question.

"I came back because I have to ask you something."

"Go ahead." She slipped her hands into her front pockets.

His gaze slipped to her belly and he didn't even mean for that to happen. It was flat, perfectly flat. She cleared her throat. He glanced up and her eyebrows shot up.

"I have a question." Man, he felt like a fifteen-year-old kid. "Are you, um, are you having a baby?"

Chapter 4

The question she hadn't even wanted to ask herself. Ryder, her best friend for as long as she could remember, was peering down at her with toffee-brown eyes that had never been more serious. He wasn't a boy anymore. She wasn't a kid.

And she didn't want to answer this question, not today. She didn't want to stand in front of him, with her heart pounding and her stomach still rolling a little. She looked away, to the field across the road. It was nothing spectacular, just a field with a few too many weeds and a few cattle grazing, but it gave her something else to focus on.

"Andie, come on, we have to talk about *this*."

"Like we talked two months ago? Come on, Ryder, admit that neither one of us want to talk about this."

He took off his hat and brushed his arm across his

forehead. He glanced down at her and shook his head. "No, maybe this isn't how I wanted to spend a Sunday afternoon, but this is what we've got."

"I don't want to talk about it. Not today."

"So you are…?"

"I don't know." She looked down, at dusty, hard-packed earth. At his boots and hers as they stood toe-to-toe in that moment that changed both of their lives. He was just a cowboy, the kind of guy who had said he'd never get married.

And she'd claimed his conviction as her own. Because that's what they had done for years. She had never been one of those girls dreaming of weddings, the perfect husband or babies. She didn't play the games in school with boys' names and honeymoon locations. Instead she'd thought about how to train the best barrel horse and what it would take to win world titles.

Babies. As much as she had wanted to pretend otherwise, her feminine side had caused her to go soft when she held a baby or watched children play. When she watched her friends with their husbands, she felt a little empty on the inside, because she shared her life with Etta—and with Ryder—but Ryder never shared his heart, not the way a woman wanted a man to share his heart.

"Andie, I'm sorry, this shouldn't have happened." He touched her cheek and then his hand dropped to his side and he stepped back a few steps.

"I definitely don't want you to be sorry." She looked up, trying her best to be determined. "Like I said, I don't know. It could be that I caught the stomach virus some of the kids in Kansas had. When I know for sure, I'll let you know."

"Let me know?" He brushed a hand through his hair and shoved his hat back in place, a gesture she'd seen a few too many times and she knew exactly what it meant. Frustration.

Well, she could tell him a few things about frustration. But she wasn't in the mood. She wasn't in the mood to spell out for him that this hadn't been in her plans, either. He hadn't been in her plans, not this way.

"Yeah, I'll let you know. Look, whatever happens, whatever this is, it isn't going to change anything." She was glad she sounded firm, sounded strong. She felt anything but, with her insides quivering. "You've always been my friend and that's how it'll stay."

"What does that mean?"

"It means I'm not going to tie you down or try to drag you into this. It doesn't change things."

"I have news for you, Andie Forester, this changes things. This changes everything."

"It doesn't have to."

He shook his head. "Are you being difficult for a reason, other than to just drive me crazy? If you're pre... uh, having a baby, it changes a lot, now doesn't it?"

She wanted to smile, because even the word brought a bead of sweat across his brow and his neck turned red. But she couldn't smile, not yet.

"I'll let you know when I find out for sure."

"Fine, you let me know. And we'll pretend that this isn't important, if that's what you really want." He turned and walked away, a cowboy in faded jeans, the legs worn and a little more faded where he'd spent a lot of time in the saddle.

He waved as he climbed into his truck and started the engine. She waved back. And it already felt different. She'd been lying to herself, trying to tell herself it wouldn't matter.

She watched him drive away and then she considered her next move. Go inside and face her mother, or stay in the barn and hide from reality. She liked the hiding plan the best. Facing Ryder and her mother, both in the same day, sounded like too much.

In the dark, dusty interior of the barn she could close her eyes and pretend she was the person she'd been two months ago. But she wasn't.

A lot had happened. She turned over a bucket and sat down. She leaned against the stall door behind her and closed her eyes. Everything had changed. Most importantly, she had changed.

On a Sunday morning in a church service at the rodeo arena she had changed. It had started when she walked out of her horse trailer, a cup of coffee in hand, and she'd heard the couple who led the service singing "Amazing Grace." She'd walked to the arena and taken a seat on a row of bleachers a good distance from the crowd.

During that service, God had pulled her back to Him. She had been drawn back into a relationship that she'd ignored for years. And it hadn't been God's fault that she'd walked away. It had been about her loyalty to Ryder.

She opened her eyes and looked outside, at a sky growing darker as the sun set. The days were cool and growing shorter. She wasn't ready for winter. She definitely didn't know how to face spring, and seven months from now.

How did a person go from turning back to God, to making a giant mistake like the one she'd made with

Ryder? And what about God? Was He going to reject her now?

She'd had experience with rejection.

It had started with her mother. She squeezed her eyes shut again, and refused the tears that burned, tightening in her throat because she wasn't going to let them fall.

"Forgive me," she whispered, wanting peace, something that settled the ache in her heart and took away the heaviness of misgivings.

She stood and walked into the feed room to look at the calendar tacked to the wall. It recorded dates and locations of rodeos. She thumbed back to the month of the Phoenix rodeo and tried to remember. She leaned, resting her forehead against the rough barn wood.

For two months she'd told herself there wouldn't be consequences, other than a little bit of time when they'd be uncomfortable with each other.

But she'd been wrong. There were definitely consequences, and this wasn't going away any time soon. She picked up the pencil she used to mark the calendar and she went through the next few months, marking through events she'd planned to attend, but now wouldn't.

Things had definitely changed.

Roping hadn't taken Ryder's mind off Andie and the possibility of a baby. His baby. He didn't need proof of that fact because he knew Andie. As he drove through Dawson after loading his horse and talking for a few minutes with friends, his mind kept going back, to better choices he could have made. And forward, to how his life would never be the same.

Ryder drove through Dawson. It was Sunday night and that meant there wasn't a thing going on and nothing open but the convenience store. A few trucks were parked at the side of the building and a few teenagers sat on tailgates, drinking sodas and eating corn dogs. Big night out in Dawson.

He turned left on the road that led out of town, to his family farm, and on past, to the house where Andie had grown up with Etta. He considered driving there and talking to her, trying to figure out what they were going to do. He didn't figure she'd be ready to talk.

Instead he pulled into his drive and drove back to the barn. As he got out, he noticed Wyatt in the backyard with the girls. Wyatt was sitting at the patio table, the girls were running around the yard with flashlights. They were barely more than babies.

And Wyatt didn't know what to do with them. That thought kind of sunk into the pit of his stomach. Wyatt had always been the one who seemed to know how to do this adult thing.

Ryder stepped out of the truck and walked back to the trailer to unload his horse. The big gelding stomped restlessly, ready to be out and ready to graze in the pasture.

"Easy up there, Buddy." Ryder unlatched the back of the trailer. He stepped inside, easing down the unused half of the trailer to untie the animal and back him out.

When they landed on firm ground, Wyatt was there. Ryder smiled at his brother and got a half smile in return. The girls had stopped running and were watching. They weren't used to horses. Wyatt had taken a job as a youth minister in Florida and they had lived in town.

"Long night?" Wyatt stepped back, watching.

"Yeah, kind of." How did he tell his brother? Wyatt

had always held it together. He'd held them together as best he could.

"What's up?" Wyatt followed him to the gate, opening it for Ryder to let the horse out into the pasture.

"Nothing."

"Right."

Ryder pushed the gate closed and latched it. The horse reached for a bite of grass, managing to act like he hadn't eaten in days, not hours. Horses were easy to take care of. They could be left alone. They didn't make requirements. They had to be trained, but he was pretty sure they were a lot easier to train than a child.

He ranched. He raised quarter horses and black angus cattle. He didn't raise babies.

Until now.

The girls ran up to them, tiny things, not even reaching his hip. He closed the gate and turned his attention to Molly and Kat. And boots. They were wearing his boots. The good ones that had cost a small fortune.

He glanced up, pretty sure that God was testing him. This was a lesson on parenting, or patience. He didn't know which. Probably both.

"We like your shoes." Molly grinned, and he was happy to see her smiling. But man, she was wearing his best boots.

The look he gave Wyatt was ignored.

"Boots." Kat giggled. The pair she was wearing covered her legs completely.

"Yep, boots." He scooped up Kat and snuggled her close. She giggled and leaned back. She looked a lot like her mom. That had to be hard for Wyatt. Kat had Wendy's smile, her dimples, her laughter.

And she was a dirty mess. Mud caked her, and his

boots. From the tangles in her hair, he guessed it had been a couple of days since it had seen a brush.

"You need a bath." He held her tight as they headed toward the house.

Kids needed things like baths, and their teeth brushed. They had to be tucked in and someone had to be there for them. They didn't need parents who drank themselves into a stupor and made choices that robbed a family of security.

He didn't drink. He had one thing going for him.

Anger knocked around inside him. The past had a way of doing that, and a guy shouldn't get angry thinking of parents who had died too young.

"If you need to talk…" Wyatt followed him up the steps to the back door, and then he shrugged. They'd never been touchy-feely. Sharing was for afternoon talk shows, not the Johnson brothers. They'd always solved their problems, even dealt with their anger, by roping a few calves or riding hard through the back field.

Every now and then they'd had a knock-down-drag-out in the backyard. Those fights had ended with the two of them on their backs, staring up at the sky, out of breath, but out of anger.

Talking about it didn't seem like an option.

"Yeah, I know we can talk." Ryder put his niece down on the floor and flipped on the kitchen light. Kat stomped around in his boots, leaving dirt smudges on the floor he'd mopped last night. "Did you guys eat?"

He looked around. There was an open loaf of bread on the counter and a jar of peanut butter, the lid next to it. He glanced down at Kat. She had a smear of peanut butter on her cheek. He twisted the bread closed.

"Did you feed the girls?" Ryder asked again when Wyatt hadn't answered.

"Molly made sandwiches."

"And you think that's good?" A three-year-old making sandwiches. Ryder screwed the lid on the peanut butter because he had to do something to keep from pushing his brother into a wall to knock sense into him. "Girls, are you hungry?"

Kat grinned and Molly looked at her dad. Ryder exhaled a lot of anger. He didn't have a clue what little kids ate. Wyatt should have a clue. If Wyatt couldn't do this, how in the world was Ryder going to manage?

"Tell you what, I'll make eggs and toast. Do you like eggs?" Ryder opened the fridge door.

"I can do it." Wyatt took the carton of eggs from his hands.

"You girls go play." Ryder smiled at his nieces. "I think there's a box of toys in the living room. Mostly horses and cowboys."

His and Wyatt's toys that Ryder had dug out of a back closet the night before.

When the girls were gone, he turned back to his brother. Wyatt cracked eggs into a bowl and he didn't look up. "I've taken care of them for a year."

"Yeah, I know you have."

The dog scratched at the back door. Ryder pushed it open and let the animal in, because there was one thing Bear was good at, and that was cleaning up stuff that dropped on the floor. Stuff like peanut butter sandwiches.

Bear sniffed his way into the kitchen and licked the floor clean, except he left the mud. Not that Ryder blamed him for that.

The dog was the best floor sweeper in the country.

"I'm taking care of my girls." Wyatt poured eggs into the pan. "And I don't want tips from a guy who hasn't had kids, or hasn't had a relationship in his life that lasted more than a month."

"That's about to change," Ryder muttered and he sure hadn't meant to open that can of worms. He'd meant to butter toast.

"What's that mean?" Wyatt turned the stove off.

"Remember what it was like, growing up in this house?"

"Sure, I remember." Wyatt scooped eggs onto four plates. "Always laughter, mostly the drunken kind that ended in a big fight by the end of the night. And then there were the phone calls."

Phone calls their mother received from the other women. Ryder shook his head, because memories were hard to shake. His dad's temper had been hard to hide from.

"Right. That's not the kind of life our kids should have." Ryder let out a sigh, because he had been holding on to those memories for a long time.

"Well, as far as I know, the only kids in this house are mine, and they're not going to have that life, not in this house. If you're insinuating…"

"I'm not insinuating anything about you or how you're raising those girls." Ryder tossed a slice of buttered toast to his blue heeler. "Wyatt, there isn't a person around who blames you for having a hard time right now."

"I guess this isn't about me, is it?"

No, but it would have been nice to pretend it was. Ryder shrugged and poured himself a cup of that morning's coffee. He ignored his brother and slid the coffee into the microwave.

"No, it isn't about you." He took his cup of day-old coffee out of the microwave. "I'm going outside."

Because it was still his life. For now.

"Not again." Andie rolled out of bed and ran for the bathroom. She leaned, eyes closed and taking deep breaths until the moment passed. When it was just a rolling hint of nausea, she sat back, leaning against the cool tile walls of her bathroom.

"I have gingersnaps."

She turned and Etta was standing in the doorway, already dressed for her day. Andie looked down at her own wrinkled pajamas that she honestly didn't want to change out of, not today.

"I'm not sure what good cookies and milk will do now."

Etta laughed. "Ginger for nausea. Although the milk might not be the best thing right now. Maybe ginger tea. Come downstairs and we'll see what I have."

The thought of ginger in tea made it worse. Andie closed the bathroom door with her foot and resumed position next to the commode. Her grandmother knocked, insistent. It wasn't a good thing, Etta's insistence, not this morning.

"Give me a minute, Gran."

"It's your mother."

Oh, that didn't make it better. Mother. Andie leaned again, perspiration beaded her brow and her skin felt clammy. She stood and leaned over the sink, turning on cold water to splash her face.

"Leave me alone."

"I can't. Etta said you're sick. Can I help?"

"No, you can't help." No one could help.

But there was a clear feeling that someone could. She closed her eyes and prayed for answers, because she'd never needed answers more. She felt as if she was on a traffic circle in the middle of a foreign city and she didn't know which road to take, so she kept driving around the circle, looking for the right direction, the right path.

Her own analogy and it made her dizzy. She opened her eyes and the swaying stopped.

"Andie?"

"I'm fine. I'll be out in a minute."

The door moved a little, like someone leaned against it from the other side. "I know you're angry with me."

The woman wouldn't give up.

And the term *angry with her mother* didn't begin to describe the hurt, rejection and fury, all rolled into one giant ball and lodged in her heart. Andie slid her hand over her stomach, wondering at the idea of a baby growing inside her, and wondering how a mother could leave a child behind.

People did things even they didn't understand, things they regretted. She tried not to think about Phoenix, but it wouldn't go away. Ryder's face, his smile swimming in her vision, couldn't be blinked away.

She had always cared about his rotten hide.

Hormones. All of this emotion was caused by raging hormones. She had to stop, to get her act together. She dried her face off and pulled the door open.

Her mother nearly fell on top of her.

"I forgive you." Andie walked past her mother and kept going, down the stairs, out the front door. Alyson's cat greeted her on the front porch. She scooped the kitten up and held it close. Not that she liked cats. But she had to do something.

The screen door creaked open.

"Are you pregnant?" Caroline asked as she stepped onto the porch. She looked so pinched and worried, Andie nearly smiled.

"I probably am." She glanced away from her mom. "I guess this is how you expected I'd end up."

"I never thought you'd be less than wonderful. I didn't take Alyson because I thought she'd be better." Caroline swept her hand over her face, her fingers glittering with gold and gems. "I took her because she was easier. You had so much energy. You pushed me."

"Pushed you?"

"I knew I couldn't be a good mother to you. I was worried I'd be a horrible mother. That would have been worse for you, wouldn't it?"

"You could have called."

"It seemed better this way. I can't go back, Andie. But I do want you to know that I'm here if you need me."

"I'm sure I'll be fine."

"Of course you'll be fine. If you'd like, I could go to the doctor with you before I leave in the morning."

The kitten hissed and clawed, wanting down. Andie let him go, watched him scamper with his scrawny tail in the air and then she turned to meet her mother's cautious gaze. "I get that you want to be forgiven, but we can't undo twenty-five years of silence with a doctor's appointment and you standing outside the bathroom door offering words of support."

"I know that." Caroline hugged herself, her arms thin. "Will you call if you need anything before I come back next month to help Alyson finish the wedding plans?"

"I'll call." Andie sighed. "If it helps, I don't hate you. I wanted to, but I don't."

Caroline nodded and tears flooded her eyes. "I'm glad."

"Yeah, so am I." Andie sat down on the steps, her mother stood, leaning against the post. "I guess what you have to realize is that I'm not ready for you to play the part of my mother."

"Right. Of course." Caroline nodded and stepped away from the post. "Thank you for giving me a chance."

"You're welcome." The kitten crawled into Andie's lap, twitching its tail in her face.

Andie watched her mother walk back into the house, and then a truck was barreling down the paved road and turning into their driveway. She groaned and wondered how a day could turn this bad this fast.

Instead of sitting on the porch, waiting for him to get to her, she got up and walked inside. From the front hallway she could smell the spicy aroma of the ginger tea that Etta had promised. And now it seemed like a good idea.

Etta turned to look at her when she walked into the kitchen. Her grandmother pointed to the cup on the counter and Andie picked it up, holding it up to inhale the aroma of ginger and cinnamon.

"Sip it and see if that doesn't help settle your stomach."

Etta flipped pancakes onto a plate.

"If it does, I want a few of those pancakes." Andie sat down with the tea and watched her grandmother. It was just the two of them, the way it had been for a long time. Even when Andie's dad had been alive, it had been Etta and Andie most of the time.

"The first plate is yours." Etta glanced out the kitchen window. "You know that Ryder is here, right?"

"I know." She sipped the tea and waited, listening for the familiar sound of his steps on the porch, the song he whistled that wasn't a song and the mew of the kitten when she had someone cornered for attention.

Chapter 5

Ryder walked up the back steps to Etta's, whistling, pretending it was any other fall day in Oklahoma. It was easy to whistle. Not so easy to put out of his mind other thoughts, more complicated thoughts.

He rapped on the back door and Etta called out for him to come in, that he didn't have to knock. He'd never knocked before, but he thought that today might be a little different. Things had definitely changed.

Andie sat on a stool just inside the door. She turned to look at him, and then shifted her attention back to the cup in her hand, and the plate of pancakes in front of her. She looked a little pale, a little green. Her hair was in a short ponytail with thin wisps hanging loose to frame her face.

How many times had he seen her in the morning? They'd taken predawn rides together, worked cattle together and hauled hay together. But today she was maybe the mother of his child. Stuff shifted inside him, trying to make room for that idea. It wasn't easy to have that space when he'd never thought about his life in terms of fatherhood.

He felt nearly as sick as she must feel.

"You're up and around early." She kept her focus on the plate of pancakes.

"Yeah, well, I have a lot to do today."

"Like?"

"First of all, I want to talk to you."

"Talk away." She took another bite of pancake.

Okay, she wasn't going to make this easy. He leaned against the wall next to the door and watched her eat. He had just finished breakfast at the Mad Cow, but that didn't stop him from thinking about Etta's pancakes. No one made them like Etta.

"Want some?" Andie offered, smiling a little. Looking a little like her old self.

"Nah, I just ate. Andie, we need to talk."

"I'd rather not. I mean, really, what do you need to say? We've covered it. We made a mistake. We were both there. So we move on, we find a way to keep being friends."

"I think I should give you kids some privacy?" Etta turned off the stove and slipped the apron over her head, hanging it on the hook as she walked out the door.

"We don't need privacy." Andie stood, picking up her empty plate. She carried it to the sink and ran water over it, staring out the window.

Ryder walked up behind her, wanting to hold her. And that surprised him. She'd never been that person to him, the person he dated, the person he held. She'd been the person who helped him keep his act together, and the friend he turned to when he needed to talk something out. He'd been that person for her, too.

"We need privacy." He stepped next to her, leaning shoulder to shoulder for a second. And she leaned back, resting her head against him.

"Okay, we're alone." She glanced up, turning to face him.

Yeah, they were alone. He took a few deep breaths and told himself this was the right thing to do. Andie was staring up at him, blue eyes locking with his. His emotions tangled inside him like two barn cats were going at it, fighting to the death inside his stomach.

"I never thought I'd do this." He'd ridden two-thousand-pound bulls, fought fires with the volunteer fire department, and he'd never been this afraid of anything.

"Do what?"

He reached into his pocket and held out his hand. "Andie, I think we should get married."

And she laughed at him. He stepped back, not sure how to react to laughter. He had kind of expected her to be mad, or something. She could have cried. But he hadn't expected laughter.

"You've got to be kidding me."

"Well, no, I wasn't." But maybe he should pretend it had been a joke. They could laugh it off and move on like it hadn't happened. Maybe she'd even tell him this was a late April Fools' joke, and she wasn't going to have a baby.

"Well, you should be kidding. You know you don't want to marry me. You don't want to marry anyone, and especially not like this."

"I'd marry you. Seriously, who better to marry than your best friend?"

She didn't make a sarcastic remark or roll her eyes, and those would have been the typical Andie reactions to his comment. Instead she smiled and he couldn't believe two months of hormones could change a woman that much, that fast.

"I'm not going to marry you, Ryder. We won't even know for sure if I'm pregnant until I go to the doctor tomorrow."

"We could get a, well, one of those tests."

She turned a little pink and looked down at the floor. Her feet were bare and she wore sweats cut off at the knees and a T-shirt. She looked young.

And he felt older than dirt.

"Andie?"

"I took a test." She turned away from him, running dishwater like nothing was different, as if this was a normal day and he hadn't just had his proposal, his very first proposal, rejected. As if she hadn't just admitted to taking a pregnancy test.

He shoved his hands into his pockets and waited a few seconds before pushing further into the conversation.

"Okay, you took a test. I guess you didn't think I had a right to know?"

"Yes, I was going to let you know." She kept washing dishes without looking at him. "I took the test last night and it was positive."

So, this was how it felt to learn you were going to be a dad. Not that he hadn't already been pretty sure, but this made it official. She reached for the ring where he'd left it on the counter. It had been his grandmother's.

She looked at it for a long moment and then she smiled and put it back in his hand.

"Save your ring for someone you love. I'm going to have this baby, and I'm not going to force you into its life, or my life. I'm not going to accept a proposal you probably planned while you were feeding cattle this morning."

She knew him that well.

"Now, if you don't mind, I have a lot to do today. Rob's coming over to shoe my horses and Caroline is going back to Boston tomorrow."

Andie was trying like crazy not to be hurt or mad. She'd never wanted a proposal like this, one that a guy felt as if he had to make. She hadn't spent too much of her life thinking about marriage, but she knew the one thing she wanted. She wanted love. She didn't want to start a marriage based on "have to."

That night two months ago was one she couldn't undo. She couldn't undo the consequences. She closed her eyes and her hand went to her stomach. As much as she had never thought about babies in connection with her life, she couldn't think of this baby as a punishment.

It was her baby. She opened her eyes and Ryder was watching her. It was his baby, too. Having a baby changed everything, for both of them. It changed who they were and who they were going to be. It changed their friendship.

If she had to do it over again, she would have walked away from Ryder that night in Phoenix. She would have stopped things. Because a baby's life shouldn't start like this, with parents who could barely look at one another.

A baby should be planned, shouldn't it? A baby

should know that it was being born into a home with two parents prepared to love it and raise it.

So what did a person do when the perfect plan hadn't happened? Andie figured they made the best of things. They counted from this day forward and promised to do their best after this.

"When are you going to the doctor?"

"Tomorrow." She washed a plate and he took it from her to run under rinse water.

"I meant, what time?"

"I'm going to leave early, probably by nine."

"I'll take you."

Andie stopped washing and took a deep breath. "I don't need you to take me."

"Why in the world are you pushing me away?" Ryder's voice was low, calm. But she knew better. She knew him better. "If you're pregnant, I'm the father. Right?"

"Right."

"So, I'm going with you. My baby, Andie. That has to give me some rights. Maybe you don't want to marry me, but I don't think you'll stop me from being a part of this kid's life."

"I'm not trying to stop you. I'm trying to tell you that I'm not expecting this from you."

Her insides shook and she felt cold and clammy as a wave of nausea swept through her again. Ryder touched her arm, his hand warm on her bare skin.

"Do you need to sit down?"

"Yes, I need to sit down and I need for you to stop acting like this."

"How do you want me to act?"

"I don't know." She let him lead her to one of the bar stools at the kitchen counter.

"Well, that makes two of us, Andie. We're both in a place we never expected to be. We're going to be parents. That's going to take some time to adjust to. Give me a break and don't expect me to know exactly what to say or how to react."

"Fine, then you give me a break and don't expect me to suddenly think of you as my handsome prince." She blinked away tears. "You've always been my toad."

He smiled and shook his head and she thought he might hug her, but he didn't. As she was contemplating the dozens of reasons why she shouldn't want him to hug her, his cell phone rang.

Andie waited, watching as he talked, as his expression changed from aggravated with her to worried.

"I'll be right there." He slipped his cell phone into his pocket. He met her gaze and his eyes were no longer dancing with laughter.

"What's up?"

"Molly's sick. Wyatt needs to run to town and get something for her. My medicine cabinet doesn't support the needs of toddlers."

"I can go with you." Andie hopped off the bar stool and grabbed her cell phone that had been charging all night. "Let me get shoes."

"You're sick."

"I'm fine. It's over now." She tried to smile, but he was still watching her. She was suddenly breakable.

He'd have to get over that in a real hurry.

"Morning sickness, Ryder. Morning, and then it goes away."

"Right. I get it."

The back door opened. Etta walked in, glancing from one to the other, clearly looking for marks of a fight.

"Where are you two off to?" Etta kicked off her shoes and set a basket of fresh eggs on the counter.

"Molly's sick," Andie explained as she leaned to tie her shoes. "I'm going over to see if there's anything I can do."

"You're going to help?" Etta smiled a little. "With children?"

"I can do that."

"Call if you need my help."

"Will do." Andie hugged her grandmother. "Oh, if Rob gets here before I get back, tell him Dusty and Babe need shoes. Not that he won't be able to tell."

"Of course."

Ryder pushed the door open and Andie walked out, past him, his arm brushing hers. And then he walked next to her. They didn't talk. When had they ever not talked? They'd always had something to say to one another, something to tease the other about.

How did she get that back? Or did she? Maybe that was the other consequence, losing her best friend.

Ryder opened the passenger side truck door. For her. She stopped and gave him a look. "Stop." She stood in front of him.

"Stop what?"

"When have you ever opened the car for me?"

"I don't know. I'm sure I've done it before. Would you just get in?"

She shrugged and climbed in. "Sure thing."

The door closed and he walked around the front of the truck to the driver's side. Her heart clenched a little, because he was sweet and gorgeous and a cowboy. For most of her life she'd just seen him as the friend she couldn't live without. Now, watching him walk away, she wondered if she'd kept that line between them because he'd insisted on just being friends.

No, that wasn't it. She was just being overly emotional. She didn't love Ryder. He didn't love her. And maybe, just maybe, the test was wrong. She'd go to the doctor tomorrow and find out it had all been a big mistake. They'd laugh and go back to being who they had always been.

Ryder didn't talk to Andie on the short drive to his place. As he eased the truck up the driveway, he let his gaze settle on the house he'd grown up in. It was a big old ranch house that his parents had remodeled. They'd added the new windows, the brick siding and the landscaping.

It had sheltered them, but it hadn't exactly been a happy home. Wyatt and Ryder had spent their time breaking horses, roping steers and looking out for each other.

They'd been in more than their share of fights. They'd broken more than a few hearts. He knew that. He could accept that he'd always been the bad boy that most parents didn't want to see walk through the door to pick up their little girl for a date.

And now he was going to be a dad. The idea itched inside him, like something he was deathly allergic to. But when he walked through the front door and saw three-year-old Molly on the sofa, a stuffed animal in her arms and her little face red from the fever that must have come on since he left the house, he thought different things about being a dad.

He thought about a kid of his own, one that he wouldn't let down.

But what if he did? What if he messed up a kid the way his parents had messed him up? What if his kid grew up too independent for its own good, or always afraid of what was happening in the living room?

The last thing he should be thinking of was a little girl with Andie's eyes.

Wyatt held Kat. "Can you watch them while I run to Grove and get some medicine?" The little girl looked like she might be nearly asleep, but when she saw Ryder she smiled. And then she held her arms out to Andie.

And Andie's eyes widened. "Oh, okay."

She held the little girl and when she looked over Kat's shoulder at him, he felt like someone who didn't belong in this picture. Andie probably felt the same way.

"I'll be right back." Wyatt grabbed his keys, shot a look over his shoulder and walked out the front door.

Something about that look had Ryder worrying that his brother wouldn't come back. He walked to the door and watched the truck drive away. "How about some lunch?"

He turned, smiling at Kat, and then Molly. His dog, Bear, was curled on the couch at her feet. As Ryder approached her side, Bear looked up, letting out a low growl. So, it had been that easy to steal the dog's loyalty? It just took being a little girl with big eyes.

"Bear, enough." At the warning, the dog's stub tail thumped the leather sofa.

Molly's eyes watered. Ryder sat down on the coffee table, facing her. "How about a drink of water?"

She nodded and sat up, still dressed in her nightgown with a princess on the front. His heart filled up in a way he'd never experienced. And then it ducked for cover, because this couldn't be his life.

Movement behind him. He turned and Andie was sitting in the rocking chair, Kat held against her. If Wyatt was running, he should have taken Ryder with him.

"Is her forehead hot?" Andie asked, her voice soft, comforting. He'd never heard it like that, as if she already knew how to be a mom.

Maybe women were that way? Maybe they had that natural instinct, and only men had to wonder and worry that they'd never get it right. The way he was worrying.

He touched Molly's head. "Pretty hot." He winked at the little girl as she curled back into her blanket, his dog curling into the bend of her knees.

"Maybe get a cool, wet cloth?" Andie shrugged. "I really don't have a clue, but it could be a while before Wyatt gets back and maybe cool water would bring her temperature down. We could call Etta."

"Wyatt will come back." Ryder cleared his throat. "I mean, he'll be back soon. It doesn't take that long to drive into Grove."

"Right." She was still holding Kat, her fingers stroking the little girl's brown hair. "Do you have a brush? Her hair's kind of scraggly."

He stood up. "I'll get a wet cloth for Molly and a brush for Kat."

When he walked back into the room, Molly was dozing and Kat had found a book for Andie to read. The two of them were cuddled in his big chair, Andie's bare feet on the ottoman.

His throat tightened and he looked away, because it was a lot easier to deal with Molly and not the crazy thoughts going through his mind.

* * *

Wyatt came back.

Andie breathed a sigh of relief when he walked through the door an hour later. He had a bag of medication and two stuffed animals. He avoided looking at her, and at Ryder. She wondered if he had thought about not coming back.

How did a person go on when the person they had loved the most, the one they had promised to cherish and protect, took their own life? She couldn't imagine his emotions, the loss, the guilt and the questions.

The questions about her mother leaving didn't begin to compare to what Wyatt must be asking himself every single day. She wanted to tell him he couldn't have stopped it. She wanted to tell him that people make choices, and when they're making those choices they aren't always thinking about how the ones left behind will feel. Wendy wouldn't have wanted to hurt him, or her daughters.

It wasn't her place. She and Wyatt had never been close. He'd been older, wiser and never up for any of her and Ryder's crazy antics.

She shifted and he moved, as if he had just noticed her. Kat had fallen asleep in her arms and Molly was sleeping on the couch. Andie looked at Ryder. Without words, he took the sleeping child from her arms and placed her on the opposite end of the couch from her sister.

Bear hopped down, looking offended the way only a dog can.

"We should get you back before Rob gets there to shoe those horses." Ryder had walked to the door. His gaze settled first on the girls and then on Wyatt. "Need anything before we go?"

"No, we're fine. Thanks for watching them."

"No problem. Call if you need me."

As they walked out to the truck, Andie slowed her pace.

"Do you think he'll be okay?" She glanced back at the house. Ryder followed the direction of her gaze and shrugged.

"I guess he will. What else can he do?"

"I guess you're right. But I can't imagine…"

"Yeah, I know."

His hand reached for hers. Andie didn't say anything. She walked next to him, his fingers tightly laced through hers. When they got to the truck he squeezed lightly and then let go. His hand was on the door handle, but he didn't open it.

Andie reached to do it herself, but he stopped her.

"Andie, we're going to figure this out. I don't know how, but we will. I guess we'll do it the way we've always faced everything else—together."

She nodded, but her eyes were swimming and she just wanted him to hold her hand again. She didn't want to feel alone. His words had taken away a little of that feeling and replaced it with hope. Maybe they would survive this.

"We should go." Andie glanced away, but Ryder touched her cheek, drawing her attention back to him, forcing her to meet his gaze. She stared up at him, at lean, suntanned cheeks and a smile that curved into something delicious and tempting.

That smile was her downfall. She should turn away and not think about her life in terms of being in Ryder's life. She should definitely look away. But his eyes were dark and pulled her in.

"We should definitely go," she repeated, whispering this time.

"I know, but there's one thing we need to do before we leave."

He leaned, his hand still on her cheek. Her fingers slipped off the chrome door handle to rest on his arm.

His lips touched hers in a gesture that was sweet and disarming. His hand moved from her cheek to the back of her neck and he paused in the kiss to rest his forehead against hers.

Andie gathered her senses, because she couldn't let her heart go there, not in the direction it wanted to go.

"We shouldn't have gone there." She broke the connection and reached for the door handle. This time he opened it for her.

"Andie, at least give me a chance to figure this all out before you give up on me."

"I've never given up on you." She touched his arm. "But I can't be distracted, Ryder. I have to make the right decisions, now more than ever."

"And you think turning down my proposal was the right decision?"

"Yeah, right now it is. It was sweet of you, really it was, but it was spur-of-the-moment and this is something that we should take time to think about."

Spur-of-the-moment was definitely a bad idea.

Chapter 6

Andie walked through the glass doors of the women's health clinic the next morning and she couldn't deny that her stomach was doing crazy flips and her palms were sweating. This time it was a good old case of nerves and not morning sickness. She rubbed her hands down the sides of her jeans and ignored the cautious look Ryder shot her as they walked across the granite-tiled lobby.

"We could skip this. I mean, the test is probably right."

Ryder laughed a little as he pushed the button on the elevator. "Right, we already know, so why bother with a doctor? I mean, who needs help delivering a kid into the world?"

Every word spiked into her heart. *Delivering. Kid. World.* This baby wasn't going to stay inside her, where it was safe, where it was a thought, something in the future. It would come kicking and screaming into her life. If Etta's calculations were correct, it would happen in May. Spring.

Andie wouldn't be riding for a world title anytime soon.

But with the life growing inside of her, that couldn't be her focus. Her old plans were being replaced by new ones. Etta was looking at paint samples and fabric for baby quilts.

It was a little soon for that.

They got off the elevator at the third floor. Andie stood in the wide corridor, staring at Suite 10. Another couple stepped off the second elevator, smiling, holding hands. The other woman's belly was round and her eyes were shining with anticipation. And Andie didn't know how to reach for Ryder's hand, or how to make this about a happy future for the two of them. The three of them.

Her own belly was still flat. Her jeans still fit. Other than nausea in the morning and a positive sign on a stick, this didn't seem real. But it was.

At least Ryder was with her. Of course he was. She knew him well enough to know that he wasn't going to let her go through this alone. He just wasn't going to be the person with adoration in his eyes, holding her hand and telling her he'd always be there for her.

He'd never been that person for anyone. She knew him, knew that he'd worked hard at never letting himself get too involved. He didn't even want kids.

That was one thought she wished she would have blocked. Too late, though, because it had obviously already been swimming around in her mind.

"We're going to be late." Ryder reached for the door and glanced back at her. "Andie, you coming with me? I'm pretty sure this doctor doesn't want to examine me."

She tried to smile. "I'm coming."

They stepped into a prenatal world of soft colors, relaxing music and mothers-to-be reading magazines as they waited. The bad case of nervousness she was already experiencing went into overdrive. It was bad enough to make her reach for Ryder's hand, tugging him close.

"Relax." He walked with her to the counter. The receptionist smiled up at him. He grinned with that wicked Ryder charm that had kept girls following him since kindergarten. "Andie Forester. We have an appointment."

"Right. Here's the paperwork for new patients, Mr. Forester." The young woman handed over a clipboard with a pen and a stack of papers to be filled out.

Ryder turned, handing Andie the clipboard. "There you go, Mrs. Forester."

She smacked him with the clipboard. "You're horrible."

He winked. "Yeah, I work at it. But you're color is coming back, so that's a plus."

She walked away from him and he followed. When she sat down in a corner, as far away from other patients as she could get, he sat down next to her. He crossed his right leg over his left knee and leaned back in the chair that had to be one of the most uncomfortable she'd ever sat in.

While she filled out paperwork, he flipped through magazines, giggling a little bit like a junior-high kid with the lingerie catalogue. She shot him a dirty look and he didn't even manage to look contrite.

Thirty minutes later, Andie walked through the doors of the exam room, alone. Other women had taken their husbands, the father's of their babies. Ryder wasn't her husband. And she couldn't face this with him.

She didn't know how to face it without him. She sat down on the examining table and waited for the doctor. And she waited. She glanced at her watch and groaned, it was way past noon. No wonder she was getting shaky. Baby needed to eat. An OB should know that.

The door opened. Andie's hands were shaking. She twirled them in the robe she'd been told to wear by the nurse who had made a brief stop some thirty minutes earlier.

"Sorry, had an emergency." Dr. Mark looked down at his file. "Good news. You're pregnant."

He said it with a happy smile that faded when he looked at her face.

"That is good news, isn't it?" he asked, pushing his glasses to the top of his head. His hair was blond and thinning, his smile was kind and fatherly. She liked him.

"It is." She bit down on her lip, trying to stop the trembling. "I'm sorry. It's not really a surprise. You can't be sick for days on end and really be shocked by the news that you're pregnant."

"But it isn't something you planned. I'm assuming it is something you plan to keep?"

Heat rushed to her cheeks. She'd never thought of anything other than keeping this baby. Her baby. She blinked a few times.

"Of course I'm keeping my baby."

"Of course." He smiled and sat down. "I'm going to

do a quick exam, but first we'll do an ultrasound. If the father is here, he can come back…"

"No, he can't. I mean. This isn't what either of us planned. We're not, we're not in a relationship."

It sounded pathetic. Not in a relationship, but having a baby. She buried her face in her hands and waited for her cheeks to cool to their normal temperature.

"This doesn't have to be the end of the world." Dr. Mark patted her arm. "It's a different path than you probably had planned for yourself. It's going to take some adjusting, to make this work out. But I think you can do it."

Andie looked up, meeting eyes that were kind, with crinkled lines of age and experience at the corners.

"Yeah, I know I can make it."

She wanted to ask him what he thought about God. She had developed a new relationship with God, and then she'd realized she was pregnant. Some people might think the baby pushed her back into church. But it had been her own feelings, her own desire to have that connection that had taken her to that service.

The baby hadn't pushed her there.

"Andie, if you need someone to talk to…"

She shook her head. "I'm fine, really. It's just a lot to adjust to."

She put on a big smile, to prove to him, and maybe to herself, that she was okay.

"Okay then, let's go for that ultrasound. Down the hall, second door on the left. I'll be right there. And we'll take a picture for dad. We don't want him to miss out on everything."

Right. She nodded and hopped down from the table.

"What about activity. I mean, horseback riding? Work?"

"Within reason you can continue activities that you've been doing on a regular basis. Of course you don't want to do anything strenuous, or dangerous."

"Got it." She walked out, down the hall to the room he'd directed her to. Alone.

She was going to see her baby, or what would soon be her baby, and she wished someone was there with her. She wished Etta had come with her. She wished Ryder had insisted. If he had pushed... She shook off that thought, because she shouldn't make him push.

Instead of having someone with her, she walked into a darkened room alone and a nurse helped her onto the bed.

A few minutes later she raised her head and watched the screen, saw the beating heart of her baby and she cried. Dr. Mark handed her a tissue.

"A healthy heart." He removed the ultrasound and the nurse wiped her belly. "Here's your baby's first picture."

Andie took the black-and-white photo, her fingers trembling as she held it up and looked at something that really looked like nothing. Except for that beating heart. Proof that her baby was alive. She couldn't wait to show Etta, and to call Alyson. She didn't want to think about Ryder. Not yet.

"Now remember what I said—make an appointment for one month from today with my colleague near Grove, Dr. Ashford. That'll be a lot easier than driving to Tulsa." Dr. Mark opened the door for her. "And try not to worry. Things have a way of working out for the best."

She nodded and tried not to attach his words of wisdom to the verse that all things work together for good. For those who trust. She had to trust. She had to believe that God would take what she had done on a night when she hadn't been thinking about Him, or trusting Him, and He would work it out for her good.

But one question kept running through her mind. Why should He?

When she walked into the waiting room, Ryder was there. He wasn't relaxed. He wasn't reading a book. He was pacing. She smiled and watched, because he hadn't seen her yet.

He had dressed up for the occasion, wearing jeans that weren't so faded and boots that weren't scuffed. He'd gotten a haircut. For a moment, that moment, he looked like someone's dad. He turned, barely smiling when he saw her. She held up the picture.

Because it wasn't her baby, it was theirs.

Ryder couldn't remember a time in his life that he'd been this nervous. And he had a pretty good feeling it was only going to get worse. For over an hour he'd been watching other women, other couples. A few couples had new babies with them.

That was going to be his life. Andie was going to get a round belly. She would need help getting up from a chair, like a couple of the women who were obviously farther along. Their husbands had helped them up, and held their hands as they walked back to the examining rooms.

He'd never seen himself as one of those men. Man, he'd never even seen himself standing next to a woman, not in his craziest dreams.

He didn't even know how to hold a baby.

Andie walked toward him, her cheeks flushed and that picture in her hand. He'd never seen her so unsure. At least he wasn't alone in his feelings.

"This is our baby." She handed him the picture. In a few months she wouldn't be wearing jeans. He tried to picture her in maternity clothes, pastel colors and with her feet swollen.

She'd hit him if she knew what direction his thoughts were taking. If she knew that he'd been thinking about being there when the baby was born and what they'd name it.

"Is it a boy or a girl?" He held the picture up and tried to decipher the dot that she insisted was their kid. "Are you sure that's a baby? Looks like a tadpole to me."

She laughed. "That's a baby. And we won't know what it is for a few months."

"Wow." He shook his head and looked at the picture again. "We're going to be parents."

"Yeah, we are."

It became real at that moment, with her next to him in a doctor's office. Andie was going to have his baby.

He slipped his arm around her waist and pulled her close, because how could he not. It felt like what a guy had to do when he found out he was going to be a dad. He hadn't expected it, that jolt of excitement, that paternal surge of protectiveness.

Five minutes ago he'd been full of regrets, full of fear, full of doubt. He still was, but a picture of a heart beating, that had to change something.

"Stop." Andie pulled loose. "You're making me nervous."

"Sorry."

"I forgive you, but you have to feed me."

He got it. And he had to stop acting as if she was someone other than Andie. He wondered how they did that, how they acted like they had acted for the past twenty-five years.

"When do we come back?" he asked as they walked out the doors of the clinic, into warm autumn sunshine.

"We don't. I visit Dr. Ashford in a month. She's at the Lakeside Women's Clinic."

"I want to go with you."

"Ryder, please stop. You don't have to do this."

He stopped walking. People moved past them and around them. Andie kept moving so he hurried to catch up with her, to walk across the parking lot at her side.

"I don't know why you're pushing me away." He pulled the keys out of his pocket and pushed the button. "Andie, we have to face this. It isn't going away."

"I know it isn't going away. But I don't want to feel like you're tied to me, knowing you'd rather be anywhere but here. This isn't who you are. This isn't who we are."

"Who are we then?"

"You're you. You're single and you love your life. And I ride barrel horses and live with my granny. That's our lives. This, having a baby, being parents together, this isn't us."

He didn't laugh at her because he'd been reading those magazines in the waiting room and he now knew all about hormones, estrogen, cravings and labor. A few months ago those had been words he wouldn't have even thought to himself. He thought he might have information overload, received after more than an hour of reading prenatal articles.

Stretch marks, whether to medicate during labor or

not, natural delivery verses C-section. He wanted the words to go away.

Anyway, he knew better than to laugh at a pregnant woman with surging hormones. She'd either cry hysterically or hurt him. And he wasn't much into either of those options.

He wasn't about to tell her that he'd much rather be at a rodeo than facing her right then. At least he knew what to expect at a rodeo, on the back of a horse, or on the back of a bull. For the time being he had to think that those days were behind him.

That meant he had to come up with something that would placate her until they could deal with this.

Cravings. The word was now his friend.

"What do you want to eat?"

Her blue eyes melted a little and she sniffled. He didn't have a handkerchief.

"Seafood."

"You got it."

That was a lot easier than dealing with the big changes happening in his life, and her body. He shuddered again as he opened the door for her to get into the truck.

As they drove through Tulsa, he glanced at the woman sitting next to him. The mother of his child. He'd never expected her to be that.

"Andie, we're going to have to talk about this."

"This?"

He sighed. "The baby. Our baby. We have to talk about my part in this."

Her hand went to her belly and she stared out the window. He didn't know if she even realized that she did that, that she touched her belly. He glanced sideways, catching her reflection in the glass. Blue eyes, staring out at the passing buildings and her bottom lip held between her teeth.

"Yeah, I know that we need to talk." She said it without looking at him. "But not yet. Let this settle, okay? Let me get it together and then we'll talk."

"Tomorrow, then, Andie. We'll talk tomorrow." About the future. About them. And about the ring he was still carrying in the pocket of his jeans.

Not that he was planning on proposing again anytime soon. One rejection a year was probably more than enough.

Andie breathed a sigh of relief as she sat down to lunch. It was officially the "tomorrow" that Ryder had talked about yesterday, and he hadn't shown up yet. She'd managed to get a lot of work done at the barn, found her favorite cow just after she'd calved. The new calf had been standing behind her, still a little damp and a little wobbly.

She'd managed to forget, for a few hours, how drastically her life would change next spring.

What Ryder needed to do was go back on the road, rope a few steer, or help Wyatt with the girls. He had to get over thinking she'd let him marry her just because. When she thought about that, about marrying Ryder, her heart didn't know how to react.

She reached for a magazine off the pile sitting on the edge of the table expecting *Quarter Horse Monthly,* and she got lace and froth instead. One of Alyson's bridal magazines. Andie picked it up and flipped through the pages. She shuddered and closed the magazine.

"What's up with you?" Etta walked into the kitchen.

She smiled and laughed a little. "Weddings make you nervous."

"White icing, white dresses, white fluff and white lace."

"It's a special occasion." Etta sat down across from her and picked up the magazine. "It's supposed to be white and frilly. It's supposed to be unlike any other day in a woman's life."

"Right, but couldn't it be white denim and apple pie with vanilla ice cream?"

"I guess it could, if that's what the bride wanted. Are you thinking of getting married?"

"Of course not. Who would I marry? And there definitely isn't any white in my future."

Andie flipped the magazine open and a strange feeling, something like longing—if she'd been giving it a name—ached inside her heart. In high school her friends had planned their weddings. They'd planned the dresses, the flowers, the reception, even the groom and where they'd go on their honeymoon.

Not Andie. She'd saved up farm money to buy the barrel horse of her dreams and the perfect saddle. She'd planned a National Championship win, and she had the buckle to show how well she'd planned.

Etta patted her hand. "You'll have a white wedding, Andie. My goodness, girl, you know that it isn't about what you've done. It's about what God's doing in your heart. This is about the changes that have taken place in your life."

"I know." What else could she say? It wasn't about white. But then again, it was. It was also about dreams she'd never dreamed. "I need to get back to work.

What's for dinner tonight? I wouldn't mind taking you out for supper at the Mad Cow."

"I'd love it. I have an order to ship off this afternoon." Tie-dye specialties, Etta's custom clothing line. She and Andie worked together when Andie wasn't on the road.

"Do you need help getting the order together?"

"No, you go ahead with what you need to get done."

Andie took her plate to the sink and walked out the back door. The weather had turned cool and the leaves were rustling in a light breeze. She walked down the path to the barn, whistling for her horses. They were a short distance away and her whistle brought their heads up. Their ears twitched and then they went back to grazing.

Dusty left the herd and started toward the barn. She would brush him first and work him a little. No need to let him get a grass belly. No reason for her to sit and get lazy, either. She'd never been good at sitting still.

For as long as she could remember she'd ridden horses. When she turned six, her dad bought Bell, a spotted pony. That summer she had started to compete in youth rodeos around Oklahoma and Texas. And she'd been competing ever since. For over twenty years.

But this next year would bring changes. She'd seen the women on the circuit with children. But they usually had husbands, too. And they didn't drag little babies from state to state.

Life's about changing—those words were in a song Etta liked.

She snapped a lead rope on Dusty's halter and led him into the barn where she tied him to a hook on the wall. He rubbed his head on the rough wood of the barn and tried to chew on the rail of the nearest stall while she brushed him and then settled the saddle on his back. She reached under his belly and grabbed the girth strap to pull it tight.

A few minutes later she was standing in the center of the arena with her horse on a long, lunge line. This was what she loved. She loved an autumn day and a horse that was so attentive it took barely a flick of her wrist or a slight whistle to command him.

Ryder pulled up the drive as she was settling into the saddle. Not that long ago she would have rode to the fence, glad to see him. But today wasn't three months ago. She blinked away a few tears and she didn't glance in his direction, but she knew he was parking, that he was getting out of his truck.

She rode Dusty around the arena, keeping close to the fence. He was restless and wanted his head, kept pulling, wanting her to let him go. She held him in, easing him from an easy canter to a walk and then she rode him into the center of the arena, taking him in tight circles. He obeyed but she knew what he really wanted were barrels to run.

As she headed back to the fence she made brief eye contact with Ryder. He was walking toward the arena looking casual, relaxed, but even from a distance she saw his jaw clench.

"What are you doing?" He opened the gate and stepped inside the arena.

"I'm working my horse."

"Really?"

"Really." She reined Dusty in, and he didn't want to be reined in. He pranced, fighting the bit, wanting to run.

When he realized it was time to work, he was always

ready to go. She held him back, though, as her attention settled on Ryder. The new Ryder.

He still looked like the old Ryder. Her gaze traveled down from his white cowboy hat to his face shadowed and needing a shave, and then to the T-shirt and faded jeans. He'd tanned to a deep brown over the summer and in the last few years his body had changed from that of a tall skinny teen to a man who worked cattle for a living.

He had changed. This Ryder didn't seem to get her. Or maybe he wanted to change her? He shook his head and walked toward her and the horse.

"I don't think you should do this."

"Why not?" She held the reins tight and patted Dusty's neck, whispering softly to calm the animal.

"You're pregnant."

"I think I know that." She glared at him, hoping to pin him down, back him off or make him turn tail and run. He crossed his arms in front of his chest, as if he was the law and she was the errant juvenile. He'd never been one to back down from a fight.

Had she really admired that about him?

"Seriously, Andie, you can't do this. It's dangerous."

"No, it isn't. The doctor said I could ride. He said I could do what I've been doing, within reason. I've got to exercise my horse. I can't let him get out of shape. And I'm not going to get hurt."

"Fine, but I'm going to stay here and watch."

"Like I need you to stay and watch. You have better things to do with your time than be my nanny."

"Yeah, I have better things to do, but if you insist on doing this, then I'm staying here."

She pushed her hat back and tried again to stare

him down. "This doesn't make you my keeper. We're not boyfriend and girlfriend. We're not going steady."

"You're right, because we're not sixteen. This is a whole lot more than going steady. This is having a baby."

"Like I need you to tell me." She closed her eyes, because they did sound like kids. She didn't want that.

Ryder stepped closer. "I don't want to fight with you."

She really didn't like change.

"I don't want to fight, either. We've never fought before."

He looked away, but his hand was still on Dusty's neck. He let out a sigh. "I'm sorry."

"You have to stop this." She backed her horse, away from Ryder because she had to take back control, of herself and her horse. "You have to stop treating me this way, like I'm going to break."

"I'm trying." His features softened a little and he smiled, a shy smile that was almost as out of place as this new, protective behavior of his.

It was sweet, that smile and her insides warmed a little. She nudged Dusty with her boots and he stepped forward, putting Ryder next to her again.

"Ryder you have to trust that I'm not going to do something dangerous. I won't put—" she stumbled over the words "—I won't put our baby in danger."

"I know you won't. This is just new territory for me. I've never been anyone's dad. I hadn't planned on it."

"That makes two of us. I hadn't planned on being anyone's mom, not like this." She slid off the back of her horse. "So, what are you doing here so early?"

He looked a little blank, as if he didn't have a real

answer. Maybe he wasn't sure why he was there. They were both experiencing a lot of that lately.

She was experiencing it at that very moment, because she wanted him to say things, about them, about the future. And she knew that wasn't them, it wasn't who they'd ever been.

And it shouldn't hurt, knowing those weren't the words he was going to say. He was probably there just to check up on her and nothing more.

She wouldn't let it bother her. She knew what to do—turn and walk away, the way she would have a few months earlier. But nope, she stood there waiting for him to suddenly say the right thing.

Chapter 7

What was he doing there? Ryder had asked himself that question a few times on the drive over to Andie's. In all the years he'd known her, he'd never had to ask himself that question.

Okay, once, but that's because he'd kissed her the night of her senior prom, a night when she'd decided it would be easier to go with him than to worry about having a date. So he'd headed home from college in Tulsa to be her date.

He laughed a little, thinking back to the two of them in the limo his dad had hired for the night. They'd taken a half dozen of their friends along for the ride and when he'd walked her to the front door at the end of the night, knowing Etta was inside watching, he'd kissed Andie.

The next day they'd made a promise never to complicate their relationship that way again. Their reasons had been good. If a relationship went bad, they knew they wouldn't be able to go back to being just friends. They'd kept that promise until that night when she'd looked vulnerable and he hadn't listened to his good sense and walked away.

He was here now because they were going to have a baby together and they needed to be able to be parents together. So it seemed as if working on a relationship was the best way to start the process. Especially if she was just going to laugh when he handed her a ring and proposed.

Wyatt had laughed, too. No matter what the situation, a woman wanted more from a proposal than some half-hearted attempt at being romantic. Ryder got a little itchy under the collar when he thought about romance in connection with Andie.

"Ryder, what is it you wanted to do?"

"I thought maybe we could go over to the Coopers' arena tonight. A few people are going to get together, buck out some bulls, rope some steers and maybe run barrels."

"You'd let me run barrels?" She grinned and he shuffled his feet and looked away, because her running barrels on Dusty was the last thing he wanted.

"I can't stop you." He stepped back from her horse.

"No, you can't."

She smiled at him, and he knew she was pushing, messing with him. That smile took him back. It was easy to remember being kids, chasing down some dirt road outside of Dawson, doing stuff kids did in the country because going out on real dates took money and a town other than the one they lived in.

They'd built bonfires and sat in groups. Sometimes

they found a parking lot in Dawson and parked in a circle, sitting on the tailgates of pickup trucks. In the summer they'd gone to the lake or skiing.

Sometimes the two had dated, but never each other. Andie had dated Reese Cooper. And today that bothered him.

Life had been a lot simpler twelve years ago. But they'd been kids, and kids didn't think about what the future held. When Wyatt had met Wendy in college, he'd never dreamed of losing her too soon. He'd dreamed of having her forever. They'd planned to be youth leaders in a church and save the world.

The irony of that twisted in Ryder's gut and he knew Wyatt had to feel a lot more twisted up over losing his wife. What Ryder wouldn't give to go back to sitting in the parking lot of the Mad Cow with a bunch of kids who had nothing more serious to talk about than the rodeo that weekend and what events they would enter.

"You look like a guy that took a bitter pill," Andie teased as she led her horse through the gate he'd opened.

"Just thinking back." And thinking ahead.

"Yeah, we had some good times, didn't we?"

"We did." He walked on the other side of Dusty, but he peeked over the horse's back to look at Andie. He'd give anything to put a smile back on her face, to make her stop worrying.

"It isn't the end of the world, Ryder."

"I know it isn't." He even managed to laugh. "I'm not sixteen, Andie. When I looked in the mirror this morning, that fact was pretty evident. Most of the people we went to school with have been married for years and have a few kids."

"We're not getting married."

She tied the horse and Ryder slid his hand down the animal's rump, ignoring the tail that switched at flies and a hoof that stomped the dirt floor of the barn. He rounded the horse to the side Andie stood on. She was already untying the girth strap.

"So, do you want to go with me?" He lifted the saddle off the horse's back and ignored the sharp look she gave him.

He opened the door of the tack room with his foot and walked inside the dark room. The light came on. He glanced over his shoulder at Andie standing in the doorway. She watched as he dropped the saddle on the stand and hung the bridle on the wall. When he turned around, she was still watching.

"Well?" He followed her out of the room, latching the door behind him.

"Yeah, sure, I'll go. I haven't seen the Coopers in a long time." She untied Dusty's lead rope and led him out the back door of the barn. "When do we leave?"

"I have to run home and get a few things done. I'll pick you up at five." He was buying more cattle and a quarter horse with bloodlines that would ramp up his herd.

"I'll be ready."

He nodded and for a moment he was tempted, really tempted to kiss her goodbye, to see what it would feel like if they were a couple. Common sense prevailed because he knew how it would feel to get knocked to the ground if he pushed too far too fast.

Instead he touched her arm and walked to the truck that he'd left idling in her driveway thirty minutes earlier. He climbed inside feeling like a crazy fool. When had he ever been the guy who didn't know what to say? He'd been that person a lot lately.

When he first got there, they hadn't been able to carry on a conversation. She had even questioned why they were fighting. He had an answer for that. Couples fought. He didn't want that to be his future with Andie. Their future.

He backed down her driveway, looking into the rearview mirror at what was behind him. Behind him, that was familiar territory. What was ahead, that was a whole other matter.

Kat and Molly were playing in his yard when he pulled up to the house a few minutes later. Cute kids, still smiling, still able to chase butterflies and blow seed puffs off the dandelions. When he thought about what they'd been through, what Wyatt had been through, he felt like an idiot for crying over his own spilled milk.

Man, life was tough sometimes. Real tough.

Wyatt was leaning against a tree watching the girls, watching Ryder pull up. He waved and stepped away from the tree. As Ryder got out of his truck, Wyatt was there, smiling a little more than he had a few days ago.

How would a guy ever smile again if he'd lost someone like Wendy?

"Some girl named Sheila called." Wyatt watched the girls, but he managed to shoot Ryder a knowing look. "Told her I'd take a message but she said she'd left messages and you hadn't called her back."

"Yeah, I'll call her in a few days. You getting settled in okay?"

"Yeah, you getting in trouble with the women? I think there was a call from someone named Anna, too. She left a message on the answering machine."

"I'll call her, too."

"Keeping them on a stringer?"

"They aren't fish."

"No, but you sure know how to haul them in like they are."

Ryder shoved his hands into his pockets and bit back about a dozen things he'd like to say to his older brother. Wyatt had always made all the right decisions. Wyatt had stayed in church, because he said it wasn't God's fault that people messed up sometimes.

In Ryder's opinion, people messed up a little more often than sometimes.

"Ryder, if you need to talk?"

Right, lay his problems on Wyatt's shoulders when Wyatt couldn't see through his grief to raise two little girls who were still laughing, still smiling. They were chasing a kitten and giggling, the sound picking up in the wind and carrying like the seeds from the dandelion that they'd picked.

"Why do you think I need to talk?"

Wyatt shrugged. "I don't know, just a hunch. You're ignoring women. And you're buying cattle."

"Right."

He was growing up and everyone was surprised. That itched inside him a little. Couldn't he do a mature thing without people getting suspicious? He guessed the answer had to be no.

"Everyone in town still going to the Dawson Community Church?" Wyatt leaned to pick up Kat who had run across the yard to him and was lifting her arms to be held.

"Yeah, I suppose most do."

"You want to go with us on Sunday?"

"No, not really." Ryder rubbed his jaw and shot Wyatt a look. He might as well get it together now. "Yeah, I guess."

Wyatt whistled. "This must be big."

Big. He knew what Wyatt meant. Something big had to happen for Ryder to be thinking about church. So, that's what people thought about him, that he was only going to have faith if God somehow pushed him into it with a big old crisis.

He pulled at his collar because it was tight and the sun was hitting full force now. It shouldn't be this warm at this time of year, just days away from October.

"So?" Wyatt pushed, his gaze darting beyond Ryder to focus on his daughters. Ryder turned to look at the girls. They'd caught the kitten.

"Yeah, it is something big." Ryder picked up a walnut and tossed it. "Andie's going to have a baby and I'm the dad."

It was a long moment and then Wyatt whistled, the way he'd whistled years ago when Ryder was fifteen and had managed to talk a senior girl into taking him to the prom. But it wasn't anything like admiration in his eyes this time. Wyatt shook his head, and he looked kind of disgusted.

"How'd that…?"

"Don't ask. It was a mistake."

"Or something like it." Wyatt watched his girls play and he shook his head again. "Man, Ryder, I just don't know what to say."

Ryder guessed congratulations were out of the question, so he shrugged. "Not much you can say."

"You going to marry her?"

"That makes us sound like we're sixteen."

"You're not sixteen by a lot of years, but she's having your baby and you've loved her since she stepped on the bus her first day of kindergarten and pushed you out of her seat."

"You can't claim a seat on your first day of school, and I had seniority." He smiled at the memory of a little girl with blond pigtails and big eyes. She'd been madder than an old hen at him. She'd been that mad more than once in the past twenty-five years.

"So, marry her, have a family together."

"We're best friends. That isn't love. And she said no."

"She turned you down?"

"Yeah." He laughed a little. "She turned me down."

A smart guy would have let it go. Especially a guy who had always been pretty happy being single. Instead of letting it go, he'd invited her to go to the Coopers'. They had always gone together.

Tonight, though, it was a date. Tonight it was step one in him convincing her to say yes to his next proposal. A couple having a baby should get married.

He repeated that to his brother and Wyatt shook his head.

"Really, Ryder, you think that's the best line to use when proposing?"

"What am I supposed to say? She's Andie."

"Right, she's Andie. But no matter what, she's a woman. Maybe it's time you realized that and started treating her like one, instead of acting like she's one of the guys."

Andie, a woman? It seemed like a good time to end the conversation. He knew Andie well enough to know she didn't want him to start treating her like a girl. She definitely wouldn't want romance and flowery words.

She was Andie. He thought he knew a little something about what she liked and didn't like.

Andie walked into the kitchen and glanced at the clock. That was the last thing she wanted to do, check the time again. She'd been doing that all afternoon, almost as if she had a date.

Ryder wasn't a date.

She walked to the back door and leaned against the wall to shove her foot into one boot, and then the other. She didn't bother to untuck her jeans.

"I think this is a good idea." Etta stood at the kitchen sink. She dried a plate, put it in the cabinet and turned to face Andie.

Andie couldn't agree on the "good idea" part. How could it be a good idea, for her to show up with Ryder, making the two of them look like a couple?

"What?" Etta poured herself a cup of coffee and held it between her hands, watching Andie.

Okay, she must have made a face of some kind or Etta wouldn't be asking "What?"

Andie met her grandmother's serious gaze, felt the warmth of a smile that had been encouraging her for as long as she could remember.

"Everyone is going to know." Okay, it sounded ridiculous when she said it like that. "That sounds crazy, doesn't it?"

Etta shrugged, her big silver hoop earrings jangling a little. "Oh, maybe it sounds a little ridiculous. I was going to say that you're not fifteen, but I don't think it matters. You're having a baby. You're going to have to face that and face people. I promise you aren't going to be able to hide the fact."

"I know that."

"So, go with Ryder and make the best of things. Make the best of your relationship because that baby deserves for the two of you to act like grown-ups."

"We're working on it."

"I know you are. And Andie, I know you're working on having faith. I want you to remember that even if folks talk a little, even if they gossip, things will work out and your friends are going to stick by your side." Etta smiled. "And I would imagine even the ones gossiping will stick by you, once they get it out of their system."

"Thanks, Gran." She hugged Etta tight and then Ryder was knocking on the door. "Time to go."

"Have fun," Etta called out as Andie went out the back door.

Ryder stepped away from the porch rail he was leaning against and tipped his hat back as she walked out the door. She paused, for just a breath of a second and then let the door close behind her. He even reached out his hand for hers. But she couldn't go there, not yet. She wasn't quite ready for this new relationship, or the new Ryder.

A year ago if he'd grinned and winked at her, she would have told him to peddle his charms somewhere else, to some other female. She walked down the steps and Ryder followed, catching up and walking next to her.

"This is supposed to be a date." Ryder pushed the door of the truck closed when she tried to open it. She glared and he smiled.

"I wanted to open the door for you," he murmured.

"You don't have to. It looks as if you already loaded

my horse." Back up, slow down. She took in a deep breath. "Ryder, I've seen you on dates, I know that side of you, the guy who charms and courts. I don't want that. I want my best friend."

"I am your best friend."

"But that guy never opened the door for me. He also didn't try to hold my hand."

"I guess that's the truth." He looked down at the ground and then back up, his dark eyes hanging on to hers. "Do you know how to go back?"

The words bounced between them like a game of pinball gone bad. They just stood there, facing each other and facing reality. And Andie finally closed her eyes and shook her head.

He pulled the truck door open and motioned for her to get in. Andie sat down in the leather bucket seat and Ryder leaned, close enough for her to catch the scent of his soap and to notice that the hair curling under his hat was still damp. She reached, nearly touching those soft curls at the nape of his neck. But she couldn't make that connection because thinking about it stole her breath and made her thoughts turn to being held by him.

That was a lot more complicated than holding his hand.

Ryder backed away, as if his own thoughts troubled him more than he could admit. He winked and closed the truck door.

They rode in silence to the Circle C Ranch, which was owned by the Cooper family. George Strait played on the radio and the breeze whipped in through open windows. Andie loved autumn, had always looked forward to the changing temperatures, the leaves turning colors and the scent of smoke from fireplaces and woodstoves.

This year she looked forward to surviving, to getting past this moment and finding the next path of her future. With a child. She watched out the window, spotting a fox chasing across the field. It distracted her, but just for a moment and then her thoughts went back again.

To faith.

Faith. She closed her eyes and tried to dig up the tattered remnants of what had felt like faith two months ago, before she knew. She'd been seeking a new beginning, thinking she could work it all out, that she'd suddenly not be angry with her mother and that she would immediately forgive. Instead she was facing a totally different set of problems.

She didn't want her baby to grow up feeling like a problem.

She wouldn't let that happen.

"Cheer up, Andie, we'll get through this." Ryder's easy comment, said with a smile.

"Of course we will." She kept her gaze on the window, at the fields and neighboring farms.

"Or we'll give up, sing about gloom, despair and agony on us, and cry in our oatmeal?"

"Stop being an optimist." She turned up the radio, refusing to smile.

Ryder turned it back down. They were on the long drive that led to the Coopers'. A dozen or more trucks and trailers were parked in a gravel area to the south of the arena and people milled around, leading horses or standing in groups talking.

"I'm going to be an optimist, Andie." Ryder slowed the truck and parked. "I'm going to be the person you count on. I might not pull it off without a hitch, but I'm going to do my best."

"Okay, we'll try this out." She reached for the truck door. "But don't get creepy on me. I want to know that some things haven't changed."

But she knew better. They both knew better.

When they got out of the truck, he met her at the back of the trailer and she could tell that he had more to say. He held onto the latch of the trailer gate, looking inside at their horses.

"Listen, Andie, we've been through a lot together." He pulled up on the latch. "We went through the mess of my pretty dysfunctional family and you stood by me. We were kids, spitting on our hands and shaking, making a deal to forget about church because of what happened."

"It was wrong."

"I know, but it happened and my dad was the reason it happened. I've been thinking a lot about faith, and church. I've been thinking that maybe we should hang tight, stick this out together."

"This, you mean the pregnancy?"

He turned red. "Yeah, the pregnancy."

"You can barely say it."

"I can say it. And I can tell you that on Sunday I'll be picking you up for church."

"I'm holding you to that. But why now?"

"Because I'm not going to be my dad. This kid isn't going to have to worry about what his parents are doing or how messed up his family is."

"It could be a girl."

"I'm okay with a girl."

"That's good, because I think it is a girl." Andie

couldn't look at Ryder, not when they were talking about their baby, their future. But they weren't discussing marriage because he didn't love her and she wouldn't marry someone who didn't love her.

What if someday he really fell in love with someone, someone he wanted to marry? What then? Or what if she fell in love? She met his gaze, those dark eyes that she knew so well, eyes she had looked into a thousand times before.

What if she lost him as a friend? She had protected that friendship for years. How did she protect it now, when they were facing the biggest challenge of their lives?

"We should go." He opened the gate and she backed up. "Andie, I mean it. I know my track record is pretty shaky, but I'm in this for the long haul."

Lights came on around the arena and someone whooped out a warning for them to hurry.

"I know you are," she whispered.

Or at least she wanted to hope. But she couldn't dwell on that. This moment, facing friends, people they'd known their whole lives, was going to take all the courage she could muster.

For a brief second his fingers touched hers, grasping them lightly and then letting go. She tried not to think about high school, about how everything had been a new experience and holding hands had been more about belonging to someone and less about really being in love.

And belonging was okay.

He stepped into the trailer and backed her horse out. She took the lead rope and moved out of his way as he backed his horse out.

"Is it too late to change our minds?" She glanced up at him and he smiled.

"I think this is pretty permanent."

"I don't mean about the baby, you goof. I mean about this, about facing people, facing questions."

"I think it's too late. We're okay, Andie."

That was easy for him to say. She'd never felt less okay in her life. But he was getting their horses out of the trailer and if she was going to live her life in Dawson, she would have to deal with looks and whispers.

Ryder tightened the girth strap on his saddle and the big roan gelding that he'd brought with him twitched and stomped his back hooves. The roan was new and Ryder couldn't even get used to the horse's name. Half the time he couldn't remember it. But the name Red worked and the horse didn't seem to care.

"I'm going to tie Dusty and head over to the arena." Andie smiled but he didn't think the look met up with her eyes the way it should.

But he didn't question her. He wasn't going to start doing that. He was the baby's dad, not Andie's keeper. He was having a hard time keeping those two things separate.

"Okay. They're going to put out the barrels later. After steer wrestling and team roping."

"I know, but I'm not sure if I'll ride him tonight. These are younger riders with younger horses. I'll just give pointers if they want, but…"

"Not be a show-off."

She smiled, this time it looked like the real thing. "Yeah, something like that."

Someone yelled his name. "Gotta run."

She nodded and he almost didn't go. But he had to ride away, to keep this moment normal. He grabbed the saddle horn and swung into the saddle, nearly reaching for her hand and pulling her up with him once he was in the saddle. Instead he held tight to the reins and backed away.

But she hadn't moved. He nudged the red roan forward, close to her and she looked up, questions in her eyes. He didn't have a single answer for her. Instead he leaned and touched her cheek.

"I won't let you down."

She nodded and he rode off, leaving her there alone.

When he got to the arena Reese Cooper motioned him forward.

"You gonna rope with Clay tonight?"

Ryder nodded. "If he needs a partner, I'm the guy."

"He thought so." Reese Cooper was one of the middle Cooper kids. And there were a few of them. Ryder had lost track but he thought there were more than a dozen kids in the Cooper clan. Some were biological, some adopted and a few were foster kids that stayed.

Clay was adopted from Russia years ago. Five years ago he hit about sixteen and every girl in Dawson went crazy over him.

Reese had always been the center of attention.

Ryder wasn't bothered by the fact that the ladies loved the Cooper clan. It meant he could live his life without too many problems from the ladies of Dawson. It did kind of bother him that Andie had dated Reese.

"You gonna ride a bull tonight?" Clay walked up, sandy blond hair and gray eyes. His chaps were bright pink, because Clay didn't care what anyone thought of pink.

"I've thought about it." Ryder settled into the saddle of the roan gelding, holding him steady because the horse hadn't adjusted yet. Obviously the animal had led a quiet life up to this point. Tonight was a real test for him, what with lights, noise and a few rangy bulls bellowing from the pens to the side of the arena.

"Come on, then, we've got bulls ready." Clay spoke with an accent. Ryder tried not to smile because he hadn't figured out if the accent was real, or just something he used as a gimmick. It just seemed that when the kid had been ten or twelve, the accent hadn't been so thick.

Ryder glanced around the arena, finally spotting Andie. She was sitting on the row of risers with Jenna Cameron and the twins. And Jenna's new baby. Funny, thinking about Jenna married to Adam MacKenzie, retired pro football player, and owner of Camp Hope. Adam and Clint, now brothers-in-law, must have brought the bulls over.

That meant they'd be over by the pens on the opposite side of the arena.

"I'll ride a bull." Ryder backed his horse away from the two Coopers. "I'm going to say hello to Clint and Adam. And when you're ready to rope, let me know."

He rode around the back side of the arena, passing a few friends who waved but didn't stop him for a conversation. They looked at him, though, as if they knew. It wouldn't be long before everyone knew.

Clint and Adam were moving the bulls through the pens and into the chutes. Clint waved and then closed a gate between two pens.

"Ryder, good to see you here." Adam MacKenzie

walked toward him. "I've been meaning to tell you how much I appreciated the help with fences at Camp Hope."

"It was no big deal."

"Seriously, though, it meant a lot to us." Adam pulled a cola out of a cooler and tossed it his way.

"I didn't mind at all. The camp is a great thing for the kids, and for this community. Gives Dawson something to talk about besides…"

Besides him, for a change.

"How was your season?" Clint had joined them. A few years back the two had ridden to events together. Until Willow showed up in town. And Jenna's boys. The two, Clint and Willow, had fallen in love while taking care of Jenna's boys.

Now that Ryder thought about it, all of their lives had been taking some pretty serious direction changes. These guys didn't seem the worse for wear.

Of course for the last couple of years, Ryder had done a lot of teasing. His friends had all fallen, and they'd all changed their ways. They were family men, now. They went to church and took care of their wives and kids.

He hadn't really envied them.

And now they were staring at him, waiting for him to answer Clint's question.

"Good, really good. Brute turned into a great gelding. I don't know if I told you, but I bought his daddy last week. I needed a good stud horse on the place."

"That sounds like a career choice," Adam interjected with a smile.

"Yeah, maybe." He glanced toward the bleachers. He knew where Andie was sitting, even if he couldn't see her clearly from where he was.

"How's Wyatt?" Clint changed the subject and Ryder

met his gaze, saw his smile shift. "I saw him drive through town the other day."

Ryder shrugged, and he didn't sit down. "Wyatt's as good as he can be. It's been a long year for him. I don't know how a guy gets over that."

Gets over finding his wife dead and their two little girls in the playpen, crying. How did Ryder convince his brother there were good days ahead? How did he tell Wyatt to have faith, when Ryder had been ignoring God for as long as he could remember?

"Yeah, it won't be easy. But he's got a whole community behind him here." Clint reached for Red's reins. "Want me to hold him while you get your bull rope ready?"

"I guess if I'm going to ride a bull, I'd better get ready. You riding?"

Clint laughed. "No, I don't think so. We've got one little girl and Willow found this little boy in Texas. He's three and hearing impaired."

Ryder nodded because he didn't know what to say. He dismounted and handed Red over to Clint. "You and Willow are pretty amazing."

"Willow's amazing." Clint had hold of the roan and the horse was flighty, more flighty than Ryder liked from a roping horse.

"Ryder, up in two."

Ryder took the bull rope that Adam tossed at him. "Might want to borrow rosin from one of the other guys."

"Got it." Ryder pulled a glove out of his pocket. At least he'd remembered that. As he walked up to the chutes, he didn't look at Andie. Instead he took the Kevlar vest that Clay Cooper offered.

"It's one of Willow's bulls. Think you can handle him?" Clay asked with a grin that didn't do much to impress Ryder. Someone needed to take that guy out back and knock some of that vinegar out of him.

"I think I can handle him." Ryder pulled on the vest.

The bull that came through the chute was a big brindled bull with too much Brahma in its DNA. He didn't like to ride Brahma bulls. Not because they were meaner, bucked harder or went after a guy. He didn't like the hump. It knocked him off balance, made it hard for him to stay up on the bull rope.

As he settled onto the bull's back, Clay snickered, like he'd meant to put Ryder on the worst bull in the pen. He worked rosin into the bull rope and then Clay pulled it, tight, so Ryder could wrap it around his gloved hand.

The bull hunched in the shoot and then went up, front legs off the ground, pawing at the front of the chute. Ryder grabbed the side of the chute and pulled himself up, out of danger. The bull went back down on all fours. They started the bull rope process again.

As soon as Ryder had the rope around his hand and the bull was halfway sane in the chute, he nodded and the gate opened. The bull spun out of the chute, nearly falling and then righting himself. Ryder fell forward but got himself back into position when the bull bucked into his hand. Foam and slobber flew from the bull's head. The force of four hooves hitting the ground jarred his teeth.

He kept forward, his head tucked. The bull jerked him to the side and his body flung off the side of the bull, his hand still in the rope. A few jumps, a few hops and then the buzzer. He jerked his hand loose and rolled.

A bullfighter, another Cooper brother, jumped in

front of the bull, giving Ryder a chance to run for his life. That Brahma bull didn't play nice. It was stomping, trying to get his feet, get his legs as he scurried to get away.

As he jumped over the fence, Andie was there. Pale, shaking and pretty darned mad. He'd never seen her like that before. He considered going back in the arena with the bull.

He dropped down on her side of the fence and walked away, dragging the bull rope behind him. She followed. He couldn't do this here with everyone watching, wondering what was going on between them.

When he got to the back of the arena, to a spot where they could talk, he waited.

Andie walked up to him, her blond hair short and blowing in the soft, Oklahoma breeze. The air was dry, but still warm and the sun was starting to set. He didn't know why, but suddenly when he looked at her, he saw someone he hadn't seen before. He saw a woman with soft edges and a look in her eyes that could have sent him running if he hadn't known her better.

They'd gone places together, all of their lives they'd been together. Tonight felt different. Tonight they were one of the couples. He shifted a little and her mouth opened, like she was going to say something, and he was afraid to hear it.

His back hurt and his shoulder throbbed. He didn't need lectures.

"Don't." He shook his head a little and her mouth closed. And he'd hurt her. He hadn't meant to do that. "Not yet, Andie."

Not yet with a rush of female emotions and words, not from Andie. She'd drown him in that stuff and he wouldn't know how to make it work, not with a ton of emotions and hormones hitting him over the head.

He couldn't think like that.

"Fine." She walked away, slim and athletic, but always graceful. He remembered her in a leotard, forced to take ballet because Etta worried that she was too much of a tomboy. She'd hated it, but he remembered going to her one and only recital. She punched him in the gut that day, because he'd told her she looked pretty.

He watched her walk away. Gut punched. Sometimes she didn't even have to touch him. And every now and then, like right at that moment, he wanted to kiss her again. Even if it landed him on the ground.

Maybe later. He let the idea settle in his mind, even imagined holding her close on Etta's front porch.

"Hey, Andie, come back."

She stopped walking, but she didn't turn to face him. "You said not right now."

"I didn't mean for you to walk away. I meant for you to give me a chance to take a deep breath."

She turned, the wind catching her hair. She held it back with her hand and waited for him to walk up to her.

"I didn't know you were going to ride a bull tonight." She bit down on her bottom lip and looked away from him.

Her dad. He wanted to swear but he didn't. She'd seen her dad broken up a few too many times. She'd always disliked it when he rode bulls, said it brought back too many memories that she'd rather forget.

"I didn't plan on it, but Clay…"

"Pushed you into it?" She shook her head, not buying it.

"Yeah, kind of. I can't believe I let a twenty-one-year-old kid get to me that way."

She wiped his face. "Dirt on your cheek."

"Right." He wiped it again, in case she didn't get it all. And because it was a lot less disturbing when he did it.

"Ryder, would you mind if we went home? I really don't feel like I can do this tonight."

"Yeah, we can go home. Stay here while I get my horse."

Andie waited for Ryder. When he came toward her on the big roan gelding, she smiled. He rode up close and reached for her hand. She looked up, and he winked. Like old times, she thought. And she needed some old times. She took his hand and he moved his foot, giving her access to the stirrup.

He pulled and she settled behind him, her arms around his waist. The horse sidestepped a few times and then trotted a bumpy trot toward the trailer. Andie didn't mind the trot, not when this was the most normal thing that had happened to her in days.

As they rode past the arena and down the drive toward the trailer, Ryder slowed the horse to a walk. Andie leaned, resting her cheek against his back, against the soft cotton of his shirt. She breathed in deep of his scent and then she felt silly, because it was Ryder.

The horse came to a stop at the trailer, but neither of them moved. Andie didn't want to move, to break the connection between them. Ryder glanced back but he didn't say anything. But his hands touched her hands that were clasped around his middle.

"You okay?"

"I'm good. This is just the most familiar place I've been in a while. You know, riding like this with you. Remember when we used to take your old gelding out at night for long rides?"

"Yeah, I remember." His back vibrated with the depth of his voice.

"Those were good times."

"They were. And they aren't behind us, Andie. We're going to have a kid. We can teach him to ride a horse, and to rope a steer."

"Her."

"Right, her." He laughed and she sighed, but then she moved.

Time to leave the familiar for what was real now. "We should go home."

"Give me your hand." He held her hand and she dropped to the ground. "Andie, we'll have more good times."

"I know." She blinked fast to chase away the tears that sneaked up on her.

Ryder landed on the ground next to her. He led the horse back to the trailer and tied it while he pulled off the saddle. Dusty whinnied a greeting because he'd been left behind, tied but not saddled. She untied him and led him to the back of the trailer.

"So, are you okay?" She handed the horse over to Ryder.

"I'll be sore tomorrow. I'm sure everyone will say that I had to leave early because I'm getting soft."

"That's never bothered you before."

"No, and it still doesn't." He led her horse into the trailer. "Go ahead and get in the truck. I'll have them settled and ready to go in a minute."

Andie nodded and she didn't argue. Tonight it was okay to let Ryder do this for her. She climbed into his truck and waited.

A few minutes later he was behind the wheel of the truck and they were easing down the driveway and then turning on to the road that led back to Dawson. It was only minutes before they reached the city limits and tiny Dawson. As they drove past the Mad Cow, Ryder slowed and pulled into the parking lot. There were a half dozen trucks and teenagers sitting on tailgates.

A dozen years ago, they had been the teenagers hanging out in Dawson, not going to Tulsa or Grove on a Friday night because the drive was too far, the gas too expensive. Dating in Dawson had been cheap and easy; hanging out in town, going to a rodeo or riding practice bulls from a local stock contractor's pen of livestock.

More often than not they ended up somewhere like the Coopers', where it wasn't for prizes or money, just for fun and practice.

Memories piled up and Andie smiled as Ryder parked his truck next to an old Ford. She understood. For a few minutes he wanted to be that kid again, wanted those easier days back. She got out with him and walked to the front of the truck.

One of the kids had set up practice horns at the outside of the circle of trucks. They were farm kids in roper boots, faded jeans and T-shirts, their girlfriends were hanging together on the back of one truck, girls in tank tops and cutoff shorts. Dawson hadn't changed in years.

The boys grouped around Ryder and Andie leaned against his truck to watch, the way she'd watched years ago. But years ago Ryder had flirted and she'd pretended it didn't matter because they were just friends.

"What are you guys up to?" Ryder took the rope that one of the boys held out to him. He ran it through his hands.

"Just hangin' out and practicing up for next weekend. Ag Days is next Saturday and the Junior Championship Rodeo." A tall boy with straw-colored hair and acne spoke up. Andie recognized him as a kid who had moved with his parents to a neighboring farm. "That sure is a nice stud horse you've got now."

Ryder shrugged off the compliment and Andie wanted to ask the questions, about the horse and when he'd gotten it. He'd never bought a horse without telling her.

She'd seen a load of cattle come in, too. The big trailer had hauled the livestock down his driveway and turned them loose in his empty pasture, the one he didn't use for alfalfa. The cattle were there, now, grazing around oil wells that pumped a slow steady stream of crude oil into holding tanks by the road.

Now he was roping fake horns, as if he was going through some kind of midlife crisis. Because of her.

Ryder looped the rope again, swinging, letting it go. It slipped through the air, landing effortlessly on the horns. She remembered watching a few minutes of an outdoor program about fly-fishing in the northern states. There had been a beauty and grace to the casting of the line. Roping, effortlessly the way Ryder did it, had the same grace.

After freeing the rope from the horns, Ryder handed it back to the kid and then gave them a few pointers. He watched as they took turns, and then he gave them more advice.

When had they grown up, she and Ryder? When had

they become the older people in town? Andie sighed at the thought of how far, and yet not so far, her life had come from the days of high school.

A dozen years ago Ryder had been one of these kids, under these same bright streetlights on the same dark pavement. Like these kids, he'd been dreaming of the future, dreaming of the best horse, the buckle, the money. No, never the money for Ryder, but winning. He'd always wanted to win. He'd won in basketball and baseball. He won in the rodeo arena.

As much as he'd won, she knew he'd lost a lot, too. His life hadn't been charmed. His parents had seen to that. And losing them, he still hurt over that loss. She could see the shadows of the pain in his eyes. There were days that he looked like the loneliest guy in the world. He had a quick smile, though. It flashed easily, creating that dimple in his chin. It was disarming, that smile. If a person didn't know better, they'd think he'd never felt pain, never been hurt. She knew better.

Two months ago she had seen the lonely look in his eyes.

A quick cramp in her stomach ended the memories. She drew in a deep breath and fought against the knife-sharp pain. Ryder turned, his eyes narrowed and he didn't say anything. He patted the boy with the straw-colored hair on the shoulder and said he'd be back soon.

As he walked toward her, she saw his fear, felt her own. Fear or relief?

She closed her eyes because she didn't want to know, didn't want to recognize the look in his eyes, or look too deep into her own heart.

"You okay?"

She nodded, because the pain had passed. "Yeah, I'm fine. But I think I'm ready to go home."

Chapter 8

Sunday morning Ryder pulled his truck up the driveway of Etta's house, fighting a serious case of nerves
that matched any that he'd met up with on the back of a
bull. He couldn't imagine feeling worse on his wedding
day, if he'd ever planned on getting married.

Going to church for the first time in over a dozen
years was definitely up there on the list of things that
were hard to do.

And that thought pulled his attention off the road and
drew it to the glove compartment where he'd tossed the
ring that Andie had rejected last week. Last week when
he'd thought having a baby meant two people ought to
do the right thing and get married. Obviously Andie
was of a different mind. And that should have cut him
loose, should have sent him back down the road and on
his way to a team roping event in Dallas.

Instead he was as determined as ever to prove to Andie that he could be a dad, even if she didn't think he could be a husband. A dad did the right thing, even went to church. He was pretty sure that's what an upstanding dad did. No, he took that back. His own dad had gone to church.

He was going to do better than that.

As he parked, the front door opened. Etta stepped onto the porch, a vision in purple and yellow, a floppy straw hat on her head. She waved with a hand that sparkled with jewelry and went on with the green plastic watering pot, tipping it to water plants that turned her front porch into some kind of crazy jungle.

He was lucky if weeds grew in his flower gardens. At least weeds covered up the bare spaces and had blooms that added some color to the place.

He got out of his truck and walked across the lawn, the grass turning brown, but autumn mums bloomed in the flowerbeds. Etta set her watering can down and waited at the top of the steps. He clunked up the steps, his boots loud on the wood.

"What has you up here so bright and early on a Sunday morning?" Etta grabbed her watering can again and moved to a planter overflowing with purple blooms that he didn't recognize.

"I guess I'm here to go to church." He glanced off in the direction of the barn, trying to make sense of the crazy turn his life had taken. A calf was mooing and somewhere a dog barked. He wondered if the animals needed to be fed and how much damage Andie would do to him if he did those things for her.

Etta chuckled a little. "You're going to church?"

"Isn't that what you've been telling me to do for the past eighteen years?"

"I guess I have. But why now?"

"Because it's the right thing to do."

"Oh, I see." She headed back into the house, carrying the green watering can. The open door let out the aroma of coffee and something baked with cinnamon. He followed Etta through the door.

"You don't think I should go?" He followed her down the sunlit hallway.

"Of course you should go." She set the can next to the back door and kicked off her slippers. "Grab a cup of coffee and a muffin. Don't take the chocolate chip muffins, those are for our new pastor."

"Gotcha." He walked into the kitchen, always at home here. He didn't have to search for a cup, didn't have to ask where Etta kept the sugar. He'd been a part of this family for as long as he could remember.

But the idea of going to church had settled in the pit of his stomach like old chili. He'd been talked about his entire life. His family had been talked about. His dad had kept the town loaded with reasons to gossip. He should be used to being a conversation piece for the people of Dawson.

He hadn't worked too hard on his own life, to make himself different. He'd dated women whose names he couldn't remember. He'd spent his teen years chased from fields by farmers who didn't want their hay crops ruined by a kid with a four-wheel drive truck.

Now it was different. He sipped the coffee that he'd poured for himself and stood at the sink, looking out the kitchen window. Etta's barn needed to be painted. He sighed and set down his cup.

"What are you here for?"

He turned, bumping his cup but grabbing it before it slid into the sink and spilled. He held it as she walked across the room. He'd never looked at her this way, in the early morning, seeing her as a woman and not his best friend. She'd always been his best friend.

Today she was definitely a woman. Her dark blue dress touched her knees and curved in the right places. Her blond hair framed her face, the color of the dress making her eyes more vivid. Her belly was still flat.

"Don't look at my stomach." She grabbed a cup and poured herself a cup of coffee.

He swallowed more emotions than he could name. She was standing next to him, not looking at him. And she was soft and feminine. She didn't smell like leather. Instead a floral scent floated in the air around her. It swished his way when she moved.

When she turned to look at him, lifting a brow and giving him a look that asked what in the world he thought he was looking at, he shrugged. And he took a step closer. That wasn't a Sunday morning thing to do, stepping closer, sliding his arms around her waist.

She wiggled free and pushed him back.

"Back off, cowboy." She moved to the other side of the kitchen and picked up a muffin.

"You aren't supposed to eat the chocolate chip muffins," he warned.

"Why not?"

"They're for the new pastor."

"Well, I'm pregnant and I'm eating it."

He shrugged again. She'd have to deal with Etta. He watched as she took a few bites, closing her eyes as she chewed. And then there were footsteps on the stairs. Andie's eyes flew open. She grinned, a wicked grin that should have been a warning, and tossed the muffin at him.

He barely caught it, and then Etta walked into the kitchen.

"What are you doing eating those muffins after I told you not to?"

Ryder glanced at Andie and her smile was a little wicked, a little sweet. He had to take the fall for her. "Sorry, I couldn't help myself."

"No, I guess you couldn't. Self-control doesn't seem to be your strongest character trait lately. Well, come on, let's go to church." Etta grabbed the basket of muffins and slid them into a bag. "You can drive."

As they walked out the door, he slid close to Andie. "You owe me."

"I don't think so."

Her voice was soft and her arm brushed his. Everything was changing. Or maybe he hadn't let himself notice before that Andie made everything in his life feel a little better, a little easier.

On the way out the door she paused for a second, closing her eyes and leaning a little toward him.

"Andie, are you okay?"

She nodded. "I'm fine. We need to go or we'll be late."

He hadn't expected to feel this way, as if he needed to protect her, even if he didn't know what to protect her from. But this was the second time in a week he'd seen that look on her face, and the second time he'd felt a stab of fear he hadn't expected to feel.

Andie sat next to Ryder on the third pew from the front of the church. Etta liked to joke that the power of

God was down front, so the people in the back were missing out. Andie felt as if the power of two hundred pairs of eyes was in the back and it was all focused on her. And Ryder. It had been eighteen years since they'd been in church together.

His father's actions had pushed them away from God. Her actions had brought them back. Because as much as she'd tried to be angry with God for what had happened to Ryder's dad, she couldn't hide from His presence or her need for this place and faith.

When it had all crumbled in around her, she hadn't wanted to run from God. Instead she'd run to Him. Which is exactly what Etta had always said would happen. And, as Etta liked to remind, she happened to be right most of the time.

"I'd forgotten what it felt like here." Ryder leaned close, his shoulder against hers. She closed her eyes and nodded, because everything hurt too much. Him never loving her hurt. Her stomach hurt. She looked forward, telling herself the pain that had started earlier meant nothing.

"It feels like peace," she whispered, wanting that peace.

"Yeah, that's what it is." Ryder raised his arm and circled her, pulling her closer to his side. The choir sang the closing hymn and Pastor Jeffries smiled out at the congregation. His style of ministry was different than that of Pastor Todd. It was less like a best friend, more like a father.

Final prayer. She needed that prayer. She need for the service to end. As the congregation filed out of their pews, down the aisle, Andie leaned forward, resting her head on the back of the pew in front of her. She took a deep breath and waited for the pain to pass.

"Honey, what's wrong?" Etta's strong voice whispered near her ear. People around her were talking.

"I think I need to leave." She stood up, ignoring Ryder's concern, his hand reaching for hers and Etta standing up behind her. "I have to go."

Panic was shooting through her, making breathing difficult and mixing with the pain that cramped in her lower abdomen. She wiped at tears that slid down her cheeks and tried to smile at the people asking if she was okay, trying to stop her with a cautious hand. Ryder was right behind her, not touching her, but he was there.

As she hurried down the steps of the church toward Ryder's truck, he reached for her arm and pulled her to a stop. Her eyes were blurring with unshed tears and his face hovered close. She wanted to sink into his arms.

"What's wrong?" His voice was hard, but barely above a whisper and his hands held her arms tight, as if she would have escaped. But escape wasn't her plan, not from him, just from the crowds of people in the church, asking questions or staring after her with questions in their eyes.

"I think I need to go to the hospital."

And then Etta was there. Andie drew in a deep breath, breathing past the stress and through the pain. It had been a twinge that morning, but had gotten worse during church.

Etta took her by the arm and led her to the side as people walked past.

"What's wrong?"

Andie drew in another deep breath. "Cramping."

"Then we're definitely going to the hospital." Etta herded them toward Ryder's truck as she talked.

"I don't want to…" *lose my baby.* She couldn't say it.

"Things happen in a pregnancy, Andie. There are different phases and pains. This could be completely normal." Etta pulled the truck door open and motioned for Andie to climb in. "You're going to be fine. The baby is fine."

Andie nodded as she got into the truck, into the seat next to Ryder who was already starting the truck, practically backing out before Etta got the door closed.

"Maybe you could let an old lady get in the truck before you start driving." Etta hooked her seat belt. "Ryder, take a deep breath and just consider this as practice. Lots of unexpected things happen when we have children."

Andie closed her eyes. Prayers slipped through her mind, getting tangled with guilt. Guilt because she shouldn't be having a baby and because, after thinking that she didn't want this, now she was going to ask God to take care of her child?

They drove the thirty minutes to the hospital in twenty. Andie opened her eyes to the flashing lights of an ambulance ahead of them, pulling through the drive in front of the emergency room. This was reality. She touched her stomach and wondered, even though she didn't want to, if she would still be pregnant when she left the hospital.

And if she wasn't… She closed her eyes against the pain that moved to her heart, if she wasn't how would she and Ryder look at one another tomorrow?

Ryder pulled up in front of the door and stopped. He glanced at her as he turned the truck off, his smile strong, the look in his eyes telling her that everything would be okay. And she was a kid again, worried that her dad wasn't coming home. But Ryder was there. Always there for her.

"We're fine, Andie."

"I know."

He was out of the truck and when she tried to step out next to him, he shook his head and scooped her up. He carried her into the building like she was a little girl with a scraped knee and she tried to tell him she could walk. He shook his head each time she opened her mouth.

"I can walk," she finally managed to say.

"I don't want you to talk."

Etta was next to them, breathing fast as she hurried to keep up with Ryder. "Don't argue. For once in your life, don't argue."

"I'm too heavy." She leaned into his neck and he held her closer, tighter. Her doctor met them at the doors to the E.R. That was the great thing about small towns, and switching to a doctor closer to home.

"What's up, Andie?" Dr. Ashford motioned them into an exam room.

"I've been cramping. It was light at first and I wasn't worried, but today it's worse."

"Okay, let's examine you and see what we can find out."

Ryder practically dumped her on the hospital bed. And then he was gone, the curtain of the exam room flapping behind his exit. Andie shook her head. So much for her hero. Her knight in shining armor. The Lone Ranger. No, wait, that was more like it. The Lone Ranger always rode in to rescue the woman and then hightailed it out of town before he could get too attached.

She couldn't let it bother her. She knew Ryder, knew why he bounced from relationship to relationship. She knew him well enough that she should have known better than to attach even the vaguest of dreams to him.

But then, he had just carried her in here. And she wasn't light.

"Andie, I'm going to do an ultrasound and examine you." Dr. Ashford stood next to the bed. "Do you want someone in here with you?"

Andie shook her head. "I'm a big girl."

But her body trembled from shock as reality set in. She was losing her baby. Ryder being with her wouldn't stop that from happening. And if she was going to fall apart, she wanted to be alone.

Chapter 9

Ryder paced across the waiting room, again. And then he sat down, again. He felt as if he'd been doing that same thing for hours. It had only been one hour, though. He bristled at the idea of waiting without any recognition of his presence here. He wanted a few answers, at least for someone to tell him Andie was okay.

He'd already asked the receptionist, twice, if she'd find something out for him. Or get someone to give him answers. She'd smiled a pained smile that he thought could have been a little nicer and told him to take a seat and she'd see if she could find something out. He'd watched and she hadn't left her desk or picked up the phone.

Etta grabbed his arm when he started to stand up again.

"If you bother that receptionist or pace across this

floor one more time, I'm going to knock you down," she whispered. And he was pretty sure she meant it.

She had a magazine in her hand, rolled up. He hadn't seen her open it and read. She kept picking up magazines, flipping through pages and then putting them down. She wasn't much better off than he was, but he wasn't about to point that out to her.

"Well, what am I supposed to do? I can't go back there. No one will tell me what's going on. What else can I do but pace?"

"Sit there and pray."

"Pray?" He drew in a deep breath and brushed his hand over his face. How much was God wanting to hear from him?

"Yes, pray. What else are you going to do in this situation?"

"I guess you're right." It wasn't as if he'd ever stopped believing, he'd just had a hard time with church after what happened with his dad. Something like that left a bad taste in a guy's mouth.

The door to the emergency room opened and the doctor walked across the room, smiling. "You can see her now."

"How is she?" Ryder stood up.

"I'm afraid I can't discuss that with you."

"What?" He growled the question, hadn't meant to, but it roared out of him, causing a few people to glance their way.

"I'm Andie's doctor and she has a right to privacy. But you can go back and see her."

He shook his head as he moved past the doctor, past the receptionist's desk and through the door that opened as he got closer. Anger had boiled up inside him, more anger than he'd felt in a long time. He tried to tamp it back down, to get control before he faced Andie. It wasn't her fault.

It wasn't even the fault of that smug-faced receptionist.

"Ryder, calm down." Etta followed him and for the first time, he couldn't listen, couldn't take her advice.

His gut had been tied up in knots and fear had shoved common sense out the door. Fear and a really healthy dose of anger were now tied together in a pretty untidy package.

He pushed back the curtain of the exam room, ready to let Andie know how he felt about not being included in the list of people who had a right to know how she was. He shouldn't have to remind her that this was his baby, too.

When he saw her, he couldn't speak. He couldn't do anything when faced with the reality of Andie curled on her side, the blue of a hospital gown over her shoulders and the white blanket up to her chin. He waited at the foot of her bed and Etta walked into the room. Etta looked at the monitors, looked at Ryder and then took a seat on the edge of the bed. She hitched her yellow purse over her shoulder and sat there for a minute.

"How are you, sugar bug?" Etta patted Andie's shoulder.

Ryder had wanted to do that. He had wanted to offer words of comfort. He hadn't known how. That was Etta's job. Besides that, he didn't know how to comfort when he was the reason she was here. He was the reason she was hurting.

And she didn't want him to know what was going on.

He wanted to throw something. Instead he shoved

his hat a little tighter down on his head and waited for Andie to say something, anything.

He'd never seen her so quiet. Never.

"I'm fine." Andie reached up to pat her granny's hand. "The baby…" She wiped her hand across her face. "I still have a baby."

Ryder closed his eyes and said a big "Thank You." That's how two weeks could change the way a guy thought about life. A man could go from living for himself, to being willing to give up everything to keep a baby safe.

On the way to the hospital, he'd had to turn off the radio. A Tim McGraw song about a man on his knees, begging God to "not take the girl" had come on. He and Andie hadn't been able to look at each other, or talk about it. Ryder had turned the song off and Andie had whispered "Thank you."

"What did the doctor say?" Etta smoothed the blankets and waited, patiently. But Ryder knew Etta. He knew patience was something she could show, but he knew on the inside she was ready to push down walls to get answers and get something done.

"Time will tell." Andie whispered the words and her shoulders shook. Ryder started to move forward, but Etta was way more qualified than he was to handle this situation.

"Well, time does have a way of doing that."

"I don't want to lose my baby." Andie turned, pulling the blanket up, avoiding looking at him. Her eyes were puffy and red and her blond hair tangled around her face, sticking to tear-stained cheeks.

When she'd lost her dad he'd been the one to hold her. They had always held each other. And now she was avoiding looking at him. Awkward had never been a part of their relationship.

Until now. And it scared the life out of him. He'd made a pretty good show of never needing anyone. And all that time he'd been lying to himself, because he needed Andie. He needed her because she was the most consistent thing in his life.

There were probably other reasons. He knew there were, but right now he couldn't put it all together. He just knew that she had to be safe. She had to be okay. And it wasn't just about the baby.

"I know you don't want to lose this baby." Etta smoothed the hair from Andie's face, as if she was fifteen, not twenty-eight.

Andie sobbed again, shuddering. "I didn't want this baby. This isn't how I would want my child's life to start. This isn't the way a child wants to grow up thinking about itself. But now... Now I can't stand the idea of losing it, of losing my baby."

Their baby. Ryder almost said something, but he bit back the words. He was definitely not experienced at female emotions. He was used to the Andie that threw rocks in the creek and could break about the rankest horses in the county. She knew how to hang on tight through some wild rides. He'd never seen her get thrown.

"Sweetheart, you don't know God's plan. I have to believe, have to pray, that God's going to take care of you and this little one of yours."

Andie covered her face with her hands and Ryder couldn't stand still, couldn't let her hurt that way. There hadn't been a moment in their lives that they hadn't gone through the hard times together.

He wasn't going to let her go through this alone.

He didn't want to go through it alone.

In a few steps he was next to her. When he wrapped his arms around her, she buried her face in his shoulder and he held her close. Etta moved and he took her place on the bed, with Andie's arms around his waist. He leaned, resting his lips on the top of her head.

"I'm not going to let you down." He brushed blond hair back from her cheeks. "I won't let this baby down."

"I know you won't."

"Andie, the doctor wouldn't tell me anything. I really need to know what's going on." He brushed her cheek with a kiss and kept holding her.

She pulled back, nodding. "I know. I'll make sure she knows that you have to be included."

"Thank you." So, he felt a little better.

The curtain moved and Dr. Ashford walked in, clipboard in hand, glasses on her head. She smiled and pulled the glasses down, settling them on the bridge of her nose.

"Andie, I'm going to release you because there isn't a lot we can do but wait. I know that won't be easy, but that's what we have. The one thing you can do is take it easy and call me if you experience any bleeding." Dr Ashford stepped forward with a tube. "Here's the cream I told you about."

"Thank you, Dr. Ashford."

"Wait a second. I need more information. Isn't there anything we can do?" Ryder reached for Andie's hand and held it tight. Man, this wasn't the way it was supposed to go. He didn't want words like *time* and *waiting*.

"At this point there really isn't anything we can do. I'm sorry to be so blunt, but miscarriages happen in the first trimester. We don't always know why and we can't always keep it from happening. At this point the baby's heartbeat is steady and so we give Andie time. And she rests."

He met the doctor's gaze, and he was mad. She was a doctor. She was supposed to do something. That's why she was there, taking care of them. "She can stay in the hospital."

"Ryder." Andie squeezed his hand.

"Andie, we have to do more than wait."

The doctor put on a patient but slightly pained smile that didn't help him feel better, it just made him feel more out of control.

"If Andie was farther along and having contractions, we could put her in the hospital or give her medication to stop labor."

"So do that." Was that his voice, out of control, unreasonable? Dr. Ashford gave him another of her "poor man" smiles. He wasn't her first time at the circus; he was sure she'd met other clowns like him.

"This isn't a situation where medication will help. This is a situation for…"

"Prayer," Etta whispered.

The doctor nodded. "I would like for Andie to take it easy for a week or two, until the cramping stops. Let's see if we can get her through the third month, make it through the first trimester, and then we'll go from there."

Andie sniffled and her chin came up, because she wasn't giving up. He wanted to feel that strong right now, but instead, he felt like a kid who didn't have a clue.

The doctor kept talking, but when the words headed

in the direction of female stuff, Ryder walked to the door. Or maybe hurried. These were words he could handle in connection to a cow or horse, but not to Andie.

He stopped at the curtain.

"I'll be waiting out here. When can she leave?"

"As soon as we get paperwork filled out. Straight home, straight to bed. She can get up to use the restroom and take showers. She can walk to the couch. But that's going to be it for now."

Ryder nodded and walked out. As he walked away he could still hear them talking, still discussing the best chance for the baby. He didn't want to hear about odds. He wanted to know that God was going to do something.

He hadn't expected that, to feel like this so soon, as if he'd push down a mountain to make sure his baby was safe. Baby. He remembered the ultrasound picture that showed something that looked like a tadpole. That was his kid in that picture.

He walked through the E.R., past other curtained cubicles, through doors that slid open as he approached, and then outside into cooler air and a light mist. He took off his hat and stood on the sidewalk with mist turning to rain. The sky was a heavy gray and the wind had died down.

For the first time he knew how it felt to need God so badly he'd bargain. He'd give himself for the life of his unborn child. He knew how it felt to be that man in Tim McGraw's song, begging God to take him, but not the girl, not the baby.

The door behind him opened. He glanced back and it was Etta. She smiled and walked over, looking up at the sky. "It's raining out here, Ryder."

"Yes, ma'am."

"You finding God out here?"

"Trying."

"He's as close as the words you're speaking. So pray hard, boy. And then get that truck and drive it up to the building so we can take her home."

"I'll do that."

She touched his arm. "Ryder, this is going to work out."

He nodded and walked away. He hoped he wasn't going to let them all down. He didn't ever want a kid to feel the way he had. Let down.

When Andie got in his truck fifteen minutes later he was thinking about how he didn't want to let her down, either. He never wanted to find her alone, crying because he'd broken her heart.

Too many times in his life he'd seen his mom that way.

"You okay?" He shifted into gear and pulled away from the hospital.

"I'm not sure."

No, of course she wasn't. He wasn't sure, either.

Andie woke up late the following morning. She knew it was late because she could hear Etta downstairs washing dishes and the sun slashed a bright ray of light across her room. She'd made it through the night. It had been a long night. Ryder had refused to leave until about midnight. That's when Etta finally convinced him that his presence wasn't going to keep bad things from happening and they all needed some sleep.

She touched her belly, because her baby was in there, still safe, still a part of her world. "Stay in there, baby."

"Keep her safe." She looked up, knowing God heard. She tried to hold on to that faith, and not to fear. Every wrong thing she'd ever done flashed through her mind, taunting her as if her mistakes were a reason for God to take this baby, to make her pay. She pushed the thoughts from her mind.

Footsteps on the stairs signaled company. She waited and then there was a rap on her door.

"Come in."

"Are you decent?"

Ryder's voice. She looked down, at the sweats she'd slept in and the ragged T-shirt. "I guess so."

He pushed the door open and she brushed a hand through her hair, hoping to look less like something the cat coughed up and then trying to tell herself it didn't matter. It was just Ryder.

"I brought your breakfast."

He held a tray with a white foam container from the Mad Cow. He put the tray down, sitting it across her lap. She knew what was in the container. Pecan pancakes. And for the first time she knew she couldn't eat them. Her stomach turned and rolled, the way it had when she'd been ten and they'd gone to Branson for vacation. The more she thought of those curvy roads and the pecan pancakes...

"Move it, quick." Her stomach roiled and she dived as he reached for the trash can and stuck it under her face. If she breathed in, she'd lose it. If she closed her eyes and didn't breathe, that wouldn't be good, either.

"You okay?" He leaned down, a little green.

"Get rid of the pancakes."

"Got it." He grabbed the tray and as he headed out

the door, she sat up. He peeked back inside the room. "Sorry about that."

"Not a problem," she groaned and leaned back on the pillows.

"I wanted to do something." He stepped back into the room, without the tray, and leaned against her dresser. He picked up a framed picture of the two of them on a pony she'd had years ago. His gaze came up, connecting with hers. "I feel like I need to take care of you."

"I don't want you to feel that way." She pulled her legs up and sat cross-legged on her bed. "This isn't us. We aren't uncomfortable, trying to figure out where we fit in each other's lives. I don't want you bringing me pancakes and holding the trash can for me. I don't want you to feel like you have to do this."

"But I do. You didn't get this way alone."

She stuck her fingers in her ears and shook her head, juvenile, but effective. "Don't."

He picked up the picture again. "It would have been easier to stay ten, wouldn't it?"

"Yeah, that'd be perfect. But it doesn't work that way."

"No, it doesn't."

"You don't have to stay here and take care of me. I know you have things to do, places to go."

"People to see?" He straightened and moved away from the dresser, a lanky cowboy with faded jeans and a hat that had been stepped on a few times. "I'm here, Andie. I'm in this for the long haul. This is the place where I'm supposed to be."

Etta popped into the room. "You're up. And you don't have to worry about a thing. Ryder fed the horses for you, and he even helped me pick the last of my green beans."

Andie swept her gaze from her aunt to Ryder. "You don't have to feed for me. You don't have to take care of me."

She didn't want to get used to him being there for her this way.

"Before you have this conversation, I wanted you to know that Caroline called. She asked about you and I told her what happened." Etta stood inside the door, not looking as apologetic as Andie would have liked.

"I wish you wouldn't have." The last thing she needed was for Caroline, her mother, to come rushing back to Dawson.

"She asked and I couldn't lie. And she said to tell you she loves you."

This couldn't be her life. Andie rubbed her hands over her face, trying hard to think about the mother who left, and the mother who had finally returned. Caroline had claimed she couldn't do it, couldn't be a mother to both of her daughters. At that moment it was harder than ever to understand how Caroline could walk away.

"It's okay, Gran." Andie smiled up at her grandmother. "Life changes, right?"

"It does change."

Etta slipped back out of the room. Andie could hear her careful steps going down the stairs. Ryder moved to the chair next to Andie's bed and sat down, taking off his hat and tossing it on the table next to him.

"You don't have to be here every day."

"You need to get over this." He raked his hand through his hair and let out a sigh. "I'm here because I want to be."

"You're here because you feel guilty, or obligated."

"No, I'm here because I'd be here no matter what the situation. When have I not been there for you?"

She could have told him that he hadn't been there for her two months ago, when he hadn't answered her phone calls. But then she remembered last night and how he'd held her while she cried, how he'd been there for her when it really counted.

He had always been there for her.

"I know," she whispered. "But this isn't easy, not being able to get up."

"I have a feeling it'll only get worse."

"Thanks." She wiped at her eyes and ignored how he shifted in the chair and fiddled with his hat, not making eye contact.

"How do you feel today?" he finally asked.

"Cagey, kind of angry and definitely tired of this bed."

He laughed. "You've only been there for about ten hours. Multiply a few times over and maybe you'll have an idea what the next couple of weeks are going to be like."

"Thanks for the optimism."

She leaned back in the bed and tried to push the days and hours from her mind. She could do this for her baby.

Ryder stood up, because he had a lot to get done, but first, he had to try one more time. He reached into his pocket and pulled out the ring that had been his grandmother's. He'd loved her, his grandmother. She had died when he was barely ten, but he remembered her smile, the way she'd listened when he told stories.

Andie focused on the pancakes that he'd set on the dresser. "I'll take those now."

"Okay." He reached for the foam container but he didn't hand it to her yet. She stared up at him, blue eyes rimmed with the dark remnants of mascara from the day before.

"Stop."

"What?" He stopped in the center of her bedroom, the room that hadn't ever changed. It still had framed photos of horses, a quilt made by her great grandmother and an antique rocking chair near the window.

Some things didn't change. And some did. No use looking in the rearview mirror when you're driving forward. An old rodeo friend had told him more than once. Greg was a rodeo clown and he raised race horses in Oklahoma City. He had a wife and kids, a real family.

People did manage to have families. He knew that. Men managed to stay married and stay faithful. Kids grew up with two parents in a home where they felt loved.

"Stop looking like that." Andie hugged her knees close to her body.

Ryder pulled the ring out of his pocket. He held it in one hand, the box of pancakes in the other and Andie's eyes widened as she watched him. She shook her head a little.

"Andie, please marry me. I haven't done the right thing very often in my life, but I really feel like this is the one time that I'm doing what needs to be done."

She actually laughed. "Seriously? That's your proposal."

He shoved the ring back into his pocket and handed her the pancakes. "What else am I supposed to say?"

"Love, Ryder. Marriage is about love and forever. Not 'doing what needs to be done.' Seriously, that's lame."

Well, thanks for that piece of information. He bristled because she was still smiling and he felt like a stinking fool.

"You'll have to forgive me if proposals aren't my strong suit. This isn't what I expected. I'm pretty sure it isn't what you expected. But we can sure do the right thing."

"I know we can, but this isn't it. I haven't put a lot of thought into marriage, either, but I can tell you one thing for certain, I'm not going to marry someone who doesn't love me."

"Love doesn't have too many guarantees, Andie. I know a lot of divorced couples who claimed to love one another. We've been through a lot together. We could make this work."

"And you'd end up resenting me. You might end up resenting the baby." She glanced up, her eyes were vivid blue and seeking something from him. He didn't have a clue what she wanted him to say.

She'd already pointed out that the proposal had been wrong. If that was the case, then he was pretty close to clueless.

"Fine, if the answer is no, then I'll live with it. But I'm this baby's father and I'm going to be here. I'm going to be a good dad."

"I know you will, Ryder."

Her eyes were soft and she already looked like someone's mom. And he still felt like the guy he'd been a month ago. Maybe she was right, he wasn't ready for this, for fatherhood.

Did other men just come equipped for this role?

"I have to go."

"Where…" She smiled. "I'm sorry, it isn't any of my business."

"I've got some bull calves that need to be taken care of. The vet's coming out this afternoon. Johnny Morgan is coming out to look at that mare I've been trying to sell."

"I wanted that mare."

"I thought you changed your mind."

She looked down and they were both thinking the same thing; he knew they were. She wouldn't be riding for a while.

Finally she smiled. "Yeah, I guess I've changed my mind. Johnny wants her for his daughter. I'm not sure that's a good match."

"I'll try to switch him to another horse then." He started to turn away, and he should have. Instead he leaned to kiss her cheek, just her cheek. "I'll be back later to check on you. Eat your breakfast."

She nodded and he walked to the door. His hand went to his pocket, to the ring that she'd rejected twice. She wanted to marry someone who loved her. He shook his head, not sure what to think about that.

If she didn't marry him, she'd marry someone else. Someday some other guy would know the right words. The thought turned around inside him. He didn't like to think of her married to another man. He tried not to picture it, her with another man's ring on her finger. His kid being raised by some other guy. What if that guy wasn't good to them? He thought if that happened, he'd have to hurt someone.

Or convince her to marry him before it happened. But the way things were going, he was far from convincing her that marriage was the right thing to do.

Chapter 10

Andie woke up to the sound of footsteps coming down the hall toward her room. Lighter steps, not Ryder's. She blinked a few times and glanced at the clock. It was one o'clock. He'd left hours ago. A light rap on the door and then Alyson peeked in. Andie brushed her hair back from her face and sat up, already smiling.

"What are you doing here?" Andie hadn't seen her sister in weeks because of schedules and because she'd needed time to adjust to having this sister back in her life. Alyson had moved back to the area, but she'd had obligations, concerts she couldn't cancel.

Alyson shrugged, "I heard from a little birdie that you might need to be cheered up."

"You have a concert in L.A."

"Not until next week. And then I'm flying home to finish up the wedding plans. And you'd better get yourself together before the end of October so you can be my maid of honor." Alyson pushed the blankets aside and sat on the edge of the bed. "How are you?"

"Great."

"You're not great. If you were great you'd have something catty to say, or you might pick a fight with me. But you wouldn't have mascara smeared to your chin…"

"Seriously?" Andie rubbed at her cheeks.

"Seriously." Alyson walked to the dresser and picked up a small mirror. She pulled a few tissues out of the box. "You might want to get out of bed and wash your face, maybe brush your hair."

"I'm on bed rest."

"Yeah, but really, you can't go a month without brushing your hair."

Yes, she thought she could. If staying in bed was a way to hide from reality, she could do it. She took the mirror that Alyson held out to her.

Andie held the mirror up and ran her fingers through her hair, untangling it and then wiping away the mascara by method of the age old spit bath. "I look worse than something that cat of yours would drag in."

"Not even close." Alyson sat back down on the edge of the bed. "Do you want to talk?"

"About what? About making a huge mistake? About being pregnant? Or about the possibility that I could lose the baby?" Andie closed her eyes. "Do you know how guilty I feel? I told myself this baby is a mistake. I was upset about being pregnant. I resented what this would do to my life." She sighed. "If you notice, all three problems were about me, about how I would be affected. And now this is happening and the only thing I can think of now is how can I keep my baby safe."

"I think every single emotion you've had is probably realistic in your situation." Alyson pushed her over a little and scooted up next to her so that they were side by side on the bed, backs against the headboard.

Etta had told them they shared a crib when they were babies and when they moved to toddler beds they had refused to sleep alone.

And then they'd been ripped apart.

"I'm worried that I have too much of Caroline Anderson's DNA," Andie whispered. "What if I have a baby and then realize that I can't do this? What if I'm the type of mom who can't handle it?"

"You aren't our mother."

"I don't know that."

Alyson leaned close and their heads touched. "I do."

Andie nodded because she couldn't get the words out, couldn't tell her sister about Ryder's proposal, about him wanting to marry her, but not loving her.

"Let me help you with the wedding."

Alyson laughed. "You want to plan a wedding?"

"I can do something. I can at least keep you from making a frilly, lacy mistake."

"Okay, I'll get the books and you can help me. I need to pick out flowers. Oh, and your dress. I'm thinking pink."

"You're not."

Alyson laughed again. "No, I'm not. The wedding is going to be fall colors."

Andie sank back into her pillow as her sister left the room, her feet light on the stairs as she went down, calling for Etta. One sister happy, and one trying to be happy.

What if she said yes to Ryder? What would their

wedding be like? Would it be a quick trip to a judge? Or something quiet on a weekday afternoon, just them, Etta and Pastor Jeffries.

As much as she'd never planned her wedding, Andie couldn't imagine either scenario. She groaned and covered her face with her hands. She suddenly wanted white lace and a man looking at her like she meant everything to him.

The way Jason looked at Alyson, not the cornered way Ryder looked at her. He hadn't ever looked at her this way, as if she was a stranger, or a problem he had to fix.

A cramp tightened around her stomach and she rested her hand there, praying the baby would stay safe, stay inside her where it could grow and be hers someday. Changes, life was definitely about changes.

She closed her eyes and thought about bargaining with God. But it wasn't about a bargain, it was about faith, about God's plan. She knew that and yet... She rested her hand on her stomach and fought against fear.

"You okay?"

Andie opened her eyes and smiled for her sister. "Yeah, I'm good."

"You don't look good."

"Pain. It isn't the same as yesterday. I think resting has helped. And the doctor prescribed some cream that is supposed to do something with my hormones."

"I'm glad." Alyson put down the pile of magazines. "You know I'll be here for you."

"I know you will." A year ago that wouldn't have been the case. But now, Alyson would be just down the road. Nothing ever stayed the same, Etta's song said. It was a bittersweet message of loss and gain.

"Ryder was down at the barn when I got here earlier."

"That's good." Andie wanted her sister to forget stories about Ryder. She pointed to the magazines as a direct hint.

"He's pretty sweet about all of this. When Etta mentions the baby, his eyes get damp. Cute."

"Right. Cute is what you want when coupled with, 'Hey, sweetie, let's get married. It's the right thing to do.' Isn't that cute?"

"What do you want him to say?"

Andie fiddled with the soft, worn edges of the quilt. Etta had threatened to get rid of it, but Andie loved it because it was familiar and comfortable.

"You want him to say that he loves you?" Alyson set books on the table next to Andie's bed. "Because you love him?"

"I don't really want to talk about it."

Alyson giggled and it wasn't like her, to giggle. Or to push. "So that's the way this is working out. You, the person who gave me advice to be careful with my heart, has lost yours."

"I haven't lost my heart."

But hadn't she? Wasn't it splintering off into tiny pieces, breaking apart each time he proposed with silly words about friendship and doing the right thing?

And as much as she didn't want her thoughts to turn that direction, she thought about what would happen to them if they lost the baby. What would happen if she said yes and then there wasn't a baby to hold them together?

The sight that met Ryder when he walked into his living room nearly undid him. He didn't need this after dealing with Andie and then working thirty head of rangy bull calves that weren't too partial to what the vet had to do with them. He stood in the doorway of his living room and stared. He counted to ten, reminding himself that they were little girls. But the little girls in question were sitting on his living room floor with sidewalk chalk, drawing pictures on his floor and his coffee table. He loved that table.

"What are you guys doing?" His voice roared a little, but he couldn't help it.

"We aren't boys." Molly stopped drawing long enough to inform him. "We're girls and we're drawing."

"That's sidewalk chalk." He scooped up the box and the chalk they weren't holding. "Sidewalk, as in outside, on concrete. Not inside on floors."

"We can wash it off." Molly kept doodling something that looked like a cat.

"Where's your dad?" Ryder held out his hand and they handed over the chalk they were still using.

Be a dad, he told himself. Be a dad. He knew what his dad would have done if he'd caught Ryder and Wyatt doing something like this. It would have started with a belt and ended with the two of them not being able to sit down for a week.

That parenting example wasn't going to work so he had to think of something on his own. He looked down at the girls. They were staring up at him, two brown-eyed little angels with smudges of pink, green and yellow on their cheeks. Kat rubbed at her nose and left a dot of orange behind.

"I need for the two of you to come with me. We're going to clean this mess up and you're not going to do this again." Ryder motioned for the two girls to head for the door.

"What happened?" Wyatt asked, looking a little frazzled. His hair was too long and he hadn't shaved since he'd rolled into town with that moving truck.

How did a guy go from dating, rodeoing, living his own life, to this? He wasn't Mr. Family Guy. He didn't *do* baby wipes, diapers and cleaning up kid messes. At least that didn't used to be his life.

He sure wasn't going to raise his older brother on top of everything else.

Get used to it, big shot. His good self smirked at his bad self; as if there had been a major victory of some sort. Rip the good life right out from under a guy and then be happy about it.

"We're cleaning up a mess." Ryder answered and he glanced back over his shoulder, at what was obviously a zoo of chalk-drawn characters on his floor and table. "Where were you?"

Wyatt shrugged. "I had to figure out what to feed them for supper. I was in the basement going through the freezer."

"Yeah, well, feel free to go to the store."

"I'll do that." Wyatt took the chalk.

Ryder walked down the hall to the kitchen, his brother and nieces following. He dug through the cabinet under the sink and pulled out wipes that promised to clean kitchen cabinets, woodwork and bathrooms. All purpose, of course. He handed it to the girls.

"What do we do?" Molly stared at the container.

He smiled, because she was little and trying to act so big. And not once had she backed down when faced with his anger. He stayed on the floor, at eye level with her.

He wanted to hug her, not punish her.

"We're going to clean up the chalk. And I'll help you."

Molly's eyes lit up a little. "Okay."

He wasn't such a bad uncle. He stood up and Molly took his hand. Kat grabbed his leg so he picked her up.

"How's Andie?" Wyatt followed him into the living room.

"I thought you were looking for something to cook?"

Wyatt took Kat from his arms. She had a wipe in her hands and she struggled to get down. Wyatt set her free to start cleaning. He stepped back, watching. Ryder lifted his gaze to meet his brother's.

"We'll just have Mad Cow again." Wyatt sat down next to Molly and showed her how to rub the chalk off the floor. "What about Andie?"

That was fine, Ryder didn't do family meals. He could slap some microwaved something on a plate, but the whole nutrition pyramid wasn't in his diet. He glanced back at the girls because they probably needed some of the stuff on that pyramid. At least Vera had vegetables at the Mad Cow.

Wyat cleared his throat, reminding Ryder of the question about Andie.

"She's doing good. I guess."

"You guess?"

"I proposed again. She turned me down again."

Wyatt moved from the floor to the sofa. "Well, how did you propose?"

"Are you the proposal expert?"

"No, but I've had more experience than you. At least with a real relationship."

"Yeah, well…"

"If you want her to say yes, you have to show her how special she is to you. You have to do more than pull out a ring and say, 'Hey baby, how 'bout we get hitched.'"

"Andie isn't about romance."

Wyatt laughed. "Have you been under a rock? She's a woman. She's having a baby, your baby. She wants romance."

"Chocolates and flowers?" Ryder hadn't ever bought a woman flowers.

"Do what you've always done. But maybe this time, mean it."

"She knows she's my best friend." Ryder showed Molly a spot on the floor that still had the smudged outline of a snake. She wiped it up with dimpled, pudgy hands. He looked at her hands and suddenly those hands meant everything. His baby would have hands like that, soft and pudgy. His kid.

But maybe his kid would have blond hair like Andie. Maybe she'd have his eyes, or his curls. He blinked and looked away from his niece, to the brother that was trying to give him advice.

"Ryder, I don't know how long you're going to tell yourself that Andie is just a friend, but there's something you ought to think about."

"What's that?" He was still thinking about Molly's hands and he wondered how Wyatt felt the first time he held his daughter. But he didn't want to ask.

"You might ought to think about the fact that she's the longest relationship you've ever had."

His longest relationship. He brushed his hands down

the legs of his jeans and smiled at Molly, whose wide eyes clued him in to the possibility that wiping dirt on clothes was bad.

"Yeah, I guess you're right, she is." He leaned and kissed Molly on the top of the head. She smiled up at him and then she went back to scrubbing.

"You think I might be right?" Wyatt got down on the floor to help his girls. "That's a huge change."

Ryder stood up, still holding the container of wipes. Yeah, huge change. But he'd had a lot of changes in his life. Not all bad. He watched the girls as they finished scrubbing his table. Change wasn't the worst thing in the world.

"I don't want to be like our dad. I don't want to mess up a kid the way we were messed up. Did you ever feel that way? Were you afraid to have kids?"

Wyatt looked at the girls. "Yeah, I was. I learned something though. If you're worried about being like him, that means you know what he did wrong. You can make changes."

Ryder wondered about that. He wondered about Wyatt and the past year, trying to get his life back.

"Take my word for it, you can do this, Ryder. But first you have to make Andie feel like you love her, like she's your sweetheart, not the woman that lassoed you and dragged you down the aisle against your will."

Make her feel like his sweetheart? He had a feeling flowers and chocolate weren't the key to Andie's heart. And he had bigger problems than that. How did he go from thinking of her as his best friend to turning her into the person he loved?

He might not have all the answers, but he did know the way to her heart. And it wasn't chocolate.

* * *

It was dark outside when headlights flashed across the living room wall. Andie glanced out the window, but she couldn't see who it was. Alyson walked to the window and shrugged.

"I don't know who it is. It's a truck and a trailer." Alyson shot Andie a knowing look. "It's Ryder."

"Why can't he give me a break?"

"Because he's worried about you?" Alyson left the room and Andie knew she was letting Ryder in, and she imagined the two would share secretive little looks, maybe whisper something about her mood.

Staying down was not easy. She kicked her feet into the couch and screamed a silent scream of protest. When the footsteps headed her way she managed a calm smile.

"What are you doing here?" She flipped off the television when he walked into the room. He stood in the doorway, his hand behind his back. His jeans had pastel pink stains down the front.

Alyson peeked in, screwing up her face. "That's nice."

Andie drew in a deep breath and exhaled. "Fine, I can play this game. Ryder, it's nice to see you."

He smiled and stepped into the room, dark hair and dark eyes, and all cowboy. Except the pink stain. Her gaze kept straying to the pink blotch. But then his hands moved.

He had flowers and a sheepish grin as he held them out to her. She wanted to laugh. He actually had flowers. Her heart did something strange, because he'd never done that before. No one had ever bought her flowers.

He hadn't even bought her flowers when he took her to the prom. Not even a wrist corsage.

"I wanted to check on you. I thought I'd see if there was anything you needed." He shrugged a little and he looked cute in jeans that had dirty smudges on the knees and a T-shirt that was a little threadbare. He didn't smell good.

"What have you been doing? You stink."

"Sorry, I worked with calves all day and then I had to go pick something up."

"You have pink on your jeans."

"Sidewalk chalk."

She pictured him on a sidewalk drawing hearts and flowers. He wouldn't have liked that image of himself.

He walked across the room with the flowers that were a little smushed and slightly wilted. She took them and held them to her nose. The rose in the bouquet flopped to the side with a broken stem. She peeked over the top of the flowers and smiled because his cheeks were ruddy from the sun and embarrassment.

"What did you have to pick up? The flowers?" She scooted up so he could sit on the couch next to her. He didn't sit down.

"No, I bought the flowers at…" He looked down, at boots covered in mud. On Etta's glossy wood floors. "I bought them at the convenience store."

They both laughed. At least they could still do that. "I love them."

"I bought you something else. I know you can't get up right now. But if you could sneak over to the window, I'll show you."

"Oh, okay."

And then he was gone. She waited a few seconds to

see if he would come back. When he didn't she hurried over to the window and looked out. He was opening the back of the trailer. Her heart hammered a little harder than before.

It was dark but the light in the back yard glowed in the night and bugs buzzed around the front porch light. Andie leaned close to the screen and waited for Ryder to walk out the back of the trailer. When he did, she laughed.

He stopped in the yard, looking up at the window, at her. He motioned to the creature standing behind him. She pushed the window up.

"How do you like her?"

"A llama?"

"An alpaca." He sounded a little offended. "You said you wanted one."

"And I do. And she's beautiful. I love her."

"Etta can knit blankets with her wool."

"For the…" She bit down on her lip for a second. "For the baby."

He nodded and then he gathered up the lead rope of the animal. "Yes, for the baby. I'll put her in the corral with hay for tonight. Tomorrow we can see how she does with horses."

She watched until he was out of sight and then she hurried back to the couch. But Etta caught her. Etta, a dish towel in her hands and a frown on her face.

"What are you doing up?"

"Ryder had a surprise for me. I just slipped over to the window to see what it was."

"And it was what?"

She laughed. "An alpaca. Can you believe he got me an alpaca?"

"I think that's about the sweetest thing I've ever heard. Now, stay on that couch and I'll make hot cocoa."

An alpaca. Andie hugged her pillow and she couldn't stop smiling. The flowers were on the table, wilted but fragrant. And Ryder had bought her an alpaca.

She'd always known that sweet side of him. He'd always done the silliest things. The sweetest things.

And she'd never been able to think about falling in love with someone else, because she'd always loved him. She had dreamed of him someday loving her, someday asking her to marry him. But the dreams had been different.

The dreams hadn't included mistakes and this wall between them. The dreams had included words of love and forever, not the words *have to*.

She'd loved him forever and no one knew her secret but her. And probably God. The two of them knew how it had hurt to be his best friend while he dated, and never women like her. Ryder had dated women from Tulsa. He had dated the kind of woman she would never be, the manicured kind who always knew how to put outfits together, always looked stylish and beautiful.

His footsteps, minus boots, alerted her to his presence. She looked up as he walked through the door of the living room, without his hat, without boots. She smiled at his bare feet and he shifted a little, like he couldn't handle bare feet in her presence.

"Etta made me take my boots off."

"It's okay, you have cute feet."

He sat down on the coffee table facing her. "My feet aren't cute. I have long toes."

"My toes look like little clubs. Etta says because I went barefoot when I was a kid. I should have worn shoes." She stopped herself from rambling more. She looked up at him. "I love the alpaca."

"Nothing says I care like an alpaca." He winked and her stomach did this funny thing that felt like flips. How often had she watched him wink at girls, and then watched those same silly females follow him, not knowing that he wasn't good for much more than one date.

One night.

But they'd done everything together. They'd gone everywhere together. She'd been his comfort zone. He'd been safe with her. Maybe too safe, she decided.

"You're right about that." She couldn't look at him, her heart ached and it hurt to take a deep breath.

"Andie, I'm sorry. This isn't the way we planned our lives, but we can make it work. I'm going to be a good dad. I'll figure out how to be good at this."

"I know you will." She met his dark brown gaze and her heart thudded, her face warmed. "I know, because I know who you are, that you're good and kind."

"I'm not, Andie. I've never been good or kind. I've been shallow and selfish just about all of my life."

"Not to me."

He reached for her hand and she held her breath as he slid his fingers between hers. "No, not to you."

His eyes narrowed a little as he stared at their hands, and then he leaned. He leaned and he slid his free hand to the back of her neck, cupping it with a gentleness that made her heart melt. His lips touched hers, leaving behind the sweet taste of cola. Time slowed down and he held her close, keeping his lips close to hers. He moved, kissing her hair right above her ear and still holding her. He whispered but her brain didn't connect words that sounded as if he meant to hold her forever.

And then Etta cleared her throat. "Hot cocoa anyone?"

Ryder scrambled back away from her, leaving her alone and cold on the sofa. He stood up, looking sixteen and ashamed of being caught necking in the parlor. Andie smiled at this side of him, the soft and vulnerable side.

"I should go." He coughed a little. "I'll be back tomorrow. To check on the alpaca, and on you."

Andie nodded and then he was gone. From her seat on the sofa she watched his truck go down the road, back in the direction of his house.

He'd bought her an alpaca, and he'd kissed her goodbye. As much as she wanted to go back to being "just friends" she knew that could never happen.

Chapter 11

Ryder hadn't gone home the night before. Instead he'd left Andie's, driven past his house and straight to Tulsa. He hadn't been sure what he was going to do once he got there, but as he'd driven past a home store, it had hit him. He was going to have a kid, and that kid needed a room. A nursery.

Kids had rooms. Babies had nurseries. He'd learned a lot last night while he'd been shopping.

Two pots of coffee later, he stepped back and looked at the wall he'd been painting. It wasn't what he'd expected, but it wasn't bad. It was pretty good considering he didn't have a clue what he was doing. This was a far cry from painting a wall white, or beige.

"What are you doing?" Wyatt walked up beside him. "I guess I know what you're doing, but isn't it a little early?"

"If a guy's going to have faith," the word wasn't easy to get out, "then he has to have faith. I'm going to be a dad and my kid is going to have the best nursery I can make."

"Green?"

"Yeah, green. For a boy or a girl." Ryder didn't look at his brother, he kept looking at the walls and he explained what the girl at the all night home store had told him. She'd said this was some shade of antique pastel green. And it would look great with cream trim on the woodwork. That's what the girl at the store had said.

He'd taken her word for it because he would have painted the room pink if it had been up to him. Pink because he couldn't stop thinking about having a little girl. As much as he'd ever wanted anything, the idea of that little girl in his arms had become the biggest dream ever.

Wyatt stepped over to the box Wyatt had placed on top of an old dresser. He started pulling out stuff that Ryder had bought on his late-night shopping trip. A train, a picture of a pony, a porcelain doll and a clown. Ryder still didn't like the clown. It looked too creepy for a baby's room. Wyatt shot him a look.

"That's the creepiest clown I've ever seen." Wyatt dropped it back in the box. "So, trains, stuffed animals and butterflies?"

"It could be a boy or a girl. We won't know for a couple of months." We, as in he and Andie. He figured it would get easier to deal with, eventually.

But he thought most people planned these things and had time to adjust, to deal with it. He was going to be a dad and that hadn't been on any of his to-do lists.

He tried not to think of Andie losing the baby because he didn't really want to think about how that would make him feel. It didn't make sense that something he hadn't wanted, hadn't planned to have, could mean so much to a guy in a matter of weeks. It felt like something he wouldn't be able to handle losing.

His kid.

The whole nursery thing had happened after he'd kissed Andie earlier. Or had it been the night before. He glanced at his wrist, but his watch was on the counter downstairs. And none of that took his mind off that kiss. If a kiss, if holding a woman could make a man change his mind about having a woman in his life forever, that might have been the moment.

"What about a bed?" Wyatt finished rummaging through the box and looked at him.

"Our old cradle and crib are in the attic. I thought I'd sand them down."

"Wow, seriously?"

Anything for his kid.

"Yeah, a baby has to have a place to sleep."

Wyatt walked over to the rocking chair Ryder had bought last night. Every time he looked at that rocking chair he pictured it next to the window and he could see Andie in it, holding their baby. For that to happen, she'd have to marry him. She'd have to live here with him and make a home with him.

That didn't seem likely because she was pretty stuck on their "best friend" relationship. He had to take the blame for that.

"You're right—a baby has to have a place to sleep." Wyatt touched the rocking chair and his smile faded. Ryder thought Wyatt probably had images in his mind that were a little harder to face. Images of Wendy holding their girls.

Ryder slapped his brother on the back. "I think we need to go break a horse or something. All of this paint is starting to get to me."

"Wish I could, but the girls are waking up. I'm going to drive over to Grove. Do you need anything from town?"

"I was in Tulsa until three in the morning. What do you think?"

"Probably not. How did it go with Andie?"

"I bought her an alpaca."

Wyatt shook his head. "Okay, maybe you don't know what you're doing."

"What? She liked it."

"Yeah, she probably did."

Ryder grinned, "I bought her flowers, too."

Wyatt shook his head and walked out of the room. "You'll never get it."

Ryder dipped the brush in the paint and finished up a small section of wall that he didn't want to leave undone. Green, for a boy or a girl. The clerk at the home store had asked him all the details, like when was the baby due and did they have a name picked out. And he'd tried to think up answers because he didn't have any.

He tossed the brush into the tray and walked out of the room. A guy who was having a baby should have answers. By the time he pulled up to Etta's he'd managed to cool down.

Etta answered the door, motioning him into the kitchen and then looking at him like he'd dropped off the moon.

"Do you want a cup of coffee or a shower?" Her nose wrinkled and she stepped back. "Take your boots off."

"I guess I look pretty bad." He looked down. The pink chalk had faded but he had specks of paint on his shirt and arms.

"Not too bad. She's in the living room."

"Has she had breakfast? I could take her a tray."

"You might lose your head. She's already sick of staying down. She made Alyson drag that alpaca up to the window, right up on my front porch."

He laughed picturing that in his mind. Alyson was about the prissiest female he'd ever met. If she and Andie didn't look so much alike, he'd say there wasn't any way they could be twins.

"She'll be glad to see me." He took the cup of coffee from Etta. "Do you think she wants anything?"

"No, she can't have more coffee. One cup a day and she had eggs for breakfast."

He nodded and walked down the hall to the living room. He knew this house as well as he knew his own and as a kid he'd probably spent more time here than at home. He peeked around the door of the living room and Andie smiled. She didn't look mean. Or angry.

"Come in." She grimaced and looked him over, top to bottom. "You look horrible."

"Thanks." He sat down in the rocking chair, still holding his cup of coffee.

"You're wearing the same clothes you had on last night."

"Yeah, I am."

"And you haven't shaved."

He rubbed his hand across his cheek. It had been

a couple of days since he'd shaved. "Andie, about the baby. What do you think we'll name her?"

She smiled and curled back into the couch. "Name her? I don't know. I mean, we don't know if…if she'll be a girl."

"But she might be."

"Yeah, she might be." Her eyes softened and she looked out the window. "I like the name Maggie."

"We could call her Magpie."

"Yeah, we could. And buy her a pony when she's three."

Andie looked at him and her smile faded. "Ryder, I don't want to do this."

"What, have the baby?" He could barely get the words out, but she was shaking her head.

"I don't want to plan. I don't want to think about names when I might lose her."

"That isn't going to happen." He wouldn't let it happen. The idea of this kid had settled inside him. The idea of Andie as the mother of his child was settling inside him, taking root. He tried to smile, for Andie's sake. "What happened to faith? What happened to trusting God?"

"I'm trying… I'm really trying, but I didn't expect this to be so hard." She bit down on her bottom lip and he'd never seen her like that—vulnerable. Her blue eyes were huge and her lips trembled.

Andie had always been the strongest woman he knew. She hadn't ever really seemed to need him, or anyone else. He always said she rolled with the punches.

But a baby changed everything.

He left the rocking chair and went to her side. She looked up, blue eyes swimming in tears that didn't fall.

"I'll have enough faith for both of us. I can do that for you. I can do that for her."

And he meant it.

Step one in being a dad, trusting someone other than himself. Trusting God. He hoped God was still in the forgiving business because if Ryder was going to work on faith, he had a lot to confess to the Almighty. He had a lot of work to do on himself.

Andie leaned against a shoulder that was strong and wide and Ryder held her close. She sniffed into his shirt and pulled back.

"You really have to take a shower."

"Sorry, I should have done that before I came over, but I had to know. Last night someone asked me what we were going to name her, and when she'd be born, and I didn't know the answer."

"Where were you last night?" Ick, was that jealousy? Andie shrugged it off. "I mean, you left here and…"

"I went to Tulsa to buy a few things for the house. And then I stayed up all night working."

She ran her hand down his arm, touching small spatters of green paint. She didn't want to take her hand off his arms. They were suntanned and strong. "Were you painting?"

"Yeah. You know, the girls are living at the house, and Wyatt."

"Oh." And it shouldn't have hurt. She should have been glad that he was doing something for the girls.

"Hey, let me get you some books. Or lunch. Would you like some chocolate?"

"Ryder, I don't need anything." She glanced out the window. "Except up from here."

"Yeah, I can't do that for you. What about Dusty?"

"I miss him. He probably thinks I've abandoned him." She wiped at her eyes. "Could you go out and check on him?"

"You know I will. But I wanted to check on you, first."

His voice was gentle but deep and he was still sitting on the coffee table, facing her. She brushed at her eyes again.

"Ryder, I'm so afraid."

"Why?"

She pulled back, looking at him, at a face she knew as well as she knew her own. She knew that dimple in his chin, the way his hair curled when it got a little too long and the way his brown eyes danced when he was amused. And she thought he should know her, too.

"Because I don't know what's going to happen. I don't want to lose this baby. It was the most unexpected thing in the world, but now…" She wiped at her eyes. "She's a part of me. She's a part of us. As afraid as I am of raising her, I'm afraid of losing her."

"I'm not going to let you raise her alone." He grinned. "Or him."

That wasn't what she wanted him to say. She wanted him to say that he was afraid. But telling her she wouldn't be alone in this, maybe he was doing his best, the best a cowboy who had never planned on settling down could do.

It wasn't like he was going to suddenly pledge his undying love to her. She was lucky he'd agreed to go to church. He had promised to have enough faith for both of them. That was good, because her faith was pretty shaky at the moment and at least he was strong.

"I know you won't." She looked out the window. A car drove down the road, a rare thing for their street at this time of day. It didn't stop.

It went on down the road, the distraction ended. And her heart was still aching because she was going to have a baby and she wanted more than anything to hear Ryder say he loved her.

"You should go. I know you have a lot to do today." She didn't want him to feel as if he had to stay and take care of her.

She wanted to get up and take care of herself. She'd thought about it earlier, before anyone was up. She'd considered sneaking out of the house and going outside to check on her horse and see the alpaca. And small twinges of pain had convinced her otherwise.

As hard as it was to stay in bed, she didn't want to take chances.

"I don't have a lot to do, Andie. I've been getting things taken care of. Today I'm here to take care of you."

She squirmed a little. "I really don't think that's a good idea."

"Why?"

"Because that isn't us."

"It's the new us." He sniffed his own shirt. "But I do need a shower."

"Ryder, really, you don't have to stay here and take care of me. I have Etta and Alyson. They'll take care of me."

Ryder stood up. "This isn't just about you, Andie, this is about our baby. I'm taking care of you and our baby."

"I don't need to be taken care of."

"Of course you don't, you stubborn female." He walked to the door. "I'll be back in an hour."

The front door slammed and then she heard him backing out of the driveway and then shifting as he headed back down the road. She picked up one of the wedding magazines that Alyson had been looking at.

White and frilly. Couldn't a wedding be practical? She was practical. She wouldn't want a dress she couldn't wear again. She wouldn't want cake that looked beautiful but tasted like dust.

If she was to get married she'd want daisies and denim. She'd want to ride off into the sunset on her horse and camp in the mountains for her honeymoon. With her baby next to her. But who was the groom in this little dream? The guy who wanted to take care of her?

Her hand went to her belly and she whispered, wondering if it was true that babies could hear from inside the womb. But a baby the size of a shrimp? She really didn't like that image.

She preferred picturing the full-sized baby, with brown hair and brown eyes. Her imagination fast-forwarded her ten years and she was still living with Etta, raising her daughter. But in the dream, Ryder was a visitor and a woman waited in his truck as he picked up his daughter for the weekend.

That wouldn't do. But neither did the other version of the dream, the one where she and Ryder were together but he resented her, resented their child because the ring on his finger kept him tied to them.

As she drifted on the edge of sleep she told herself that wasn't fair. It wasn't fair to Ryder that she was putting him in the role of villain. Ryder had always been honorable. He had always been there for her.

But having a baby, neither of them knew how to approach this mountain. She had made mistakes in her life, mistakes that she knew God had gotten her through, helped her to overcome. As she laid there she thought about her baby and she couldn't call a child a mistake.

The baby was a choice they had made. It might not have been the right choice, but it was one they would work through. And it would never be the baby's fault. She would never let that happen.

A truck door slammed and she jumped but then settled back onto the couch. She listened to boots on the wood front steps, a rap on the door and then Ryder walked into the living room. He had shaved and his hair was damp and curled a little.

"Wake up, sweetheart, you're going outside."

"What?" She sat up, but she didn't reach for the flip flops on the floor next to the sofa.

"I'm going to work Dusty, but I thought you'd like to go. You can sit on a lawn chair out there."

"You think that would be okay?" She reached for her shoes.

"Don't stand up."

"What?" She held her shoes and then he was standing in front of her, leaning to pick her up.

"I'm going to carry you." He scooped her up and she grabbed quick, wrapping her arms around his neck.

"I'm too heavy."

"You're not heavy." He laughed and jostled her, shifting her. "No, you're not heavy. I've picked up bales of hay that weigh more."

"Thanks, I'm a bale of hay." She leaned and he did smell better. Soap, aftershave and the minty smell of toothpaste. He turned a little and they were face-to-face, practically nose to nose.

"You're not hay," he whispered. He touched his forehead to hers and then looked away, his arms tensing, holding her close.

What was she to him? Okay, she got it, she wasn't hay. But if she asked, what would he say? Best friend, pain in the neck, or was she now just extra baggage that he wasn't sure how to handle?

Andie wasn't heavy. She held him tight, her arms around his neck, and her head close to his. He carried her down the hall and into the kitchen. Etta was sitting at the table with a basket of yarn, knitting needles in her hand and something partially made. She looked up as they walked into the room.

She set the knitting needles and yarn on the table and stared for a moment before shaking her head. "What do you think you're up to?"

"Going outside." He stopped at the screen door and waited for Etta to tell him he was crazy and why he shouldn't do this. But the more he thought about Andie stuck in the house, the more he knew he had to get her outside.

"She has to stay down," Etta warned.

"I'm not going to let her walk, just letting her get fresh air. We can't keep her locked in the house for nine months."

Andie moved in his arms. "I don't think I'll be on bed rest for seven months."

"Well, probably not, I'm just saying that you could use some fresh air."

Etta shook her head again. "I think the two of you were meant for each other."

Meant for each other.

Ryder couldn't respond to that. He pushed the screen door open with his hip and slid through. Andie pushed to keep the door from hitting them on their way out. She was easy in his arms, and he'd never thought of the two of them as a couple. As "meant for each other."

Or maybe he had. Maybe he'd pushed it from his mind because it was easy to be her friend and the idea of breaking her heart had been the thing that scared him the most. He'd never let himself think about the two of them together. She had always been his best friend.

He'd picked safe.

"What?" She quizzed as he sat her down in the lawn chair, cradling her close as he settled her in the seat.

"Nothing."

"Whatever. I think I've known you long enough to know when nothing is really something. You're jaw is clenching because you're grinding your teeth. You do that when you're mad about something."

"I'm not mad."

"Are too."

"Not right now, Andie. I can't have this conversation with you right now."

"Yeah, I guess we're talked out."

No, he thought they probably had plenty to talk about, just nothing they wanted to talk about. "When's your next doctor's appointment?"

"Next week." Her hand went to her belly and she looked away from him.

"Are you," he squatted next to her, "are you having pains?"

She drew in a deep breath. "Some twinges, but nothing too bad. Sometimes I'm afraid…"

He'd never heard her admit that before. "I know, me, too. But I'm praying."

"You're praying?"

"Every time I take a breath." He couldn't stop looking at her belly, because his baby was in there. He'd never thought it could change him like this, that child and Andie needing him.

"One of us has to be strong, Ryder."

"You can count on me." He stood and she was staring up at him. "What do you need me to do with Dusty?"

He backed away, hoping she'd let the conversation end.

"I think lunge him in the arena. He doesn't like it when you ride him." She pulled her sweater closer around herself.

"Yeah, I seem to remember the last time I rode him. I think I still have the scar on my arm where he dumped me."

She smiled at that and picked up the cat that had left the barn and was circling her chair. When her smile faded and her eyes clouded over, he knew he should have left when he had the chance.

"Ryder, what if I lose the baby?"

How was he supposed to answer that? Two months ago having a baby was the farthest thing from his mind. And now she wanted to know what they'd do if she lost it? Having that baby meant changing his life in ways he hadn't planned.

Now, not having it felt like the change he didn't want to face.

"We're not going to lose the baby." He bent and kissed the top of her head. "I'm going to catch Dusty."

She might have whispered "chicken" as he walked off. He couldn't be sure of that, and he wasn't positive it wasn't just his own thoughts calling him names.

But yeah, he was a chicken. That was something he was just now figuring out about himself. He was a big old chicken. He was afraid of conversations with obstetricians. He was afraid to talk about having kids with Andie.

He was not afraid of a horse. He whistled and Dusty didn't even lift his head. That horse was not going to make him walk out into the field and catch him.

Chapter 12

The house was quiet. Andie hated the quiet. She hated being inside. She hadn't been out since the day Ryder had carried her outside to watch while he worked Dusty. He'd meant it to be a good thing, but instead it had ached inside her, watching him work her horse.

At least she'd gotten to go out.

Since then it had been daily visits. He showed up with food from the Mad Cow or movies for her to watch. He'd sat with her while she dozed. He constantly asked how she was and if she needed anything. Her heart was getting way to used to him being around.

Today it was raining, a cold rain that blew leaves against the windows while thunder rumbled in the clouds. And everyone was gone. Alyson was in Tulsa with Etta, getting the finishing touches on her dress. Ryder was selling off a herd of year-old steers. She'd promised she would stay on the couch. She had food. She had a thermos of cold water.

She had cabin fever like nobody's business.

Somewhere in the distance a dog barked, the sound getting swallowed up by thunder and rain beating on the roof of the porch. Andie strained to listen. She heard it again and then a cow.

Normal farm sounds, she told herself. Dogs barked and cows mooed. The only thing that wasn't normal was her, and the fact that she couldn't go check and see what was going on.

The barking got louder, more frantic.

"Okay, I can't sit here." Andie picked up her cell phone and slipped her feet in tennis shoes by the door. She grabbed a jacket off the hook on the wall and walked outside. For a moment she stood on the front porch, protected from the rain. Of course the dog stopped barking when she walked outside.

Andie walked off the porch and headed across the yard, in the direction of the most pitiful mooing she'd ever heard. Her stomach twisted, because she didn't know what she'd find, and because she shouldn't be up.

But she hadn't had pains for two days. That had to be a sign that things were getting better. She was close to finishing her first trimester.

She scanned the fence, looking for the cow and the dog. They were quiet for a minute and then it started again. The dog barked an excited bark, not angry. Picking up her pace she headed for the clump of brush and stand of trees near the corner of the fence. The dog barked again. And then she saw the cow on the ground. It bellowed, low and pitiful, sides heaving. The dog was crouched on the ground, tail wagging. It turned to look at her, tongue hanging out. It didn't leave the cow.

Now what?

Andie slid between two rows of barbed wire and approached the cow, talking quietly to calm the poor heifer. "I know, it's scary, isn't it? Poor thing, you don't know what's happening to you."

The cow looked up, her eyes huge, her mouth opening in a pant that became a low moo. Andie squatted next to her, running her hands over the animal's heaving sides. Cows never picked good weather or good conditions to calve. And if they were going to have problems, which they often did, it always happened at the worst possible time.

Andie had pulled a calf two hours before her senior graduation. That's how life worked on the farm. She'd pulled a calf, and then she graduated from high school.

But this was different. A cow in distress, but Andie's baby, needing a chance, needing to be safe.

One hoof was out. Andie couldn't begin to guess how long the cow had been down or how long she'd been trying to push this baby out.

It was her first calf and she was obviously going to be like her mother, having difficult deliveries. But Andie couldn't help her. Any other time, but not today. It wasn't a difficult decision to make. It really felt like the only decision.

Etta had ordered her to call Ryder if anything happened, or if she needed anything. He had his cell phone on and was just minutes away. This qualified as an emergency, as needing something. She let out a sigh, because she hated having to call him away from what he was doing. To take care of what she needed to have done.

But this wasn't about her. It was about the baby.

She stood up.

The dog, a stray that had showed up in town a year or so ago hurried to her side, wagging his entire back end. He hadn't run the cow, she was sure of that. He'd just been sending out his own alert. He sat down next to her, proud that he'd done his job.

Andie pulled out her cell phone and dialed. Ryder answered after a few rings.

"Andie?"

"Ryder, I have a cow in labor. I think the calf is going to have to be pulled."

"Are you outside?"

"Yes, I'm outside." She wiped rain from her face but it kept coming down, soaking her hair and clothes. "I had to see what was going on."

A long pause and then he spoke. "Andie, get back inside."

She could hear sounds in the background. Laughter, conversations and dishes rattling. It riled her that he was ordering her back into the house. When had he ever done that?

"I can't leave the cow."

"You have to leave her." His voice got loud, firm. "I'll be there in five minutes."

"Fine." She slid the phone back into her. "Help is on the way, girl."

The cow mooed and raised her head. "You're right, I'm not going to leave you alone."

No one wanted to be alone in a situation like this.

Andie backed up to a tree that was just a few feet away. It gave her a little protection from the rain, a little shelter. But the whole time she stood there, waiting, she felt mad and guilty. She didn't want to feel either.

Ryder grabbed the ticket for his lunch at the Mad Cow and reached into his pocket for his wallet. He was trying to look casual, as if this was something he did every day, getting calls from Andie and leaving in the middle of lunch.

But lately, nothing was what he'd been used to doing every day. He looked at the guys he'd had lunch with— Clint Cameron, Adam Mackenzie, Reese Cooper and a couple of others. They were all taking their lunch break at the Mad Cow. A few of them were getting ready to go to the livestock auction. Reese was getting ready for the rodeo finals in Vegas. They were all still living the lives they were comfortable with.

Without warning, Ryder's life had become something so upside down he didn't recognize it. Church yesterday with Wyatt and the girls and afterward he'd taken lunch to Andie. A couple of weeks ago he'd found out he was going to be a dad. And each and every day he was climbing up the biggest mountain of his life, trying to find his way back to God and his way forward in this situation with Andie.

For a while it had been like wearing someone else's boots. But he was adjusting. And everyone at the table was looking at him as if they thought maybe he was going to lose it if they didn't hitch him to an anchor.

Clint reached for the ticket Ryder was still holding.

"You go on, that sounded like something that needs to be taken care of. I'll buy your lunch."

"Andie has a cow down." He picked up his burger to take it with him.

"Do you think you'll need some help?" Adam Mac-Kenzie grabbed the ticket from Clint and pulled out his wallet. "I'll get lunch."

Clint laughed. "Will he need help with what, Andie or the cow?"

Ryder threw money on the table for the tip. "You guys are hilarious. I don't think I'll need help with either."

Reese, chair tilted back on two legs, was grinning. And Ryder kind of wanted to hit him, because Reese had dated Andie back in their college days. He'd dated her and cheated on her. It had mattered then, it mattered more now.

"I never thought you'd be the guy falling like this," Reese finally commented. Clint jerked his chair back and Reese scurried to get his feet back under him as the chair went to the floor with a crash that had people staring and Vera running from the back.

The owner of the Mad Cow glared at them and then she headed toward Ryder with foam containers. "Are you heading out?"

"Yeah, Andie called." He shot Reese a look. "She has a cow down. I need to run but Adam's buying lunch."

"I wasn't worried about you skipping out on a bill, Ryder. I was worried about Andie. I saw you here and I know Etta's in Tulsa, so I made Andie up some of my special cashewed chicken. Take this to her. And let me have that." She grabbed a napkin out of the holder on the table and reached for the burger he was about to take a bite of. Before he could object she opened the Styrofoam and put the burger inside. "There, now you're all set to go. And you'd better hurry or she'll be hooking up a pulley to her truck and pulling that calf on her own."

"I know." He kissed Vera on the cheek. "You're the best.

He pulled into Andie's a few minutes later. She was sitting on the porch, out of the rain. She didn't stand up when he pulled up to the house. Worry knotted in his stomach. He should have ignored her when she said she didn't need him here. He could have found someone to do his work at home and he could have sat with her while Etta was gone.

He jumped out of the truck, grabbing the container of food before he shut the door. Andie crossed her arms over her front and glared as he hurried toward her. She was mad. He guessed that was a plus.

"What took you so long?"

"Had to get our food." He felt the need to defend himself. "And it didn't take that long. Here's your lunch. Vera made you some of her cashewed chicken."

She took the container from him. "The cow is over there, near the corner post and that clump of brush."

"She'll be fine, Andie. Why don't you go inside?"

"I couldn't sit in there. I'll sit on the porch. This isn't walking around. This isn't doing something." Her hands clenched into the sleeves of her sweater.

"I know." He took a few steps back to keep from holding her when he knew being held was the last thing she wanted. He knew her, knew she was close to tears that she was fighting hard against. There were times to hold a woman and let her cry. He knew this wasn't one of those times.

"I'm so tired of this." She brushed her hands over her face and didn't look at him. "I'm so tired of not being able to take care of things. And having to call someone to take care of things I can usually take care of. And then there's the guilt because I got up to see what was wrong."

"It's okay to be sick of this, you know."

"But the baby…" she began.

"Is going to be fine. You're going to be fine."

"You don't know that," she insisted.

Now was when a man held a woman and let her cry. He sat down next to her on the wicker bench that always creaked with his weight and she leaned into his side. He heard the cow mooing and tried to ignore it.

"Andie, we're almost to the three month mark. What have we got, another week or two?"

"Yeah."

"So, we're going to make it." He held her and felt her tense and pull away.

"You have to go deliver that calf. I can't lose that calf."

"I'm going."

He hurried out to his truck and found rope, a coat and some old towels. He kept the metal toolbox on the back of his truck stocked with just about everything he might need in an emergency. As he dug around inside the box he found a rain poncho that he'd never taken out of the package. Now that was prepared.

The dog greeted him as he walked across the yard. The scruffy looking terrier cross was mud-caked but happy. He'd never seen a dog like this one, one that always looked as if it was grinning. He guessed if everyone in town was feeding him, he'd be pretty happy, too.

The cow was still laboring. He climbed the fence and eased toward her. The wild look in her eyes warned that she wasn't going to be pleasant about dealing with him. Good thing she was nearly worn out. That was a bad thing, too. It meant she wasn't going to be a lot of help pushing this calf out.

"How is she?" Andie had moved to another seat on the porch and she leaned out. He knew it was killing her, this inactivity, and not taking care of her farm.

"She's having a baby, Andie. Now give me a minute." He looped the rope around the tiny hooves that were trying to poke out.

It wasn't the worst case he'd ever seen. It wasn't going to be the easiest. He probably should have taken Adam up on his offer to help.

"Do you want me to call for help?" Andie asked.

He shook his head and she'd have to deal with that answer for now. The cow tried to get to her feet but couldn't. Oh man, that wasn't what he needed. He turned back to Andie and she was still leaning out, still watching.

"Call Clint."

He got the calf delivered before Clint got there, but the cow was still down. "Momma cow, we need you to get up and take care of this baby."

It happened sometimes, a cow got down, got sick and that was just the end of it. He couldn't look at Andie, sitting on the porch. He knew she'd be out there fighting to save that heifer if she knew what he suspected.

Clint's truck pulled into the driveway and Adam was right behind him. Ryder had never had a sentimental day in his life, but right at that moment, it was a pretty good feeling to be from his hometown. It was good to be where people knew him and where he didn't have to go far to find a helping hand.

The two were armed with calf starter in a bottle for the calf, several bottles of medication and a needle to give the cow the necessary shots. They climbed the fence as Ryder dried off the calf. It was the most pitiful looking little black baldy calf he'd ever seen. Black with a white face, its sides were caved in from dehydration and it kept coughing from the gunk in his lungs.

"That's a shame." Clint had lowered himself next to the cow and he injected her with antibiotics. "She's a good little heifer."

"Yeah, and if we don't do something, Andie's going to be down here trying to get her on her feet." Ryder took the bottle that Adam carried and pushed it into the little calf's mouth. It moved away a few times and then finally started to suck. It didn't take long for the little guy to put down the two liters of milk.

"Let's see if we can get her on her feet." Adam grabbed the rope that Ryder had used to pull the calf. It was soaked and muddy. "What do you think?"

Ryder shrugged, so did Clint. Clint took the rope and put it around the cow's neck. Ryder was dealing with a calf that now thought he must be mommy. It was sucking at his jeans and at the hem of this T-shirt. It would have been cute if buckets of rain hadn't been falling on them and the momma cow hadn't been on her side in a puddle of water.

They were heaving on the cow when Andie came traipsing across the yard again.

"What are you doing up?" Ryder was in the process of sliding a rope under the cow's middle.

She stopped at the fence and watched. "I had to check on her because I know you aren't going to tell me everything."

"Andie, you have to get back on the porch. If Etta comes home and you're standing down here in the rain…" He stopped. "You know, it doesn't matter what Etta is going to say. You're an adult and you know better."

"Tell me how she is."

"She's going to die if we don't get her up."

"Ryder." Clint's voice was a little softer and Ryder thought that had to be Willow's influence. When had Clint Cameron ever been the guy with the soft touch. "Andie, we'll get her up and if we can get her in the trailer on my truck, I'll take her home and work with her. We'll get her back on her feet. You might have to bottle feed that calf, though."

"Thanks, Clint." Andie shot Ryder a smug smile. "Now I'll go sit back down. Just consider this my shower for the day."

Ryder watched her go. Rain was pouring down, and a crack of thunder gave him the motivation he needed to kick it up a notch. He had no desire to be standing under this tree when lightning hit.

Clint pulled on the rope, heaving and out of breath and Adam helped Ryder push the back end of the cow as she fought to get up.

She was finally on her feet.

"Let's take her out this corner gate right to the trailer." Clint leaned to catch his breath.

"We can take her to my place." Ryder didn't have his trailer, but they could put her in Andie's.

"Ryder, you have enough going on right now with Wyatt at your house and Andie needing you here. Let us do this one for you."

"I can manage."

"I didn't say you couldn't." Clint pounded him on the back. "But I'd say you've got your plate pretty full right now. And the next few months aren't going to get any easier."

"That's great to know."

Clint laughed, but he was still working, still moving the cow and working with her. "Yeah, well, that's how life is. When you think you've got it all figured out and think you know your next move, God surprises you with something huge. But seriously, it's about time you and Andie realized what the rest of us have known forever."

"Known?" He'd never had such a hard time forming sentences.

"Yeah, known." Clint shot him a look like he really should be getting it. "You and Andie haven't been far from each other's side in years. And when you thought Reese hurt her, you broke his nose."

"He deserved that."

"Yeah, he probably did." Clint led the cow a few wobbly steps toward the gate that Adam had opened. "But most guys wouldn't bust their buddy's nose for just any girl."

"She's…" He wasn't going to get baited into this conversation. Clint and Adam shot one another knowing looks and Ryder decided to ignore them. The odds of him taking the two of them were pretty slim, so it made sense to load the cow and forget this conversation.

He walked away from Clint's trailer telling himself that this was just part of his new life. Every guy in town was dating, getting married or recently married. And they didn't want to suffer alone.

Andie reheated Ryder's cheeseburger up while he changed out of his T-shirt into a button up shirt he found behind the seat of his truck. When she heard him coming down the hall she poured a cup of coffee and sat it next to the plate.

Domestic. She'd never been one of those females, the kind that loved to cook and clean. She could make a decent burger or pancakes, she could brew pretty terrific coffee, but she had never seen herself as June Cleaver or Martha Stewart.

Ryder walked into the kitchen, stopping at the door. He eyed her, eyes on the meal and the coffee, and then back to her. She ignored him and poured herself a glass of milk, because she'd had her cup of coffee already.

"You should be sitting down. I could have done this. I could have made coffee." He didn't sit down.

"I wanted to do something for you. You've been doing everything for me for the past couple of weeks."

"That's because you've needed me to be that person, Andie. There's been plenty of times you've taken care of me."

"Yeah, but this is just not right, all of this sitting and letting people wait on me."

"You're not doing it because you're lazy. You're taking care of our baby. And I'm taking care of you." He pointed to the hall and she knew what that meant. "Back to the parlor, sweetie."

She grabbed her milk and walked past him down the hall. He followed a few minutes later with his coffee and plate of food. When he walked through the door she was back on the couch, her feet up, the pillow over her face.

He had the nerve to laugh.

She tossed the pillow at the end of the sofa. "You think this is funny?"

"I think you're suddenly a drama queen and you're not very good at it."

"How's my cow?"

"Clint thinks he can save her. You know how it is, Andie. She's in bad shape. The calf drank, though. We got some colostrum for him and added it to the milk replacer in the bottle."

"Thank you." She hugged a pillow to her stomach. "I'm sorry I had to call you."

"I'm not." He finished his burger and set the plate down. "Now, tell me what I can get you? Chocolate? Books? Something to drink?"

"Nothing." She pointed to the obvious. "I have books. I have magazines. I have the TV remote. The only thing I don't have is my life. I shouldn't resent that, should I?"

"I think it's probably natural."

"I don't want this baby to feel resented. What if she can feel it now, that I'm sick of sitting. I don't blame her, though. This is my fault. This whole pregnancy is my fault. You didn't ask for this to happen to you. If it wasn't for me, you'd be on your way to Vegas to the finals."

"Andie, I'm not blaming you. And this pregnancy isn't your fault. We, I think that's how this works. I made a decision to stay here. This is where I need to be. The finals aren't that important."

"Right. And you'll never resent that a night with me changed your life? This is exactly what we were worried would happen. We can't go back to being friends. I'm not even sure if we can go back to being us."

He moved to the table, the place that had become his in the past couple of weeks. She met his gaze, the dark eyes that always looked at her as if he knew her better than anyone else knew her.

"Andie, we'll make this work. We'll deal with it."

"Right, that's what we'll do, deal with it." She leaned back away from him, against the cushioned arm of the sofa and she closed her eyes. "I need to take a nap. That's one of the symptoms of the first trimester of pregnancy, being tired."

"I'm not leaving."

He got up and moved to the cushioned rocking chair a short distance away. He looked out of place in Etta's parlor and in that prissy chair. She smiled, watching him try to get comfortable. He stretched jean-clad legs in front of him and crossed his legs at the ankles. His hat was low over his eyes and he crossed his arms in front of him.

She was the one needing a nap and he'd probably be asleep long before her. If she even fell asleep. Mostly she wanted an excuse to stop talking about their lives and how everything had changed.

One thing hadn't changed. She loved Ryder. But Ryder thought she was nothing more than his best friend.

And the mother of his baby.

Chapter 13

Something woke Andie up. A bad dream? A bad feeling. She turned and she was on the edge of the sofa. She moved back to keep from falling off. It took her a minute to put it all together, to remember that it was Tuesday and Etta was in Tulsa with Alyson. She sought the person who had been there with her when she fell asleep.

Ryder was still in the rocking chair. His head was bent forward, his hat covering his face. Soft snores drifted across the room. She smiled and curled back into the blanket that hadn't been on her when she fell asleep. And she tried not to think about it, about him hovering over her, covering her with the afghan that had been folded at the other end of the sofa.

Pain slid through her abdomen, catching her by surprise, taking her breath.

That's what had awoken her. It hadn't been a dream. It hadn't been just a bad feeling. She rubbed her belly and waited for it to end. It didn't. The cramping wrapped around her lower abdomen and held on.

"No," she whispered but it woke Ryder.

"What?" His voice was groggy his eyes a little foggy from sleep.

She needed a minute, just a minute to get her thoughts straight.

"I'm cramping again." She met his gaze and his brow furrowed. "It's my fault for going out to check on the cow."

"We left you here alone. I should have stayed with you." He stood. "We aren't going to sit and talk about this being someone's fault. We don't know what this is, or even if there's something that could be done to stop it."

"I know." Her heart tightened with dread, because she knew that there was nothing a doctor could do, not at this stage in her pregnancy.

He grabbed her shoes and a jacket that she'd left on the other chair. "Come on, let's go."

"Go?"

"To the E.R. Andie, we're not going to sit here and do nothing. We'll call Etta on our way."

"I don't want to call Etta. Alyson deserves to have this day without me interfering."

"Alyson would want you to interfere if…"

If she lost the baby. Andie slid her feet into the shoes he set on the floor for her and then she let him hold the sweater for her to slide her arms into the sleeves. They felt like a couple. She closed her eyes against another sharp wave of pain, and a similar one that invaded her heart that asked her what became of them tomorrow.

"I don't want to lose my baby." She looked up at him, not wanting to need him, but she did.

He sat down on the sofa with her. He touched her cheek and turned her to face him. "I know."

His kiss was sweet, gentle, and it made her feel strong. It made her feel loved. And she knew that wasn't what he meant to do with that kiss. She sighed into his shoulder and he hugged her close.

"Let's go, Andie."

She walked out the door at his side, her hand on her belly, her baby still safe inside her. And thoughts invaded, because she knew that when she returned to this house, everything might be different. The last thing she saw was the pile of clothes on the table next to the door, the little baby clothes that Etta had found in the attic, and an afghan that Andie's mom had tried to crochet years ago—when Andie was a baby.

The E.R. was bustling with late afternoon activity. Rush hour in Grove always resulted in plenty of minor fend-benders the nurse informed them as they got Andie settled in a bed.

"You can't leave me this time." Andie waited until the nurse left and then she grabbed Ryder's hands. "Don't leave me."

"I'm not going anywhere."

"Please, don't be angry with me."

He sat down on the edge of the bed. "I'm not angry, Andie, I'm worried. This is my baby, too."

"I know."

"Do you? Because sometimes you act like you're in this alone. And you're not. We were both surprised by this, but I'm no less invested in this pregnancy than you are." His voice cracked. "That's my kid. It isn't something I planned, but after a couple of weeks, a guy starts to get used to the idea."

"I'm so afraid that this is God's way of punishing me."

He rubbed his thumb over her fingers. "Andie, you thought being pregnant was punishment. Now you think God's punishing you with problems. Why? Do you think God is sitting up there waiting for you and you alone to mess up so He can come up with new ways to punish you?"

"Consequences?"

"Yeah, okay, consequences. But you're wrong about this." He leaned close, touching her cheek. "Your whole life you've worried about being good enough. That's your mom's fault. And your fault for blaming yourself for her skipping out on you."

"If I'd been easier…" She choked on sobs that came in waves and Ryder grabbed her up and held her close.

"She messed up, not you."

"How does a mom walk out on a kid?" She leaned into his shoulder and all of the pain of her childhood came out, all of the feelings of being defective. Ryder held her tight, rubbing her back.

"You're not your mom."

"No, I'm not." She wiped at her eyes and moved away from him. "But if I lose the baby, you're off the hook."

"Oh, so now I'm your mom?"

"I don't know, Ryder. I don't even know what I'm feeling right now." More tears rolled down her cheeks and this time Ryder didn't hold her. "This could be the last day that I'm pregnant."

"I choose to have some faith, Andie. So, I'm not going to play this game with you."

The curtain opened and Dr. Ashford walked in. Ryder moved off the edge of the bed as the doctor washed her hands and pulled gloves out of the box on the table next to the bed.

"When did this start?" Dr. Ashford glanced at the curtain and motioned a tech into the room with a portable ultrasound.

"An hour or so. I woke up and was cramping then."

"Have you been staying down?"

"As much as possible. I had a cow get down today."

"She called me." Ryder shot her a look. "Andie, you walked out into the yard and then back to the house. This isn't your fault."

Dr. Ashford smiled at him and then turned her attention back to Andie. "He's right. Now isn't the time to blame yourself. Now is the time to see what's going on. Any bleeding?"

Ryder stood up. "I'll wait outside."

"No. And, Ryder, stay. I don't want to be alone."

He sat back down. "I'll stay for the ultrasound."

Dr. Ashford slid a heart monitor over her belly and smiled.

"There's that heartbeat." She paused, frowned and moved it again. "Oh."

"What?" Andie's heart squeezed painfully and she watched, waiting for Dr. Ashford to smile, to say something.

"Let's get that ultrasound in here before I make any big announcements."

Andie leaned, waiting. And praying. Because she needed faith. And she needed God. She wasn't going to believe lies that she was being punished or tossed aside because she wasn't good enough. Old wounds. She tried to tell herself it was time to let them heal. It wasn't easy.

Dr. Ashford squeezed cold gel on her belly and reached for the ultrasound. The tech stood back as the doctor moved the gizmo over her belly, finding the baby, settling on the heartbeat. The doctor nodded and moved the ultrasound a little to the right.

Another heartbeat.

"You're a twin, aren't you?"

"Yes." Her heartbeat was echoing in her ears, beating in unison with the two heartbeats on the ultrasound.

"Andie, you're having twins."

"But there was only one."

"Yes, well, there wasn't only one, but we didn't hear baby number two the last time we checked."

"But they're okay?"

"Andie, they seem to be very okay. I want to do a blood test and keep you here tonight."

"Here, in the hospital?"

"For the night, yes."

Andie's body trembled and she reached for Ryder. His hand tightened around hers.

"Andie, we're having twins." His voice shook a little.

Two babies. Her life had changed, and then changed again. She looked at Ryder, and to her, he looked a little cornered. And that wasn't what she wanted.

She didn't want him stuck somewhere he didn't want to be, including in a relationship he'd never planned to have.

Dr Ashford left them alone. She was going to arrange for Andie to have a room for the night, and she thought they might need to catch their breath. She made the last comment with a smile as she walked out the door.

Ryder whistled a lot whistle. "Wow, this is it. Not only are we going to do this, but we're going to have twins."

"I'm sorry."

"Why are you apologizing? Andie, we've talked about this. I'm a part of this. I'm the dad. You aren't having a baby, we are having a baby. Two babies."

"Exactly. The guy who didn't want to get married or have kids is now going to have two."

"I know." He sat back in the chair and tried to think about that. "You're going to be on bed rest for a big part of the next seven months."

"Dr. Ashford didn't say that."

"No, but that's the way it works."

"Stop."

He stopped. He knew when a woman was at the end of the emotional rope swing and about to go off. Andie was dangling.

"We have to get married." He said it with as much conviction as he could, because it was going to take conviction to convince her.

"Excuse me?"

"Married, Andie. We can let Alyson and Jason have their day, but I think we should plan on a Christmas wedding."

"Haven't I already told you no, twice?"

"Yeah, but…"

"But we don't even know yet that the babies are okay. Have you thought of that? Have you thought about putting that ring on my finger and then…"

She could lose the babies.

Of course he hadn't let his thoughts go there. He was a little upset that she would. And he told her so as he stood up.

"Andie, you're emotional. I guess I'm pretty emotional right now, too. But this is crazy. Those babies deserve for us to be married."

"I don't want a proposal that's prefixed with 'this is the right thing to do.' Ryder, just go."

"Go?"

Dr. Ashford walked into the room. "Problem, kids?"

"No, no problem." Ryder grabbed his hat. "Her grandmother will be here in an hour."

"Oh, okay."

As Ryder started his truck, his better self told him to go back and wait. But he couldn't. He was so mad at Andie, he knew he'd say the wrong thing if he stayed. She didn't need that right now. He didn't know what she needed. Definitely not anything he could give.

He'd done his best. He'd proposed three times.

He should have at least stayed to make sure everything was okay after the blood test. But he'd seen the babies, seen their hearts beating. Two of them.

That took a guy some time to adjust to. Two beds. Two ponies. Two frilly pink dresses and two infant carriers in the back of his truck.

Maybe she was right. He wasn't ready for this. He'd been doing the right thing, or what he thought was right, by proposing. But was that really the best thing for them, and for the babies?

Andie was in a darkened hospital room alone when Etta walked through the door, smiling like summer sunshine. Andie looked up, trying to smile back. She'd never felt less like smiling in her life.

She'd chased Ryder out of her room and she was afraid she'd chased him out of her life. But it was for the best. She didn't want him tied to her by guilt.

"Sugar bug, what in the world is going on? I went to the E.R., but they said you'd been moved up here and they didn't know anything."

"Dr. Ashford wants me to stay a night or two, just to keep an eye on the, on the…" she sobbed "…babies."

"Babies?"

"As in two. I was barely adjusting to the idea of one, and now there are going to be two. Two heartbeats, two little babies growing inside me."

"Which explains a lot. Where's Ryder?"

"Home." Andie pushed the button and raised the back of the bed.

"Now, I didn't expect that. He told me he'd wait with you, that he wouldn't think of leaving you alone."

"Yeah, well."

Etta set her yellow purse on the table next to the bed and poured a glass of water that she drank without offering it to Andie. Her lavender-and-gray hair was windblown and her red lipstick was smudged.

"Well, explain to me why Ryder went back on his word. Because Ryder usually keeps his word."

Yes, Ryder did keep his word. And if he promised to be at her side forever, he'd be there. Even if it wasn't where he wanted to be.

"I told him to leave. I am not going to keep him hooked to my side this way. I'm not going to use this as a way to force him into my life."

"Well now, that's new. I didn't know you wanted him in your life."

"Not like this, I don't. I don't want proposals that start with 'the right thing to do.' I want love." Tears streamed down her cheeks. "I want frilly stinking dresses, fluffy dry cake with jam stuck between the layers and a lot of people crying and wiping their eyes with lace hankies."

"Hormones."

"Probably." Andie took the hankie her granny dug out of her purse.

"You love Ryder. Andie, that's nothing to be ashamed of. It's been as clear as the nose on your face for as long as I can remember. It's just that you've spent a big part of your life playing it safe and pretending you were just his best friend."

Because she kept him in her life that way. The one way to run Ryder off would have been to let him know how she felt. Ryder had always run from females who were looking for forever. He had good reasons, she told herself, even though she knew he was nothing like his dad. He was nothing like his mom.

And now he'd be in her life as the father of her babies. They'd share weekends. They'd share school pictures. And her heart would break someday when he found someone he loved and wanted in his life forever, someone who got a real proposal.

"Andie, you're going to have to work this out. You're going to have to tell Ryder. Because I'm a pretty good judge of things, and I think he loves you, too. He's just afraid to love anyone."

"I know." She knew about his fears, not about his feelings for her.

"The other thing you have to work out is your relationship with your mother. She called and Alyson told her what is going on. She's flying in tomorrow."

"To help Alyson with the wedding?"

Etta shook her head. "No, to be with you."

Dr. Ashford knocked lightly on the door and stepped into the room. "Etta, did Andie tell you her news?"

"She did. We're so excited."

Dr. Ashford's gaze landed on Andie. "Are we excited?"

"Scared to death is probably more like it." Andie flipped off the TV because it was just noise.

"I think that's probably normal. Andie, a pregnancy like this can be hard on relationships."

Andie shook her head. "There isn't a relationship."

"Oh, there is one, whether the two of you want it or not. You're going to be parents and you're going to start out with double the joy, and double the work. That's a relationship."

"It isn't the end of the world." Etta patted her arm, her smile big, like she meant what she said.

All Andie knew for sure was that she felt sick.

Dr. Ashford touched her arm. "Andie, if you need anything, don't hesitate to call. I know things look a little frightening right now, but I promise you'll adjust. You have months to get used to this. And babies have a way of helping us to grow into parenthood."

"Yes, in most cases." Every single time Andie thought of parenting, she thought about her mother. And she didn't want it that way, with that memory hanging over her head.

Her mother would be there tomorrow. For her. The same woman who walked away, and now she was trying to walk back into Andie's life. She closed her eyes and breathed deep, fighting the sting behind her eyelids as tears tried to push through. She wouldn't cry.

Etta touched her arm and Andie opened her eyes.

"You'll be a good mother. And you're going to have plenty of help." Etta smiled in a way that said she understood.

"Andie, let me know if you need anything." Dr. Ashford patted her foot and walked out the door.

"Alyson is with Jason." Etta sat on the edge of the bed. "She wasn't with me when Ryder called. But I called to tell her what is happening. After that your mother called and Alyson explained the situation to Caroline."

"Call Alyson and tell her she doesn't have to come over. She and Jason have so much to do in the next month."

"I'll tell her, but I can't guarantee she won't come over."

The door opened a few minutes later. Andie's heart jumped a little, expecting it to be Ryder. Because he wouldn't stay gone. He'd never stayed away for long. It wasn't him, of course it wasn't. She had told him to go. It was a nurse's aid with a dinner tray. The young woman set two covered dishes on the table and opened the container of milk.

"Dr. Ashford told me to bring food for you and for your grandmother."

"Thank you." Andie raised her arms and the aid moved the table across the bed.

She was hungry, but she didn't know if she could eat. Her heart was still breaking, because she hadn't expected to want the person walking through her door to be Ryder. She hadn't expected it to hurt this much when he left.

Etta sat down in the chair next to the bed. She thanked the aid for their food and waited for the young woman to leave.

"Andie, I don't know what is going on with you and Ryder, but I know the two of you will work this out. You'll find a way to be parents to these babies. And I think you'll both do a good job at it."

"I hope you're right."

"Oh, honey, when have I ever been wrong?" Etta winked and then her smile faded. "Goodness gracious, what kind of food is this?"

Andie managed a smile, but it was hard to smile when she didn't know when Ryder would be back. She wouldn't let herself think the worst—that he wouldn't come back.

Chapter 14

Ryder Johnson didn't run. Or at least he'd been telling himself that for the past few days. But it really felt like running. He'd taken his cue from Andie, and he'd run. It wasn't sitting too well with him. He'd called himself things like "yella" and "coward." But it was hard to shake off pretty serious changes to his life, and to Andie's.

He was going to be a dad—to twins. Every single time he thought that, which was often, it felt like a punch to the gut. But it wasn't all bad. He was adjusting. And it was starting to feel a little better, the idea of those two babies in this house.

Since he'd left the hospital, he'd been working on the nursery. The room was painted, all but the trim around the door, and he'd ripped up the carpet. Antique green with antique ivory trim. He didn't get all of these antique colors. His mom had worked hard to make this house look French country and anything but antique.

Ryder stepped back, wanting to see how the room looked from the door, as a first impression. He wasn't very creative, and he wasn't much of a painter, but he thought it looked pretty good. He wondered what Andie would say.

Not for the first time in the past couple of days he thought about calling her. But he wasn't going to push. He'd said what he had to say and now she had to come to terms with things, with life, and with them as parents.

When he left the other day he'd decided they both needed a few days to adjust and think. He had to admit to being knocked on his can with everything that had happened. First the pregnancy, and now twins. He shook his head and looked at the room he had meant for one baby.

Now he thought about how it would be to have the babies here part-time.

He put the brush down and walked around the room, trying to picture it with Andie here, and babies in that crib he was sanding down out in the garage. A room, a crib, a rocking chair and babies. He told himself not to put Andie in this room, not even in his imagination. Babies, yes; Andie, no. But he couldn't stop thinking about her in this room, in this house and in his life.

Floorboards in the hallway creaked. He turned and Wyatt walked in. He stopped just inside the door and nodded what Ryder hoped was his approval.

"You got it done. I guess that's why you've been up here with the door closed for the past two days." Wyatt wiped a streak of green off the trim at the door.

"Yeah, almost done. Still have to do the trim around the door."

"Word around town is that Andie Forester is having twins."

Ryder hadn't talked to his brother much since the night he came home from the hospital. He'd come home, gone out to the barn and knocked around the old punching bag they had in one of the stalls. That was one thing their dad had done for them. He'd taught them to box. He'd given them an outlet. So after his fight with Andie he'd come home and put on boxing gloves.

"Yeah, we're having twins."

"Wow, that's huge."

"Thanks." Ryder put the cap on the paint.

"Is she going to marry you?"

"Nope. She says I have to say something other than 'I think we should.' I'm not sure what she wants from me."

Wyatt laughed, really laughed. "You can't figure it out? You know, everyone in this town thinks you're the ladies' man. But you're really just the guy who dated a lot of women. You know, to be honest, I've never figured out why you didn't date her."

"Because we're friends. I didn't want to mess that up by dating."

Wyatt had said it best; Andie was the longest relationship Ryder had ever had.

But he had messed it up. Instead of dating, he'd taken advantage of her when she'd needed him the most. He'd done a lot of praying about that, and he'd needed a lot of forgiveness.

"This isn't about protecting your friendship." Wyatt picked up the brush and stroked it across an area that looked smudged. Now that Ryder looked a little closer, maybe it was. He'd never said he was a painter.

"Well then, oh wise one, what do you think it is?" Ryder was about to get those boxing gloves again. It wouldn't be the first time he and Wyatt had settled something in the backyard under the security light.

Wyatt shrugged. "I guess I'd say you're selfish. You didn't want to lose your best friend so you never put yourself out there to see what other kind of relationship you could have with her."

"I asked her to marry me." Ryder growled the words and then he took a deep breath and made his words come out a little quieter. "I asked her to marry me and she said no."

"You asked her like it was a solution to a problem."

"Yeah."

"Yeah? You're an idiot if that's all you can say. You're a clueless idiot and you don't deserve her."

"I'm not clueless… I know exactly what I feel." He stopped, shocked by his own words, and not surprised that Wyatt was smiling.

"Really, what do you feel?"

"I'm not going to hurt her." Ryder looked away from his brother. "I don't want her to be Mom. I don't want to start out thinking we can conquer the world and then someday realize we don't even like each other."

"I guess if you start out thinking someday you'll fail, or things will go south, then you're probably doomed."

"Yeah, I guess we are, but I love her too much to have her hurt that way."

"You love her too much to marry her and be a dad to those babies of yours. Like I said, idiot. You're not our dad. You're the guy who has been in this room for two days, painting it some prissy looking shade of green. You're the guy who has been down in the garage sanding a crib by hand."

Wyatt tossed the brush in the bucket and walked out of the room. Wyatt was getting it together. He'd even taken the girls to church. Ryder would have gone after him but he figured his older brother was figuring out his own life.

He had proposed to Andie by telling her it was the right thing to do. No wonder she was ticked off. And he'd left her in the hospital alone.

It would take a lot of paper to list the mistakes he'd made in his life. And now, at the top of the list was the way he'd treated Andie.

Somehow he'd make it up to her. He'd find a way to show her that he loved her and that he wasn't going to let her down. He wasn't going to be the man who walked away from her. He wasn't going to walk out when things got tough.

But those were words he had to share with her. As soon as he got this room ready. He wanted to show her that he hadn't walked away and forgotten about her. This room was for her.

All this time working up here and he hadn't really thought about it that way. He'd been fixing a room for the babies. That meant having those babies living here, with him. And that meant Andie.

He couldn't picture this room without seeing her in it. And it was that image, man, that image of her, with her blond hair and the sun shining through the window that made him want to have her in this house forever.

Because he loved her. He hadn't ever, not once in his life, let himself think those words about Andie. But he'd selfishly kept her tied to his side in the place of best friend.

Now he was going to find another way to keep her in his life. And he wasn't going to use the words that had gotten him thrown out of her hospital room.

Andie walked out to the barn. It was great to be able to come and go again. She'd tried not to overdo it, but it had been hard to remember that she still needed to take it easy. She wanted to go everywhere and do everything. She wanted to buy baby clothes in matching sets and pretty pictures for the walls.

The thoughts were pretty out of place in her life. Etta called it nesting and said it would get worse as she got closer to her due date. She shuddered to think about it, about how bad it could get.

She'd had the same bedroom furniture, the same quilt, the same pictures on her walls since as far back as she could remember. And why? Because a girl didn't plan her wedding, or talk about children, when she was in love with her best friend and she knew that he had no intention of ever settling down.

She wondered how much he resented her for taking away his freedom.

Dusty whinnied when he saw her. He trotted up to the fence, his gold coat glimmering in the evening sun. He pushed his head at her, demanding attention and a treat. She pulled baby carrots out of her pocket and held them out to him. He sucked them off her hand, barely moving his lips.

And then she saw the alpaca. She laughed and tears slid down her cheeks. She touched her belly. "That's your dad's idea of romantic."

It wasn't chocolates or roses, although he had brought wilted flowers with the alpaca. But it showed how well he knew her, and how much he cared. He'd bought her an alpaca, a silly thing she wouldn't have bought herself.

"I can't believe he bought you an alpaca." Alyson walked across the yard, pretty and feminine.

Andie tried not to compare herself to her twin. But she did look down at her faded jeans tucked into worn boots. Two peas in a pod, they weren't. But they were connected. Andie should have hunted her sister down. It wasn't fair, that Alyson didn't know about them, but they'd known about her. They should have found her.

But Andie had been too stubborn. She'd decided, without any proof, that Alyson knew about them but didn't want to see them.

She was bad about that assuming thing. She had assumed, for a lot of years that her mother didn't care about her. She was learning now, since Caroline's arrival the previous day, that maybe more connected them than Andie had thought.

Last night they'd talked about how it felt to be Caroline, leaving her life in the city, trading it for life in Dawson. And then having twin girls.

Last night Andie learned that her mother suffered from chronic depression. And she learned, from her mother, that the biggest difference between them was that Caroline had never felt like a part of Dawson. She had been the wrong fit for Andie's father.

But Andie and Ryder had always been here, always loved their lives here. They knew each other. They knew one another's dreams and goals.

Caroline had helped Andie see that. In a conversation that had been a little stiff, a little formal, Andie had learned about herself from her mother.

"Yeah, an alpaca." She finally answered Alyson's question. "What did you say Jason bought you, a baby grand?"

"Yeah, but Jason knows that I wouldn't have appreciated an alpaca. I think Ryder probably knows how much you'd love one. And you do, right?"

"He's the cutest, sweetest thing in the world."

"The alpaca or Ryder?"

Andie laughed at her sister's very obvious attempt at bringing the conversation back to Ryder. "The alpaca."

"Yeah, of course." Alyson leaned across the fence and scratched Dusty's neck. The alpaca walked toward them, a little slow, hesitant. "How do you feel?"

Andie shrugged. "Good, really. No more cramping. For now, no bed rest. I'm not looking forward to that last trimester. But Dr. Ashford assured me that if I take it easy now, maybe the last trimester won't mean a lot of bed rest."

"That's good to hear. You aren't a good patient."

"Thanks for that." Andie reached to pet the alpaca she'd named George. "I guess I need to try on my dress this week."

"That would be good. The seamstress says she can leave a little room. In case you've gained weight by the end of the month."

"I don't plan on doing that."

Alyson touched Andie's belly. "I have bad news for you. There's a little pooch here now."

"That's water weight."

"Of course it is. But about Ryder..."

"This had to come up, didn't it?" Andie turned away

from the alpaca and they headed toward the house. "Did Etta send you out? She's been after me for three days. Your…our mother has been after me."

"The two of you not talking isn't going to solve anything."

"I never said that I'm not talking to him. He left. He didn't come back." Okay, she'd kind of wanted him to leave at the time, but he didn't have to stay gone.

"Tell him you love him. Give him the opportunity to do the right thing." Alyson said it with such conviction, looping her arm through Andie's as they walked back to the house. "He deserves that honesty from you if you're going to be good parents together."

"Yes, he deserves to know." That she loved him. But once the words were between them, what happened then?

She had no idea. She didn't think it would change anything, though. There were some realities that mattered and wouldn't change. The fact that they were going to have twins was a big reality. He was going to be a dad. She was going to be a mom.

But the two of them together? She wondered if maybe she was being stubborn. She had been called stubborn once or twice. Maybe loving him was enough?

Maybe him loving the babies and being a good husband, being her best friend, was enough? Her heart picked up speed because she'd never felt more like God was showing her something, as if He was really showing her an answer to her prayers for herself and Ryder.

There were starting places in life. Most of those starting places had a lot to do with trusting God, even with a situation that you didn't know how to tackle, or how to face.

"I have to go." She walked through the back door of the house and grabbed her purse off the kitchen table.

"You have to what?" Caroline had walked into the kitchen. Andie paused in the doorway, because it still took her by surprise to see her mother in this house.

"I have to go talk to Ryder."

"Really? Are you done with the silent treatment?"

"I'm done. We have to come to an understanding. I think the understanding is that we're going to be parents and maybe 'I think we should' is a good enough reason to get married. For our babies."

"Oh." Caroline walked to the coffeepot.

"What?"

"Well, I'm glad you're putting the babies ahead of yourself." She poured her coffee and turned.

Andie stood at the door, not sure how to have another conversation with her mother. They'd never discussed the important things in life. They'd barely discussed more than the weather in the three times that they'd met. Except last night, when they'd gotten to know each other a little.

But it still felt like a new pair of boots. She wondered if that would always be their relationship?

Andie guessed probably so if that's all she expected. She breathed a little and let go. Because Caroline wasn't going away anytime soon.

"I love him." Andie slid the strap of her purse over her shoulder and she wondered if her mother saw the parallel between their lives, the way she was seeing it.

"I know you do." But Caroline had never approached anything with faith. Andie was holding fast to hers.

"I know you believe I'm doing the wrong thing. But in my heart I know that going right now and talking to

Ryder is the right thing to do. I know that we have to stop being stubborn and be parents."

Caroline smiled. "You're doing the right thing."

Andie nodded and left. She hadn't needed to hear that from her mother, she already knew it. But it shifted things. A small empty space in her heart closed up a little.

Ryder carried the sanded cradle into the nursery. He planned on painting it that same ivory color. He thought that'd be the right color. First he had to figure out what kind of paint to use. Babies chewed on things. He knew that. Even toddlers chewed on stuff. He'd found Kat chewing on the kitchen cabinet.

He turned at a noise and smiled. Kat was sitting in the doorway, watching. She had a paintbrush and was pretending to paint the door. Fortunately she didn't have paint.

"Good job, Kat."

"Ryder, you have company," Wyatt shouted up the stairs.

Ryder had thought he heard a car come up the drive a few minutes earlier. He brushed his hands down the front of his jeans and wiped dust off his shirt. It might be Andie. Or it might not.

He wondered just how bad a guy could look after getting just a few hours sleep over the last few days. He raked a hand through his hair and hoped for the best. When she came up the stairs, he was waiting for her. Kat was still sitting in the doorway, smiling at her pretend paint job.

"Hi." Andie stopped in the hallway, smiling, looking from him, to Kat, to the open door.

"You look good. I guess it feels good to be out of the house."

"Really good." She shrugged. "It might not last long."

He let his gaze slide to her belly. In a few months he'd be a dad. To twins. Andie was going to be the mother of his kids. And she'd never looked more beautiful. He wanted her to know that.

He took a few steps and when he was close enough, he ran his fingers through her hair, and pulled her closer to him, holding his hand at the back of her neck.

"You look beautiful." He whispered words that he'd never said to her before. And he should have. His teen-aged attempts at being cool had included phrases like, "You look hot."

But she was beautiful.

"I'm beautiful?" She blinked a few times and shot a look past him. He turned, smiling at Kat who watched with all of the attention she typically focused on her favorite princess cartoon.

"Yeah, beautiful. I've been meaning to tell you that."

"When you were stumbling over words like, 'Hey, babe, how about you and me get hitched?'"

"I should have told you that you're beautiful and then said 'Hey, babe, how about if we get hitched.'"

"Not much better." She touched his cheek. "You look beautiful, too."

She stole his breath with those words and that moment. He had too much to say to stop now and hold her the way he wanted to hold her. If he didn't back up he'd never get the words out.

"Ryder, I'm here because I've had time to think, and I want to marry you. I want to raise our babies together." She bit down on her bottom lip. "You don't have to love me, but I love you. I've loved you for as long as I can remember, but I didn't want to lose you by saying something that would push you out of my life."

He hadn't expected that. She could have said almost anything and he'd have been fine, but he hadn't expected love. Or that she'd marry him. And he didn't even have to love her back.

He'd done that to her. All of his macho words about staying single and never falling in love had put these ideas into her mind.

Kat was giggling and she couldn't understand their conversation. He shot her a look and it didn't quell her two-year-old joy an ounce. She was beating on the door, grinning her kind of toothless grin.

Ryder turned back to Andie. "That's it, you love me? And now we can get married?"

Andie hadn't expected that reaction. She swallowed the lump that lodged in her throat. Maybe it was too late for those words. Maybe he'd changed his mind after her third rejection. Not that she blamed him.

And then he smiled. That smile that shifted the smooth planes of his face and took a girl by the heart, holding her tight so she couldn't escape if she wanted to. Andie didn't want to escape that smile or what it did to her heart.

"Andie, I want you to see what I've been doing." He took her by the hand and led her into the bedroom, past the very smiley Kat.

Andie had felt like crying a few times since she'd walked up the stairs and saw Ryder for the first time in three days. But this room, it undid her emotions. Emotions that were raw and close to the surface overflowed when she stood in the center of a room he had planned out and painted.

For their babies. He didn't have to tell her that this was a nursery. The colors and the box of nursery items said it all.

"This is beautiful." She walked around the room, stopping at the rocking chair next to the window. She pictured herself in that chair with her babies.

In this house.

She pictured late night feedings and a lamp glowing softly in the dark. She was holding her babies and Ryder was standing in the doorway, watching. He was leaning against the door frame, his hair a little messy and his feet bare.

She liked him like that. And she liked images of herself in this house.

"Why are you smiling?" Ryder had walked up to her and he leaned in, slipping his arm around her waist and pulling her close.

"I love the room." She touched his shoulder, sliding her hand down to his. "I love you."

He leaned, resting his forehead against hers. "I want you to marry me."

Okay, that was better than his earlier proposals.

"I'll marry you." She swallowed all of her fears, emotions that could become regret and she said it again. "I'll marry you. I want us to raise these babies together, to give them a home where they feel loved and protected."

"What about you?" He was still standing close.

"I'm sorry?"

"What about loving you?"

"You're my best friend."

Ryder reached into his pocket and pulled out the

same ring he'd tried to give her three other times. But this time he held on to her hand and sank to one knee. He raised her hand to his lips and kissed her palm. He turned her hand over and slid the ring into place.

"Marry me, Andie. Marry me because I love you so much I can't breathe when you smile at me like that. I want to be more than the father to our babies. And I plan on having a bunch of them. I want to marry you because I love you."

"You love me." She dropped to her knees in front of him and cupped his cheeks in her hands. "You're not just saying that?"

"I'm not just saying that. I love you. It was easy, being your best friend and not worrying about hurting you or losing you. But I love you and I was hurting you. I hurt you by not being honest with you or myself."

"We're both pretty stubborn."

"We are." He lifted her hand and his ring glinted on her finger. He brushed a kiss across her knuckles and then he pulled her close and kissed her again.

Andie closed her eyes, letting her heart go crazy with his words. He held her close and his lips brushed hers again and again and then moved to her ear.

"We have an audience?" He motioned toward the door with his head.

Andie glanced that direction and smiled. Kat was standing at the door, holding it and watching, her thumb in her mouth.

"That's going to be our lives," she whispered.

"Yeah, I think I'm going to like it a lot."

She was going to like it a lot, too. She was going to love living in this house, being his wife and loving him as he loved her back.

Epilogue

Ryder woke up, wondering why Andie wasn't next to him in bed. It didn't take him long to find her. She was sitting in the rocking chair in the nursery. Her foot was on the cradle in front of her, rocking lightly. But one of his daughters slept in her arms. Both of the girls must have woken up.

He stepped into the room and peeked into the cradle at the sleeping, month-old baby girl. Her hair was blonde, like her mother's hair. She slept on her side, her fist in her mouth.

The other baby was her identical sister. They were both blond with eyes that might turn brown. Or maybe blue. He'd insisted on matching pink sleepers.

"Which one is eating?" He peeked but couldn't tell.

Andie looked up at him, her features soft in the dim light of the lamp. She smiled and he would have done anything for her. He would do anything for her. Every moment since she'd married him and moved into his house, their house, had been better because she was part of his life.

And they were a family. In this house they were a family. With Wyatt and the girls in their own place—but always around, at church when they sat on the pew with Etta, Jason and Alyson, they were a family.

"They're your daughters and you can't tell the difference?" she teased.

"No, Mrs. Johnson, I can't. So, who is this?"

She lifted the baby girl and handed her to him. "This is your daughter who needs to be burped while I feed her sister."

He peeked at the tag inside the sleeper. "Ah, my darling Mariah."

"Exactly. And Maggie is about to get her midnight snack."

"This is actually her 3:00 a.m. snack."

He pulled the second rocking chair next to Andie's. That had been a necessity when they'd found out they were having twins. Two rocking chairs. Two cradles. One crib because Andie and Alyson insisted the babies sleep together. And stay together.

These two little girls would never be split up. They would be protected and they would have parents who raised them with love and security.

Ryder was working hard to keep that promise to his wife and to his little girls.

"I love this room," Andie whispered into the quiet of the room.

"Me, too. I love waking up and having you here. I've never loved this house more than I love it right now."

"Do you know what I love?" Andie shifted her nursing daughter and turned to look at him. "I love looking up and having you standing there, watching me. I dreamed about that the day you proposed. I dreamed of seeing you standing there, your hair messy and your feet bare."

"Really, Mrs. Johnson, I had no idea."

"No, you have no idea." They leaned close together. The kiss was sweet and a promise of something wonderful and lasting.

"I've always loved you, Andie." She cuddled her baby close and smiled, because nothing in the world felt better than being loved by her best friend and knowing that their children would grow up in a family where two parents loved them and they were there for them. Twenty years ago she had pulled petals off a daisy and prayed the last petal would tell her that he loved her. And he did.

* * * * *

Dear Reader,

Welcome back to Dawson, Oklahoma.
Andie Forester's story really started with Alyson's story (*The Cowboy's Courtship*). It was there that we met the twin sisters and got to know Andie a little bit.

I was excited by the story that unfolded for a heroine who quickly became one of my favorites. I felt as if I knew Andie. But as her story unfolded, I realized it wasn't going to be as easy to write as I had assumed.

I didn't undertake this story, or the subject, lightly. I hope that you'll trust me when I say that I prayed about this and labored over the words and how to handle this very delicate subject. People make mistakes. Each of us has done something that we regret, but obviously we can't go back and undo what we've done. So we move forward, we seek God and we find a way to move forward in grace and with faith.

That's exactly how Andie and Ryder handle their situation. I hope you'll fall in love with these two characters the way I've fallen for them. And come back soon for Wyatt's story.

Many blessings,

Brenda Minton

We hope you enjoyed reading
this special collection.

If you liked reading these stories,
then you will love **Love Inspired**® books!

You believe hearts can heal. **Love Inspired**
stories show that faith, forgiveness and hope
have the power to lift spirits and change
lives—always.

Enjoy six new stories from
Love Inspired every month!

Available wherever books and
ebooks are sold.

**Uplifting romances of faith,
forgiveness and hope.**

STEPLI

JUST CAN'T GET ENOUGH?

Join our social communities
and talk to us online.

You will have access to the latest
news on upcoming titles and special
promotions, but most importantly,
you can talk to other fans about your
favorite Harlequin reads.

Harlequin.com/Community

 Facebook.com/HarlequinBooks

Twitter.com/HarlequinBooks

Pinterest.com/HarlequinBooks

Love the Harlequin book you just read?

Your opinion matters.

Review this book on your favorite
book site, review site, blog or your own
social media properties and share
your opinion with other readers!